MW01686886

# CAST INTO THE FIRE

CAROLYN CHAMBERS CLARK, EdD, RN

Vista publishing, Inc.

Edited by Mary Ann Liotta, RN

Cover Design by Thomas Taylor of Thomcatt Graphics

Vista Publishing, Inc.
473 Broadway
Long Branch, NJ 07740
(908) 229-6500

This publication is designed for the reading pleasure of the general public. The novel is based on incidences described in historical treaties regarding the Inquisition in Spain and the Salem Witch Trials in Salem, Massachusetts. The characters are fictional. The healing aspects are based on the author's research and professional practice of nursing.

Printed and bound in the United States of America

First Edition

ISBN: 1-880254-19-0
Library of Congress Catalog Card Number: 94-60685

| U.S.A. Price | $14.95 |
|---|---|
| Canada Price | $20.95 |

# DEDICATION

*To all nurse mavericks --- past, present and future*

**ACKNOWLEDGMENTS**

Many thanks to Charlotte Andersen, my creative writing teacher, who encouraged me to write this book and get it published. She was also a help getting me to hone my descriptive skills and finding reference books of the period.

Sandy Oestreich has been a true friend and colleague. She seems to delight in wading through my manuscripts and giving me the gift of her fine editorial pen.

Carolyn Zagury, my publisher, deserves a big thank you. I believe this story needs to be told, and Carolyn has given me that chance.

The reference librarians at the St. Petersburg Main Library are always helpful, always patient---even with the most outrageous of my requests. Thanks.

Tony Auriemma, my husband and helpmate, not only gives me the emotional space to write, but provides support, and even helps me reason out a plot point or two. Thank you, my dear.

June 1994

Carolyn Chambers Clark

St. Petersburg, Florida

## MEET THE AUTHOR

Carolyn Chambers Clark, Ed.D., R.N., A.R.N.P.

Carolyn Chambers Clark earned a B.S. in Nursing from the University of Wisconsin-Madison, a Masters Degree in Psychiatric/Mental Health Nursing from Rutgers, the State University, New Jersey, and a doctorate in Nursing Education from Teachers College, Columbia University, New York City. She is an Advanced Registered Nurse Practitioner (ARNP) in Psychiatric/Mental Health Nursing and was admitted as a Fellow to the American Academy of Nursing in 1980.

She is the Editor of *ALTERNATIVE HEALTH PRACTITIONER: THE JOURNAL OF COMPLEMENTARY AND NATURAL CARE* and is listed in WHO'S WHO OF AMERICAN WOMEN.

Carolyn's work experiences are extensive and varied. She has thirty years of experience as a clinician, educator, consultant and psychotherapist. She has taught thousands of nurses at the baccalaureate, graduate and continuing education programs, learning systems and articles.

In 1980, Carolyn founded THE WELLNESS INSTITUTES, offering wellness workshops, consultation and a health promotion newsletter. Since 1980, she has been the editor/publisher of *THE WELLNESS NEWSLETTER*, which she developed to fill the void of self-care information.

Carolyn is a member of the Nurse Healers-Professional Associates, Inc. She writes about, and since 1972, has been teaching therapeutic touch---one of the procedures used by wise women, like Ventura, for centuries---at the basic, graduate and continuing education levels for nurses. More recently, she began teaching the lay public the procedure. Carolyn is also an independent practitioner at Bay Area Psychological Services in St. Petersburg, Florida. She provides therapeutic touch, guided imagery and self-hypnosis, in addition to traditional psychotherapy.

# AUTHOR'S NOTE

Throughout history, those who are classified as different or nonconforming have been punished, especially if they present a threat to the ruling classes. This book is about one group of bright healers, precursors to nurses, who were lightyears ahead of the medical men of the day. These iconoclasts were tormented, tortured, burned at the stake or hanged, to serve as examples for generations of maverick women to follow.

The novel is based on incidents described in historical treatises about the Inquisition in Spain and the Salem Witch Trials in Salem, Massachusetts. Some of the characters have elements of real people described in the many books I consulted. The healing aspects presented are based on my research and my own practice as a nurse. The rest of the characters have sprung from my imagination.

"If a man abide not in me, he is cast forth as a branch and is withered: and men gather them and cast them into the fire, *and they are burned*.

John XV. 6

EXURGE DOMINE ET JUDICA CAUSAM TUAM PSALM. 73

# CHARACTERS

## Spain, 1669-1671

Alonzo - Member of the underground who helps Richard escape from the dungeons.

Anna - Ventura's mentor who teaches her healing and herbology.

Capita - Ventura's dog.

Miguel de Castro (el Doctor) - Threatened by women healers who save patients he has given up for dead, he joins with the Inquisitor General to brand them as heretics and have them burned at the stake.

Jozeph Delgado - A volunteer rower on the ship, Santa Isabel, who befriends Richard and saves his life after a shipwreck.

Dulcinea - A servant in the da Fonceca house.

Elvira - Member of the underground. Passed as a man to lead a more liberal life.

Teresa da Fonceca - Ventura's mother.

Antonio or Tonio da Fonceca - Ventura's father who allowed her freedom in her youth, but disowns her when she joins Clara's underground group.

Ventura da Fonceca - Daughter of a wealthy landowner who leaves her family and Xavier, her betrothed, to pursue the forbidden life of a woman healer.

Salvadore Gago - A friar and member of Clara's group who infiltrates the Inquisition to be its Clerk, thus gaining useful information for the underground.

Cecily Hasleton - Richard's aunt who takes him in and helps him escape Spain.

Richard Hasleton - English sailor who joins Clara's underground group, meets and falls in love with Ventura, saves her from death and marries her.

James Henriques - A wealthy landowner and Xavier's father.

Rafaella Henriques - Xavier's ugly sister.

Xavier Henriques - Ventura's betrothed, a wealthy landowner who betrays her after she calls off their engagement.

Dom Francisco de Hernandez - The Inquisitor General.

Diego Lopez - Ventura's friend, a tobacconist who is garrotted for disliking pork and changing his personal linen on Saturdays.

Pablo Olivedas - Helps Richard and Jozeph after the shipwreck.

Clara Rodriguez - Leader of the underground of healers and free thinkers who is burned at the stake as a heretic.

Hernando Sorell - District Commissioner and parish priest of a town near Gibraltar.

Mario do Valle - Member of the underground; a sexually-liberated woman and free thinker who teaches Ventura about the Church's corruption.

## Journey to the New World, 1671-1672

Arawaks - Indians living in Jamaica with whom Alvaro and Ventura trade.

Ann Bonny - Captain of the Pirate's Revenge.

Diogo Dias - Captain of the Merchant Cadiz.

Maroons - African slaves living in Jamaica, set free when the Spaniards flee to Cuba.

Jack Rackham - "Calico Jack" - Captain, with Ann Bonny, of the Pirate's Revenge.

Alvaro Ribeyra - Steward on the Merchant Cadiz.

Mary Read - A pirate on the Pirate's Revenge.

Verity - Ventura and Richard's daughter, born on the Merchant Cadiz.

## Salem Massachusetts, 1673-1696

Reverend Bigginson - Joseph Boyes' superior who sends him to Salem Village to help Cotton Winthrop.

Bituba - Cotton Winthrop's Barbados slave; lover of Jim Indian.

Joseph Boyes - Minister of Salem Town; part of the court during the witchcraft trial of Verity.

Charters - Richard's friend during the whaling voyage.

Sigrid Cloyce - A healer who befriends Ventura and helps her.

John Corwin - Puritan who falls in love with Ventura and plots to win her from Richard.

Abagail Goodfellow - Elizabeth Winthrop's eleven-year-old cousin who accuses Verity, among others, of being a witch.

Mrs. Griggs - Ventura and Richard's landlady.

Reverend Nicholas Hale - Called by Cotton Winthrop to help with his daughter's bewitchment; becomes part of the court that tries Verity.

Benjamin Hanover - A physician who tells Cotton Winthrop his daughter is bewitched.

Mary Hazzard - Free-thinking woman who is forced out of town for saying people can speak directly to God without going through a minister.

Jim Indian - Cotton Winthrop's slave from Barbados; lover of Bituba.

Henry Jordan - First mate on the Boston Frigate, Richard's sister ship.

Andrew Martin - Helps Ventura when she falls from her horse and is injured.

Sam Pritchard - Dockmaster with whom John Corwin plots.

Mrs. Sidle - Town gossip in Salem Village who helps Cotton Winthrop.

Oliver Stone - Governor Easty's assistant who is sent to Salem Village to observe the trials and eventually stop them.

Absalon Winthrop - Verity's sweetheart.

Cotton Winthrop - Minister of Salem Village.

Elizabeth Winthrop - Cotton Winthrop's nine-year-old daughter who is talked into accusing Verity and others of being witches.

George Venable - First mate on the Salem, Richard's whaling ship.

Governor William Easty - Governor of Massachusetts who stops the Salem Witch Trials when his wife is accused.

# BOOK I

## Seville, Spain

## 1669

# CAST INTO THE FIRE

*Seville, Spain*

1669

## 1

Something important was happening ahead in the square that April morning and Ventura da Fonceca had to find out what it was. She had guessed something was astir from the anxious murmurs of the servants in the back hall after breakfast, and seen their pinched faces closing up when she asked for particulars. That was when she had set her jaw and wheedled Xavier into bringing her to the center of town so she could find out for herself.

The spicy smells of hot sausage, unwashed bodies, horse dung, and oranges filled air, but they didn't bother Ventura. She was used to them. What did trouble her was the turbulent crowd and the snatches of clipped conversations swirling around her. "Official announcement---" said a short man, stabbing at the air with his gold-headed cane.

"It can't happen here---" said a heavy woman from behind her black fan.

"You're so naive---" said her companion, fingering his mustache nervously.

Ventura couldn't figure it out. What announcement? What couldn't happen here?

"Xavier," she coaxed, "can't we get closer?" She whispered in his ear, tugging at the arm of his waistcoat.

The eyes of the stern-faced man by her side turned disapproving. "Ventura," he said in a deep voice that was nearly a growl, "that's just not proper." His lips tightened into a scowl. "We should leave now, before anything happens."

Ventura tugged harder on his sleeve. "But what could happen?"

Ignoring her question, he turned to his sister, a thin woman whose head poked forward like a turtle out of its shell. She had huge nostrils and a rim of coarse black hair above her lip. "Rafaella," he commanded, "take this girl aside and talk some sense into--"

Before he could finish, Ventura slipped her arm out of his and dashed forward. Excitement rose inside her as she moved swiftly through the crowd. Nothing was going to stop her, not her long skirt or the stiffness of her waist cincher or even the jeers and jabs from the crowd as she pushed her way past them. Streams of black hair sprung out from under her silk mantilla, but she paid them no mind.

A thunder of hooves, and a stone-faced driver jolted his cart in front of her, urging his horses along with a whip. Jumping back, she caught her breath, then surged forward when he sped past.

The church bells clanged suddenly and a hush fell over the crowd. Everyone's eyes turned to the Casa de Ayuntamiento, the imposing building on the square where two carved female figures atop its high columns gleamed in the late morning sun.

Ventura heard a faint voice reading in a strident cadence and she pushed ahead. She could not yet make out what the voice was saying, but the tone of his voice sent a quiver of fear through her.

Then she saw him, an ugly old man in a tall-crowned hat and bobbed gray hair. Lines of bitterness curled around his mouth and his back hunched over the pages he held. He stood at the top of the steps of the Casa, nearly blending in with the scrolled figures carved in the niches of the dark wooden door.

His nasal voice carried over the crowd. "...direct, command, require and admonish that within the space of twelve days, that they should reveal it unto us if anyone know, see or have heard that any person is reported to be a heretic or a witch."

Skirts rustled as a few more brave souls pressed forward. The ugly man's voice droned on "— or if any is suspected especially of such practices as to cause injury to or save and deliver men, cattle, or the fruits of the earth, to the loss of the State."

A hand slapped the face of a small whimpering boy, cracking above the monotone voice just before the little one started his wail of protest. The nasal-voiced man crooked his neck and a fierceness flowed out of his eyes, silencing the crying child. Clearing his throat, the man continued, "The edict is signed," he paused and looked down his nose at the crowd, "Dom Francisco de Hernandez, Inquisitor General, Francisco Lopes Cazado, el Doctor, and Salvador Rodriguez, Notarius."

The hush that had overtaken the crowd during the reading changed into confused murmurs and then into a din of questioning voices. Some women whimpered and made the sign of the cross on their chests, while a few men raised clenched fists. The guards moved in swiftly, pushing back the crowd and yelling at them to disperse.

What could it all mean? Surely Xavier would know. Ventura turned to ask him, but then she remembered how she had bolted from his side to get to the front of the crowd. She grimaced and shook her head. This was the kind of thing sure to displease him. She could almost hear his intimidating voice in her ear: "As my betrothed, you are expected to follow my lead, consult me in this kind of thing, not take impulsive action." Her cheeks burned even more in dread of the tongue lashing he would give her.

Her eyes searched the crowd, darting here and there, looking for Xavier's tall thin frame and probing eyes. He had been wearing the purple waistcoat, hadn't he? With that Cavalier hat he was wearing, he should stand out in the crowd.

She thrust through the waves of people, her body twisting and turning, finding any empty space to move into. Fear gripped her throat. He couldn't have left without her. Then again, it would serve her right if she'd been too bold.

Then she saw his face and scolding eyes. She was in for it now. She dropped her head, bravery disappearing under his hot glance. He would be impossible on the way home. She wished more than ever that her father had never arranged their marriage.

Xavier grabbed her elbow and pulled her through the crowd. He smelled of sweat and lamp oil and his eyes radiated smugness. Anger built in her gut and rose to her throat. "Not so fast, Xavier," she muttered. Ignoring her, he shoved her along. Ventura pulled her elbow away.

"What has come over you, Ventura? You could have been hurt." But it wasn't concern, it was anger because she had left his side, dared to take the lead, dared to do what she wanted to do. She glanced at Xavier's sister for reassurance, but Rafaella dropped her eyes.

In some ways, he was so like her father, chastising her for her independence. "You'll never get a good husband if you insist on being so brazen. You must submit," her father had said.

Sweeping her past knots of people, Xavier tried to hurry Ventura along, but she heard bits of conversation. "Thirty were relaxed..." said a young man in breeches.

"The Malleus Maleficarum says..." whispered a nearly toothless seller of broad-sheets, clutching handwritten parchment to his chest.

"Many Marranos will burn..." said an estate bailiff with shoulder-length hair.

Their comments spurred her on and she couldn't stop herself from asking, "Xavier, what does it all mean?"

He pulled her away from the crowd. "Hurry along now, I promised your father I'd have you home before dusk."

But even his sullen eyes did not stop her. "I want to know what those people were talking about."

His eyes were black disks in a sea of sallow skin. "What people?"

He knew, he must. "Those people we passed. They were talking about being relaxed, and something called the Malleus Maleficarum. What did they mean?"

He shook his head. "There you go, always wanting to know things you should be innocent of." He sniffed, an air of judgment descending from his nostrils.

A flicker of rage passed through her. "Come on, Xavier, just tell me a little." She used the teasing, coaxing voice she had heard her mother use with her father. She hated playing these games with Xavier, but if she showed her anger to him, she would get nothing but a tight-mouthed answer and a vise-like hold of her arm.

Xavier was so strange. He only told her things if she acted coy and hid her true feelings. She wished it wasn't that way, but it was, and she would have to get used to it if she was going to be Señora Henriques.

His eyes softened to drab and he loosened his grip. "All right, I'll tell you a little, but just a little." His lips curved into a half-smile. "But walk a little faster. Try to keep up with Rafaella." She nodded and his voice took on a lecturing tone. "The Malleus Maleficarum was written by the beloved sons of Pope Innocent VIII. It says that woman is not meant to think alone, because as we know," he turned and looked at her with accusing eyes, "when she thinks alone, she thinks evil."

Ventura's cheeks burned and another flash of anger flared in her chest. She opened her mouth to protest, then closed it. If she spoke too soon, she'd never find out what she wanted to know. "What about witches?" she demanded. "I've never seen one, but my mother told me one of them cured my Uncle Joseph." Rafaella gulped, then flushed.

Xavier tilted his chin arrogantly and his eyes mocked her. "That's just the point. Women aren't supposed to be curing anyone. That is the province of el Doctor, is it not, Rafaella?" He turned to his sister, coaching her with his eyes, his voice booming in Ventura's ears.

"Of course, dear brother," said Rafaella softly, her lashes fluttering.

But why shouldn't women cure? Her mother had called the witch a wise woman. And she was a wise woman. She did something el Doctor could not do: cure her uncle. She turned her head and looked at Xavier. "What's wrong with women curing?"

"It's forbidden!" He flung his arms out in disgust. "How could you even question it? These pagan witches meet in groups to spread their vicious lies. They come together by the thousands on festival days." Xavier's face reddened to the color of her mother's ruby pin and his voice shook with anger. "They don't worship God as any self-respecting person does. They use magic potions and who knows what else." He strode down the street, dragging Ventura behind. "Enough questions now. You should be thinking about our wedding. Have you talked to your mother about the church?"

Ventura barely heard him, she was picturing witches dancing around and chanting, their hands full of vials steaming with colored vapors. What kind of rituals must they have that the church wanted so desperately to stop them? Her mind burned with questions. "Xavier," she said tentatively, patting his arm with her hand.

"Umm, hmm," he said absently.

She tried to sound matter-of-fact. "What is relaxation?" She flinched when he opened his mouth, hoping he wouldn't scold her. Instead he answered her calmly. Men were such strange creatures.

"Relaxation is when the Church turns the witches and heretics over to the authorities for punishment. The Church frowns on the shedding of blood, but the heretics and witches must be punished, mustn't they, Rafaella?" His sister nodded, the tiny green ribbon in her dull hair shaking in agreement.

"What is relaxation? If no blood is shed, what is done?"

His voice was steady. "Why they are burned at the stake, my dear. Tortured first to obtain names of other witches and heretics, and then burned at the stake."

Ventura shuddered. Burned? What a gruesome, slow death. What must it be like to be roasted alive? Could they smell themselves burning? Maybe they passed out from the heat before they died. Her face contorted in confusion and abhorrence. "Isn't that a bit severe?"

"One does not question the wisdom of the Pope." He stared at her with a look in his eyes that told her there would be no further discussion on this point.

She sighed and looked away, fighting back the tears. How could he accept such cruelty without question? But then, he never questioned anything. If the Pope said it was so, for him it was so. And Rafaella, poor unmarried ugly duck - she agreed with whatever her brother said.

Ventura needed more information before she made up her mind. But that was exactly what got her into so much trouble. If only her mind was not so inquisitive.

She remembered the wise woman who had helped her uncle. "You mean all those branded witches or heretics are burned?" If there was even a chance that would happen, she'd never tell the priest about it. But what if Xavier made her tell, or if he told himself? What kind of trouble had she started now?

"Well," he said, rubbing his chin, "I've never really witnessed a burning. Usually only royalty is invited. But I did see a few garotted when I was in Portugal." He sniffed again. "Come along now, enough questions for today." With that, he hurried her down the street.

Garotting. That was almost as bad as burning. Imagine some dirty thug putting his fat, greasy hands around your neck and squeezing the last breath out of you. It was hard to believe it could happen, but Xavier had seen it. Of course, not in Seville. Seville was more civilized.

She couldn't resist asking, "Why would they burn the Marranos? They're Christians. They don't go in for secret rituals. I've seen them in church."

Resentment quavered in Xavier's voice. "That's true enough, but they are Jews and Moslems. Just because they've accepted baptism, don't let them fool you. My father has seen what they can do. They've risen to powerful posts in Seville, and for all their talk of being Christian, in their hearts they are still heathen."

They reached her home within minutes, Xavier and Rafaella saying a hurried good-bye. Ventura was in a hurry, too. Feet thudding, she raced up the outside steps. She glanced up to the second floor, past the family crest, to her mother's bedchamber.

The heavy metal knocker fell with a resounding clunk three times on the door before a young servant girl opened it. Ventura pushed inside and ran toward the stairs. She took them two at a time, pushing handfuls of her skirt out of the way as she went. She arrived breathless at the second floor and burst into her mother's bedchamber. A heady smell of roses greeted her.

Her mother swiveled from the mirror. Her voice was a warm caress. "Do not run, Ventura. A lady does not run."

"Mother! Mother! You'll never guess what I saw!"

Her mother stood up, the purple silk of her dress whispering across the floor. Teresa da Fonceca's face was delicately made, pale with smooth lips and dark blue eyes. Her raven hair coiled tightly behind her head showed off the gold at her earlobes. "Calm down, Ventura, you'll bring on a bad humor." Her mother arranged a stiff curl beside her ear.

Ventura shook her head. "Good humors. Bad humors. I don't believe in any of it."

"Don't be silly, Ventura. The doctors have studied at the university and they know all about the complexions and temperaments." Her hand smoothed the rigid stomacher at her waist.

Ventura sighed. "They study logic at the university. What good are Plato and Aristotle to the sick? All they offer us are bleeding by leeches or orders to eat less garlic or cabbage."

Her mother shook her head and clicked her tongue. "Now, you know when you eat too much garlic your bile goes red."

"How do I know that? I've never seen it, but I have seen el Doctor. What a clumsy, stupid man. Remember when I had a toothache and he touched a needle to a caterpillar and then to my aching tooth? It didn't help at all. Besides, he smells of onions and has greasy hair and dirty fingernails." Ventura pointed at her mother. "And he leers at you."

"Now Ventura---."

"He even tried to rub against me in the doorway." Ventura swallowed in disgust. "Afterwards he pretended he had only been clumsy, but I know better."

"Child, what an imagination you have---."

"But mother, it's true, and you should have been in the square today. There was a man reading an edict. It was nailed to the door of Casa de Ayuntamiento. Everyone has twelve days to bring forth the names of all witches and heretics."

Her mother drew a sharp shocked breath. "Santa Maria," she made the sign of the cross, "So it's happening here, too."

"What's happening here, too?" Ventura pulled at her mother's sleeve. "Do you know about relaxation and the Malleus Maleficarum, too?" She stamped her foot in irritation and started to pace the room. "Does everyone know but me what's happening in Seville?" She whirled around and threw her hands to her head before she collapsed in her mother's arms.

Teresa da Fonceca stroked her daughter's forehead. "I know about it. I wish I didn't." Ventura jerked her head back and looked at her mother. "Your Aunt Isabel wrote me from Portugal. Hundreds of women have been burned at the stake and thousands come from the countryside to see the spectacle. They call it the auto de fe. Not very Christian if you ask me, but the Pope says we must protect against heresy from within and without." She released Ventura, crossed herself, and looked up toward the religious figures carved in relief on the ornamental ceiling.

Ventura jumped to her feet. "But what about the wise woman? Are you going to report her?"

"I don't know, dear. I'll have to discuss it with your father. I'm not sure what to do." She shrugged hopelessly, shaking her head.

Ventura grabbed her mother's chin in her hands. "But you can't report her. She helped Uncle Luis. She can't be a witch, can she?"

"Your father says the Malleus Maleficarum affirms even women who do good are witches. Curing is for el Doctor."

"But you don't believe him, do you? Well, do you?"

"Well---."

"Mother," she said in an agonized voice. "That sounds just like Xavier."

"Did he say the same thing?"

"Yes, and he was so sure and stern about it." Ventura turned on her heel and started to walk away. "Well, I'm not so sure," she said loudly enough for her mother to hear.

"Ventura. Ventura! Where are you going?"

"I'm going out to the garden. I need to do some thinking." Ventura hurried down the stairs, past the ornate gold frames holding the likeness of all the da Foncecas. The back door opened with a creak to a cool evening breeze and the sweet odor of flowers. She looked out across the arcade patio.

Softly yapping, her dog, Capita, ran to her side. Ventura stood silently, feeling the cool, grainy surface of the scrolled column beside her. "Come, Capita," she whispered, wandering out to the stone fountain. They stood together, watching the slender tinkling waterfall. Aroused from their stupor by their presence, two brown doves took flight, whiffling the air with their feathers.

"You don't believe mother, do you, Capita?" The dog's wrinkled paw plopped down on Ventura's foot, then she yawned and nuzzled into Ventura's leg.

Ventura lifted her head heavenward and raised a silent prayer. "Please, Blessed Virgin, help me decide what to do." Then she waited silently, thinking about the man on the square who had read the edict. Her heart gave a cry of sadness for all those who had died. For all those who were about to die.

Capita barked and Ventura kneeled down to pat the dog's silky head. She whispered in Capita's ear, "We have to find out more, don't we? And we must hurry!"

# 2

The library door was not completely closed, and Ventura could hear her parents' anxious voices. She stood against the door, holding her breath, pressing her ear to the opening.

The words were muffled, but she heard, Marrano and garotted. They were discussing the Inquisition! She thrust open the door and ran inside. "Who is being garotted? When? Why?" Ventura demanded, passing the well-polished desk in the corner and the chairs and couches of the best wood and richest silks and brocades.

"Ventura! Listening in on others' conversation is very rude," said her mother softly from her apple green chair in the corner. Capita raised her head from her nestling place on Teresa da Fonceca's knee and barked. "Antonio," her mother's voice pleaded, "Maybe we should tell her, caution her. She must know these things before she does something foolish."

Her father stood by an intricately-carved fireplace, looking grand in his heavy cloak, tight silk breeches and the sparkling gold medallion that hung nearly to his waist. He was a handsome man with flashing dark eyes and tightly waved black hair that nearly touched his shoulders.

He stroked his chin, considering. Finally he said, "Very well, Ventura, I will tell you, but you must promise not to get involved in this. Now, promise me."

She swallowed. A tingle of guilt washed over her. No, she wasn't going to promise anything until she learned more. She smiled at him. "But father, why are you questioning me like this?"

"Because I know you, my daughter. You are an inquisitive señorita. I know how you are always sticking that pretty little nose of yours in things that do not concern you."

His eyes glimmered with affection, making her bold. "Tell me, father. What has happened?" She walked over and put her hand on his arm. He smelled of horses and apples.

He touched the thin mustache above his lips nervously. "Don Simoa, our neighbor, has reported a New Christian for his Judaising."

"Who? Who did he report?"

He squeezed his daughter's hands gently. "It was Diego Lopez."

Her shoulders rose and fell in a sigh. "The tobacconist? The man who used to give me sweets when you took me with you to buy tobacco?"

Her father's face flushed and he looked away. "Yes. I'm afraid he has lapsed into his old ways."

She knew Diego. He was a Christian. How could anything bad happen to him? She looked into her father's eyes. "What do you mean, lapsed?"

"He will be garotted tomorrow in the square."

Her eyes were a blur with tears. How could something so terrible befall Diego, the gentlest man she knew? Her knees went weak and she sat down heavily on the nearest couch.

"That's one thing I don't understand, Tonio," said her mother. "Didn't he confess to changing his personal linen on Saturday and disliking pork? Why wasn't his confession enough to save him from dying?"

Her father shrugged. "It was enough to save him from burning, but not from dying." He started to pace." I am not the Pope, I do not make the rules. He will be garroted tomorrow at the auto de fe and I can do nothing about it." He stopped pacing and looked deep into his daughter's eyes. "Now, Ventura, under no circumstances are you to go to the square! No circumstances, you hear me?" Anger was in his voice, but there was a hint of challenge there, too.

Her voice caught in her throat, then rushed out. "But why shouldn't I go to the square? Everyone else will be there. Why can't I go?"

Her father's dark eyes searched hers. "It's too dangerous. Not long ago, Juanes de Burua, the carpenter, was knocked down and badly hurt by the crowd at the auto de fe. You could be hurt, badly hurt. Promise me you won't go."

"Oh, father, why would I want to go to a garotting?" She didn't want to lie to her father, but she had to see first hand what was going on in Seville.

***

Early the next morning, she crept out of the house, leaving her mother a vague note about visiting one of her friends for the day. When the heavy front door closed behind her there was a finality to it that almost made her go back inside. But the sun shimmering down the buildings, making quivering patterns on the stones below, drew her ahead. Steeling herself, she took a deep breath and hurried down the street.

She was barely a block away when a tide of peasants nearly swept her away with them. A chasm of fear opened up inside her. They pushed and shoved her to the side, cursing and shouting to one another, saying something about hurrying to the auto de fe. They were foul-smelling with pale flashes of agitation and passion jumping out of their eyes. Her heart beat fast and sluggish in her throat. Maybe she shouldn't go after all. Maybe father was right about the trip being dangerous.

No. She must go. She had to find out.

She followed the noisy peasants to the square. Heart pounding, her feet clicked along the stone street. Poor Diego. What was to become of him? The overwhelming sweet smell of the flower sellers' rose-laden carts made her head reel. Why was Diego being singled out? What was the Church up to? She hurriedly touched her forehead, chest, then her left shoulder and right shoulder, lowering her head in case God might think her too bold.

Peasants were streaming toward the square from all directions, looking as if they'd slept outdoors. Ventura picked her way through the crowds. The country women and maidservants smelled of body odors, while the inn-serving maids eyed Ventura, calling out to her in vulgar tones. Farmers smelling of manure and hay eyed her too, but in a different way. Ventura pulled her mantilla around her face, put her head down, and hurried on.

Nearing the square, she saw a procession winding its way through the streets. Men carried staves with brightly colored pictures of Jesus on the cross, the Pope and various saints. One of the tall priests brandished a gold emblem. Behind them plodded the parish priest and his monks. Plump and winded, church choristers sang psalms in a minor key that reminded her of a dirge.

A line of barefoot men and women walked behind, their faces dull with depression and hopelessness. They smelled of death and sickness. Some wore long yellow robes with black St. Andrew's crosses on them and they carried lighted candles. Others wore the sack cloth of penitence with figures of devils and flames painted on them.

The crowd started to chant: "Burn! Burn! Burn!" Priests trudged by carrying doll-like effigies of dismembered bodies with grotesque faces on long poles. "No more dolls. Bring on the live ones to burn!" shouted a tall man with a frozen smile and grim eyes.

Ventura turned her eyes heavenward and a vile sickness beat within her heart. "Oh, God, forgive the angry voices for their unchristian words," she muttered, crossing herself. Finishing her prayer, she opened her eyes and searched again for Diego, but all she saw were more priests, some carrying small coffins of the ones who had died in prison. Behind them came six condemned men with straps around their necks. "Whip them!" shouted a fat man with sweat glistening on his face.

Ventura shuddered. How cruel the Church was, and how cruel the crowd. Mumbled rosaries and a few hoarse shouts of prayer to Jesus or Mary punctuated the chants for blood. Well-dressed men and priests on horseback came by. Even greasy el Doctor was there, carrying a standard with a green cross on it. He saw Ventura and winked at her, a leer plastered on his face. She crossed herself and looked away.

Growled psalms mingled with screams and moans from the condemned. Peasants jeered and cheered as the procession moved past. Then she saw Diego, head down, body shriveled. She screamed his name and was nearly pushed into the parade, but warm hands pulled her back. "Are you all right?" whispered the pleasant-faced, plump woman in a scarf and long-flowing clothes. She had surprisingly soft features and lively eyes full of compassion. Her hands were bold and coarse like a laborer's, but something vital stirred beneath their surface.

A guard nearby glared at Ventura and the woman whispered to her: "Keep your voice down. The Church does not look kindly on sympathizers."

Ventura looked at the woman. "But I'm no sympathizer. I know Diego, he's---."

The old woman shook her head sadly. "Thousands of people have died so the Church won't lose its monopoly on tithes and sacraments."

"You mean the Church would force people to believe in Catholicism and silence those who don't?" Before the woman could answer, a cart thundered up the street and careened toward them. At the last instant, the woman's strong arm grabbed Ventura and pulled her safely to the side. The cart flew by, depositing its cargo of exhumed corpses in front of Ventura. She screamed, a shriek as thin and sharp as a shard of broken glass. The smell of decomposition was putrid and sulfurous. Grinning lips smiled in a worm-eaten head. She screamed again and the guard took a step toward her, the sharp edge of his lance glinted, coming within inches of her face.

The old woman stepped forward and said to the guard, "I stepped on her foot with my cane. She won't do it again." The guard nodded, withdrew his weapon and retreated into the crowd.

The old woman sighed with relief and turned to Ventura. "You mustn't show any sympathy or anything but glee. Otherwise you'll be branded a sympathizer and that's only one step above a heretic in the Church's eyes."

Ventura couldn't believe her ears. Her heart chugged away, making breathing nearly impossible. New ideas and images forced their way into her brain, confusing her, choking the breath out of her. The comforting arm came around her again and she leaned against the old woman until her mind cleared.

"The ceremony is starting," said the woman's soft voice. "Look there. The ones to be burned are on the highest scaffold. The ones below will be reconciled today."

A pulpit and temporary altar, both draped in black, stood between the two stages. To the delight of the crowd, a dark stocky man in a black robe held up a cross. Those around her cheered and raised their arms in approval. The din was so great Ventura had to cover her ears with her hands.

When the crowd finally quieted, the stocky man began to speak. Ventura couldn't hear all the words, but "solemnly defending the Catholic faith and supporting the Inquisition" came to her loud and clear. In one voice, the crowd shouted approval, nearly knocking Ventura down as it swayed and pushed forward. Only a few raised silent prayers to the Almighty, crossing themselves with panicky hands as they asked for forgiveness for the torturers.

A man in purple bishop's robes moved to the altar and began a sermon. His angry voice carried over the crowd, spewing a torrent of insults, his thin hand pointing toward the condemned. He read for a long time from a green velvet book, calling out the names of the accused.

One by one the penitents were led to the altar and the man read their sentences. A small child sat on her father's shoulders in front of Ventura, clapping and laughing while the bishop droned on.

Ventura couldn't digest it all. Exhumed bodies. Garotting in the square. Peasants shouting enthusiastically. The Church dressing people in holy robes and sentencing them to death for little more than common behavior made a sick feeling creep up inside her. Images of the spectacle burst in her mind. Then everything went black.

***

The fires were consuming her. The devil leered from el Doctor's face, his voice came out of the bishop's mouth like an utterance from hell and his hand held the guard's lance.

Ventura's eyes fluttered open. An angelic face framed in a radiant light leaned over her. The face came into focus. It wasn't an angel at all, it was the old woman who had spoken to her in the square. Ventura looked around her. She was in a tiny cottage. The room smelled of spices, herbs and garlic. A cool cloth touched down on her forehead. "What happened?" she murmured and tried to sit up.

"You fainted. These goings-on are a bit much for any but the sadistic and depraved. I only went because my friend, Sophia, was being garotted and I could not stay away." A look of pain came over her face, then vanished. "By the way, my name is Clara, Clara Rodriguez." Before Ventura could introduce herself, the old woman hobbled away to a short stool by the fireplace.

The room held few trappings of wealth---no ornate scrolls, garlands or shells carved in the furniture or fireplace, no silk draperies, and only crude wooden furniture. Yet there was warmth there and comfort. The fire snapped and hissed, lighting the room and illuminating Clara's face. Hanging from the fireplace was a steaming metal pot. The smell of a pungent stew reached Ventura's nostrils, making her realize it had been hours since she'd eaten.

A crudely-made wooden box with a leather carrying-strap stood in the corner. Several long shelves on the wall opposite the fireplace held tightly-sealed jars with labels that read: Digitalis, Belladona, Ergot, and Peppermint.

Clara smiled, stood up and put some of the stew in a deep clay dish, before she hobbled back to the bed. "Here, have some of this. It will warm you and balance your energy."

When she laid the bowl in Ventura's hand, a mysterious raw force touched her. She stared at Clara's hands, then she looked in the old woman's eyes and saw the strength reflected there.

Awed, she swallowed. "Is this your home?" She took a mouthful of stew. It tasted of potato and basil and felt warm in her stomach.

Clara's voice was vibrant and low. "Yes, this is my home and my work-space. Sometimes it's our meeting place."

Ventura glanced back at the jars. "What kind of work do you do?"

"I'm a healer."

"A doctor?"

"No, a healer. I work mostly with herbs." She pointed to the shelves holding the well-sealed jars. "This one will help a woman deliver her baby with less pain. This one will relieve gas in the stomach. This one is for fever and gangrene. Each one has a use in my practice. And of course, I use my hands. My hands help people heal." She looked down at them proudly. "I consider myself to be a channel for God's energy."

Ventura considered Clara's words while she finished the stew. Somewhere in the back of her mind, Ventura heard Xavier's words warning her that women were forbidden to heal, but she pushed them farther back, covering them over with questions she needed to find answers to. "You don't believe in humors, Clara?"

Clara smiled. "Humors! They just don't make sense. I believe in what I see with my eyes, smell with my nose, and touch with my hands." As she spoke, Clara pointed to her eyes and nose, and then touched Ventura on the arm lightly, leaving a trace of warmth behind.

Ventura set the empty bowl down on the table beside her. "But what about the Church's teaching that women can't be healers?"

"I know what I do is dangerous, but I have to help people. I have a gift. My hands are Godgiven and I'm going to use them, even if el Doctor and the Church say I mustn't!"

Ventura nodded. She and Clara had so much in common. It certainly wasn't their age and, from the looks of her home, it wasn't their backgrounds. It was inquisitiveness and daring they shared. She must learn all she could from this woman.

There was no question in her mind. She would start a new life, one that might mean suffering and poverty, but that would be a meaningful life. Swallowing her fear, she blurted out, "My name is Ventura da Fonceca and I want you to teach me all you know. Will you do it? I want to learn everything!"

Clara smiled and put her hands on Ventura's shoulders, sending a tingle of warmth coursing down her arms. "I would love to do that, but you must take time and think about this. Joining my group means danger and risk. Some have already been tortured and burned for heresy and witchcraft. It is not an easy road even if we are not discovered. There is much ignorance and illness that you will be exposed to, and country folk cannot pay much. Most only come to us after they have spent their money on el Doctor."

"I don't have to think about it. I know." Ventura looked into Clara's eyes and they both nodded.

"Very well. When you have rested, I will take you home. Come here tomorrow evening at seven o'clock and you will begin your course of study."

Ventura didn't want to leave Clara. Her mind bubbled with questions about healing.

Finally Clara said, "Your family will be worried. You must go." For some reason, Ventura did not protest. If Clara said it, it must be true.

At home, Ventura lay awake most of the night thinking about what had happened to her that day. She offered up a prayer of thanks to the Blessed Virgin. Tomorrow she would begin her new life. Only when she fell asleep did the frightening images of the exhumed corpses come back to torment her.

## 3

All the next day, Ventura's thoughts were on Clara and the meeting that was to take place that evening. Several times she caught her mother watching her inquisitively, her dark eyes questioning. Before her mother could ask, Ventura said, "I'm going to evening mass."

Pulling her mantilla around her for warmth, she hurried down the narrow winding streets to the poorer section of Seville, her feet echoing hollowly in the shadows. Clara's house was one of the many attached two-story houses. Laundry and colorful flowers hung from its windows.

Ventura arrived early, but Clara didn't seem to mind. She showed the young woman into the room with the fireplace. "I'll be back in a few minutes," the old woman said, smiling.

The room caught the gleam of the fire, sending bursts of rosy bloom along the walls and happy crackles into the air. Ventura sat down on one of the stools and gazed intently at the jars of herbs, wondering which one was for stomach upset and which one for childbirth pain.

The front door banged open and an attractive woman in her late twenties flounced over to the fireplace . She was tall and angular with a face full of fun. An aura of jasmine surrounded her. Her luxuriant hair was piled on top of head and cobalt light gleamed from her enormous eyes. "Hello, I'm Maria do Valle," she said in a voice that was low and sensual. She pulled up a stool and sat down next to Ventura, her dress rustling when she arranged it beneath her. "Don't you just hate these skirts?" she said, slanting her open palm beside her mouth as if she were telling a secret.

Ventura nodded. "Yes, I'm always complaining to my mother about how ridiculous the fashion is. I think Clara dresses the right way."

Maria wrinkled her nose. "A little too plain for my taste, but she has the right idea." She smiled and her clear eyes presented a direct challenge: "If you like the way she dresses, why don't you dress that way, too?"

Ventura was startled and confused. But weren't Maria's words exactly what she'd thought many times but been afraid to act on? But she'd do it now. Tomorrow she'd alter her dresses or have some new ones made. If she were going to start a new life, she'd need a more suitable wardrobe. She glanced at Maria who was staring into the fire. "You're here to learn about healing, too?"

"Mmmm. Sort of," said Maria, winking at Ventura from behind her silk handkerchief. The lavender feather in the back of her hair fluttered and her curls bounced back and forth when she spoke. The red flower clipped to the bosom of her dress barely covered the cleavage between her breasts when she leaned toward Ventura and spoke in a low voice. "People come here for other reasons, my dear," she said, lifting her eyebrows and winking again.

"What other reasons?"

"It's fashionable for ladies of intrigue and danger to meet here." She sniffed, her nostrils quivering. "Women of high social standing are drawn to this group. It is not only healing that goes on here." She winked again, confusing Ventura even more. "My dear, you don't know? Is this your first time here? But then it must be. I have never seen you here. I would have remembered your pretty face."

Maria smiled and pulled her stool closer to Ventura. "You see, any woman who thinks alone, thinks evil, according to the Malleus." Ventura nodded, remembering the words Xavier had spoken.

A slight pout curved Maria's lips. "That includes women who think progressively about sex. You are aware of the Church's preoccupation with sexual crimes."

"Yes---" said Ventura, not wanting to appear stupid for not knowing.

"Then you know that the Church associates women with sex, and all pleasure in sex is condemned because it could only come for the devil. Lust in men is always blamed on us, my dear. We are the temptresses, are we not?"

Ventura nodded, her head spinning with new ideas.

"We women of sexual pleasure are in jeopardy just as healers are. They lump us all together as witches. The Church even makes the woman look bad in the wonder of childbirth."

Ventura leaned toward Maria. "They do?"

"My dear, your priest must have sermonized about how during intercourse the male deposits in the female a little person complete with soul which is simply housed in the womb for nine months, without acquiring any of the attributes of the mother." Marie's eyes snapped with anger. "If I had carried a child, don't you think it would have at least some of my characteristics? The Church's position on this, as on many other things, is simply ridiculous."

Ventura sat staring at her companion, mouth open, mind trying to take in all Maria had said.

"Their teachings on the matter are outrageous!" Maria fanned her flushing face with her handkerchief. "Especially the one about a pure infant not being safe in the womb, and being in danger until it reaches male hands when it is baptized by a priest and is ensured the salvation of its immortal soul. Hmph! Who do these self-righteous men think they are?"

Ventura nodded. It *was* the men in the Church who decided everything. But then, the Pope was a man. Suddenly, things Ventura had accepted all her life as truth were question marks.

Never stopping to think if she were committing blasphemy, Ventura nodded her agreement with every word Maria spoke. "Then, of course, the fact that we have the audacity to meet regularly in groups frightens the Church. They want to keep us separate and afraid, not trusting each other, so then we will cling to the Church for help. Witches serves a very useful purpose. With the peasants blaming them for crop destruction and plague and even famine, the Church and State are seen as protectors, rather than as the ones responsible for disasters, or as the ones charging ever-increasing tithes and taxes without providing any of the help we need."

Ventura shook her head, trying to keep all the new ideas straight. These were revolutionary thoughts that made her heart beat like a frightened animal, while her mind hungered for more. What Maria said explained the burnings and the peoples' obvious glee in seeing so-called heretics punished. They saw the authorities as their protectors, punishing the guilty.

"A few condemned screams and unfair trials do nothing to reassure me!" Maria's eyes flashed.

"But aren't only heretics punished?"

"My dear child, have you read the Listas? Defenseless old women, lower-class midwives, healers, old men and children and the poor are on them. These are the ones without power to speak."

"But aren't there some nobility on the lists?"

"I've been to every auto de fe. That name, in itself, is a misnomer. Now I ask you, how can burning be an act of faith? Pah! Such liars and thieves." She brushed back a clump of hair from her brow. "Only three times has a member of nobility been accused and in every case, not one was executed!"

Maria sighed deeply. "But enough of my lectures. My goodness, I do get fired up, don't I?" She laughed and touched Ventura's arm. "You think about what I have said and decide for yourself. That is the only way. Now let me tell you about pleasanter affairs."

"Pleasanter affairs?"

Maria smiled coyly. "Yes, my love affairs. They are, shall we say, notorious throughout the province." She fanned her face. "You haven't heard rumors about my exploits?"

Ventura thought a moment. She knew nothing at all about love or affairs. Her mother had evaded her questions, telling her Xavier would teach her everything she needed to know once they were married. Ventura looked at Maria and said, "No. I haven't heard anything about your love affairs, but then I don't go out often."

"Well, perhaps you're too young. At any rate, the rumor is that I have ceded." She fluttered her fan in front of her face and then dropped it below her chin. "The more malicious say I've sold my favours. But, then, I can count theViceroy himself and many of the proudest colonial hidalgos as my lovers. I sit, or should I say lie, very close to the seat of power."

Maria's voice erupted into a chuckle that shook her curls in a waterfall of auburn color. She tapped Ventura's shoulder with her gold-edged fan. "I must be very careful to keep up on the latest information and rumors. It is not unlikely that the Inquisitor General will try to unseat me soon, and people who come here have the freshest information on that point."

Before Ventura could register her shock or utter a word, another beautiful but very young woman entered the room. She couldn't have been more than a few years older than Ventura. She was slender, with hair piled atop her head in thick black waves, and a small defiant nose between her wide cheekbones.

Maria turned and smiled a secret smile at her friend. "Elvira, my dear, what intrigues have you been up to?"

Elvira sauntered over, her silk skirt rustling as she bent over to kiss Maria on the back of her neck. "My dear," giggled Maria, "in public?" They both laughed loudly and Ventura felt uncomfortable as if some secret joke had been told that she did not understand. She looked back at Elvira and found beautiful green eyes eyeing her body carefully before she smiled approvingly at Maria. Ventura had no idea what had happened, but she felt a tingle of excitement pass through her body before her cheeks turned burning hot.

Elvira snickered. "What have you done, Maria, brought us a delicious new temptress?"

Maria shook a finger at her friend. "Naughty Elvira. Leave the girl alone. She is here to learn from Clara, she's not a hermaphrodite like you. One never knows which sex you are!"

Ventura's whole face went hot. Maria smiled. "Why look at this poor child blush. Look what you've done now, you bad girl," she said, rubbing Elvira's arm slowly. "She is a bad girl, you know," Maria said, turning to look at Ventura then back at Elvira. "Tell her about yourself, Elvira."

Elvira sat down on a stool next to Ventura, straightening her bodice in a way that was more like a caress. Maria whispered in Ventura's ear. "It's quite a story, my dear, one that will enhance your education in such matters."

Elvira yawned and said in a bored voice, "I'm not telling anything. Where is Clara anyway?"

Maria batted a hand at her friend. "Creeping around somewhere. We're early, you know."

"Well, I'm going to find her," said Elvira, getting up and leaving the room.

Marie giggled." Yes, Elvira's quite a woman, or should I say, man."

"Man?"

"Yes, it's hard to keep up with her. She was married right and proper when she was fifteen. Even had a son. but then she wearied of the female role and seduced the mistress of the house."

"Her mother-in-law?"

"So they say. But that's not all." Maria's fan fluttered. "So bold was she that she seduced several other women before she truly took on the male role."

"The male role?" Ventura gulped her words, hardly believing what she'd heard.

"Yes, indeed. She served as a soldier during the Morisco rebellion in Granada, worked in a hospital at Madrid and even gained a surgeon's certificate."

"She's a doctor?"

"Of sorts. Being a professional man requires a regular domestic life so she found herself a tantalizing young thing and proceeded to propose. Of course the girl's family was suspicious of the bridegroom's hairless face and feminine manners. She would have pulled it off except the family finally insisted Elvira be examined by a doctor."

"What happened then?"

"He found her out, of course. She may have acted like a man, but underneath it all, she is a woman." Her laugh echoed through the room. "Unfortunately for her, the physician happened to be the doctor for the Inquisition and he turned her over, claiming she'd made a pact with the devil."

"But she wasn't burned or garotted?"

"No, you saw her in the flesh." Another low laugh. "She is perfectly fine. Personally, I think she seduced someone and received a lesser sentence."

"What kind of sentence?"

"Two hundred lashes and ten years hospital service without pay. She's still serving that sentence, but she comes here to learn from Clara. She's not in favor with humors and thinks Clara's healing measures are better."

Ventura sighed. She had never met such women. Women who spoke their minds so directly and acted on their feelings. Women who dared to be different. Before she could asked any more questions, the room swelled with men and women of all shapes and sizes, all of them chattering noisily. Some took up seats on the floor, others on the wooden bench or on stools.

Clara came in then, carrying jars and papers in her arm. She stood opposite the bench, leaning on her cane. A hush fell over the group and Clara began. "Before we start the healing class, there are some announcements. For those of you who have never been here before," she look into Ventura's eyes and smiled, "welcome." You will be starting your education in things having to do with the Inquisition, for if you take the path of a female healer, you will surely be in danger from them. So, think well before joining us."

Clara looked back at the group. "In fact, my friends, we must all be more vigilant. Violente Maria, a member of our group since last year has just been taken by the guards to the dungeon." A few people cried and someone moaned loudly.

"Another attempt by the Church to deflect attack from themselves," said a young grim-faced man sitting on the bench.

Clara nodded. "I'm afraid so, but the peasants won't believe it. The Inquisition serves the Church, the State and the peasants well. If it didn't, it would not survive." Murmurs of agreement rippled through the room.

Ventura looked at each person around her. There was a bond between them like she'd never seen. Even her own family were more concerned with their own private thoughts and day-to-day conventions. These people were alive in a way that was new and exciting.

The moans turned to wails and an old woman with white hair was led from the room by a humpbacked man. Clara sighed. "For those of you who do not know, that was Violente's patron." She sighed again. "Violente will no doubt be tortured until she confesses to heresy. We can only hope that she does not reveal the name of any of us gathered here."

A murmur of fear passed through the group. Clara held up her hand and the room grew quiet. "Let this not dissuade us from the important work we are doing here."

"We must continue, only we must be most careful. Avoid talking about our work to others, especially if you suspect they represent the Church or the State. Those of you who are healers, be especially careful that no physicians are in attendance when you practice."

A young woman opposite Ventura stood to speak. She was so beautiful and stately in her long white gown that Ventura could not take her eyes off her. Her skin was clear and fair, her blonde hair flowing softly down her back. Even her deep-set blue eyes immediately commanded attention. She spoke in a clear, crisp voice. "Clara, I was treating my client, Miguel Vicente, the other day and a physician was in attendance. He had come to see my work because he was amazed at how well Miguel is healing. The doctor told me he had tried everything he could think of and the man was still in agonizing pain. I tried the healing salves and even the Ergot I used for his wife's birthing pain. Nothing worked. Then I moved my hands above his body the way I've seen you do and within minutes, his pain lessened and he slept. The doctor was astounded and begged me to teach him. Should I?"

"Anna, that is a difficult question." Clara's face contorted in concern and anguish and the animation drained out of eyes. "You will be putting yourself in jeopardy if you do teach el Doctor. On the other hand, teaching our skills to others means more people can heal."

Clara started to pace. A few minutes later, she stopped and looked back at Anna. "The best I can do is to tell you about the dangers. Then you must make your own decision in the matter."

Anna sat down, but Ventura kept watching her. Ventura wasn't sure if she was attracted to her beauty, her stateliness, or her words. The only thing Ventura knew for sure was that she had to talk to Anna.

The room was abuzz with whispering for several minutes before everyone quieted down. Then Clara asked, "Any more announcements?" When there were none, a sigh of relief passed through the group, making Ventura think that most announcements contained very bad news.

Clara shared her new treatment for heart palpitations: hawthorne berries. She passed a jar around for healers to take samples from. "Remember, now," she cautioned, "do not use dried foxglove anymore, the effects are too hard to control. Don't forget to keep a diary of any observed effects. Use your eyes and ears to observe, but always ask your clients for their reactions."

When all the questions about the new herb had been answered, Clara turned to Anna and said, "Come, let us show them what I am teaching you."

All eyes were riveted on the front of the room. Clara seated Anna in a chair facing the others. "God has given us the talent to use our hands to heal. But when we don't awaken and use it, we forget how. First we must protect ourselves. Think of a shield of God's heavenly light surrounding you, allowing you to open up to healing energy. Feel it flow from heaven into your heart and down into your hands."

The room seemed to relax into the light. This was what church should be like, a communion of spirits. There were no candles, jewels, altars, stained glass, splendid garments, priests, sin or damnation here. Clara brought love and caring with her, and Ventura was sure that here resided God's presence.

Excitement and pleasure coursed through her when her palms started to tingle with warmth. She knew God's heavenly light had entered them. "I feel it! I feel it!" she shouted, then covered her mouth, feeling heat rising on her cheeks.

The others smiled encouragement and gave her reassuring glances. These people weren't the least like Xavier or father: no criticism, no suppression, no playing of games here.

Clara's fingers were positioned a few inches away from Anna, and she moved her hands down Anna's body and beyond her feet in a sweeping motion. The old woman's hands flowed so gracefully, they seem to be moved by some invisible force. When Clara finished, she turned to her audience. "Now you try it on each other. Look for cold or heat or tingling spots. Try to balance the energy so it flows evenly and smoothly throughout the body."

Maria waved Ventura over. "You want to try, don't you? Go ahead, I'm yours."

Ventura nodded and moved her hands slowly down Maria's body, feeling cold at Maria's neck and heat near Maria's stomach. She held her breath and asked, "Do you have any pain anywhere?"

Maria burped. "I shouldn't have had that sausage."

Ventura smiled. "Anywhere else?"

Maria rubbed her forehead. "You know, I feel one of my headaches coming on."

Ventura hugged Maria. She had been right. Her hands had found what ailed Maria. She was very young and knew little of life, but she could be a healer. It was clear to her now. It was as if God had reached down and shown her the path she was to follow. There would be no turning back now.

***

"I'm Ventura de Fonceca; I've been dying to meet you," Ventura said to Anna after the meeting. "I just know we'll be great friends."

Anna looked at her, surprised. "Well---well---" she said, finally smiling and taking Ventura's hand. "Yes, you have the touch. We will be friends."

Clara looked at them both with approval in her eyes. "Anna, you shall be Ventura's patron. Take her with you on your visits tomorrow." She put her arms around both young women. "Teach her well." She looked into Anna's eyes. "I think she has the hands and heart to be a great healer."

Ventura felt a surge of warmth and satisfaction. All her life her parents had been preparing her for marriage and protecting her from life. She stared at Clara in wonder. This woman believed that she, Ventura da Fonceca, could do something, be someone.

She was more at home here than she was with her parents. She felt like pinching herself to make sure she wasn't dreaming. But it was real. It was happening and she was very happy. Happier than she was with Father. Happier than when she was with Capita on the patio. Much happier than she could ever be with Xavier.

Clara was called away then to talk with a tall man in black who stood by the door, so Anna pulled Ventura over to the pot of hot coffee. Ventura accepted the warm brew from her new friend. "How long have you been studying with Clara?" she asked.

"Two years now. She healed my father. He fell down the stairs and el Doctor could not get it to heal. His leg was swollen and hot. El Doctor gave us no hope. We heard of Clara's work and sent word to her. She came and put green leaves on the wound. She said the green in the leaves would help. Then she used her healing hands. In a week he was up and about. From that day, I devoted myself to study with her."

Ventura felt a tug at her heart and tears came to her eyes. The rest of her life fell away as if it had never happened. It was her past. This was her future.

She would study night and day. She would be the best student Clara and Anna had ever seen. She would be at Anna's side every day, learning. She grabbed Anna's hand. "When will we begin? Where? How do I prepare?"

Anna smiled at her and said softly, "Wait. One question at a time. I will meet you here, at Clara's, tomorrow morning when the church bells chime for mass." She looked at Ventura's clothes. "Come in comfortable clothes. That tight-waisted, wide-hipped dress won't do. Our work calls for bending and stretching."

Ventura nodded. "I'll find something. Is there anything I have to bring?"

"Just yourself. Rest well, for you will need all your energy and a clear mind for tomorrow."

***

Ventura hurried home, her lips repeating over and over: Please God, let father be busy in the library or out for dinner with mother.

The meeting had changed her and she wondered if it showed. Would Mother see it? She clicked her tongue. There she went again, trying to figure out the impossible. She'd just have to wait until she got home and see what happened.

She hurried past the young girl who opened her front door, then turned around to ask, "Where is my mother?"

"In her bedchamber, Señorita."

So they hadn't gone out yet. Maybe she could tiptoe past and not be discovered. She took off her shoes and held them in her hand. Through the partially-closed door, she could see her mother at her toilette. She was dressing for an evening out. Her long black hair was pulled behind her ears and clipped in place with a bright red flower. Her thin shoulders gleamed in the table light and her black silk dress billowed out around her high-backed chair.

She was smiling at her image in the mirror, pinning a golden brooch to the middle of her breast. Her gold rings twinkled in the light. She was dressed in her best clothes. That meant they were dining with someone of power.

"Ventura? Is that you?"

Ventura froze in the hallway. Now she was in for it. "Yes, mother, it's me." She pushed the door open and went inside.

Her mother put another gold ring on her finger. "Where have you been? Mass was over hours ago."

Ventura cleared her throat. "I took a walk by the river." She stared at her mother, wondering if her lie would be detected, but her mother seemed more interested in adjusting a curl in her hair than in talking to her daughter.

Ventura got up and went to her room. It was her refuge, the place where she kept her treasures, where she went to feel better when the world outside bothered her. She walked past Zuberans' painting of lemons and apples, went over to her bed table and touched the small ring her grandmother had given her before she died. Perched on the bed was the small rag doll she had loved since childhood. She picked it up, clutching it to her. Then she bent down and opened the old wooden chest, releasing a burst of lavender. Her fingers rummaged at the bottom until she found the soft leather of Guido's rein. He had been her first horse and she had cried for days when he had broken his leg in one of her furious cross-country rides.

Her hand closed the top firmly. That part of her life was over. Maybe she should go back and talk to her mother. No, if she spoke of the group, she would put them in danger. She sighed and slid to the floor, cradling her doll. Everything had suddenly become very complicated.

# 4

Ventura woke with a hint of guilt in her breast, but she pushed it away and hopped out of bed. Her oldest dress would look just fine without the circular barrel hoop, barrel sleeves and stomacher. She ripped them out and stuffed the extra material in the back of her wardrobe. Her mother would be upset, but that was the least of her worries. Ventura put on the dress and her only pair of flat-heeled shoes, muttering to herself because the toes were too pointed to be comfortable.

When she was finished, she took down the long mantilla her grandmother had given her. She felt so grownup, pulling the soft silk over her gown. At least if the threads gave way in her dress after all that ripping, she'd be modestly covered. A few minutes later, she tiptoed down the steps.

Ventura arrived at Clara's door just as the morning bells for mass started to toll. Anna came down the narrow street from the opposite direction, her shoulders capped in sunshine, skin glowing. Over Anna's arm was slung a crude wooden box on a leather strap, just like the one in Clara's corner.

Anna wasted no time on pleasantries. She motioned Ventura to follow her down an even narrower street. Soon Ventura was gasping for breath, trying to keep up. Anna giggled and slowed down. "You'll get used to walking and your body will strengthen."

Each time Ventura took a step, her skirt slapped against her leg and she stopped to look behind her, sure something was wrong. Her hair started to slip out from under her mantilla and perspiration popped out on her upper lip. Anna didn't seem to mind the sudden stops and starts of her companion, she just hummed a pleasant tune and walked gracefully along.

They left Seville and soon were in the country. It was a shimmering day, alive with promise. They followed the river at first. It ran smoothly, dropping down through glittering shallows beside a shrubby bank. Above was a green plateau where calves were fattening and trees putting out their sticky buds. To the south was a richly-flowered meadow, its vivid colors alive in the sun with color and sweet fragrance. In the distance, a farmer cultivated his field, his back bent from effort.

They followed the road until it dissolved into dust, then they took a path worn in the grass. They had to beat through the brush until they arrived at a stone wall dense with smells of mold. They turned and scuffled up a thorny hill. Breathless, they reached the top, spying a sunbaked cottage below.

"First, we'll visit Brites Valenca and her new baby," said Anna. "I helped with the birthing last week."

Ventura had never seen anything born, let alone a baby. It had to be some kind of miracle. "I wish I'd been there," she told Anna, "what did you do?"

"You'll see very soon. Not much after that, you'll be delivering your own babies. It is a special event. A joyous occasion. My favorite work." A smile of peace settled on her lips.

"What am I supposed to do when we go inside? Are they expecting me?"

"One question at a time. For a few weeks, you watch. When you feel ready, and you'll know when that is, you will begin to practice. For now, just watch and listen."

Relief flooded over Ventura. She wasn't ready to use her hands yet. Perhaps she wasn't as bold as she thought. There was more to this healing business than just laying your hands on someone. For now, she would be content with watching. Soon enough she would begin the work.

Inside the cottage, a young woman of Ventura's age sat by the fireplace on a crude wooden chair, rocking a crib with a squalling infant in it. The walls were bare, the chairs worn and sagging, the rug faded. The young mother was too thin for her sex and looked like a young girl with no breasts.

She shouted to Anna above her baby's cries, "I am so glad to see you. I don't know what to do with little Gaspar. He cries all the time."

Anna set down the wooden box and began rummaging through it. When she found what she wanted, she looked at Brites and said, "Don't worry. I have something in my case for that. This is Ventura, she's studying to be a healer."

Brites managed a weak smile when Anna handed her a handful of herbs. "Heat some water and make a tea from this." While Brites made the tea, Anna laid her hands on the baby's forehead and abdomen until his crying changed to hiccups and then to sighs. After the baby had his camomille tea and was fast asleep, Anna gave Brites some more herbs and said, "Brew some of this for all three of you, it'll help you all sleep tonight."

When they were ready to leave, Brites paid Anna with a sausage and a piece of cheese. "Just right for our lunch," said Anna, motioning Ventura out the door. To Brites she said, "I'll be back next week to check on you and Gaspar. Stay well."

Their next stop was old Belchior da Sylva. His tiny cottage was tucked among rocky slopes studded with scrub and dwarf juniper. An old woman in a white scarf and apron came running out to meet them. "Come quick! Belchior is in severe pain!" Her withered hands flew through the air waving them on. "He has not emptied his bowels for days now. I am afraid he is dying. El Doctor has been here, but he offers no hope."

They followed the old woman inside to a tiny bedroom that smelled of dirt and sickness. Old Belchior lay on a soiled mat, moaning softly. He tried to move when he saw Anna, but he couldn't. His face was lifeless, the color of old veal.

"Where does it hurt?" Anna asked. He pointed to his abdomen and moaned again. She moved her hands in an inverted U, over and down his belly, loosening the blockage while encouraging him to picture the food moving down and out of him. Old Belchior's face soon began to relax and Anna nodded to his wife. "The channels are opening up. He will be better now."

Belchior's wife paid Anna with three gold coins she took from a blue jar on the mantel. They left the house and continued down the road. They picnicked in a meadow among the daisies, sating their hunger on rough bread and cheese, then drinking from a small stream. Several times they stopped in the road, taking samples of weeds and ferns, or picking berries.

By the end of the day, Ventura had witnessed Anna giving Isabel Nunes peppermint tea for her indigestion, Sebastian Ferrayra, the grated bark of the willow tree for his fever, and Joanna Carvalno, green mold from cheese for her pus-filled finger. When they stopped for a rest by a stream, Anna handed her a book of herbs and cures.

Ventura paged through it, fascinated. "Could I borrow it?"

"It's the only one I have, but I'll let you take it until tomorrow." Ventura took the book and they walked back to Seville. Ventura chattered constantly, asking questions all the way. "Why did you use willow bark? Does peppermint have other uses?" On and on she asked. Anna just smiled and answered in a calm, encouraging way.

The church bells chimed six when the exhausted pair stopped at Clara's for coffee and more talk. They nibbled on bread and sweet berry jam until darkness fell. Then Ventura jumped up and hurried out, clutching Anna's book. "I'll be back tomorrow," she called behind her.

She ran into the misty street, scrambling toward her house on panicky feet. Maybe she would be fortunate and find her parents out for the evening with one of the local dons. That would make it easy for her to slip in unnoticed in her hideous costume. Ignes, the young maid who usually opened the door was slow in answering her knock. Ventura waited on the cold stone steps, her heart beating with fear while she rehearsed every excuse she could think of for being late.

"Evening, señorita," said Ignes, pulling the heavy door open.

"Are my parents---"

Her father's angry voice boomed through the hall. "Is that you, Ventura?"

"Yes, father." Her mind started to picture what was about to happen as she hurried toward the sound of his voice.

He eyed her with horror in his eyes when he saw her beautiful silk dress ripped and torn and the worn mantilla hanging over it crookedly. "What are you wearing? Have you been accosted?"

"No, father I-I--" She hesitated, unable to think of a single good reason for the way she looked.

He motioned to her. "Come over here. This is unforgivable, out on the streets so late, in the dark, alone, and wearing beggar's clothes. What will our neighbors think?" He paced in front of her, his hands behind his back and his head bowed down. Finally he stopped in front of her and said, "Well, what is your explanation?"

The time had come to tell him that she was living a life that stood firmly against all he had taught her. Without a second thought, she burst in, words tumbling out. "I'm learning to be a healer. You wouldn't believe how exciting it is. It's what I want to do with my---"

Before she could finish, a stinging, burning force exploded in her head and sent her reeling backwards. Red and yellow spots shimmered in front of her and she nearly fell to the floor. Then she saw her father's hand rising to strike her again.

Her mother came shrieking down the stairs. "Antonio! Antonio! Stop!" She stepped between them, grabbing Ventura into her arms. "Antonio, what are you doing?"

"What am I doing? What is your daughter doing shaming the family? Look at her, dressed like a street woman and talking nonsense about being a healer. Well, I won't have it. I won't have it! Not in this family!"

Ventura tore herself from her mother's arms and screamed, "Shamed the family? It is you who shame the family by not speaking up when our friends are being murdered for no reason. It is your precious property you fear losing." She saw the look of hurt on her mother's face and the violent anger in her father's eyes before she ran up the stairs and slammed the door behind her.

She was alone now. She had taken a stand and there was no turning back. Her pillow muffled her cries until the house grew quiet. She knew her mother wanted to come and make amends, but her father would forbid it. There was only one thing to do.

She rose and began packing a cloth bag full of her things. She ripped the hoops out of several of her dresses and packed them along with her diary, the book Anna had given her, her travelling desk, writing materials, and some jewelry she planned to sell for food. When she was ready, she walked slowly over to her grandmother's ring, kissed it, and put it on her hand. It was the one thing she would keep with her always.

Slowly she crept down the stairs, heart wrenching with the agony of being torn from her family. She whispered a silent prayer to God, asking for his blessing. Capita awoke from her snoring by the fire, and ran to lick her hand and then scuttle behind her mistress. Ventura hugged the dog and whispered through her tears, "No, Capita, you cannot come."

The door clicked shut behind her. The breath of the night flowed before her and she stood, shivering, pulling the long mantilla closer to her body. There was only one place to go — to Clara's.

Lanterns burned green and orange on the street an she started in their direction. Her heart lurched in her chest when she spied a man in a dark cloak, but he turned the corner ahead of her and she was alone again.

Hurrying, she turned up Clara's street. The old woman answered Ventura's knock, candle in hand, gray hair standing out in clumps around her head. Clara's warm hand came around Ventura's shoulder. "Come in, my dear, come in."

***

Xavier Henriques called on Señora Teresa da Fonceca that afternoon. There were some final arrangements for the wedding, and he wanted to have his say in them. The dowry had already been set and their place of residence had been found near to the da Fonceca's. He must force his decisions on Ventura today so there would be no question who was to be the boss in their household. Ventura was becoming entirely too independent these days, and he had to quell it before she became unmanageable.

His mother-in-law-to-be sat on a silk couch, looking extremely beautiful in a fern green dress that flowered out around her like a luxurious pelt. Despite her beauty, there were lines of fear and worry gathered in her face. It would be rude for him to mention them. She would talk if there was something to be said. He could count on women for that.

"I'm glad you are here, señor," she said, her voice cracking with emotion. A trembling hand offered him a tray of tiny cakes. "Ventura---" her voice broke off and tears glistened in her eyes, "---Ventura is not here."

He felt a knot of anger growing inside. How dare she play games with him now? "Not here? But we were to finalize our wedding plans." He snorted to himself. Just like her to forget. Women were so unreliable in matters that concerned the mind.

"I know she should be here---with you---" She took out a silk handkerchief from her sleeve and wiped her eyes. "I'm sorry to have to tell you, but she's gone. I don't even know where."

He jolted back in his chair, startled. "What do you mean, señora?" There had to be something wrong with Ventura's mother. Maybe she was the reason Ventura had become so flighty.

Señora da Fonceca gulped back her tears and said, "She and her father had an argument last night and this morning when I went to wake her, I found her bed had not been slept in and some of her clothes gone." She put a hand to her brow. "Oh, what will we do?" she whispered, bursting into sobs.

A sick feeling started inside him. What would he do? This kind of thing was very bad for one's reputation. Engagements were seldom broken in Seville. "Gone?" he shouted, "How could she be gone?" Ignoring the Señora's tears, he stood up and walked to the window. "There must be some mistake," he said finally, turning to face her, "are you sure about this? Maybe she went to visit a friend or to mass to light a candle."

"This is no mistake! She is gone. She screamed at her father. I've never seen her like that. She said she is going to be a healer." Ventura's mother shook her head, a dazed look on her face.

"Healer? My Ventura? But---but--we are to be married---"

Teresa da Fonceca shook her head and sighed. "I do not think there will be a marriage. I have never seen her so. You must find her and bring her home before she does something that cannot be forgiven. Already her father threatens to disown her. Imagine, the daughter he loves."

"Where is she learning this healing? I will go there and demand to see her."

She shook her head sadly. "That I do not know, Señor. If I did, I myself would go. Please, please, ask, find out. Bring my daughter back to me."

He left Teresa da Fonceca sobbing on the couch. Women were no good in such matters. He would find Ventura. His feet took him swiftly down the steps and toward the square. Surely someone there would know something that would lead him to Ventura.

The square was alive with fruit and vegetable carts and men standing around in breeches and bolero jackets. Many were of the lower classes, but Xavier pushed aside his disgust and walked up to a group of them. They eyed him suspiciously when he said, "I'm looking for a healer. Someone who teaches the forbidden. Do you know of such a person?"

Most turned away, but not before Xavier caught a glimpse of knowledge in their eyes. They knew, but fear pulled them away. But, who could blame them, healers were tainted with heresy and no one wanted to be accused of that. Only one old woman, plump as a goose and half-blind, spoke. "So it is information you wish, Señor." She put out her palm and ran her fingers together as if she was already stroking a coin or two.

He sighed and reached for a few pesetas. When he placed them in her hand, she smiled. "Thank you, señor, the poor bless you." With that, she turned and moved away.

Zavier raised his voice for all to hear. "Now don't you forget old woman, you promised some information."

She turned back, smiling a biteless grin. "Oh yes, señor. Let me ask you this first." She yanked at his sleeve, pulling him away from the crowd. "Do you want to become a healer?"

He didn't want to be branded a heretic, but if he answered wrongly, she might not tell him anything. He nodded and said, "I do want to learn to be a healer, but keep your voice down. I don't want anyone to hear."

She smiled again. "It is an honorable idea. Come, I will show you the place." The old woman pulled him along, touching the sides of buildings to find her way. "I am nearly blind, Señor, but certain things one does not forget." She took him to the street where Clara lived and said, "There, that is that house of the healer, Clara Rodriguez." Before he could ask any more questions, the woman turned and shuffled away.

He went up to the door and knocked. No one answered, but he kept knocking. Finally, he turned and started to walk away. He felt eyes watching him, but when he whirled around, there was no one at the window and no sign of anyone even living there.

Before he left, he made note of the address. He would be back.

***

Clara watched the young man's retreat from her meeting room window. "Ventura, come look. Do you know this man?" she whispered.

Ventura tiptoed beside her friend and stared out. There was no mistaking the tall, thin frame she knew so well. Her voice was at once distressed and irritated when she answered. "Yes, it is my betrothed, Xavier. Don't let him in. Never let him in. That part of my life is over."

Clara led her into the room by the fire. They huddled together, neither speaking for a moment until Clara said, "It is dangerous that he knows. He could bring much trouble to you, my dear."

Ventura sighed and leaned against Clara's shoulder. "Yes, I guess it is starting now."

Clara nodded. "I warned you it would. Perhaps you want to change your mind. If you go back home now and give up the healing sessions, perhaps your family will take you back. Later, there is no guarantee."

Ventura shook her head. "Never. I'll never go back there. My father is crueler than I thought possible. And my mother---she pretends to be on my side, but she does only what he says."

They sat silently for a few minutes, Clara stroking Ventura's cheek softly. Finally the young woman looked into Clara's eyes and said, "But what about you? Now that he knows where you live, he could bring the soldiers. He could start trouble for you, too."

Clara nodded and sighed. "I have lived with trouble for many years. My life is almost over. I have accomplished what I set out to do---teach others. Now I have you and Anna and a legion of others who will carry on my work if I am taken. No one will ever stop us. The ideas and practices will live on no matter how hard they try to end it."

"But why won't they leave us alone? We mean them no harm."

"They are terrified because our ideas are better than theirs. Their cruelties toward us show what pitiful creatures they are. Even though they invoke his name, God knows who are his helpers and who are the hypocrites."

Ventura did not answer. She could only crouch closer to Clara and wonder if she had made the right decision.

***

Leaving Clara's front door, Xavier headed back in the direction he had come. He would not be so easily dissuaded. Ventura had made a mistake, but it was not yet irrevocable. He would find her and persuade her to come home. Maybe they would get married sooner than planned. That would stop these silly ideas that were in her head about being a healer.

He was mumbling to himself as he entered his home. His father, James Henriques, was waiting for him the courtyard. Xavier's father was not a demonstrative man. He was aloof and polite, and had taught his son to be the same. Both of these characteristics had been useful to him in his quest for acquiring ever more land. He had learned how to use the patronage of the enchufe system. He had friends at court and he had woven an invisible web of indebtedness about them.

He waited in the courtyard, learning against one of the tall columns, admiring the splendor of his home. He was tall and thin, like his son, with a thick mustache and a gloomy look about his eyes. "Someday all this will be yours, my son, along with the lands I have acquired. You will build it to even greater magnificence." He pulled absent-mindedly on his short beard, a habit he engaged in when he was thinking about his wealth.

Finally, noticing Xavier was starting to walk away, he called, "My son. how go the wedding preparations?"

Xavier turned and said, "Father, there is a problem."

James nodded. "Ahhh, your intended is getting cold feet about the wedding. Well, she will be fine. I remember your mother---." He crossed himself quickly on the chest and forehead. "God rest her soul. Did I ever tell you she almost broke the engagement the day before our wedding?" He laughed deeply and slapped his son on the shoulder roughly. "Of course, she came around the next day and we were married. Don't worry, Ventura will be fine, too."

"That's not the problem. She's run away to become a healer."

His father's eyes clouded to a murky brown. "What? That can't be! She's from a very good family. Dom da Fonceca is well-known for his wealth and manners."

"That may be," said Xavier, brushing a twig from a nearby ledge, "But Ventura has a mind of her own, as I am swiftly finding out."

"What's that? Mind of her own? Go get her my son, talk some sense into her empty little head. I tell you, women today are not like the ones in my generation. They are too inconstant, too independent."

Xavier sighed. "I went to get her, but no one answered when I knocked on the door."

"Mmm," said his father, pulling on his mustache, "perhaps you should break the engagement."

"I've thought of that, but then we will lose out on the acquisition of all of Dom da Fonceca's land. It was a good match because of the land. I knew that once we were married, I could shake the silly ideas out of her head. I still can."

His father shook his head. "Not if she has already brought shame and embarrassment to her family."

"You may be right father," he said cautiously, not yet ready to believe it. "Her father is already threatening to disown her."

"There it is, then. If he disowns her, you will have no part of his lands. Think, boy. Your future depends on it. And my honor." His father's voice carried an undertone of threat. Xavier was too smart to cut himself off from his father's good will. If he dared to do that, his future would be very shaky indeed.

Xavier spoke clearly and firmly. "I will handle this, father. There will be no disgrace for the Henriques' family."

His father nodded. "Good. Good. I am proud of you, my son." Xavier turned to go. "One more thing, Xavier. Mark well this name, Dom Francisco de Hernandez. He is the Inquisitor General. If she is in league with these healers, it is only a matter of time before she is exposed. If she is labeled a heretic, can you be far behind if you are her intended?" Xavier shrugged. His father held up a warning finger. "Separate yourself from her. If you cannot, go to Dom Francisco and he will deal with her directly."

Xavier went inside to brood. Point out Ventura as a heretic? Never. She was the beautiful woman who excited his body and mind as no woman ever had. True, she was headstrong and too independent, but a heretic? He didn't think so. It was just another of her diversions. She would soon tire of it all and come back to him. He had time. He could wait.

# 5

Ventura placed loaves of crusty bread on a wooden platter while Clara hung extra coffee pots around the fireplace. Ventura's eyes watched the door. The meeting would soon start.

A click of the door and Maria burst in, fluttering her fan and giggling through her gossip. A beautiful young girl in blue with eyes soft as a fawn's came in, awkward, embarrassed. Elvira followed a minute later, walking in majestically, shaking her auburn tresses flirtatiously toward the new young arrival.

"Elvira's at it again," chuckled Maria, her fan whipping furiously beneath her chin. Ventura was only half-listening. Since Xavier had come to Clara's door, she lived in constant fear he would return.

The room filled quickly and the meeting began so Ventura had little time for her thoughts. Immediately after Clara began to read the announcements, they heard a loud clatter at the door. Several rose to answer the knock, but Clara raised a hand. "I will answer it. Please, close the door to this room and remain quiet. If it is who I think it is, you will not want it known you are here."

Whispers followed Clara out of the room. Someone closed the door and barricaded it. Then they all huddled together, listening.

There was a clank of metal, a scuffle of feet and then a voice. "In the name of Dom Francisco de Hernandez, Inquisitor General, I arrest you for the crime of witchcraft."

Ventura's mouth opened, but no sound came out. Terror and dread registered on the faces around her. Feet shuffled across the hall outside and the front door slammed shut.

She gave a wail of dismay. Struggling to her feet, Ventura tried to run to the door, to Clara. But strong-armed men seized her and held her back. A rough hand clamped over her mouth and a man whispered. "Quiet. You can't stop the inevitable. We'll go on with the work." Twisting, turning, gasping for breath, she kicked and struggled, but the men were too strong.

Eventually, the arms released her and she slowly moved toward the window. Clara's bent body was walking lamely among six soldiers. Ventura's hands gripped the cool ledge, holding on against the nausea that wracked her.

Outside, people in the streets made way and onlookers' necks twisted to see the procession. Two soldiers held Clara's arms tightly and hurried her along, their eyes unfocused, cold. The clank of soldiers' metal and the hard crunch of feet echoed down the stone street.

Ventura ran for the door, but three men blocked her way. "You cannot follow. It is best to let her go," said a man with one eye. Ventura pushed against them, but the line would not give. Whimpering, she turned and staggered back into the meeting room, a sick, cold feeling seeping through her.

She was alone again.

Then a warm hand came around her shoulder. "Why don't you come and stay with me?" Ventura looked into Anna's clear eyes.

Ventura shook her head. "No, I will stay here and go on with Clara's work. Tomorrow I'll go to the prison to see her."

Anna's voice cautioned her. "I warn you. Stay away. If they think you are her friend, they'll put you in prison, too."

"But they can't do that. I've done nothing wrong. I don't even practice healing yet."

"Worse things have happened." Anna's face darkened and Ventura could see the lines of pain around her eyes.

Ventura tightened her jaw. "I have to do what I have to do."

Anna touched her arm gently. "Just be careful, my friend."

***

The soldiers were coming to get her, their armor clanking. She must get away! She ran, but they were gaining on her, their heavy boots pounding on the stone street. A cold hand clamped down on her shoulder and she turned. His eyes were the eyes of a corpse, putrid and sulfurous below a worm-eaten head. "No! No!" Ventura screamed.

She jolted awake and scrambled out of bed. Dawn threaded its colors in the window, drawing away the darkness, but not the fear. Somewhere near, church bells tolled, and Ventura fell back into her bed. It was a dream, a bad dream. Heart thumping, she lay there, not sure what to do.

Then she got up, dressed and filled a wooden basket with cake, cheese and fruit. Clara must be somewhere near the square and she was probably hungry. It was not yet fully light, but already there were merchants in the square, setting up their wagons and baskets. Their lusty laughter resounded against the stone buildings. A few early shoppers were there too, picking through yesterday's limp flowers and moldy cheeses, trying to make the best bargains.

Head still foggy, Ventura walked up to a man with a pleasant face who was squeezing an orange. "Do you know where they take the accused heretics?" she asked.

He grabbed her arm and pulled her to the side. "Be careful how loudly you speak," he whispered. "The Inquisitor General has spies everywhere." He pointed to an impressive building. "They are there, in the Palace of the Inquisition."

She looked up at the tall building. "But I thought that was the Church of Our Blessed Mary."

He nodded sadly. "It was, but the Church has become very political these days. It is said there are secret dungeons below the marble floors where unspeakable tortures occur. I've heard tell there is even a statue of the Virgin. She is studded with spikes so she can inflict a fatal embrace to all that are brought near her."

Ventura shuddered and headed for the Palace, wondering what terrible things must be happening to Clara. She walked up the first set of steps. Two guards at the landing looked down at her, lances extended, barring her entrance. She held up her basket and said, "I have some food for a friend of mine who was taken by the soldiers last night. Can I see her?"

The soldiers eyed her and raised their lances with a clank. The old one with an eye patch mumbled to his comrade. From the way they laughed, she knew it was not a respectful comment. "What is a pretty señorita like you doing worrying about heretics?" said the young one.

The older soldier grabbed the basket and said gruffly, "Are you family?" His face was so close she could smell his acrid breath.

"No, she's not family," said the younger one, eyeing her up and down.

"Does she have any family?" asked the older one, as if his companion might know.

"She has no family," shouted Ventura.

The older one toyed with a piece of bread in the basket. "Well, we have to find her family. They will have to pay for the cost of torture and trial."

Ventura stared at him, shocked, wondering what kind of court made victims pay for their own torture. "She has no money."

The younger one took an apple out of the basket and took a bite. "What does she have? Property?"

Ventura wanted to grab the basket away and run inside, but she was pinned in place by two big men. Instead she said, "She has no property. Only some books and papers." Ventura felt the blood rushing in her ears, knowing she shouldn't have told them about the books. They would surely seal her fate. She tossed her head and said, "Of course the books are simple things. Nothing of importance."

The old one scowled. "That is for us to determine. Now, what is this friend's name?"

Ventura thought quickly, inventing a name she shouted at them before she turned and flew down the steps. "Maria Henriques---her name is Maria Henriques!" When she got to the street, she ran even faster, not stopping to look back. She had been a fool to think they'd let her see Clara. Now she'd wasted money on food that would probably end up in some guard's stomach.

She arrived at Clara's out of breath. She spent the rest of the morning thinking about what to do. Just as she was about to go out, she looked out the window and saw a young boy in front of the door. He couldn't have been more than twelve years old, but he was dressed well and had an intent look on his face. She opened the door, wondering what he wanted.

His voice was too loud for his small body. "Señorita da Fonceca?"

She answered him hesitantly, "Yes, what is it?"

"I have a message for you from Señor Henriques."

She took the message and handed the young boy a small cake for his trouble. He ate his sweet meat, waiting patiently for her answer. She tore open the message and read:

*My Dear Ventura,*

*I know you have been under a great strain of late. That is why I have forgiven you for your behavior yesterday. If you still want to marry me, you will return today to your parents' home.*

*I look forward to seeing you very soon.*

*Sincerely Yours,*
*Xavier Henriques*

She folded up the message. Not even a "Love, Xavier" or an "I love you". How could he think she'd come back to such a cold man? She sighed. Her life with him was over.

She almost tore up the note and threw it in the fireplace. But then she had second thoughts. Maybe she could enlist his help with Clara. She gave the young boy another cake and went inside to her desk. She dipped a sharpened quill in her bottle of ink and began to write. She had to bring him to Clara's, but she didn't want to raise his hopes that their marriage would still take place. She finished the note, hurriedly sealed it with wax, and gave it to the small messenger.

Within an hour, Xavier's tall frame was at her door. His eyes glistened with anticipation when she let him in, but then his nose wrinkled with contempt when he eyed the spare surroundings. "I hope you've come to your senses," he said, "and are ready to come home with me now."

She shook her head and said, "Please sit down, Xavier. I have something to ask you. I need your help."

He smiled a tense half-smile she knew so well and took the most comfortable chair in the room before he said, "What kind of help do you need?"

Ventura sat down on a stool across from him. "Clara, my teacher, has been arrested and will probably be charged with heresy. I need your help to get her released."

He waved an impatient hand. "What have I to do with matters of Church and State?"

She leaned closer, hoping to be convincing. "You're a wealthy landowner," she said, "you have power."

His smile broadened, but took on a condescending look. "But, if I tried to interfere in matters which do not concern me, I would lose my power."

Her voice became louder, more frantic. "But they do concern you. At least they concern me, and if we're going to be married---."

His smile faded. "Give this up and come home. You are shaming your family and me."

Her voice rose in anger at him. "I am not giving Clara and her teaching up. I am here to stay!" She stood up, feeling her body quiver. "The engagement is off!"

He stared at her for a moment, as if he wasn't sure whether he'd heard wrong. Then a look of anger took over his face and he stood up and stomped out, not even once looking back.

"Good riddance!" she said to his back. Not stopping to answer, he slammed the front door behind him.

***

Bewildered, Xavier stumbled down the street toward Dom da Fonceca's home. Seeing his face, the servant girl admitted him immediately.

Ventura's father greeted him by the fireplace. "What news have you brought, Señor Henriques?" He glanced toward the door as if he were looking for Ventura.

Xavier cleared his throat and said, "The news is not good." Antonio da Fonceca's face fell into lines of helplessness. "She has broken the engagement and claims she will stay in that despicable place she calls a house."

The older man's body trembled and a look of fury descended over his face like a dark curtain. "Then I shall disown her! This very day. She will see nothing of my lands. She is no longer my daughter!"

Teresa da Fonceca hurried into the room. "Antonio, what's happened?" Her frightened face carried a glimmer of hope until she saw the look in her husband's eyes. Then the light went out of her heart and tears poured down her face. She swooned in her husband's arms. Xavier stood by uncomfortably, watching his carefully planned life crumble.

***

"It is unanimous, then. Anna will be our leader until Clara is released!" Clara's meeting room resounded with shouts of approval and hand claps. Ventura's heart beat wildly. At last something good was happening. Perhaps this would all turn out all right after all.

A warm smile lighting up her face, Anna stepped to the front and began to speak. "My friends. These are perilous times indeed."

Many in the group shook their heads in agreement. A few voices shouted, "Yes, Yes!"

Anna continued, "It may not be safe to meet here any longer." A hush fell over the crowd as if they already knew something terrible was to follow. "News has just reached me that Clara has been branded a dogmatiser."

Whispers began and turned into a few howls. Ventura couldn't help shouting, "What is it? What does it mean?"

Anna turned a calm face toward Ventura. "It means she will probably be relaxed."

"Relaxed! Burned at the stake? Not Clara, it couldn't be. We have to do something!"

"Yes, yes!" cried several in the crowd. Maria's fan fluttered furiously and the pink feather in her hair quivered as she agreed.

Urged on by the crowd, Ventura stood up. "We must make a plan and rescue her. We cannot allow her to die. Not our Clara." Hot tears tracked down Ventura's cheeks, yet something inside her swelled strong and confident.

"But what can we do?" said a little man with a wart on the end of his nose.

Out of the crowd came a deep voice. "Death to the Inquisitor General!"

Dead silence filled the room, then whispers and claps. Finally hurrahs and shouts of glee followed. "Yes! Kill the Inquisitor General! Death to the Inquisitor General!" They danced around the room chanting it over and over until they were exhausted.

Anna finally held up a hand. "Wait. Who will do this? I am not a killer. Who is among us? We are healers, people who save lives, not take them."

Not even stopping to think, Ventura's voice came out, challenging her mentor. "But can we allow something so evil to live? This man is destroying all that is good in Seville!"

A man with a British voice stood up and shouted. "Ventura is right!" The crowd turned to look at him. He was a striking figure, lean and tall with thick blonde hair falling nearly to his broad shoulders. His body was full of vitality and his face was craggy and bearded with the deeply-lined forehead of one who had thought much and suffered. His voice was deep and stirring. "Perhaps it is time to stop the evil that has taken over Seville, let them know we will not stand for it any longer!"

A few muttered agreement. The young man looked around the room until his eyes found Ventura's. The strength of him, his intelligence and authority struck her like a physical force, making her pulse quicken and her mind reel.

She fought to regain her composure. From the look of him, this man was only a sailor and not half as handsome as her father, but there was something about him that drew her.

The crowd buzzed and someone shouted, "Yes! He is right!" Others whispered, "Who is this man? Where did he come from? Is he one of us?"

The sailor began to talk again. "I am Richard Hasleton and I sail on Her Majesty's ship, the York. I met Clara in the square one day and we talked for many hours about the work she does and the corruption that lies festering in Seville. She invited me to come here tonight. I am sorely distressed that she is in prison. I want to help." The pain from his words burned in his face. Ventura stared at him in fascination. This fellow seemed to care about others and was not afraid to show it. Here was the kind of man she'd been waiting for. So unlike Xavier.

A short fellow with one leg stood up and started to talk. "Perhaps some of us could detain the Inquisitor General's men while the rest rescue Clara."

There was a long silence, then, "Yes, yes, Claudio has a good idea," said Richard.

A stocky man with an earring stood up. "I am Ignatio Nunes, a man well-versed in fighting. I will detain the Inquisitor General while the rest of you fine lads rescue our dear Clara.

Maria stood up, her fan fluttering nervously. "Elvira and I can use our feminine wiles to put off the guards."

Elvira stood up and grabbed Maria by the arm. "We will need a special potion, one that will put the guards out cold."

An old woman with a whiney voice called out, "But how will you get them to drink it?"

Elvira laughed a deep, sensual laugh and Maria fluttered her fan seductively. "Leave that to us. When we are through, there will not be a guard standing."

Ignatio Nunes nodded and pulled out a dagger. A lock of black hair fell in his eyes when he said, "I will find Dom Hernandez and hold him at knife point."

Richard jumped to his feet again. "And I will lead a group to the dungeons. We will find Clara and take her to safety." There were shouts of joy and celebration. Their beloved Clara would be among them again.

A mysterious man in black rose to speak. "I can draw you a map of the palace and its entrances. I have been there many times and have traveled to the dungeons."

Ventura stared at him, wondering how he could know so much about the dungeons. She wanted to ask him many questions, but there was no time. Plans must be made.

Richard held up a hand. "Since there is no way to know when Clara will be relaxed, we must act quickly. Those of you coming with me, step to this side of the room and we will plan our part."

Ventura strode over to the table and sat down with the men. Richard began to speak. "We shall meet by the back gate of the dungeon tomorrow at dusk."

A wiry man nudged Ventura and said, "Ladies over there."

Ventura shook her head. "I want to go to the dungeons. I must make sure Clara is all right. I've already been to the Palace. I know where the guards are."

Richard turned his startling blue eyes on her and smiled. "I cannot allow that. It is too dangerous for a woman to go."

Anger burned inside her. A minute ago she was ready to swoon into his arms, now she wanted to kill him. "I don't care what you think, Richard Hasleton. I'm going."

Ventura felt a tug on her arm and turned to see Anna by her side. "No!" shouted Ventura. "I'm not going with you and do what a lady does. I'm going to the dungeons to get Clara!"

The men beat on the table with their fists and laughed. Feeling her face go hot, Ventura jumped up and ran to the other side of the room. Although they couldn't hear her, she shouted, "You may think you've won because you are big and brawny, but we shall see. " She set her mouth and pushed away the tears blurring her eyes.

Elvira put a hand on her friend's shoulder. "Don't be silly, dear. It's dirty and smelly in the dungeon. Hardly a suitable place for a beautiful woman."

Ventura just sighed in disgust, putting her head down on the table. The others coaxed her with their words: "Come, help us, Ventura. You and Anna know the most about herbs. We must find the most powerful one there is, something to put the soldiers to sleep for hours."

Anna opened Clara's healing book. "We need your help, Ventura," she said in a soothing voice.

Slowly Ventura raised her head. "I will help you because I want to, not because some dumb sailor says I must." She wiped her nose on a handkerchief and soon forgot about Richard Hasleton as they poured over the book.

A few minutes later, Anna rose and went to Clara's shelf. She took down some small cloth bags and a jar of yellow powder. "Here, fill these," she told the women, "there must be enough powder in each bag to put one hundred men to sleep."

While she filled her bag, Ventura's lips worked, rehearsing what she would say to that impudent sailor. When the bags were all full, they gave them to Elvira and Maria.

Ventura turned to shout her anger at Richard, but the room had already emptied of men. She nodded her head decisively. He would hear from her soon enough.

***

The next afternoon, Ventura went to the square. She milled around, looking for the right shop. About four o'clock she found a secondhand clothes merchant and rummaged through his bins. They smelled of soiled clothes and body odor, but she finally found some black breeches her size, a shirt, a long black cloak and a wide-brimmed hat. She paid the shop owner with the last of her pesetas and left.

She spent the next few hours at Clara's, waiting for sundown. When the time was right, she pulled on the men's clothes and hurried to the Palace of the Inquisitor.

The streets were quiet. Everyone had left the square. Ahead, she saw only two guards in front of the entrance. She turned right and made her way around to the back, inching her way along. Ahead was an incline that could take her to the top of the wall. Slipping and sliding, her feet nearly losing their footing more than once, she persevered and finally crawled to the top. Then, lying very still, she looked down over the wall. She watched the entrance, straining to see Richard and the other men.

It seemed like hours before she heard muffled whispers and the clap of soft shoes against the street. She squinted. It was them. No time to waste. She slid over the wall, jump down the last few feet, and stood triumphantly in front of Richard.

"What's this?" he whispered in a strained British accent.

"I'm coming with you," she whispered back.

Realizing there was no time to argue, the men looked at each other, shrugged and motioned her to join them. "The dungeons occupy all three floors," whispered Richard. "There is no way to know for sure which one Clara occupies, so we must cover all three."

Ventura's eyes traveled up the building, past the vaulted galleries. It was a huge structure with a gigantic edifice. Richard put his hand up, "Come now, and do it quietly."

They moved swiftly toward the entrance and were upon the half-drugged guards before the men had time to react. Elvira and Maria had done their job well.

Richard and the others blind-folded the guards, bound them, took their keys and were inside in minutes.

Richard signalled them to spread out along the damp walls of the dungeon. The pungent odor and damp mossiness beneath her fingertips sent a shiver up Ventura's spine. Holding her breath, she waited until he gave the sign for them to follow.

The walls were irregularly lit with huge candles. Richard took one of the brighter ones down and led the way, his keys clinking while he opened cell after cell. Ventura and the other men surged behind him. The smell of unwashed and sickly flesh was almost overwhelming. They found nearly one hundred living victims of all ages and both sexes in cubicles. They were all naked and weak, and some moaned in pain.

On the second floor, Richard opened a cell door and Ventura gasped. Clara gazed back at her. The old woman was filthy and there were burns on her arms and face and a look of pain deep in her eyes. Richard held the lit candle to her face, but Clara moaned, covering her eyes from the light.

Along the walls were carved names. Beside them were lines and notches, indicating the number of days of their captivity. Ventura took a step forward and tripped. Reaching down, she picked up the fragment of a monk's garment. Her foot hit something hard and heavy. A scream nearly escaped her lips when she looked down. There, lying on the dusty floor, was a human bone.

She stepped over it and took the old woman's hand. "Clara, it's me, Ventura," she whispered, putting her arms around her friend.

They embraced for a moment before Clara said, "You must go." Her voice was so weak and tired, Ventura almost did not believe it was hers. "They will catch you and put you here with me."

Ventura shook her head. "You are coming with us." She pulled off her cloak and wrapped it around Clara's body.

Richard pulled them both out of the cell. "We must hurry!" They trotted along the tunnel behind him, back toward the exit door. Then they were outside, their feet crunching along the gravel. A wagon pulled by two powerful horses waited ahead. Strong arms placed Clara in the back of it and covered her with a blanket. Ventura pushed the men away and whispered into Clara's ear, "Keep safe."

Richard pulled her back just as the wagon rumbled away from the city toward the countryside. Ventura's knees gave way then, and Richard pulled her close. She felt his breath on her face and the strength of his body straining against hers. "You," he said playfully, "You could have ruined the whole escape."

Her lips were inches away from his and her senses were reeling. She pulled away. "But, I didn't. Clara's safe, and you were wrong!" Before he could answer, she was on her way, heels clicking down the street.

***

Richard Hasleton stood speechless, watching Ventura stride away. What a headstrong young woman she was. She had actually dared to come with the men and help Clara escape. There was too much fire in her eyes and too much passion in her speech. She would be a handful of trouble.

Yet, there was something about her. Something that drew him to her. She was unlike any woman he had ever met. The women he knew were shy and required gentle admiration. They were like precious jewels. This one was all brimstone.

That tingling when he held her. It had taken his breath away. He smiled to himself and wondered if he'd ever see her again.

***

Ventura slept well that night. Her dreams were of a blessed reunion with Clara. A loud knocking awakened her from her blissful sleep.

"Ventura! Open up!"

Still half-asleep, Ventura crawled out of bed. "What is it?" She peered through the window at Anna's agonized face.

Ventura opened the door and stood looking at her friend. Anna pushed inside. "The news is bad and there are too many ears in the street."

Ventura led her friend to a chair. "What is it?"

"They have recaptured Clara. The men who drove the wagon must have been paid off by the Inquisitor General. She is back in prison and scheduled to be relaxed today."

"Today? But, what about the auto de fe?"

"I think they're afraid she'll be rescued again."

"Of course she'll be rescued again. We'll get Richard and---"

Anna shook her head. "No! It's too dangerous. It's probably not safe to even be in Clara's house. You'd better pack your bags and come to my house."

"They wouldn't dare bother me. My father is wealthy and powerful."

Anna's eyes dulled. "Do not be so sure of yourself. It is being said the Inquisitor General knows Clara owns this house and he will be coming to take it in payment for her torture and trial. You do not want to be here when that happens."

Ventura nodded. "Very well, I will stay with you tonight. Now, what about rescuing Clara?"

"I have spoken to Richard, and even he won't risk it."

"Then what will we do? We can't let them kill Clara!" Ventura grabbed her friend's arm tightly.

Anna sighed and tears filled her eyes. "There is nothing now that can save her. They are already readying the Place of Burning outside the city walls in the Campo de Tablada. It is a gruesome sight. They have dragged effigies and the bones of those who have escaped the stake by death in prison there. Already wood is being piled on pyres. They have even invited honored guests and a special stage is being erected for their convenience. I heard talk on the square. Spectators are paying high prices for windows with a good view."

Ventura's heart felt sick. "What is the sickness that brings them to see their brothers and sisters burn?"

Anna shrugged. "Curiosity, probably. Spectacle. Maybe the sight of the wood burning and smoke blowing fools them that the Church is doing something for them. I do not know." She put her face in her hands and sobbed. "I don't understand it either, but I see the ghoulish delight on their faces when they talk about relaxations. They have become their entertainment."

Ventura's stomach tightened. How could people be so heartless? What had happened to her city? She did not have the answer, she only knew she did not believe anyone deserved to burn at the stake.

That evening, after promising to return to Anna's, Ventura crept outside the gates of the city, hoping to find some way to save Clara. The procession to the pyre had already begun. The condemned prisoners moved wearily to their death, some on horseback, others walking with their hands manacled behind their backs, their feet echoing hollowly against the stone. All wore pointed headdresses and sack cloths painted with red devils and leaping flames. Many moaned in pain, others repeated psalms and prayers. Friars in brown capes and sandals walked beside the prisoners, begging them to confess their heresy so their souls could escape perdition. Their mumbled words of guilt and penitence floated in the chilly night air.

The procession entered a large circle of stakes. Around the perimeter, sitting eight feet above the ground were spectators who had paid high prices. Some of them were eating and drinking. The smell of their sausages and hot bread wafted through the air. Others who had come for the show, pointed at the prisoners and laughed crudely.

At the highest point of the spectators' stand, the Green Cross, emblem of the Inquisition, was illuminated by throngs of lanterns. As Ventura moved closer, the smell of burning wood almost overwhelmed her. Then she saw the red flames leaping above the burning fires.

A screaming, barefooted woman was forced onto a bed of burning coals. Some near her whimpered and cried. Others looked dazed and numbed, as if they were having a bad dream.

hose book is it?" He shoved a small volume into the shipmaster's

master shrugged. "I've never seen the book."

d smiled smugly. "A likely story. One of my men found it in your

master shook his head. "I've never seen that book in my life."

d winked. "I'm sure the Inquisitor General would be happy indeed ve it. He would put you up on charges before you could turn this Then he lowered his voice and smiled, "But seeing you did give us overlook it if you pay 200,000 pesetas."

master's face turned gray. "What? We can't afford that. We're a e have are some provisions."

d nodded and looked unimpressed. "I don't believe you, but let me ave." The shipmaster grunted some orders and in minutes, ten ses and six tubs of butter appeared. The guard looked over the sure this is all you have?"

master nodded. "That's it."

t, but we may be back." He signalled to the other guards and the s swiftly taken off the ship.

guards left, Richard laid on his mat, thinking about Ventura and might both be in. If the Inquisitor's men had been at the ship and net was gathering.



Servants with sweat-greased faces and short breeches worked around the stakes, their wiry bodies piling four-foot poles into the stacks of wood. When they finished, they led victims to their handiwork, then strapped them down, beating them if they would not stand still. Honored guests stood nearby, ready to light the pyres, holding their fancy robes away from the sputtering oil.

Ventura's frantic eyes searched the stakes for Clara. A burst of sulfur and leaping flames and the first pile was lit. Flesh sizzled and hair burst into puffs of white smoke. Gasping, Ventura stumbled away on weak legs. Then everything went dark and the sky spun into the earth.

She lay on the ground, unable to move, until Richard's face came into focus. She tried not to let him see the relief she felt. After all, he was a bossy sailor who thought she was just a stupid little girl. But he didn't seem to care what she thought of him because his arms came around her, strong and warm. She fought against the urge to let him help, pummeling him with her fists. "Leave me alone," she shouted, "I have to save Clara!"

He shook his head sadly. "We are too late. Look there, she already burns. He took her hand and pulled her to her feet. "Come, now we must leave this place and save ourselves."

Dazed and blurry-eyed, she let him lead her through the crowd. She pulled out of his reach as they neared Clara's house. Hearing the scuffle of feet and defiant shouts, she pulled out of his reach. Four guards came out of the door, talking loudly and carrying books and boxes. Richard grabbed Ventura's hand and jerked her around the corner. They stood breathless, watching the men.

Richard whispered in her ear, "You can't stay here anymore. You'd better go to Anna's."

She pulled out of his reach and ran up the steps, bursting into the house through the open door. The usually neat rooms smelled of perspiration and pillage. Bottles and papers were strewn all over the floor. Books had been torn out of their covers and left to lie in heaps in the bed and on the floor. Cupboards hung open on their hinges, their contents either broken or damaged. Ventura's heart lurched with fear when she couldn't find the herb book.

She ran to the bed and looked in the crevice behind the headboard. In the dim light she could barely make out something dark and square. She reached into the opening and felt its binding. When her fingers slowly inched the book out, her voice erupted in a shout of joy. "They didn't find it. I still have it!" She hugged the book, then kissed its cover. At least she had the book. From it she would learn Clara's secrets.

Richard's anxious voice rasped in her ear. "Hurry and pack. Those soldiers may come back." She nodded and put the book in her bag along with her clothes. When they closed the door behind them, she knew she would never be back.

Anna was waiting for them at her small cottage. She smiled her welcome and said, "Come in. I have put a pot of coffee on the fireplace and there are some freshly-baked cakes."

Ventura couldn't eat anything and barely sipped at her coffee. Richard stayed for a while, then Ventura asked him to leave. Much later she told Anna what she'd seen and they both cried about Clara, wondering aloud what would happen to the healing group.

***

Richard left Anna's house whistling. As sad as he was about Clara's death, his heart was warm when he thought about Ventura. Not only was she beautiful, she was brave and determined. But she was also too impulsive, too exasperating, and too independent. But even so, she had the ability to make him feel totally alive and supremely happy. How that could be, he didn't know, and although she hadn't given him any reason for hope, he felt completely optimistic. The crisp sea air only enhanced his mood and by the time he reached the docks he was almost dancing.

Maybe that was why he didn't hear the commotion aboard ship as he approached it. It wasn't until he was halfway up the gangplank that the image of Ventura faded and he saw the groups of soldiers standing on the dock. They whispered, faces full of anger and surprise.

Richard ran up the gang plank, wondering what the commotion on deck was about. Three of the hands were preparing the artillery when he ran up to them. "What's happening, mate?" he asked the nearest one.

The red-faced man pointed to the men standing below them on the dock. "We are preparing to be boarded. A delegation of inquisitorial and royal groups have asked to come aboard."

"What for?"

"They think we have important books and the Inquisitor doesn't like that a bit."

Richard was bothered by the mate's remarks. He had heard about other ships being searched, but never had a ship he was on been examined. He wondered if it might have something to do with his association with Clara and if it was becoming dangerous to be near Seville.

He stepped back as the mate lit the artillery charge and fired a three-gun salute. Standing at the bottom of the ramp, ready to board, were the Inquisitor General's men and the King's officers. A leader from each group marched toward the other one and stood talking. Then, the King's representative backed away and



his men quickly dispersed. The competition f
and the Inquisitor General's men came marchi

The door to the galley swung open an
of beer. They carried them to the Captain'
Richard went to his cabin and waited. Withi
face came in and began poking around in Ric
and asked Richard, "Where have you sailed fr

"England," said Richard, seeing the ha
heard about the suspicion that followed Bri
Catholic.

The guard's voice was hard, distrusti
port?"

Richard tried to sound calm. "I left ho

The guard rummaged through a stack
you met or traded with?"

Richard thought quickly. "We met the
traded with neither."

The guard looked at him as if he didn
head to the side and asked, "Are there any c
from England, Flanders, Germany or France?'

"I am from England. I believe the ca
too."

The guard withdrew his hand from
"What Christian doctrine and what prayers of
what saints are besought against peril?"

Richard smiled at the guard. He had
correct answer and he recited it without paus
the cabin walls. The captain had alerted
images on paper that could be interpreted as
on his walls were a map and a painting of a sh

The whole examination took only a f
formality than substance. The guard left and
outside his door, going toward the captain's
sounds of drunkenness begin.

There had been no attempt to search
physical impossibility anyway. He had heard
orgies and extortions were tossed in so a b
Nevertheless, before the guards left, they dra
your book?" growled a surly-faced guard with

"No," said the shipmaster, remaining
game. He leaned his skinny body against th
speak.



"Then w
chest.

The ship

The gua

cabin."

The ship

The gua
to know you h
ship around."
those beers, I'l

The ship
poor ship. All

The gua
see what you
hams, five che
supplies. "You

The ship

"All rig
merchandise w

After th
the danger they
at Clara's, thei

# 6

The next day Anna insisted they go to the countryside to gather herbs, because their supply was low. But Ventura wasn't fooled. Anna wanted Ventura out of Clara's house and the only sure way to do that was to get out of Seville.

They went late in the morning. "You can only gather herbs after the dew has exhaled, and it must be a day when the weather is clear and dry," lectured Anna.

Ventura nodded, concentrating on the warm sun on her shoulders and the cool breeze on her face. Lilac scented the air and the dark soil smelled strongly of spring, and today, that interested her infinitely more than the story of herbs. They wandered through cool cork forests, inhaling the damp moistness, before trudging up onto the sand, and climbing the bare rocks to obtain a view of the farm fields below. After picking a few berries, they followed the trail past lush olive groves and fragrant orchards, drinking at a spring near a stubbled mud road.

Farther along, the grass turned rough, then dropped into a cool valley. The meadow beyond was a mass of brilliant color. Ventura ran to it, stopping to pick blossoms that smelled of sun and sweetness. "Take some," said Anna, "they're chamomille. We use the tea for stomach upset and nervous exhaustion." Ventura stooped down and picked more of the herb flowers, tucking them in the small cloth bag she wore on her shoulder.

"Here are some sweet roots," said Anna excitedly, pulling up the small shrub to let Ventura inhale the sweet licorice. Anna nodded. "This one is good for sore throat and---"

Before she could finish her sentence, Ventura heard a shout. She turned to see a young man running toward them. He was muscular and tan with the sun-creased skin of a farmer. "Come quick!" he shouted, "My wife, Isabel---the baby---it is coming!"

Ventura and Anna ran behind him, down the dusty road to a nearby cottage. The smell of a wood fire filled the air outside the small abode. Inside, it was a small structure with only a rounded gap in the wall between the living room and the kitchen. There was a woodsy stuffiness in the house, with its earthen floor only partially covered by worn straw mats. It was the home of a poor family, but scrupulously clean and neat. A fire burned low in a small fireplace in the corner.

Here and there, in cracks and crevices on the wall were small religious pictures, momentos and crucifixes. On a ledge across from the door lay a young woman. Her eyes were large and fearful and her abdomen swollen with child. She moaned and twisted her body, while perspiration dripped from her face.

"I will wait outside," said the farmer, looking relieved that they had arrived to take over the vigil.

Anna sent Ventura to brew some Ergot tea. Then she went straight to the young woman in the bed, took her hand and introduced herself. "The tea Ventura is making is for your pain," she told the young woman.

In the kitchen, Ventura filled a heavy iron pot in the kitchen and hung it on a hook above the fire. While the water heated, Ventura heaped more wood on the fire. Then she took a large mug from the table and poured the steaming liquid over the herbs.

"Has your water broken?" Ventura heard Anna ask when she returned to the bed and set the steaming tea on a rickety table.

The young woman's eyes were full of fear. "I don't know."

Anna smiled. "You'll know when it breaks. Can you stand up?" Anna helped the woman out of the crude bed, holding her tightly around the waist. "Walking will help with the labor. The baby must come down and out of you. If you lie down it is harder." She walked with the woman, stopping for Isabel to take brief sips of the tea Ventura had brewed.

Out of her bag, Ventura took a small black notebook she had made by binding small papers and leather together. It was her healing book and it contained all the notes of what she had learned from watching Anna work. Ventura had copied most of Clara's ideas into it, so it was already quite thick.

She sat down on a stool next to the bed and took out a quill and an ink-pot from the bag hanging from her shoulder. She knew she would never remember everything she saw, and someday, when Anna wasn't there, she'd have to help with a birthing.

When Anna tired of walking the young woman, Ventura took over. "Something's happening," moaned Isabel.

They both looked at the young woman and saw a clear liquid gushing from between her legs. Anna nodded. "The water bag has broken. The water is clear, that is a good sign. The baby is healthy. Everything will happen very quickly now."

For the next few hours, Isabel was nearly incoherent, yelling out, twisting her body and calling out to the Blessed Mother for help. She even cursed Ramon a few times for doing to her what she now had to endure.

The whole time Anna stayed calm, telling Isabel not to push and giving her a rag to pull on when the contractions got worse. Ventura was just finishing her notes when Anna tapped her on the shoulder and said, "Take some basil out of my bag and make up another cup of tea. She'll need it soon."

While Ventura made the tea, Anna told Isabel to blow out through her mouth. When Ventura came back from the kitchen, the baby's head had come out and its tiny shoulders were starting to turn. Anna put her hands beneath the baby and waited. In minutes, the baby lay wrinkled and crying in her arms. "He's fine," she told Isabel, "two arms, two legs, ten toes, ten fingers."

With expert movements, Anna washed and wrapped the infant in a warm blanket and put him to his mother's breast. Her finger gently traced his small cheek until he grabbed hold of the nipple and began to suck. A smile of satisfaction spread across Isabel's face as she watched her son taking his first meal.

Anna handed Isabel the tea and said, "Drink this. It will help you deliver the afterbirth."

In minutes, a bloody mass emerged that reminded Ventura of raw liver. Anna examined each piece of it carefully. "We must be sure all of it comes out. Come and see, Ventura, so you will know what to look for."

Ventura watched Anna tie the afterbirth with a piece of cord before bundling it in the blanket with the baby. "It will keep him warm, she said, patting the baby's cheek softly. "The cord will dry and fall off soon enough." When the baby was sleeping, Anna sent Ventura out to get his father.

Hearing the news, he burst inside. Ventura followed just in time to see him kiss his wife's forehead and touch his son's tiny hand.

While the family got to know its newest member, Anna took several pinches of comfrey, fennel, nettle and alfalfa and left them in a cup on the table. "These will help you make more milk for the baby," she told Isabel. Before they left, Ramon pressed several pesetas into each of their hands and said, "It is all I have, but you have given me my son and so I give it to you."

Anna and Ventura left the modest cottage and headed home. Ventura felt hopeful for the first time since Clara had been taken away by the guards. Something new and shining and wonderful had entered the world, and she had been part of it.

***

Ventura sat chatting with Maria, waiting for the next meeting of the healers and freethinkers to begin. Flirtatious as ever, Maria pointed out a mysterious man in black as her next target. "But he's a man of the cloth, isn't he?" said Ventura, pointing to his friar's habit. He looked familiar. Then Ventura remembered he was the man who had helped with the map of the dungeons.

Maria fluttered her fan devilishly. "So, he's of the cloth. It wouldn't be the first time, you know."

Ventura giggled, never knowing when Maria was teasing her. "We'll soon find out. Here he comes."

The friar had warm eyes and a booming voice that rang with laughter. "Maria," he said, taking her hand, "are you telling this poor child lies?" Maria smiled and tapped his shoulder with her fan.

Ventura watched them together, sensing his strength. He turned and looked into her eyes. "Señorita," he said, taking her hand, "I am Salvadore Dago, Clerk for the Inquisition."

Ventura stared at him. "You're the Clerk for the Inquisition? What are you doing here?" Her eyes searched the room for a place to hide. Had he come to arrest her and everyone there?

Maria chuckled. "You're as full of the devil as I am, Salvadore." she turned to Ventura. "He's one of us, my dear. Don't be afraid. He's infiltrated the Inquisition. Salvadore is a defender of our ideas, are you not, Salvadore?" Her fan moved furiously under her eyes.

He looked at Maria from beneath thick eyebrows and the saddest gray eyes Ventura had ever seen. "That is correct, my beautiful woman. I am a defender."

Ventura stared at him, perplexed. "But I thought the Inquisition was led by the Church."

"That's true, my beauty, but some of us have been persecuted by our own Church."

Ventura shrugged. "How can that be?"

Maria tapped Ventura on the arm with her fan. "You are an inquisitive child, aren't you? Salvadore was a Professor of Religion at the University of Alcala, but he has seen the light. Haven't you, my dear man?"

The cleric nodded. "I have seen the horrors the Church has committed in the name of God. Sometimes I wonder if the Almighty looks down and sighs in deep regret that the human race was ever created. We are, after all, the only species that kill its own, barring a few birds and insects who eat their children. But that is probably for a very good reasons, certainly not for power and aggrandizement!" He stopped abruptly and smiled at Maria. "But I do go on," he said, his face turning red.

Maria fluttered her fan in encouragement. "You are only saying what we all believe."

Ventura could not stay quiet any longer. "How did you come to work for the Inquisition?"

He shrugged. "The group needed someone to infiltrate, learn about what is happening inside, provide information. My family has been a trusted friend to the Inquisitor General. It was only predictable that I should come to the post of Clerk." He sighed. "It is truly depressing work, but useful to the cause, so I do it." He gave Ventura a sad smile.

Maria fluttered her fan. "You do it, my good fellow, because it gives you access to some of the most beautiful women in Seville."

Ventura burst in with, "Maria! Are you suggesting that Salvadore, a friar, would be interested in women?"

Maria smiled slyly. "My dear, you are so naive. Shall I tell this young thing about the goings-on, Salvadore?"

He shrugged and walked away, a broad smile on his lips. Ventura turned and looked at Maria. "What goings-on, Maria?"

"I'm not sure your young ears are old enough to stand the shock." Her fan beat with a taunting rhythm on her hand.

Ventura pulled on Maria's arm, nearly forcing her to tumble off her high heels. "Now tell me, Maria."

Maria arranged a curl and said, "Stop pushing me. I'll tell you, but settle down." She flapped her fan at Ventura. "Now, I'm not sure about Salvadore, mind you, but he is an attractive man, is he not?"

"Yes, he is, but what goings-on are you talking about?"

Maria's eyes sparkled. "Well, the Quietists are the most famous cases."

"Quietists? I don't think I've ever heard of them. What are they about?"

"Complete annihilation of self. They abandon themselves entirely to God, allowing free expression to every idea and impulse which comes to them. Some of them even maintain that the body can only receive merit for withstanding temptation if systematically exposed to it. Sensual priests have been known to exploit their position to manipulate the most vulgar of sexual orgies. I've never seen any myself, but I've heard tell---"

"What have you heard?" Maria tittered and fluttered her fan. "Maria, do stop teasing!" Ventura stamped her foot in frustration. Although she felt a flush on her cheeks, she was burning to know more about things she had never heard about.

"My, you are a fiery one! Very well, I'll tell you, but don't pass it around." Maria fluttered her fan nervously. "It is said that religious hysteria or craving for notoriety sometimes occurs in women, and some can be easily led to be credulous followers. Of course, you know the Inquisition is against sexuality in any form." She sighed. "It is always such times that bring out the worst sexual practices." She fluttered her fan. "You know of Saint Beata of Piedrahita."

"Yes, a popular patroness. What about her?"

"Well, she is said to have claimed that she was in a very real sense, the bride of Christ, in whose arms she was nightly dissolved in---"

"Dissolved in what?"

Maria fluttered her fan seductively. "Why dissolved in love."

"Really? What else do you know?"

"Well, there is the case of a group discovered in Gundaljara. They were headed by a lay preacher, I believe his name was Pedro Ruiz de Alcaraz, or something like that. Anyway, he taught that sexual union was union with God, that mental prayer alone was necessary, and that confessions, indulgences and good works were unnecessary. Then of course, there was Francisca Hernandez, a woman after my own heart."

"What did Francisca do?"

"I believe she was in league with a student of Salamanca named Medrano, who was subsequently admitted to the Holy Orders. Before he was, he claimed that neither all the evil women in the world nor all the devils in the next could move him to commit carnal sin."

Ventura wanted to know more about everything Maria knew. She tapped her friend's arm excitedly. "Maria, what did Medrano do?"

"It's rumored he would lie in bed with Francisca night after night. He asserted that male and female devotees could fondle one another naked, without qualms, for it was not clothing, but intention that mattered. Now I tell you, is that not a juicy bit of gossip?"

Before Maria could say another word, Richard Hasleton appeared. Ventura was so caught up in watching him, that she did not even realize Maria had left her side.

"Ventura," he said in that deep voice that seemed to melt her resolve. "I've been thinking about you."

Her eyes moved from his face to his muscular shoulders and back again and a wave of giddiness struck her. "You have been thinking about me?"

His eyes darkened. "I've had another adventure. This time aboard my ship." He told her about the Inquisitor's guards.

She searched his eyes for a sign of reassurance, but reflected back into hers was the fear she felt. He took her hand and squeezed it tight. Her heart thudded as she remembered the soldiers at Clara's.

***

Miguel de Castro, el Doctor, sat outside the splendid office of Dom Francisco de Hernandez. As a physician, he was the perfect person to be called to testify against healers and midwives. And that was only right. After all, women moved according to superstition, it was a known fact. Whereas men, and especially physicians like him, were moved by logic. Men were the experts in matters of the mind.

Of course, there were times when he questioned his own. When he thought about that, his nose began to itch and a squeamish feeling took over his bloated stomach. Those were the times when the leeches or the broths of black snake or the incantations did not work.

Then there were the rumors of the female healers and how they had cured the patients he had given up on and left to die. Of course, those were only rumors.

He didn't know for sure they were even true. He had come upon a healer once, and she had told him some interesting things about herbs. But everyone knew herbs were disgusting things that grew in the fields. How could they cure anything?

What had astounded him the most was when she laid her hands on the man. He couldn't see her actually doing anything other than putting her hands on him, but the man quieted down and a wonderful state of peace flowed over the face that had a moment ago been racked with pain. It had to be magic, though. Witchcraft. Some kind of bedevilment.

If it was, it was his duty to take a stand, tell someone in authority. That was why he'd written the letter to Dom Francisco. He was only doing his duty.

***

On the other side of the door sat Dom Francisco de Hernandez, Grand Inquisitor. He knew el Doctor was waiting, but it was custom to let people wait. It was expected of the head of the Inquisition. If people thought they could just get in to see him like that, where would his power go? Besides, he had to think about a few things first.

One of them was the inner conflict he felt when gazing around this palace of a place he was forced to live in. Here he was, an ascetic, used to living in a small, dingy cubicle. Yet now, as Grand Inquisitor, he had to maintain the dignity of his office. Of course he didn't want to, and every time he saw a symbol of his office, he felt a little nip of guilt deep inside. He quickly pushed these little nudges away.

Then of course, beside the dignity of his office, there was the matter of his subordinates. He had a bodyguard of fifty mounted Familiars and two hundred infantry. Even his subordinates were allowed ten horsemen and fifty archers apiece. The salaries of each of these men had to be recouped out of his own efforts. It wasn't difficult to seize victim's homes and possessions once they were imprisoned in the dungeons. Many of the imprisoned were poor and had few possessions. That was why he had to increase his efforts to find the heretics. He needed all his men for a solid defense force. After all, only a week ago he had been held at knife point. His life was in constant danger. He lived in perpetual fear of assassination.

He hadn't slept well again last night and his eyes burned as he looked past the heavily brocaded curtain to his courtyard beyond. He could almost smell the sweetness of those beautiful roses. His gaze wandered among the vines and blooms as he thought about his recent activities.

He had been very successful at his job, and his job was to put heretics to the stake. How else was one to cleanse and purify their immortal souls? He pulled at his chin with something resembling religious fervor. He could almost smell the burning flesh. Ah, how wonderful to be doing God's work!

Since coming to Seville, Dom Francisco had concentrated his energies on the Jews. His task was a large one because they were all guilty by virtue of their fidelity to their ancestral religion, which was a standing affront to Christianity, to Christians, and to Jesus Christ himself. No matter that Jesus Christ himself had been a Jew. There were explanations for that, explanations that Dom Francisco had long since forgotten.

Now his quest, nay his anger, was focused on the Jews. His thin body suddenly stiffened in his high-backed chair. There had been so many he had sentenced to the stake. So many that one day God, or a suitable representative, would congratulate him for the fine job he'd done.

His thin hands fingered the piece of paper on his desk. It was only since receiving el Doctor's recent letter that he had even thought about the dangers the healers might bring. He knew so little of them. Only one of their numbers had been relaxed, a stupid old woman named Clara something or other. But now, according to el Doctor, there were many of them and they met regularly, probably plotting his assassination. He had to find out and deal with them, cleanse them too, if necessary.

He signalled to one of his soldiers to bring el Doctor in. The click of the door and soft thuds of shoes and the man stood before him. He wasn't prepared for the foolish appearance the physician presented. Bloated belly from too many sweets and creamed dishes, greasy hair that clung in clumps around his elephant-like ears, and stumbling feet that brought him nearly in a collision with the cleric's desk before he slumped back into a chair.

Dom Francisco cleared his throat and glared at el Doctor. Although a physician had much power, it was nothing compared to the Inquisitor General's and it was up to him to maintain that illusion of power at all times. He rattled the letter in front of him. "I am in possession of the letter you sent to me. I want you to tell me in detail about this healing group and what kind of danger they may present for me."

El Doctor nodded and began talking in a most annoying voice. "These so-called healers are the followers of Clara Rodriguez. One of their member practices out and out witchcraft. I have seen it with my own eyes. Of course, one does not trust only to one's senses, but I was there, I swear it!"

Dom Francisco looked across the desk at his visitor, feeling a look of disdain grow on his face. Was this man a total fool, asserting something and then contradicting it in the next breath? He waved his hand at el Doctor impatiently and sniffed, wishing the meeting to be over. "Go on."

El Doctor's words flew out of his mouth. "They rely on their hands rather than on faith or doctrine. Can you imagine? They are religiously passive as women are meant to be, but actively inquiring, using their senses to cure. Now as you well know, this evil, which is of the devil, creeps in by all the sensual approaches." He leaned toward the Inquisitor General familiarly until Dom Francisco sneered at him and the physician withdrew his heavy body, still talking. "As we both know, the devil places himself in figures, he adapts himself to colors, he attaches himself to sounds, he lurks in angry and wrongful conversation, he abides in smells, he impregnates with flavor and fills with certain exhalations all the channels of understanding."

Dom Francisco waved his hand angrily. He knew the passage from St. Augustine, Book 83. What other new evidence did el Doctor have? This was all so tiresome. "Get to the point. What other information do you have?"

El Doctor picked at his chin. "I saw one of the healers put her hands on a man and a strange look came over his face. I did not see exactly what she did, but it was surely witchcraft."

"You saw her put her hands on the man. Was it done in a lustful way?"

"Oh no, Dom Francesco, she was trying to heal the man. And I think she did. And we both know that women are not supposed to heal. It is better for a physician to do wrong than for a woman to heal."

Dom Francisco stroked his chin thoughtfully. "You are right about that. Women are not to heal. This is important information, but I need more. I need to know where this healer group meets and what others are involved in this sinful behavior."

El Doctor smiled a smile that said it would be a pleasure to have the Inquisitor General indebted to him. His voice rose with fervor. "I will find out what I can and report back immediately." Dom Francisco nodded and rose, indicating their meeting was at an end.

***

Miguel de Castro hurried out of the Inquisitor General's office. He rubbed his hands together, mouth watering at the thought of the task ahead. He knew about the network of espionage that surrounded the Holy Office. It was a formidable weapon. Together with the Edicts of Faith, which invited families to denounce each other, and the Confessional system which enforced it, nearly the entire population of Seville was implicated in the Inquisition.

Of course there were abuses, there were bound to be abuses in any system as large and long-lived as this one. He had personally known a youth so desirous of insinuating himself into favor that he had denounced by name no less than 121 of his relatives and friends.

There were also rumors of ridiculous stories that had been told that somehow resulted in arrests. Some were the rantings and ravings of madmen and women, but all voices had to be taken seriously, even if occasionally one or two innocents were harmed. The larger purpose, preserving the Holy Church, was maintained, and that was what really mattered.

Miguel chuckled to himself. Of course there was Luis de Carvajal, that sweet-talking jailbird, who gave information about a secret congregation he alleged existed in Seville. Luis told the Inquisitor's men that his own Paymaster of the army met with the group to scourge ceremonially images of Christ and the Virgin Mary. What heresy. But the Paymaster had been brought to justice. There had been ample confirmation. Parents even testified against their children and sisters to put an end to their awful sufferings while the trial dragged along. It took five years before they finally found out Luis' story was simply a spiteful invention. It was almost humorous that he had single-handedly fooled the forces of the Inquisition, but they had eventually found him out, and only a few unfortunates had suffered.

It was fascinating to see how the Holy Office persevered in its pursuit, collecting evidence, sometimes for years, until it was ready to pounce on a victim. But that wasn't unusual, sometimes it took a long time to extract, often under torture, the exact piece of information that would implicate the victim. The idea of the machinery at the Holy Church's disposal, and his now prominent place in it, made him tingle with excitement.

An integral part of the works were the professional spies. Their activities extended as far as the bounds of the Peninsula, maybe farther, and to North Sea ports where Spanish merchants imagined they were beyond the prying eyes and attentive ears. But they weren't safe. Nobody was.

Miguel de Castro's heavy legs hurried out of the Inquisitor General's suite. He hastened to find a knowledgeable guard who could point him the direction of a spy who could find the meeting place of these healers. Bringing their immortal souls to justice was now his main concern.

***

Ventura's heart pumped madly. She waited in the square, searching for the sight of Richard's face. To take up time, she wandered through the flower stalls, inhaling the sweetness of the blooms. Her eyes were never far from the awesome cathedral and its chiming bells.

Then she saw him coming toward her and her heart increased its pace until she felt something between a delicious excitement and a fluttery faintness. He took her arm. "Ventura, I'm so glad you've come. There's news." He guided her behind an overflowing flower cart. They stood behind the brilliant blooms and he said, "I've heard Miguel de Castro, a physician of some power and pomposity, has put out feelers to find Anna and the healing group.

The climate inside Ventura changed from springtime to winter. A storm raged inside her. It was mostly fear, but swirling in its center was anger. "Why can't they leave us alone? Wasn't Clara enough?" Her voice had risen so loud, a few pairs of eyes nearby turned to stare at her.

Richard grabbed her arm and pulled her down an alley. "Quiet now, someone will hear you. I do agree with what you say. Our group does nothing but good and the only reason they harass us is because they fear us."

Ventura pulled her arm out of his reach. "But we're not interested in power. All we want is to be left alone."

He nodded and said, "You know that and I know that, but the Church fears anyone who they even think could generate any support. That is how desperate they have become."

A familiar voice boomed toward them. She turned to see Xavier walking with Rafaella. His voice was laced with sarcasm. "Good morning, Ventura," he said.

Ventura moved toward them, reaching out her hand. "Good morning, Xavier, Rafaella. I want you to meet---"

Xavier jerked on his sister's arm. "I have no desire to meet this man." He looked at his sister and said, "Come, Rafaella, we are expected at home." Without another look at either of them, he yanked his sister down the narrow lane.

Richard turned to Ventura. "Who was that madman?" he asked.

Ashamed that she even knew Xavier, Ventura pretended to be picking out a bouquet. "I have no idea who he is," she said angrily.

Richard chuckled and leaned in front of her to pay the merchant. A wave of giddiness blazed through Ventura. What were these strange feelings Richard caused in her? She shrugged them off. Whatever they were, she was just going to have to learn to overlook them. She had things to do in this world, important things, and swooning over Richard Hazleton was not one of them.

***

Xavier Henriques jerked his sister along behind him, hardly noticing the slight resistance she made. Using gigantic steps, he covered the distance to their home in record time, all the while mumbling to himself, "How could she be so bold to dare to introduce me to another man? Didn't she know my honor was at stake? And all this only days after breaking their engagement. Probably best rid of her. She would never make a suitable wife anyway."

He tried to console himself by mumbling to himself, but the real hurt, his honor, was yet to be assuaged. By the time they reached home, he was grinding his teeth and thinking of ways to teach Ventura a lesson.

A servant girl met them at the door. El Doctor was waiting in the small parlor. It was a richly furnished room, but lacked warmth, holding the close, cold odor of books. A bronzed bust of Xavier's grandfather frowned down on all who entered and staid gray drapes hung partly open at the windows.

Oblivious to the atmosphere, Miguel de Castro sat in a soft chair between two fireplaces, his hands and mouth full of lemon cake. In front of him was a silver pot of steaming coffee.

Xavier nodded to himself. The presence of the local doctor could only mean one thing: someone in the house was ill. Since his mother's death, only he, Rafaella and his father resided there. Rafaella had been with him, so it had to be padre. "My father is ill?" he said, not bothering to say hello to el Doctor.

The physician answered without swallowing, his words garbled by an overly-full mouth. "Just a small thing. Your father has been bothered with foot swelling. I have seen to him, and he is resting upstairs. Here, have a lemon cake."

Xavier refused the sweet, but poured himself a cup of coffee and stared out at the gardens. He hated to be forced into a situation of making small talk, especially with a man like Miguel de Castrol. El Doctor prattled on, asking about Ventura and other matters that were none of his business.

El Doctor wiped his hands on his breeches and refused to be put off. "How is your intended, the lovely Ventura?"

Xavier coughed into his hand. "I don't know how she is, nor do I care. The engagement is off."

The physician slurped coffee from his cup. "You don't say. Has she done something to dishonor you?"

Xavier looked away, unwilling to answer. He didn't want to be reminded of the shame and embarrassment he had felt when Ventura had nearly thrown him out of that healer's house, let alone when he had seen her in the square with that sailor.

El Doctor took another cake and kept on talking, giving the latest Seville gossip. Xavier barely listened until he heard something that interested him. "The Inquisitor General is looking into the women healers in Seville," the doctor was saying. "They're growing in numbers here. They practice little more than witchcraft. I believe what they're doing is little more than a cover for their lustful wishes." To emphasize his final words, the physician belched loudly.

Xavier stared out into the gardens, trying to forget how repulsive he found the man. "How does the Inquisitor General plan to find these healers?" he asked.

The physician smiled, showing the cake crumbs lodged between his front teeth. "Strange you should ask. I am quite close to Dom Francisco these days."

"And---?" said Xavier, his voice rising with irritation.

"And, I'm sure the Edict of Faith as well as the confessional will bring in some of them. If that doesn't work, our Inquisitor is readying a spy network that will cover the city." He panted like a pig in heat, obviously enjoying the discussion.

Xavier pulled on his chin. "I may have some information for the Inquisitor."

"You?" said Miguel, raising an eyebrow.

"Yes, I happen to know a woman who is learning to be a healer."

The physician nodded, a look of pleasure coming into his eye. "I'm sure Dom Francisco will be more than pleased to know about this. Perhaps you can tell me the name of this woman and I will keep it in the closest confidence until I speak with the Inquisitor."

Xavier shook his head. "The name I will keep for the Inquisitor General. You may tell him, however, that I do have valuable information."

El Doctor finished his cake and said a hurried good-bye. Xavier watched the physician leave with his belly jiggling and his beady eyes full of anticipation. For a second, but only for a second, Xavier wondered if he had done the right thing.

***

Miguel de Castro hurried to the Palace of the Inquisition. His news would not keep. He had to see the Inquisitor General immediately, before Xavier could share his information and take all the credit. Hurrying toward the square, he pictured the beautiful Ventura. Her luscious body beckoned to him whenever he was around her. Now she was free, no longer engaged to Xavier Henriques. Perhaps he could call on her. He knew her mother and father well, so there was no reason he shouldn't mention the matter to her father the very next day.

When he reached the Palace, the outer guards recognized him and admitted him without hesitation. El Doctor's large feet plodded heavily across the inlaid marble mossaic toward the Inquisitor General's suite.

Two guards directed him to sit in the high-backed chair across from the magnificent door that opened into Dom Francisco's office. He sat down and stared at the fluted panels and elaborate ornamentation on it. It looked like silverplate to him, but what did he know of such things?

He stared at the door, but his mind was concentrating on the words he planned to used to tell the Dom his news. Eventually, he grew impatient. What was going on behind that door?

Of course Dom Francisco was a busy man, with many people to see, but he was busy too. Besides, his stomach was growling and a foul humor was taking over his mind. Who did the Inquisitor General think he was, keeping him waiting. Probably on purpose just to show him who was in charge. He started to chew on his fingers, a habit he had long ago given up.

The door finally opened and two guards emerged. They marched over to him and led him into the Inquisitor's office. While he sat waiting for the Dom to look up from his book, he began to get the feeling that maybe he was doing the wrong thing. He was about to rise and leave when the Dom looked up and said, "Yes, what information have you got for me?"

El Doctor cleared his throat and tried to look impressive. "It is very important information, information related to the subject we discussed the last time we met."

A look of disgust flooded over the Inquisitor General's face. "Well, get on with it. I don't have all day."

All thoughts flew out of el Doctor's head and he gazed at the Dom, speechless. Finally he said, "I don't know exactly how to begin---"

"Begin at the beginning."

El Doctor chuckled to himself nervously. "Begin at the beginning. Yes, yes, of course. Fine advice." He took a shaky breath and said, "Earlier today I had a conversation with Xavier Henriques, and he informed me he knew of a woman healer. Of course I offered to transmit the name to you, but he said he would do it himself. I tried and tried to find out the name of the woman, but he would not tell me."

The Inquisitor General grunted and dismissed Miguel with a wave of his hand. "Fine, then I will speak with Señor Henriques about this myself."

On his way out, el Doctor turned back to look at the door to the Dom's office. If he had played his part correctly, maybe some small dropping of favor would come his way.

***

The next morning Xavier Henriques arose early. The morning mass bells were still ringing when he left the house. Xavier stopped at the nearest chapel to receive a blessing, then hurried on to the Inquisitor General's quarters. If he worked this right, perhaps he could trade the information he held. As long as there was no way to trace his connection with the Inquisitor General, there would be no retaliation from that lusty-looking sailor, and there might even be a way he could increase his land holdings.

"Señor Henriques," said the Inquisitor General with a smile on his face when Xavier was admitted into his office. "How nice of you to come."

Xavier made a small bow. "Dom Francisco, it is a pleasure to see you. I have come because I have some information that I believe may be of interest to you."

The Inquisitor General nodded and waved Xavier to a seat. "What is the nature of this information, Señor?"

Xavier cleared his throat. "I understand you are looking for women healers."

A glint of interest shone in the Dom's eyes. "Yes, what news do you have?"

Xavier leaned forward in his chair. "I know of a woman who is studying to be a healer. In fact, she was studying with the woman, Clara, who was recently relaxed."

The glint in Dom Francisco's eyes turned into a burning fire. "Where is this woman?"

Xavier felt his stomach tighten. "I---let me be frank. It could be very dangerous for me if it is known I mentioned the woman's name. She has important friends."

The Inquisitor waved a hand. "I understand completely. Let me reassure you. Heretics are never allowed to know the names of their accusers. Where would I be if I did not protect my sources of information?"

Xavier let out a sigh of relief. "That makes me feel much better, but there is still something. A very delicate matter."

The Dom smiled benevolently. "Your confidences are safe with me, young man. I assure you, there is no danger."

Xavier licked his lips. He did not want to appear too greedy. "Is there a possibility of---"

The Inquisitor's words caressed the air. "What? What is it?"

"I just wondered if there would be a---a reward." He leaned back in his chair and stared at the Dom, feeling perfectly confident. "You see, I'm a landowner and could profit from increasing the number of lands I own. You know how it is. I have peasants who are not paying their dues and the ones who do are too cunning. They try to force a re-fixing of the land division."

The Inquisitor General raised an eyebrow and his voice lost its sweetness. "What has all this to do with me?"

Xavier's voice quavered. "Well, I thought---you might see your way---that is, to give me more land."

The Dom's eyes narrowed. "More land? Do you realize I do all this work, from sunrise to sunset, with no salary. Any lands or possessions I receive from the prosecution of heretics goes to provide salaries for my guards, my associates, my notary and much more." He slammed a fist on the giant desk in front of him. "Do you think I take any of this for myself? If it were up to me I would live in a cubicle half the size of this room, but I must do this. It is my duty to do this work."

Xavier's eyes traveled around the room. The Inquisitor General nodded. "You think that because I work in this splendor that I have lands and possessions I can just give away? No, no. It is not so. All this is for appearance sake only."

Xavier felt the anger of the man taking hold of his belly and twisting it into a tight knot. "I'm sorry Dom Francisco, I didn't mean---"

"You didn't mean---but did you know that all I have to do is---" He clicked his fingers together and Xavier shuddered in his chair. "A snap of my fingers and two guards will be in here to put you in manacles and drag you to the dungeon beneath my feet. And you will stay there until you rot!" Dom Francisco jumped to his feet and shook his finger in Xavier's face.

Xavier's mouth was dry as cotton and his legs trembled uncontrollably. The Inquisitor General stared at him and shouted, "Now tell me, who is this woman healer. Tell me or you'll be in my dungeon within the hour."

Xavier did not hesitate. "Ventura da Fonceca. Her name is Ventura da Fonceca."

Dom Francisco's voice turned soft and coaxing. "Very good, now where might I find the señorita?"

# 7

Ventura's mother dabbed a tear-soaked handkerchief at her swollen eyes. Her daughter was lost to her and she was helpless to do anything. She had pleaded endlessly with her husband to take Ventura back and forgive her. But each time, he had refused.

He was such a stubborn man! She had prayed ceaselessly to the Virgin, her frightened hands continuously fingering her rosary beads until she had almost given up hope. Then it had come to her. She must go see Xavier. Surely he would help. Together they could convince Ventura to return home and then all would be as it had been.

She waited until she heard Antonio telling the maidservant he was going out on business. Then she slipped away to Xavier's. A pale-faced young girl showed her into the small winter parlor. She sat staring out over the formal gardens, her mind rehearsing explanations and counter-arguments.

She was concentrating so hard on her thoughts that she failed to hear Xavier enter the room. She jumped a little when he said, "Señora da Fonceca." He smiled and took her hand. "How good to see you. I was afraid that once my engagement to your daughter was broken, I would no longer be viewed as a friend by your family."

Teresa da Fonceca's heart skipped a beat. She had to be very careful how she worded what she was about to say. Everything depended on it. She took a deep breath and said, "I came here today to plead with you. I have lost my only daughter and my husband will do nothing to help. I know you love Ventura. Please, please." Tears welled up in her eyes. "Please help me."

Xavier let go of her hand. "Señora, I understand your wish, but I cannot help you. She has shamed me and trampled on my honor. There is nothing I can do." He turned and stepped back toward the fireplace.

Teresa reached out a hand. "Please. Out of your love for Ventura, please help us!"

For an instant she believed he heard her, then his eyes went dull and his body turned away. "There is nothing I can do that I have not already done," he said.

***

Antonio da Fonceca was already in dinner dress, his tall frame leaning slightly forward to warm himself by the fire and read the tiny figures printed on the page he held in his hand. But even the gentle snap and hiss of the wood and its warmth could not soothe him tonight.

Nor could the increase in money from the peasants occupying his lands in Andalusia cheer him. Before dinner there would be some unpleasantness. He had met el Doctor in the square that afternoon and promised to have a drink with him before they left for Dom Refrasio's estate. El Doctor was an unpleasant man and the last thing he wanted to do was have a drink with him. Somehow, through manipulation and flattery, el Doctor had talked Antonio into a drink. Now, Antonio was regretting the obligation.

Upstairs, his wife was preparing for their dinner with friends. Antonio kept thinking about her. The dinner at the Dom Refrasio's had been planned by him because he knew his wife was grieving for their daughter and he thought a good meal in pleasant company might help.

The list in his hand dropped into his lap and he sat staring into the fire. He grieved for Ventura, too, but in his own way. She had dishonored the family and this was the time-honored way to deal with family members who shamed the family. He certainly wasn't going to go against such well-established practices. After all, what would become of society if he just did whatever his heart told him?

Antonio had just returned to his list when a voice at the door startled him. "Good evening, Dom da Fonceca," said el Doctor. Antonio smiled at the physician, watching the ugly man settle into the soft chair offered him by Dulcinea, the head maid. She scowled at Miguel until he removed his soiled toe from the edge of the couch.

"Bring us some food, Dulcinea, in case the good doctor has not eaten." Miguel's eyes instantly filled with a look of gluttony. Once Dulcinea had set down a platter, the physician chattered away, sloshing down wine and talking through mouthfuls of meat and cake. Finally he said, "I've heard about your daughter's engagement. Let me be the first to express my sympathy." He cocked a finger at his host. "But perhaps it is all for the best. Maybe you will look favorably on me now." He picked up another cake and said boldly, "I would like to request her hand in marriage."

Anger crept into Antonio's voice. "Of course I would be very pleased by the prospect, but Ventura is no longer with us. I've disowned her."

El Doctor set down the cake he had been eyeing. "Disowned her---"

Before Antonio could answer, he heard someone banging on the front door. Only bad news came wrapped in that kind of din. He jumped from his chair, knowing in his heart that Ventura was involved.

He heard a loud voice asking to see him and was aware of the scuffle of heavy boots outside the door. In seconds four guards burst inside, their armor and helmets ablaze with reflected light from the fire. "Dom da Fonceca, we are authorized to bring you in for questioning," said one of the men.

Antonio stared at them, his heart pounding. "Questioning?" he repeated.

The guard nodded and stepped forward. "Yes, in the matter of Ventura da Fonceca, heretic." Before he could answer, two guards grabbed his arms and dragged him out of the house.

***

They were in the big room by the fireplace, sitting at a well-polished pine table. While Anna refilled their supply of healing potions, Ventura placed them in the wooden box. The home they shared was small, only two rooms, both sparsely furnished with wooden furniture and brightly-colored cloths and spreads. Dried flowers hung in baskets from the ceiling and a coffee pot simmered on the stone fireplace.

They were preparing for their daily visit to their clients, filling cloth bags with the dried herbs and flowers they had gathered. When they had almost finished, they heard a loud knock on the door. Ventura jumped, sure it must be Xavier. Anna pattered quickly to the door. The sturdy body of Salvadore Gago stood waiting, his black robe thrown back over his shoulder.

The three of them sat at the table, drinking coffee and talking about their work. Finally the monk turned to Ventura. "I have some bad new for you, my dear," he said, his eyes turning gray with sadness and his voice resonating with worry.

Blood thumped in her ears and the image of Richard Hasleton flashed before her. "It's Richard, isn't it?"

Salvadore shook his head and placed his hand over hers. "It's something I came across while taking notes for an interrogation. Antonio da Fonceca is a relative of yours?"

A soft moan escaped her lips. "Father? It's my father?"

He nodded, his hand tightening over hers. "Your father and mother have been taken to the palace and are being interrogated and probably tortured for information about you. The Inquisitor kept repeating your name and asking where you were. El Doctor, Miguel de Castro was taken also, but he was released. The rumor is he now works in the torture room with the Inquisitor."

Ventura jumped to her feet. "We have to do something."

Salvadore stood up and put an arm around her. "That would not be wise. They have probably implicated you and in that case, you are in grave danger. You will have to leave Seville today or risk imprisonment."

Ventura's mind was a jangle with confused thoughts and images. The world she had carefully built after Xavier was crumbling around her again. Then she remembered Richard and bolted for the door.

Anna was on her feet, shouting. "Where are you going?"

"To the docks," yelled Ventura, just before she slammed out of the house. She ran along the street, not even sure where the docks were. It was not the kind of place a woman of her class went, but things like that did not concern her any more.

She hurried to the square, the center of information for the town. If only she could remember the name of Richard's ship. It was something simple and British. The York. That was it, the York.

She had to be careful who she asked. There was no way to tell who was a spy for the Inquisition. She spied an old woman selling flowers by her cart. A little dog yapped by her side. From the loving tone of the old woman's voice, Ventura knew she would do her no harm. "Excuse me señora," Ventura said, "but can you tell me the way to the docks?"

The woman smiled and pointed to the Palacio de Monterrey. Ventura craned her neck and saw three masts of a tall ship. Her feet took her swiftly toward the water where she scoured the docks, asking sailors here and there for Richard's ship. No one knew where it was, although a few asked her to join them on their ships.

An old sailor motioned to her. He only had one leg and a purple patch covered his left eye. He sat on the dock, next to a pint of whiskey, his hands busy whittling a piece of wood. "So you're looking for the York, señorita. Well, you're too late. She had to sail out of port. Been boarded again by the Inquisitor's sailors. It was a swift departure, you can bet on that," he said, winking at her.

Ventura sighed, a sinking feeling taking over her chest. "Do you know where she's sailed to or when she will return?"

The man shook his head. "No, but she'll be back when it's safe to enter this port again." He eyed her up and down and asked, "What's your name, señorita?"

The sun's shadows were lengthening and soon it would be dark. The docks were no place for her now. She tore open the message and read it as she walked toward the square.

*My Dear Ventura,*

*I hope this letter will pass into your hands. There was not time to see you, or I would have told you this in person. We must flee Seville or most certainly fall into the hands of the Inquisitor.*

*I promise I will return once the danger is past. Take care, for the Inquisitor has tightened his grip on us all. Destroy this letter once read or risk being found with it.*

*Fondly,*
*R.*

Clutching the letter to her bosom, she hurried along. She had gone no farther than a few blocks when she heard the military cadence of many feet on the stone road. Over her shoulder she saw the line of guards in their dull armor, the late day sun gleaming off their lances.

A guard in the front shouted at her. "Señorita da Fonceca, we have come to take you to the Palace. Do not try to get away, the Inquisitor General wishes to talk to you."

The moment she had feared so long had come at last. She stood frozen, her heart pounding in time to the soldiers' feet on the stone. All was lost now. But even when the guards grabbed her by the arm and dragged her away, she forced herself to concentrate on the letter she had tucked inside her dress. As long as Richard was alive and she was alive, there was hope.

The church bells chimed doom while the clank of soldiers' metal and the hard crunch of their boots on stone echoed in her heart. A crowd gathered and stopped to watch, their faces full of fear at what was about to happen.

The guards marched Ventura up the steps of the palace. The heavily-ornamented door banged closed behind her, sending a shiver up her back. The guards led her through a great hall and down a corridor into a damp and cold room that smelled of mildew and unwashed bodies. Against one wall was a ceiling-high crucifix. Next to it was a round window with a heavy curtain partially closed against the light. In the middle of the room, on a six-inch platform, stood a large, dark refectory table.

The Inquisitor General sat at the head of the table in a high-backed, heavily brocaded chair with tassels. He wore long black robes and a three-cornered black hat. His sunken eyes glared at her, then dropped to the sheaf of papers on the table.

Salvadore Gago, Clerk of the Inquisition, sat next to the Inquisitor General, but he kept his eyes on his notes. The Inquisitor General motioned her to a wooden bench on his left. Knees quivering, she moved toward it.

She was so terrified, she barely heard the words spoken to her. "Señorita," said the Inquisitor General, "do you know why you have been arrested?"

"I have done nothing wrong."

The Inquisitor General shook his head and sighed. "In this Holy Office, it is not customary to arrest anyone unless sufficient evidence is available to confirm that she has said or done, or seen others do, something which is contrary to our Holy Catholic Faith."

Ventura stared at Salvador, but his face remained impassive. At that moment, she understood that he could offer her no help. The Inquisitor's voice rose, "Now, tell me, do you accept the doctrine of the immortality of the human soul?"

She nodded. "I accept it."

"Good. Then nothing that happens here, no earthly discomfort, can affect that." He glanced down at the papers in front of him on the table, then said, "Now, all will go well if you confess."

She stared at him, unsure of what to say. Finally she said, "Confess myself of what? I have done nothing wrong."

"That is for us to decide, señorita."

"Very well, what am I charged with?"

The Inquisitor stared into her eyes and smiled. "Most men and women charged here, show fear, yet I detect none in you. Aren't you afraid?"

It surprised her that she felt no fear. She stared back at the Inquisitor. "I am not afraid."

He pointed a finger at her. "You don't fear God's reprimand?"

She shook her head. "I have done nothing to be reprimanded for."

He chortled to himself. "Very well then, are you a man?"

She sat up a little straighter. "Of course I'm not a man. Surely you can see that for yourself." She stared at him thinking what a stupid man the Inquisitor General must be.

His voice was cunning, soft. "Have you been practicing healing?"

She nodded. "Yes, I am learning to be a healer."

"Are you aware that only men heal. It is forbidden for women to be healers."

She felt a sliver of fear crawling up her spine. Perhaps she should not have confessed to being a healer.

His voice echoed around the room. "Your immortal soul is damned for what you have done. Do not place the burden of continuing this interrogation on me. Confess yourself and obtain absolution."

She looked at the Inquisitor. How dare he hold her like this and ask her to say that helping people was a sin? She opened her mouth and said, "You want me to confess so you can burn me at the stake like Clara Rodriguez!"

"Ah, so you know the heretic, then."

"I know she was a wonderful woman who cured many people el Doctor had given up to die."

His eyes shifted to hers. "Let us go back to this matter of relaxation." He rubbed his hands together slowly. "Do you believe the mortal body is filthy, dirty and sinful?"

"I believe in sin."

"And you have sinned. But your body can be purified through death and you will gain everlasting life."

Death. She shuddered, thinking of the smell of flesh burning at the stake.

"Become one with God. Give up your earthly torment, confess and go to the stake."

There was a gleam in his eyes as he talked about burning her at the stake. She stared at the Inquisitor, believing he was truly mad.

"Become one with God. Give up your earthly torment. Through burning you will be freed of your heresy. You will be wrapped in flames of love and forgiveness." He stood up. "I have pleaded with you and used reason. But I will plead no more. Confess your sins!"

She looked him in the eye. "I have not sinned."

"Then you doom yourself."

She stood up and shouted. "And you doom yourself by hoping to take away the power to heal by killing me. It will go on without me."

The Inquisitor snapped his fingers. "Guard! Guard!" Two burly men quickly entered the room. The Inquisitor pointed at Ventura. "Take her to the torture chamber and let us see if she tells the truth then!"

Ventura shivered, the meaning of what was happening becoming clear. Her words had had no effect. Only torture and pain lay ahead. The last thing she remembered seeing was the glint of anger and madness in the Inquisitor's eyes. Then the floor changed places with the ceiling and everything went dark.

***

Cruel hands stripped off Ventura's clothing and bound her with a coarse cord. Standing in front of her was the Inquisitor. Beside him stood a hooded man in black. His muscular arms were sweat-greased and he smelled of death and destruction. The Inquisitor turned and pointed at Ventura. "Vexatio, show her the ways we use to aid in confession."

The hooded man nodded, his eyes and mouth slits in the background of black. The vexatio moved to a triangular frame in the corner of the filthy room where an emaciated man with sunken eyes laid. He was stretched and bound so that he could not move. The vexatio turned the crank to the windlass half a turn until the wrists and ankles of the man cracked from the pressure. The old man cried out in the most horrible of screams, a scream that bounced off the stone walls and echoed in her ears.

She screamed at the Inquisitor. "Stop it! Stop it! I see what the torture does!"

The Inquisitor nodded and turned to the vexatio. "Good. Now show her the strappado. The vexatio nodded and walked to another corner. A woman with her hands tied behind her back dangled from a rope attached to a pulley and windlass. The muscular man released the rope an inch and the woman fell with a jerk to within inches of the ground, her hysterical screams echoing in Ventura's ears.

The Inquisitor shouted to Ventura from his seat in a high-backed chair elevated a foot above the proceedings. "Are you ready to confess now, Señorita da Fonceca?"

She swallowed hard and said weakly, "I have nothing to confess."

The Inquisitor nodded and motioned to the vexatio. "Start the punishment of the burning. Few can refuse the purification of the fire."

Shocked, Ventura looked around dumbly. The vexatio grabbed her arm and yanked her to another corner where a fire had been started. Two guards shoved her body down onto the floor, manacling her feet, rubbing their bottoms with a vile smelling oil before extending her legs toward the blaze.

The Inquisitor jumped down from his chair and bent down over her, his coarse breath raw in her face. "Now, señorita, confess your sin or your feet will be thrust into the fire. With that grease on your feet, you will burn very quickly and soon you'll know both the horrors and the delights of the fire."

Her lips quivered and she offered up a prayer to Jesus. Then she fainted.

***

Ventura awoke in a small dark cell, her feet chained to a musty wall. She felt no pain. When she bent over to inspect them, she found no signs of burning. The Inquisitor had only shown her the torture this time. Next time he would not be so obliging.

Sometime later, a small cup of water and a crust of bread were pushed into her cell. She grabbed for them hungrily, then dropped them both on the floor, screaming and jumping back when she almost drank an insect floating in her cup.

Hours later, a flickering glow came through the tiny window in her door. "Yes, this is the cell of Señorita da Fonceca," said a deep voice she thought she recognized.

Ventura crawled along the floor toward the light, stopping to rub her gritty palms into her burning eyes. Two men were outlined against the door by a flaming torch. Dom Francisco's voice came through the grate. "Are you ready to confess your sins?"

Ventura cleared her throat of the dusty air and said, "I have not sinned and I will not confess."

The Inquisitor laughed and turned to a guard. "Then, bring her to the torture chamber and we will see if she can be persuaded." He did not wait for them to follow, but turned and walked away, his footsteps echoing behind him.

A guard entered her cell and loosened her chains. Then he grabbed her by the arm and dragged her down the darkened corridor. The screams of pain grew louder as they approached the torture chamber.

Once inside, the guard forced her into the center of the room, holding her arms so they could be bound behind her by the vexatio. Out of the corner of her eyes, she saw Salvardor Dago, his notebook and pen in hand, ready to record in detail everything he observed. Next to him sat el Doctor, Miguel de Castro. When he saw her, his face blanched white and a gasp escaped his fat lips. Then his eyes traversed her naked body in an especially horrid way.

The Inquisitor walked toward her, stopping in front of her feet. "Let it be known," he said loudly, "that el Doctor is here to enforce sufficient moderation in the application of torture. Let it further be known that should the victim die or suffer grievous bodily harm under torture, this must not be imputed to the Holy Office, but to this woman who may fail to take the opportunity to tell the truth."

The Inquisitor stepped back and signalled to the torturer. The vexatio tightened a cord around her arms and twisted them. "Are you ready to tell the truth?" shouted the Inquisitor.

Ventura remained silent. The cord cut into her arms like a knife. Ventura screamed out, "I have nothing to confess." Thoughts like small silvery minnows swam before her in a great dark sea of pain as the cord twisted even tighter.

The Inquisitor smiled. "Loosen the cord."

Ventura's eyes darted to Salvadore. Her pain was reflected in his eyes, but she knew he could do nothing to save her.

"Confess your sins!" shouted the Inquisitor.

"Loosen the cord and I will tell you what I know," said Ventura through dry lips.

The Inquisitor smiled, a dirty, demanding smile. "Tighten the cord, vexatio."

Ventura's breath came in raggedy bursts. "Oh my God, loosen the cord!"

The Inquisitor shouted back at her. "Confess your sins."

Ventura gasped and screamed. "Loosen me for the sake of God. Tell me what I have to say." Streams of panic flashed through her body in white hot bursts. "I did it. I did whatever you say I did. Now, loosen the cords. I have nothing else to tell. Oh! My arms! Release me and I will tell."

The Inquisitor smiled. "Now we are getting somewhere. Confess your sins."

"I don't know what my sins are. Tell me what I must confess."

"Take her to the potro," shouted the Inquisitor, waving the vexatio away. Ventura was dragged to the triangular frame and strapped down. A sick feeling of terror crawled over her body. How much more pain could she stand, she wondered. She stared up to the ceiling, past the wet stone and dark mold.

The vexatio turned the handle and spasms of pain tore through her. "Stop!" She stared up at the ceiling, her lips mumbling, "Mother Mary, deliver me from torture."

The Inquisitor's voice rose above hers. "Confess your sins and you shall go free."

Jaw clenched against the pain, she murmured, "Tell me what it is you want me to say and I will say it." Just when she thought her arms and legs would be torn from their sockets, the cord was released and a funnel was jammed into her throat.

"Confess your sins," said the Inquisitor.

She could not reply. Nor could she stop the torrent of water that poured down her mouth. She couldn't breathe and her lungs burned as if acid was eating away inside her. Her belly would soon burst, it was so full of water. She closed her eyes, feeling Death was near. She could almost see the Holy Spirit descending from Heaven.

Then the pain ended and a voice somewhere deep in her head said, "Take her away, she is exhausted. Bring her back in four days when the limbs have stiffened. Then she will be more amenable to the rack."

She didn't remember the trip back to her cell. It was almost a pleasure to be chained to the wall and left alone. Sometime later the shakes began, twisting her body, ripping at her, banging her against the hard surface of the wall. She shook, violated and helpless, then fell into a deep sleep, only waking when food and water were thrust into her cell.

For the first three meals she could not swallow the bread and even a trickle of water down her throat brought the most excruciating pain. After that, she managed the water and a few bites of water-soaked bread.

Sometime later she awoke to the fire of the torch in her face. Her fingers pulled away spider webs and she swallowed again and again against the pain in her throat. The guards dragged her down the corridor to the room of tortures. Hands tied behind her back, weights were placed on her feet. Freezing perspiration poured off her body at the thought of what was to come.

Very slowly she was raised to the ceiling of the chamber, her head dangling dizzily beneath her feet. "Blessed Virgin," her cracked lips muttered. She closed her eyes tightly, not daring to look below. She hung for several seconds, suspended in the air, then, without any warning, she careened through space. In that instant, she knew her body would be sent crashing into the floor. "Dear Jesus!" she shouted. Eyes closed tightly shut against the impact, she waited. But there was no crash. Instead, the cord ripped her to a halt and she dangled three inches above the floor like a puppet on a string.

"Confess your sins!" shouted the Inquisitor.

"Yes, I've sinned. I'm a healer! I ask God's forgiveness for my sins," she screamed, half-delirious with pain and fear. Somewhere, in the back of her dazed mind, she knew then that burning at the stake would be her punishment. She had branded herself a heretic and she would burn.

Tears streamed out of her eyes. She knew not whether they were from relief that the torture was over or from fear of what lie ahead.

Back in her cell, she ate her crust of bread and prayed. Then she fell asleep, but was awoken by a familiar voice. "Ventura," it called, "wake up." At first she thought she was dreaming, but then the voice turned more insistent. "It is I, Salvadore."

She sat up and rubbed her eyes, trying to still her feverish mind. "Salvadore," she whispered toward the door, "is that really you?"

His voice dropped to a whisper, too. "Yes, it's me."

"Have you come to rescue me?"

He was silent for a minute, then his voice came at her sad and apologetic. "I can't release you or I'd be branded a traitor. I must not be found out or who will help all the others?"

Her mind could not accept what he said. "But you must get me out of here. They will burn me now for sure. You have it in writing that I confessed to being a healer. That means they will charge me with heresy."

"No, they won't. That is why I have come to see you. They will wait twenty-four hours before they read your confession to you. If you do not ratify it, they will continue to torture you until you do. What you need is time. I am trying to reach Richard Hasleton. When I do, I am sure he will come to rescue you."

Her agony-racked mind tried to understand the words. "Richard? Richard is coming here? To save me?" The image of him, his strength and vitality came before her and the remembrance of all she had endured floated away. "Yes, Salvadore. I will do what you say." She fell back to the floor, and for the first time in days, a feeling of happiness surged through her. She would live now. She had to live until she saw Richard again.

After that, the days and nights merged into a succession of tortures and hours spent in the cell. They pricked her skin with hundreds of needles and seared her back with a hot iron until the smell of her own flesh burning was acrid in her nose. She lost track of how many times she was on the rack or dangling from the ceiling. She did not even remember much of the pain. Even the Grand Inquisitor's taunts or the agonized screams of those around her did not touch her. She held Richard's smiling face in front of her and he was all she saw. It was only after they had untied her and dragged her wounded body back to her cell that she realized it had been her own voice screaming.

***

The order to weigh anchor was given just as Richard scrambled back up the ramp. Before the ship could get under way, the Inquisitor's guards marched up the gang plank, armor rattling, lances at the attack. They were coming and there were too many to ward off. Richard pushed and shoved, battering at them like a ram, forcing a soldier with a shiny scar across his face into the swollen brine below. Two hefty hands grabbed Richard from behind and forced his aching wrists into irons. Arms yanked out at his sides, he was marched through the streets to the Inquisitor's Palace.

Young children, dirty-faced and tattered, pointed and laughed until their parents pulled them back and shushed their voices. Richard reached the Palace of the Inquisition just as the church bells clanged six. He was flung up the steps and brought to the courtroom of the Holy Office. He entered the room and was shoved in front of the refectory table. The face of Salvadore Gago stared back up at him. He gave no sign of recognition, but deep in Richard's mind ran the hope the clerk would help him.

The room had a mild odor of decay. The Grand Inquisitor sat in his black robes, his voice raspy and accusing. "You must divulge all sins. Clear your mind of everything that is troubling you."

Richard grunted, then said, "The only thing that is troubling me is how I'm going to get out of here."

A burly guard stepped forward, his beefy hand raised to strike. But the Inquisitor waved him back and said, "We know you have committed many crimes against the Church."

Richard started to reply, but a hump-backed brute silenced him with a resounding slap across his face.

The Grand Inquisitor's mouth swelled into a smile. "You are part of an outlaw healing group." The monk's voice vibrated with indignation. "You have sealed your fate by helping a known heretic escape."

His voice went on, cajoling, pleading, chastising, until Richard thought he could stand it no longer. Still he listened, wordless, breath hissing through his teeth.

Waving his hands in the air, the Inquisitor ordered, "Bring that crucifix over here." Salvadore jumped up and lifted a small wooden Jesus. "Offer it to him. See if he will take the symbol of our Holy Church." Salvadore held up the wooden cross, gave an earnest, pleading look, then thrust the crucifix in front of Richard's face.

Anger rushed up from deep inside Richard and his hands clenched and unclenched. For the first time in a long time, he felt the urge to strike someone. He closed his eyes, trying to push back the bursts of red anger flashing before his eyes. But it was useless. Unable to control himself over this sham of justice, he turned, lunged for the Inquisitor and spat in his face.

Two sullen guards jumped on Richard and hauled him out of the room. They pummeled his body with their fists while they dragged him down several corridors. The way was dimly lit, but by keeping track in his mind of the number of turns, Richard figured they were traveling around a square.

They dragged him up a flight of stairs and pitched him into a filthy cell that smelled of moldy tile, stale urine and sweat. The metal cell door clanged shut behind him and Richard sighed.

A small patch of dusty light fell on his face and he looked up. There was a breathing hole barely visible above him. It let in a glimpse of midnight sky. He stared up until his neck ached, then he stumbled around, reaching out to touch the walls, finding the dimensions of his new home.

His hands felt along the cold, damp surface, tracing the names of those who had been there before him. In one of the corners he tripped over a skull and other human bones.

Eight steps took him to the end of each wall. In the center of his cell, his feet stumbled over a badly worn straw mat. On one of the walls, his fingers found a small listening hole, its edges rough and gritty. When he put his ear to it, he heard the soft, scurrying sounds of feet. It had to be a secret corridor, but where it went, he had no idea.

Days passed and he scratched on the wall to mark the coming and going of guards bringing his sparse meals. When he wasn't eating or resting, he had his ear to the listening hole. One night, after he had been beaten and his back throbbed with pain, he lay in the corner, huddling against the wall. The cell was hot and still and he was feeling especially hopeless.

Then he heard a muffled voice coming through the hole. It was Salvadore! He would be saved at last. Sweating with effort, he dragged his stiff body to the wall. "Richard, is that you?" the clerk whispered.

Joy bounded through him. "Yes, it is I, Richard!" His eyes blurred with tears. "I knew you'd come."

Salvadore's voice rasped in his ear. "I can't do much. I only come to bring you bad news. Ventura da Fonceca has been here for several weeks."

His heart raced threadily. Ventura's image floated before him. His lips refused to form the words. Finally he said, "Is she---?"

"No. No. She's alive. But she has endured great punishment and so little food."

Richard offered up a silent prayer, then said, "Thank God. Where is she now?"

"Not far from here. She is in a cell on the first floor. She doesn't enjoy the luxuries you do. She has no breathing hole and no mat on the floor. I've drawn up a map for your escape. I cannot help you, but you can reach safety if you follow the plan. I will push it through the listening hole now. Somehow you must find enough light to read it. Good luck and God bless you. You will not hear from me again."

Richard's hands groped along the damp floor. A flash of panic ran through him when he couldn't find it. Seconds later, his hand touched the dry parchment. Tears filled his eyes and he clutched it to his breast.

He slept that night with the message folded tightly in his hands. As soon as the first rays of light came in from the ceiling hole, he began to read, squinting to make out the words.

> *Tonight the usual gaoler will be replaced by A.G., one of us. He will take you to V's cell. The map below gives her location. Once you are loose, you are on your own to escape. It shouldn't be too difficult, for it is Holy Week and all is fiesta. The guards will be full of drink and you can slip through the crowd and leave the city. Chew and swallow this note once you have memorized the location of V's cell. If I am discovered, all is lost.*
>
> *S.*

# 8

All had been quiet for more than an hour in the secret corridor behind Richard's cell. Then footsteps scraped outside and a burning torch flickered through an opening. "Are you ready?" whispered a man's voice.

Richard stood silently for a moment, not sure if this was the man who would take him to safety, or one of the Inquisitor General's spies. Finally Richard spoke in a hesitant voice. "Who is it?"

"It is I, Alonzo." Keys clanged in the lock and the door swung open. A stocky man stood outlined against the opening, grinning. "Come along, time is short," he said, bending down quickly to undo Richard's leg irons and rub life back into the stiff limbs. Alonzo smelled of sweat and last night's wine but he was a welcome sight.

He pulled Richard to his feet and threw him some coarse garments. Richard pulled on the shirt and breeches, biting back the pain of the cloth against his wounded body. "Put these on, too," said Alonzo, pushing a pair of sandals into Richard's hand.

The two men made their way along the dank corridor, following the curve of stairs down and around toward Ventura's cell. Richard's heart clacked in rhythm to the flop of his sandals on the stone steps. Soon he would see her again and all would be well.

Alonzo stopped abruptly. "Which way, Señor? I was only told she was on ground level."

Richard led the way, looking right and left at every juncture for guards. At the last turn, loud voices echoed off the stone walls. Alonzo put out a hand and they stopped in their tracks. The voices were coming closer. Alonzo grabbed Richard by the arm and yanked him back around the corridor. They stood waiting, listening to the sound of their breathing and the voices coming toward them.

The guards passed by, stumbling with drink and laughing at the latest joke about the Inquisitor's nose. When he was sure it was safe, Richard poked Alonzo and they hurried around the last turn. Silently counting the cells, Richard led the way until they stood in front of Ventura's cell.

Alonzo unlocked the door quickly, but it took both of them to pull it open. The cell reeked of a foul smell. Using the torch to guide him, Richard searched until he found a body. His heart quivered in his chest with the thought she might already be dead. Then he was on his knees, patting her icy hand and mumbling, "Ventura. Ventura."

She moaned softly, then gasped his name. He pulled her body into his arms while Alonzo bent down to undo her leg irons. Screaming in agony, she pulled away. "They've hurt you. My God, what have they done to you?" He kissed her hair, her forehead, her chin, his body shaking with joy at seeing her and with anger that she had been violated. Gently, he picked her up and stood her on her feet. "I'm taking you out of here right now. No one will hurt you again."

Richard yanked the gown from Alonzo's hands and, using great care, he inched it down her body, his hand muffling her screams from the pain. "Hurry," whispered Alonzo, "the guards will be here soon to check on her." Richard picked up Ventura and carried her through the musty corridors to the back entrance, following Alonzo's torch.

Their guide waited for the all clear signal, then he led them outside. "Hurry now, the wagon is waiting past the square by the Giralda. I say good-bye to you now, and may the blessing of God go with you."

Richard grabbed Alonzo's arm. "Thank you, my friend, I don't know how to---"

Alonzo nodded and smiled. "Just go. Your escape from this hellhole is my reward."

Richard nodded and hurried toward the square. Once there, he saw people everywhere, chattering and pointing. A procession of white-hooded penitents and altar boys in heavily-brocaded robes passed them. Women in fine lace with high combs in their hair stood next to men in fine cloaks of wool, watching. The smells of cooking sausages and oranges were almost overwhelming, but Richard pushed along, moving through the crowd.

"Is she ill?" asked a fleshy woman in a lace mantilla.

"She is with child," mumbled Richard, pushing past. If only it were true, he thought, looking down into Ventura's face. The idea that they might someday have a child together brought a new energy to him and he moved along the stones more quickly.

Ahead lay the light of the Giralda. "Just a little more," he whispered into Ventura's ear.

A horse neighed and a smiling driver appeared out of the shadows. "Richard Hasleton?" he said, his grizzled hand pointed toward a cart.

"So glad to see you," said Richard, placing Ventura's body in the back of the cart.

Before he could climb aboard, he heard the clank of armor and four guards stepped out of the shadows, their lances pointing at his throat. One of them pulled Ventura onto the ground. She screamed and Richard reacted automatically, springing at the guard. But two of the armored men overpowered him and jerked his hands and feet into manacles. He tried to shut out Ventura's moans from his mind as he was separated from his beloved and dragged out of the way.

The darkness of his lost hope echoed in the footsteps of their forced march back to the Palace. Onlookers stared and whispered. A few clapped their approval. When the door to the Inquisitor's dungeon banged behind him, he let out a sigh of desperation. He lay in his cell that night, dreaming of what might have been if they had escaped from Seville.

The scraping of heavy shoes and armor woke him. Four guards dragged him out of his cell and into the torture room. Salvador sat in the corner, his hand busily scribbling his notes. Richard was propelled onto the strappado and tied down. A signal from the Inquisitor and the guard pulled on the rope. It squeaked and whined against Richard's body, raising him to dizzying heights, before he careened down, to within inches of the floor.

"Who helped in this escape?" shouted the Inquisitor, his squalid breath hot in Richard's face.

Richard bit his lips and shook his head in refusal. "Again!" shouted the Inquisitor. Again his body was raised, then pitched perilously close to the floor. "Who aided you?" shouted the Inquisitor.

Three more times he was raised and dropped before they released him, his body a jumble of bones and muscles, all shaking and burning inside the sack of his skin. He could not stand and so the guards had to carry him back to his cell.

The next morning, when the paltry rays of light sifted through from the ceiling hole, guards entered his cell and yanked him off the floor. They heaved him down the corridor and toward the courtroom of the Holy Office. The heavy wooden door creaked open and Richard was deposited inside.

The room smelled of old papers and suffering. Three men sat at the heavy wooden table: the Inquisitor General, Salvadore and a tall, sallow-faced man with a trim mustache. The guards jerked Richard forward and shoved him onto a wooden bench. The Inquisitor's thin fingers shuffled through the papers in front of him on the table. "The fiscal has drawn up an indictment based on the statements of witnesses against you and the facts that have emerged from our preliminary inquiries."

The fiscal cleared his throat and there was an unease about him as if he might tiptoe away to some unknown task. His long white fingers selected a paper and he began to read in a nasal voice. "The type of heresy this prisoner is accused of is holding the Reformed faith. His crimes are as follows: holding the Reformed faith, refusing to abjure the Reformed faith, accosting the Inquisitor General, attempting to escape from the Inquisitional Palace." His thin body turned toward Richard. "How do you answer to each charge?"

Richard cleared his throat, forcing a thin stream of air out from between his bruised lungs. "It is true that I am of the Reformed faith and have no instruction in the Catholic faith. As to accosting the Inquisitor General, I did spit at him after two hours of questioning." Richard turned his eyes toward the fiscal. "My patience was at an end." He coughed into his hand. "I did attempt to escape from the dungeon, but then, any sane man would have."

The door to the courtroom squeaked open. An old bent man waddled in. There was a fringe of gray hair around his baldness and stains like crushed purple under his narrow eyes. His skin held the waxy pallor of long illness. His breeches were too large for his thin legs and he drowned in his shirt. The man took a seat beside Richard, his hands shaking uncontrollably from either drink or a nervous disorder.

"This is your defending lawyer," said the fiscal. "Here is a copy of the charges against your client," he said, sliding the indictment toward Richard's lawyer. "You may confer with your client for a few minutes, but you cannot leave this room." He sniffed and sat back in his chair.

The fiscal looked at Richard. "I exhort you to beg for mercy and penance for all charges."

Before Richard could answer, seven men in long black gowns entered the room. Their hair was bobbed and smoothly dressed with curls arranged neatly above their foreheads. Each one carried a book and walked solemnly to a seat at the table. The Inquisitor General introduced the bishop's representative and the theological and legal advisers to the tribunal. Then he turned to Richard. "We are now ready to proceed to trial. All witnesses have ratified their previous statements, confirmed them and have made any necessary corrections and amendments."

The Inquisitor looked at the fiscal who rose and shuffled through more papers before he picked one and began reading. "In this month of May, the year of our Lord, 1670, a certain person stated that at the square you were seen trying to flee the city and that you had with you a heretic, Ventura da Fonceca."

He thrust his head toward Richard, mustache quivering above half-closed lips. "Is this true?"

Richard nodded and said, "It is."

"In this month of May, the year of our Lord, 1670, a certain person stated that you engaged him to provide a horse drawn cart for your escape from the Inquisitor's Palace. Is this true?"

Richard paused a moment. Alonzo had engaged the driver, but if he said that, the jailer's life would be in peril. Richard cleared his throat, then said, "I didn't actually engage the cart, I---"

"In this month of May, the year of our Lord, 1670, a certain person," the fiscal glanced at Salvadore, "stated that you did willfully spit in the face of the Inquisitor General. Is this true?"

Richard swallowed. "It is, but---"

The fiscal ignored him. "Pass these down to the defending counsel," he said. The papers were passed from one pampered white hand to another until they reached their destination.

The Inquisitor's eyes roamed the room, then settled on Richard. "What is your defense against these charges?"

Richard's lawyer rose and his near-sighted eyes squinted in the direction of the Inquisitor General. His hands shook even more convulsively and his voice was but a hollow drop in the huge room. "We submit the unnamed witnesses were hostile toward the defendant, nay, were his mortal enemies and their words can be brought into question."

The Inquisitor nodded and waved away the lawyer's words. "Let it show the esteemed counsel has made the usual objections," he said, his face a mask of scorn. After a moment of silence, he looked at Richard. "Do you have any person who could come forward to confirm these objections?"

Richard's mind twisted around the question. If he named anyone from the underground group, they might be imprisoned, too. Sure he would sentence anyone to prison with his words, he shook his head.

The Inquisitor nodded. "No persons to come forward."

Richard's lawyer gave him a disbelieving look, then started to cough convulsively.

The Inquisitor leaned forward and regarded Richard across the table. "Are you sure? Investigations you request will be undertaken to the extent that they might benefit the case."

Richard shook his head. "No witnesses." His lawyer gagged and held a soiled handkerchief up to his mouth.

The Inquisitor smiled benevolently. "Do you or your defense counsel have anything to add?"

Richard looked at his counsel, then shook his head. "Nothing to add," said the lawyer, looking down at the table.

"All right, then. The secretario del secreto will read out the report." Salvadore's deep voice read out the summary of what had just taken place in the court.

When he finished, the Inquisitor General turned to his advisers for their verdict. "Guilty!" said the bishop's representative. "Guilty!" rang out six more times around the table. A film of cold sweat covered Richard's forehead. Now that the moment of penance was here, Ventura's distant voice echoed through the corridors of his mind.

"The verdict calls for a penance." A secret smile rippled across the Inquisitor's lips. "You will serve for two years, unpaid at the oar in the galley of the Santa Isabel." The advisers and court lawyer rose and filed out quickly. Two guards grabbed Richard and pushed him roughly out of the court.

He lay awake that night wondering how he could escape or at least get a message to Ventura to let her know he was leaving. Through the breathing hole high above his head, he watched the sky turn from midnight blue to gray and still he had no plan. His meager breakfast of bread and water had barely settled in his stomach when the guards clanked in, placed him in full irons and marched him to the Santa Isabel. He walked up the ramp wondering if he would ever see Ventura again.

***

Ventura lay on the damp stone, her thoughts full of Richard. Her mind wove around his image and fired unanswerable questions at her. For one full day, she did not rise from the floor. That evening, pushed in under the cell door with her crust and water, was a message.

*Richard sentenced to two years at the oar of the the vessel, Santa Isabel. Pray for his mortal soul.*

A scream formed behind her lips, but she fought it back, allowing only salt tears to wash down her face and track down her neck. Then panic squirted in her mouth like the bitter juice of a lemon. Deep inside her came the conviction that she would never see him again. There was nothing to delay for anymore. Richard was not going to rescue her. She had only herself to depend on now.

The next morning the guards arrived early, sweat-faced and muscular, with lewd looks and wandering hands. They pushed and squeezed her, forcing her down the corridor toward the courtroom of the Holy Office. It was her turn and she gave little resistance when the door creaked open and unkind hands shoved her inside.

The Inquisitor General looked up from his table when she entered the room. "This is the fiscal," he said, pointing to a short fat man in a black robe with a puckering mouth.

The fiscal rose and began to read the charges against her in his slow, plodding way. "On this 5th day of May, 1670, in Seville, in the courtroom of the Holy Office of the Inquisition, his Worship, Inquisitor Dom Francisco de Hernandez, holding morning Audience, summoned to appear before him Ventura da Fonceca, with whom this Process deals. And that she might in all things speak the truth, and preserve secrecy, she was told to take oath on the Holy Gospels."

The fiscal motioned to the Clerk who presented a Bible for her to place her hand upon. "On which she placed her hand," said the fiscal," and having taken oath accordingly under seal thereof. She has testified on countless occasions that she is a healer, but has refused to sign a document abjuring her heresy and returning to the fold of the Holy Catholic Faith and the Holy Mother Church of Rome. In addition, she has, with the sentenced heretic, Richard Hasleton, attempted escape from the Holy Inquisition Palace." He turned his small eyes on Ventura. "How do you answer to these charges?"

A cloud of rage eclipsed the hopelessness Ventura felt. How dare they sit in judgment of her good acts? She would never confess heresy. Let them burn her. Her death would stand as a testament to the act of a righteous person in a corrupt society.

She lifted her shoulders and said loudly, "Guilty. Guilty to both charges." Then she turned and looked defiantly into the Inquisitor's sneering face. "Guilty, and I'd do it again!"

Dom Francisco's face turned from a gray dinginess to a pale white. Except for the scratching of Salvadore's quill on parchment, the room was deathly silent. A minute later, the Inquisitor called out, "Bring in the jury. We will have done with this one soon enough." In seconds, the jury of Dom Francisco's advisers filed in. They marched crisply to their seats, their black robes whipping behind them.

On a signal from the Inquisitor, they sat down. Before they could begin, the door swung to and in rushed ten men and eight women, all shouting and yipping. Behind them followed four baaing sheep and three yelping dogs. Taken off balance, the guards stood gaping, their lances shoved to the floor by the onrush.

"What is that? What is going on?" shouted the Inquisitor, his three-cornered hat knocked askew by one of the peasants.

The fiscal threw up his hands. "I don't know, your eminence."

A ripple of laughter skittered through the room. "We've come to testify for Ventura da Fonceca," said Isabel, her linen hat fluttering above her dark tresses, while the babe on her hip kicked wildly. "Ventura is a wise woman who should not be punished. She has done for us what el Doctor has been unable to do."

An old man stepped forward and shook his cane at the Inquisitor. "Yes, yes, she does good. Do not make her do penance!"

A brown-spotted dog ran around the refectory table and plunked down on the Inquisitor's foot. "Get these animals out of here!" shouted the cleric.

Sweat-faced and swearing, two guards chased after the dog, but tripped over a sheep. Purple as a beet, the Inquisitor waved his arms and shouted, "Get these people out of here!"

Keeping a straight face, Salvadore shouted above the din, "But aren't they witnesses, your eminence?"

"Witnesses?" said the Inquisitor, his voice a grumble of anger.

The tall man who had remained silent to this point stood up, "Yes, witnesses," he said. "As the lawyer for the accused, I say we must listen to their words."

The Inquisitor sat back into his chair, his voice mumbling and growling while Ventura's lawyer asked each person to speak and bear witness.

A young woman in a white linen cap stepped forward. "I am Brites Valenca of the province of Andalusia. Ventura da Fonceca has come to my house many times. Once she saved my life and the life of my baby by helping with the birthing." She wiped her hand on her white apron. "As you know, your eminence, physicians are only for the wealthy. But what of us? We are the Lord's people too, and we need help." Her green eyes flashed.

"A rumpled old woman pushed forward. "I am Señora da Sylva and Señorita da Fonceca has more than once stopped the pain of my poor husband, Belchior, when el Doctor had given up on him. But she did not give up on him. Belchior, bless his soul." She made the sign of the cross. "He was so sick señor, he could not pass his food. Surely he would have died had she not come to help. I owe a debt I can never repay to her." She wiped huge tears from her eyes with the well-worn red kerchief she wore around her neck. The others who had come to witness for Ventura patted the old woman on the shoulder and mumbled agreement or shook their heads fervently.

Ventura smiled at them, feeling a burst of elation. Maybe she would be freed. After so many witnesses in her favor, how could the Inquisitor give her a penance?

"I am Isabel Nunes," said a woman in a dress of thick cotton the color of moss. "Ventura helped me with my indigestion. It kept me awake for days, but she knew what to give to soothe me." Isabel rubbed her abdomen. "She is truly a wise woman."

The old man with the cane shouted at the Inquisitor. "I am Sebastian Ferrayra. She gave me a drink for my fever."

"And me," said a small, shriveled woman with a face full of history and a squeaky voice. "Would you believe this finger was puffed up big as my wrist, all green and swollen with pus." She moved forward, thrusting her hand in front of the Inquisitor's face. "I thought I was going to lose my finger, but she and the other wise woman, they cured me. It was a wondrous sight, your worship, a wondrous sight." A black dog barked and jumped into the woman's arms, to the delight of the peasants.

"All right. All right," said the Inquisitor, his voice returning to a controlled chill. "Has everyone had his say now?" Everyone nodded. "Good, then you may leave my chambers."

He motioned to the guards and the baaing sheep, barking dogs and all the peasants were ushered out. When the room was once again quiet, the Inquisitor held up a document. "I have another piece of evidence. It is a petition to me from el Doctor, bewailing the worthless and presumptuous woman, Ventura da Fonceca. It asks for relaxation of the woman for attempting to usurp the practice of medicine. This petition also declares that the charge is not that Señorita da Fonceca is incompetent, but that as a woman, she is forbidden to cure."

Ventura's elation evaporated. There was no defense against such a charge. The male physicians had decided they would be the only healers. It mattered little that they were clumsy in their work and condescending to their peasant patients. El Doctor and the Inquisition had made a pact and Ventura was locked out of it.

The advisers nodded and whispered, "Forbidden to cure." The pages were passed down the table to the fiscal who looked them over and then handed them to the other advisers. When all had seen the charges, the Inquisitor pointed to each in turn. "What is your advice?"

"Guilty," said the round-faced adviser loudly, his flabby chin waggling agreement.

"Guilty," said the man with bulbous eyes and pure white hair.

"Guilty," said the adviser with an off-center nose.

"Guilty," said another adviser through crooked teeth.

"Guilty," said the fat adviser, punctuating his words with a belch.

"Guilty," said the bishop's representative from behind his gray beard.

The Inquisitor nodded. "So, guilty it is. Now, what is the penance?" He rubbed his hands together in anticipation.

Shuffling papers and whispers filled the room. Finally the bishop's representative said, "Relaxation. She has not repented from her sin. She must suffer the purification of the fires." His great smoldering eyes gleamed.

Ventura's brain froze with terror and a cold finger of dread passed over her. Before she could react, a guard pulled her out of the room and she was quick-walked to the door. Dazed and not remembering, she was led back to her cell.

***

Richard stood looking into the broad expanse of the Guadalquivir River, inhaling the familiar musty smell of the wet docks and the moist air of the sea. Rough hands shoved him up the galley ramp and he took his last look at Seville. On the other side of the water was the Moorish Torre del Oro. In the distance soared the cathedral, with La Giralda towering above, its hundred-year-old wind vane turning in the breeze.

Ahead was the Santa Isabel. She was a small sea-going ship propelled by oars and occasionally by sail. She was not a bad ship, seven or eight times as long as she was wide, her hull rising less than three or four feet above the water. She narrowed down considerably fore and aft and a deck covered her entire length. Above that was a long guard-bridge. Up and down that marched galley-masters, their long whips whizzing and snapping above their heads at the oarsmen, while a drummer beat a cadence.

He sighed, realizing this would be his home for two years. The call to begin rowing echoed down the deck and the ship turned, heading out of the harbor toward the sea. "Move on," said the gruff voice of a guard while he shoved Richard to his post at one of the thirty-foot oars. Richard gagged, inhaling the stench of the hundreds of unwashed and diseased bodies.

The rail-thin man next to him was already being whipped into swifter action. The scourge cracked and then sliced into the man's raw back. His eyes were sunk deep in his head and his skin was the color of dirty cotton. He was sick, possibly dying, and only a soft moan came from between his cracked lips.

The galley-master's assistant took no notice, keeping his eyes on the chains he used to secure Richard to the oar. The man rowing opposite him gave him a toothless grin. "We are a smelly lot, are we not? Do not worry, your nose will adjust," he said with a wink.

"Soon, I hope," mumbled Richard.

"You there, no talking," said the galley master as he passed by them.

"Don't let them bother you," said the man next to him, "I'm Jozeph Delgado and who might you be?"

Richard introduced himself, then they both stood to push the oar to the count of the drum stroke. Very soon soreness stretched across Richard's back and hands, then red knobby blisters formed on his palms. An hour later, panting heavily and back aching, Richard opened his mouth to receive a piece of wine-soaked bread onto his paper-dry tongue. He chewed, the sweet wine running down his chin like a red river.

Jozeph winked. "Wine with our meals. Not bad, eh?"

Richard gave him a weak smile. "And how did you come to be here?"

"Would you believe I volunteered to serve for a year on the galley?" Their bodies moved to the next drum cadence. "Times are tough. At least here I get two pairs of trousers, two shirts, an overcoat of red cloth and a sou'wester for winter wear." Jozeph's thick arms took up the slack from Richard's tiring ones. "They throw in a red cap and two blankets to keep us warm here on the bench when the wind is chill."

Richard stared at his comrade in disbelief. "You mean you chose this on purpose?"

Jozeph nodded. "It's better than the bagnos."

"The what?" said Richard from between clenched teeth, his body working to meet the oar.

Jozeph spoke in time to the drum cadence. "The bagnos are ghastly prisons where they lock us up when we're not at sea. I have no trade and I was in and out of jail anyway. At least here I get some food. There it was bread and water. Here they let me grow my hair, not like that poor man over there. See how his head is shaved? He's a criminal. The slaves," he pointed to two other men on the oar, "they wear their hair in a short tuft so they can be recognized if they try to escape."

The galley-master wandered by and Jozeph clamped his mouth shut. A piece of wine-soaked bread was stuffed in the mouth of the thin man next to Richard, but it was left lying in his open mouth. The man moaned and slumped back, eyes lolling crazily. The galley-master was on him in a minute, whip whizzing above his head, then crashing down on the man's back.

The whip slashed down two more times before the galley-master gave a sound of disgust. Then he picked up the man as if he were a useless piece of wood and threw him overboard into the swirling water. "Let this be a lesson to you lax ones," he cried to the oarsmen.

The galley-master's words brought a new vigor to Richard's arms, giving him a burst of speed until the man with the whip passed by. Between drum cadences, he asked Jozeph, "What is that thing around your neck?"

Jozeph nodded. "You'll soon have one, too. We're supposed to take this wooden pear in our mouths so we do not cry out too loudly when we're wounded or being whipped or dying. But our galley-master isn't that strict. He knows we talk, but he won't bother us as long as we row steadily."

"What happened to you, poor fellow?" said Richard to the man across from him whose ears and left foot were missing.

The man looked at Richard, his yellow eyes dull in a charcoal face. "They got me for escaping." He groaned and pulled against his oar. "First, they cut off my right ear." He fell down into the seat, a look of relief on his face. "The next time they took my left ear. Last year, my left foot." Richard winced when he looked at the wound oozing yellow-green pus from under its dirty rag covering.

They rowed for another hour before a skinny galley slave slapped a slab of salted meat, a piece of hardtack and a wedge of cheese into Richard's hand. Black things crawled along his food, but he closed his eyes and ate. A horn beaker was thrust into his hand and he struggled to swallow the slimy liquid that smelled of mold. He must stay alive. He must!

The cadence continued. When they entered the sea, the waves gradually increased in strength, until the boat listed and lurched. "Storm coming," said Jozeph, pulling the blankets over them. The wind whistled on the deck, pouring buckets of briny water from the raging sea on their already soaked and shivering bodies.

A huge wave crashed over them and the rowing cadence stopped. Through the blur of water, Richard saw the drum flip overboard into the sea. The galley-master dropped his whip and stumbled against the wind into the hold of the galley.

The waves rose and thundered around them until the ship leaned dangerously to starboard. The galley-master and his assistants reappeared. They tugged valiantly at the rower's chains, freeing men so they could go aft to keep the ship afloat. Very slowly, with the weight of one hundred men leaning in opposition, the ship creaked, laboring until it righted itself.

Then an even bigger wave exploded over them, taking Richard's breath away and forcing frigid salt water into his eyes and mouth. He raised his arms to signal Jozeph, but the man was lost in the next downpour. The next wave hit Richard like a roof falling on him. Beneath him, the ship gave way with a large crunch and he fell to the deck. Fighting against the torrents of water raining over him, he stood up again and inched his hands up the oar. The water rose until it was up to his neck and he sputtered and gagged as the sea tried to force its way inside him.

His hands clutched for something to steady himself with. The deck seemed to disappear in foam, but a second later, the ship surged up between the waves, gushing water from all sides.

The ship plunged down again and he wondered if it had gone under for good. But up it came, then sank down again into the watery abyss.

A few minutes later, he was above the waves, watching wooden crates from the hold bobbing in the surf like toys. He grabbed onto one of the larger ones and held on, while the rest of the cargo scattered across the sea's furious surface.

Part of the deck appeared on the crest of the next wave. Richard let go of his life raft and swam to it, gasping and ripping through the debris. The deck was connected to a piece of peeling hull and looked like a crudely-carved boat.

Jozeph's call came to him, sounding far away, unreal. His friend's face appeared and then his body, swimming in the frothy brine toward the sea-made boat. Richard forced himself onto it, grabbing hold of a piece of oar. Seconds later, Jozeph appeared and Richard reached down, pulling his water-soaked friend aboard.

They lay side-by-side, gasping for breath. The next time Richard opened his eyes, the midday sun beat down, burning into his skin. The only relief from its oppressiveness was a stiff, warm wind.

Richard's left leg throbbed and ached. He sat up and pulled down his stockings, finding a deep moon-shaped wound on his ankle. It had stopped bleeding but was ringed in dried salt.

Time passed slowly. By mid-afternoon, the wind died down. Richard looked in the sky, hoping to discover their location. Neither the green sea nor the cloudless sky gave him a clue.

Jozeph lay half-asleep, a drugged look on his face. Richard's lips burned and had already split from the salt. His legs rolled and pitched beneath him on their half-submerged deck-boat. The sun seared into his face and shoulders, but he kept a watch for land or any sign of life. He watched so hard that his eyes burned and he had to look away.

That evening he looked up, using the stars for guideposts. He found Ursa Minor and breathed a sigh of relief. At least he had a small handle on his location in the universe.

The night moved slowly. Huge black sea creatures passed near them, their fins and tails slashing through the water. Richard cringed and rolled toward the center of their little boat. Later, his body began to shake. Whether from fear or loneliness, he did not know. Jozeph seemed so far away, on the other side of the raft, and lying so still, he could be dead.

Then came a blast of fire and the sun burst onto the horizon. Jozeph woke and began to chatter. "What I wouldn't give for a piece of that wine-soaked bread, my friend." Hunger jerked in Richard's stomach at the mention of food and he looked away.

They took turns watching the horizon for the sign of land or a ship, and submerging themselves in the water to keep cool. By midday, the torture of thirst was upon him. Hours went by and his parched sore throat yearned for wetness. He looked down at the miles of water around him. If he could just dive in, that would quench the thirst and stop the plague of intense heat.

He stood and took a step forward. A hand grabbed him by the back of the neck and forced him to sit. "Don't go in, the sea creatures are there," Jozeph's voice mumbled.

Richard panted, "The heat, the sun."

Jozeph nodded. "I know, but you must fight it."

Richard reached down with a cupped hand and took a drink of sea water. It felt cool and soothing going down, but the thirst persisted. His friend's hand clamped on Richard's wrist. "Easy now, the salt will make you sick." Richard laid back, angry and sullen.

"Stay calm now. Do not let the sun fry your brains. The sharks are there, waiting for you. Come, let us talk some more."

Richard shuddered and turned with a grateful look. "Thank you. I think I was a little crazy for a minute there."

Jozeph waved it aside. "Ah, it comes and it goes in times like these." They watched the horizon together for a minute, then Jozeph said, "You speak such good Spanish. How is that?"

"My mother was Spanish. Only my father is British."

"That explains it then. I myself never learned another language."

"I am glad I speak Spanish. If I didn't, I probably would not have met Ventura."

Jozeph cocked his head. "You speak with seriousness when you speak of her."

Richard's voice cracked with emotion. "Yes, I love her, but what good is that now, I will never see her again."

Jozeph shook his head. "One never knows in this life. We must all keep hope."

Richard stared at his companion. "How do you keep your hope after what you've been through?"

"Hope for something better is what keeps us alive, my friend, is it not?" Richard smiled. How lucky he was to be sharing the raft with Jozeph.

He dozed off for an hour or two and woke up with a terrible thirst. He eyed the water, his throat dry and tight.

"Best not to drink the water, my friend," said Jozeph, "it will only make you thirstier."

"I know, but all I want is something wet and cool." He reached down and took another handful out of the sea. Tipping his hand to his mouth, he let the soothing liquid ride down. The thirst was still there, but the tightness disappeared.

Late that afternoon, Richard glanced over the side of the raft. When he spotted a shark fin, terror gripped his body. Heart thumping, he watched, sure the beast would kill them. "Jozeph! Jozeph! Shark!" His shipmate peered over the side, fear in his wide eyes. Minutes passed and the creature did nothing to harm them. It swam by playfully, flicking their raft gently with his fin.

"Look Richard, he wants to play." They laughed together and Richard felt a twinge of hope they might survive after all.

At twilight, fish of every color swam by the raft, all curious, all frisky. Then a brief metallic flash and a spurt of bloody water flew in the air. He looked again, pieces of fish floated in the sea. "Come, get yourself some dinner," shouted Jozeph, hanging on the edge of the raft, hands grabbing frantically for the pieces floating by.

Richard dove for the other side of the raft to try his luck. The more frenzied their attempts, the more quickly the tidbits slipped through their waiting fingers. Angry and hungry, they fell back in the raft, poking each other, arguing about whose fault it was that they did not have dinner that night.

By the next afternoon, the sun burned into their skins, covering them with painful red blisters. Richard's chest ached deep beneath his shoulder blades. In desperation, he scooped up another handful of water and drank thirstily.

That night, Richard had a visitor. Ventura came on board, bringing a basket of meat and wine. They talked for hours. When she left, she promised to return the next night. Although he knew she was only a vision invented by his delirious mind, it gave him great comfort to think she would return.

The next day a flock of seagulls glided over the raft, their mournful cries strong in Richard's ears. The birds dove into the sea for their lunch, ruffling their feathers before soaring high above the raft. His mouth watered at the thought of eating one.

When one of the smaller ones flew down and landed on the raft, Richard motioned to Jozeph. They crawled toward the bird, waiting for the right moment.

Richard's hands crept closer and closer until the tiny neck was in his hands, its body pulsing against him.

He looked in the shiny dark eyes and hesitated, then hunger and thirst overwhelmed him and he broke the neck with a crack. The feel of warm bloody feathers and the strong odor of raw fish nauseated him and he could not eat it He threw the bird to Jozeph who pulled it apart with a single jerk. Richard looked away, his stomach turning at the sight of the pink intestines and blue veins.

Jozeph ate around the feathers, his eyes wild with hunger. When he finished, he dipped his mouth into the ocean and drank. Richard sat staring at the bird's head, lying stiff and bloody on the surface of the raft. After a while, it did not disgust him so much and he began to wonder what use could be made of it. He scoured the boat for a line or hook, but found none.

Before he knew it, the sky darkened and evening was upon them. He feared he would soon die of exhaustion when a harsh wind swirled up, crackling past his ears and pitching their small boat about. Much later, a black rain cloud passed over. Then the wind died down and a sliver of moon came up.

Ventura did not visit that night and he fell asleep sobbing. When he awoke, the sky had turned pink and lavender. Richard rolled his body to the edge and took a long drink from the sea. When his eyes looked up at the horizon, he saw a long, heavy shadow. It could be just be another trick his mind was playing on him. But no, it grew and deepened.

It had to be land. Using all his strength, he inched over to his shipmate. Jozeph sat up, rubbed his eyes and looked in the direction of Richard's finger. "Land, it's land!" he shouted.

He grabbed Jozeph and hugged him. Tears ran down their cheeks and they giggled and pointed and waved.

A surge of hope coursed through them and they hurried to the oar. "We must break it off and row toward shore," shouted Jozeph. They jerked and pulled, but the oar only loosened, creaking loudly.

Jozeph shook his head and smiled. "We must be meant to drift toward land, my friend. Let us wait and see." The waves pushed and tugged at their raft, nudging them toward shore. Then the wind switched and they moved in a parallel course to the land.

Richard nudged his companion. "We'll have to swim. Are you up to it?"

For an answer, Jozeph dove in and started to paddle. Richard watched his friend for a moment, then he ran to the edge of the raft and plunged in. The cold liquid rushed over his head, but he kept moving his arms until his feet touched sandy bottom.

Before him, rich green foliage peppered the shore, poking branches out dark and shiny above the water's edge. The landscape was harsh, full of roughly-hewn rock and scrub juniper. He stumbled, then crawled ashore, eventually reaching Jozeph's outstretched body.

He fell down next to his friend on the warm, damp sand, too exhausted to move. The ocean crashed onto the beach and echoed against the rocks and the bitter spray covered his aching lips. But all he knew and all he cared about was that he was safe.

Somewhere far away he heard the bark of a dog. Then he closed his eyes and didn't open them until he felt a tongue licking his face. Barely able to see, he squinted up. Next to the dog stood a short brown man in dirty breeches and a soiled cotton shirt. He spoke to Richard in strange words that sounded foreign, yet familiar.

"Señor, help us," Richard whispered with the last of his voice, then he lost consciousness.

***

When Richard came to, he was in a sun baked cottage, lying on a cool ledge. Jozeph was opposite him on another ledge, mouth open in a loud snore. A black crucifix and a weathered picture of a ship hung on the wall. On a rack nearby, stood a picture of two people. One face was a younger version of their rescuer, the other a likeness of a woman with round solemn features and shiny black hair.

Across the room, a burning log snapped and hissed in the fireplace. Above the stone mantle hung an old rifle, rusty from disuse. "Are you hungry, señor," asked their host. The gloss of health spun across his face and his eyes were blue as bottle glass. Richard nodded weakly. Minutes later, or maybe hours later, Richard opened his eyes and the man was there, placing a bowl of steaming broth on the table next to him.

The man put gentle arms around him and helped Richard to sit up. His head spun with dizziness, but with supreme effort, he managed to take a sip from the bowl. The hot liquid ran inside him, warming and vital. After a few sips, the man laid him back gently on the bed and Richard fell asleep.

Sometime later, he jerked awake. Framed against the lighted door he saw a black silhouette. The room smelled of wine, lamp oil and good cooking. Richard rubbed his eyes and the man from the beach came into view. His leathery face radiated concern. "I am Pablo Olivedas," he said smiling. "I have been worried about you and your friend."

The smell of something minty and fresh filled the room. Pablo's hands rubbed soothing salve on Richard's skin, taking special care to pull away the burned skin without hurting him.

Whenever Richard awoke, his body hot and sore, Pablo was always there with soothing broths and salves. Days merged into nights and he vaguely recalled being bathed with warm oil and soothed with camphor. His strength came back slowly and the stiffness receded. One day he awoke to the smell of roasting chicken and felt hunger for the first time. He ate his portion greedily, sucking the bones dry before he fell into a deep sleep.

The next day he was able to sit up without Pablo's help. The old man told him he was a widower who lived alone and that the woman in the picture was his wife who had died ten years ago. Pablo talked on and on as if he hadn't seen another person for years. Richard smiled and nodded agreeably, glad to hear human conversation.

One morning Richard awoke and found he was alone in the cottage. He heard the distant bleat of goats and the bark of the dog. Pushing against the bed, he managed to get to his feet and take a few steps before he stumbled into a chair. He sat for a few moments, breathing deeply, perspiration heavy on his forehead. When his head cleared, he stood and slowly made his way outside. There, in the brilliant sunshine, stood Jozeph and Pablo, their faces glinting brown in the light.

"Where are we?" asked Richard, his voice still gravelly and his throat still scratching with soreness.

"There is Gibraltor," said Jozeph, pointing to a city in the distance. "Isn't it beautiful?" Jozeph fell to his knees, bent down and kissed the earth.

Richard smiled. "Yes, it is beautiful. Especially since I believe I have relatives nearby." He turned to Pablo. "Do you know the Hasletons?"

Pablo's eyes lit up and an appreciative smile crossed his lips. "Of course, señor, everyone knows the Hasletons. They are a rich and powerful family in Gibraltar."

Richard nodded. "Good. I want to go there as soon as you can take me. I'd walk, but I don't think my legs would carry me yet."

Pablo took Richard's arm. "Look how you shake. You must rest now. I will take you to Gibraltor in a few days." The two men guided Richard toward the cottage.

Richard stopped walking and turned toward Pablo. "Jozeph, too?"

Jozeph laughed, a deep, boisterous laugh. "Pablo needs someone to help him work his fields and I do not wish to be captured and return to the bagnos. It is safer for me here. Here," he said, spreading his arm in a wide arc, "there is plenty to eat, no galley-master and I am free to walk where I please. This is paradise, is it not?"

Richard nodded. "I guess you're right, but there is someone I must see."

Jozeph smiled. "The lady you spoke of on our ocean cruise."

Richard managed a weak smile. "Yes, the lady. Perhaps, if things go well, I will return here and settle. Either way, I can never repay you for your help."

"Repay me? It is me who should repay you. You have given me much by journeying here with me. Without you, I would have jumped overboard many times. It was only you who kept me sane." Jozeph put his arm around Richard and clapped him on the back warmly.

Two days later, they embraced outside the cottage and said their final good-byes. From his seat on the back of Pablo's cart, Richard watched his shipmate until he was a black dot against the gray sky.

Then he turned his thoughts to what lay ahead. The day smelled of dust and rain and he wondered what would happen to him if it stormed. Each rut the donkey cart hit sent waves of pain up Richard's leg, but soon they were on the flat road and he forgot his discomfort. The dark sky split open then and bright sun emerged.

Olive groves were everywhere and the sweet scent of apple blossoms filled the air. Shaded by cork trees, the road rose gradually before they bumped across a rugged mountain pass. On the other side, a city glistened in the sun and a strong dry wind tickled across Richard's face. Another city, shrouded in mist, stood beyond a narrow strip of clear blue sea.

"It is Tangier," cried Pablo. "They are our twin guardians of the sea." The old man pointed excitedly. "We are near to the Hazleton estate now. I used to work for Señor Hasleton, so we should be able to gain entrance." The cart clacked up to a high-gated property before the donkey hooves were muffled by green boughs and fallen leaves.

They only stood outside the gate for a few minutes before a tall man in peasant dress came out. He had a paunch and a weather-beaten face and a suspicious look in his eye.

"I'm here to see my uncle, Winston Hasleton," said Richard. The peasant looked at Richard's ragged clothes and sun-scorched body and squinted down his nose at him. Then he turned bloodshot eyes on Pable and frowned, trying to place him.

"Ah, you recognize me. I am Pablo. Remember when we pulled the tree out of the road?" The gatekeeper showed his yellow teeth in a smile and shook his head agreeably. Pablo nodded and said, "My friend, Señor Hasleton, has been shipwrecked and has come to seek help from his family."

The gatekeeper gave a little bow and said, "Yes, yes, right this way."

Richard turned and said his good-byes to Pablo. "I will send you a reward for your help," he called to the man after he was heading for his donkey.

Pablo turned and grinned, "Your health is my reward, señor." Then he winked, raised his hand in salute and jumped into his cart.

Richard felt suddenly alone and lonely. He followed the peasant, his feet echoing hollowly along the stone walk. Pablo and Jozeph had been true friends and he would probably never see either of them again. He could not help but feel sad about that.

The heaviness in his chest lifted a bit when he was led into an immense room that felt familiar, like home. The odor of a morning fire hung in the air.

While his feet clicked slowly over festive blue tiles, his eyes drank in the richness of the paintings and furniture.

Before he could ask about his uncle, a door to his right burst open and a raven-haired maid with a heart-shaped mouth ran to meet them. "Please be seated, señor," she in a warm, inviting voice. She led him to an enormous blue chair overlooking the gardens. Blooms of every color and stone fountains gaily carved into figures of fishes and animals danced before him.

A melodius voice filled the silence. "My dear boy." He turned to see a frail, birdlike woman whisking into the room, her velvet gown standing out around her stiffly. He jumped to his feet. "Is it true you've been shipwrecked?" she asked, her intelligent dark eyes smiling at him. Her features were aristocratic, yet her face flickered with exuberance.

She reached out to grab his hand with affection, fingering the gold ring he wore. She nodded, "You truly are Richard Hasleton." Her smile was warm and affectionate. "If you're Richard, then I, of course, am your Aunt Cecily." She gave him an even smile. "I gave you your grandfather's ring when you were quite young. Do you remember?"

He felt embarrassed when he said, "I don't remember."

"You were here with your mother, playing in the gardens. You said you wanted to take the bear fountain home with you." She tossed her black curls and giggled. "But you may have been too small to remember." She patted his hand. "You were such a little boy."

He looked around the room. "I don't remember, but yet the house does seem familiar.

"You were a very small boy." She smiled at him again. "And now you are a man." Her fingers touched the gold locket around her neck, opening the tiny latch. She showed him the small portrait of his father painted inside on white porcelain. Looking into Richard's eyes searchingly she said, "Yes, yes, I see your father's eyes." Slowly her glance covered the rest of his face. "And his chin." She snapped the locket closed and looked down at his raggedy clothes and blistered body. "Of course you are badly in need of a bath, some soothing salve and rest. But then you will be just fine."

She signalled to a servant by the door. "Ramon, help him to his room." The man shuffled forward. He was all head, like a fish, and wore an intense smile which he directed at the floor. The dizziness came back and Richard grabbed for the man's arm. "I'll see you after you've rested and eaten," called his aunt's voice after them.

It wasn't until several days later that Richard emerged from his room. By then the dizziness was gone and his legs barely wobbled. The maid with the heart-shaped mouth led him into the breakfast room where his aunt was drinking tea and nibbling daintily on toast. "This is much better, Richard." she patted a seat beside her and he sat down. "That will be all, Sophia," she said, dismissing the maid.

Richard turned to the small woman by his side. "Where is Uncle Winston?

Her eyes clouded and she handed him a tea cup. "Then you don't know."

"I haven't been in touch with---"

"He died last year. It was a riding accident. He was up on the cliffs and his horse shied." Tears formed in her great dark eyes. She pulled a lace handkerchief out of her sleeve and brushed them away.

"I have been sailing and haven't gotten my mail for months. I'm so sorry, Aunt Cecily."

She looked past him toward the garden. "It has been lonely in this big house without him." She looked at her nephew, eyes shining. "But now I have you and we shall have many things to talk about." She passed him a plate with tiny wedges of toast on it.

"I'm afraid I won't be much consolation. As soon as possible, I'm off to Seville. Actually," he said, taking a bite of toast," there is a woman there, a woman I intend to marry, who has been wrongfully imprisoned and I plan to go there and help her."

Cecily leaned closer and her shiny hair released a sweet perfume. "Who is this woman? Is she Spanish?"

"Yes."

She nodded. "Like your mother."

"No, she's nothing like mother. Ventura is a free spirit. A beautiful, free spirit."

She glanced at him. "Yes, I can see she is important to you." She poured more tea into his cup. "Now, how is it that I can help you?"

"Aunt Cecily. You are so perceptive."

A smile like a shaft of warm sunshine touched the corners of her mouth and she passed him a plate of sausages. "Winston used to say that too," she said, her eyes misting over.

"What I need is transportation back to Seville. Can you manage that?"

"Of course, the stables are full of fine horses. You can take two of your uncle's finest and hitch them to a cart. Talk to Henry at the stables." She turned to face him, her curls bouncing as she did. "Now you will stay a few days, won't you?"

"I'm afraid not. I leave tomorrow. Time is of the essence. Ventura is in great danger and may be under torture."

His aunt's face broke into lines of distress and her cool hand reached over and gripped his wrist tightly. "Torture? What is going on in Seville?"

"Not much good. The Inquisition is imprisoning thousands of people on the whim of the Inquisitor. I believe him to be mad."

***

Squinting to see in the early morning light, Richard looked at himself in Aunt Cecily's long gold-edge mirror by the wall. He pulled the wide brim of his green hat even farther down on his forehead, nearly obscuring his eyes. That would do for that, but what about his chin and blonde hair? He was certain to stand out among the dark-haired Spaniards in Seville. Impatiently, he pushed the stiff shirt collar up around his chin, tying the heavy black cloak more tightly around his neck. He nodded at his reflection and hurried out.

His aunt stood at the front door, next to Sophia and Ramon. "Oh dear, here he comes. Now who has that parcel?" she whispered. A cloth-wrapped bag was shoved into her arms. Aunt Cecily turned and handed it to her nephew. "These are clothes for your Ventura. If she's been in prison, she will need them."

"Aunt Cecily, I can't---"

"Of course you can, now you just be careful."

He smiled and took the parcel, leaning down to kiss her cheek. She smelled of apples and goodness when she hugged him and he almost didn't want to leave.

Eventually he stepped outside, arm-in-arm with his aunt. They headed for the cart parked by the door. A pair of horses stood waiting, tails flicking against the flies. The stallion was tall, three hands taller than any he'd seen. It was black, shiny and powerful, with a curved neck and flaring nostrils.

Next to him, lithe and supple, stood a spirited chestnut with glossy limbs and savage eyes. Beside the cart stood Henry. He was a scrawny man, with hair poking around his seamed and polished face. He laid his fingers aside his mouth and said, "These are the best horses we have. Watch out for the black one, he's a bit frisky, but they will see you well to Seville."

Richard gave his aunt one more squeeze, then he climbed into the cart. The door to the house opened and Sophia ran out, giggling. She handed Richard a lunch basket which he placed on the seat beside him. Then he took the reins and slapped the stallion's rump. The cart lurched forward and Richard turned to wave. "Come back if you can!" shouted his aunt, her silk handkerchief fluttering good-bye.

The horses broke into a canter, their hooves skimming the earth, lather building quickly on their necks and backs. He urged them on and they responded to him as if they knew the importance of their journey. The trip to Seville was long, but the closer they got to the city, the faster he drove. It was as if an invisible cord was drawing him toward Ventura.

# 9

Ventura sat on the floor of her cell, shivering. She had been awake all night, unable to close her eyes. For every time she did, images of Clara burning at the stake haunted her. All night a monk had sat with her, his rosary beads clicking in the damp must of her cell.

Now it was the morning of her auto de fe and soon she would be at the stake. Then it would all be over---the torture, the hunger, the loneliness, the fear.

It was not yet sunrise when she heard the armor-covered feet marching down the corridor, coming to get her. They stopped in front of her cell. The key turned loudly in the lock and the heavy door swung open. Someone tilted a lamp into her face and she gasped and looked away from the strong light. Two strong arms lifted her to her feet roughly, pinning her arms and chest against her. Two more arms released her leg irons and pulled a long robe over her head. Someone placed a tall pointed hat on her head, manacled her arms in front of her and pulled her into the corridor.

The light burned into her eyes and the soft voice of the monk beside her begged her to confess. She walked uncertainly into the dimness, but the soldiers pushed her along the dank corridor. Trembling with fear, she looked down at her robe and the black St. Andrew's cross. If the flames pointed down, she had escaped the stake by confession and would only be walked through the streets in humiliation. Maybe the Inquisitor had somehow taken pity on her.

Yes, there were the flames, but in their midst were the devils, casting heretics into the fires of hell. Terror gripped her throat like a vise when she realized she would burn.

Her body went numb then, and the trek through endless corridors turned dreamlike. It was almost as if she was sleepwalking, turning left and right until they reached a familiar room, the courtroom of the Tribunal.

The door was open. Inside the Brothers of the Inquisition waited.

Lamps glowed eerily in their faces. They sat at the refectory table or stood in small circles with other penitents, offering platters of cakes stiff with fruit, stuffing their own mouths with the sweet food. Ventura shook her head, a sound of disgust escaping her mouth when a platter was extended to her.

How could she eat now? How could anyone eat now?

The sun's first rays came through the windows. Bands of salmon and violet glowed above the horizon just as two soldiers grabbed her arms and led her with the others out into the street. Two Brothers of the Inquisition marched up and took their positions, one on each side of her. Their voices rang out nonstop, urging her to confess her heresy.

Heart thumping in fear, she slowly lifted her eyes. Small altar boys carrying lighted candles led the way. Church bells clanged a lament, while crowds along the way shook their fists angrily or clapped in anticipation of seeing her burn. The procession made its way snakelike, along the road. Those to be punished by whipping wore scourges around their necks. Some whimpered and cried out above the rumble of the monk's urgings.

Ten delinquents followed. The painted symbols on their garments and caps showed they were to be reconciled, not burned. Staggered among their number were effigies and boxes of those who had already died during torture or trial.

Ventura walked in the next group. All wore sambenitos and tall headdresses covered with figures of devils and flames. Half of them were women. Several appeared only in effigies carried on long poles. The dizzying smell of disease and destruction was all around her.

Ventura glanced behind at Salvadore. As Clerk of the Inquisition, he rode on horseback. His deep-set gray eyes did not acknowledge her. But then, how could they? He must continue his work as a spy and to do that he must not show sympathy for the condemned.

She sighed and looked behind Salvadore. A plodding mule came next, carrying the velvet-covered document chest, the container of the sentences that would be read out at the auto de fe. Behind him rode the Inquisitor General, face proud, eyes glazed with self-righteousness. His left arm bore the green cross, standard of the Inquisition.

The procession moved slowly toward the square. Rough arms led her to her seat in the back row, the one reserved for those to be burned. Some of the condemned bore the look of the resigned. Others swaggered forward with the utmost fury in their eyes. She wondered what was to be read from her face.

The Dominican Prior's voice rang out in sermon. He had been the one to speak the loudest guilty verdict against her. He looked past the penitents, dark eyes staring out into the crowd, voice full of anger and accusation. "Penitents! By the bowels of the Lord, become converted to the Holy Catholic Faith. Let not the devil possess your body and soul!"

His voice quieted when he held up a large gold cross. Then he asked the rowdy spectators to raise their hands and swear solemnly to defend the Catholic faith and support the Inquisition.

The din was overwhelming. The crowd roared its approval. Ventura's eyes searched for a familiar face. A flash of sun on a well-angled face and her heart leapt with the possibility it was Anna.

One by one the penitents were led to the pulpit to hear their fate. Then it was her turn. She knew what was to happen to her, but when she actually heard the verdict said aloud, tears poured out of her eyes and a ferocious anger seized her.

"You hypocrite!" she screamed. "Is this God's work, killing innocents?" Her voice was drowned out as the prior's voice raised in volume and guards came quickly to return her to her place.

The reading of the sentences went on for hours. Ventura's lips moved constantly, speaking with God, reminding Him that she had only tried to help others.

The sun was beginning to cast shadows across the back of the Prior before he finished, and still there was no sign from God. Ventura and the others who were to be relaxed, were then transferred to the hands of the secular authorities, so that punishment could be carried out.

A soldier stood on each side of her and she was led out to the place where the faggots and stakes stood ready. Beside her walked a monk, his voice first soft and sweet, consoling, then louder and more harsh as he admonished her, demanding she confess.

She was led up the stake and the crowd roared its approval. The soldiers pushed back the mob who threatened to impose their furies on her. She saw several faces, all of them contorted into anger at her, as if she had perpetrated some personal injury on them.

All around were exhumed corpses and heretics in effigy, with grinning lips and moldy foreheads. Penitents around a burning pyre moaned and cried out to God. Ventura stared into the crowd. The colors, angry faces, shouted psalms and condemnations melded into a collage of terror. She stood detached, above the crowd and its entertainments. A vision of Richard coming through the crowd on a black stallion came before her, bright, brilliant.

She knew it couldn't be him. He was on a ship somewhere on the ocean, but the idea brought her peace as she readied herself to die.

***

Richard's cart neared Seville and his mind grew feverish with plans and questions. What if this escape was doomed and it ended as his ill-fated rescue of Clara had? Urging the horses ahead, he forced the doubts out of his mind.

The cart clattered into the city and the sounds and colors of the festival were all around him. A minute later, a penitent in a mitre and sambenito caught his eye, making him realize this was no festival.

Then he could smell the burning wood and roasting flesh and he knew it was an auto de fe. Ventura's auto de fe.

Pressing the horses around the back of the Inquisitor's Palace, he jerked the cart to a halt, and grabbed a Lista out of a woman's hand. There it was: Ventura da Fonceca, sentenced to relaxation.

A moan of agony escaped his lips and he bent down to unfasten the black stallion. Jumping onto the horse's back, he patted its neck and said softly. "You'll have to carry us both, boy." Then, raising a silent prayer to God to help him through the crowd in time to save Ventura, he dug his heels into the stallion's flank.

They moved swiftly through the crowd, his hands pushing people back, his eyes riveted on the burning pyres. Through the blur of faces, hers stood out. She was being led to a stake only a few hundred yards in front of him. He leaned down, grabbed a lance out of the hands of a weary soldier and rode full speed toward her.

Reaching her side, he pushed the soldiers back with the weapon, and pulled Ventura out of their arms and into his. She gasped and flung her arms around his neck, then they rode away, never stopping to look back. The crowd cheered, some drunk with wine, others ready to applaud any action that pleased them.

Behind him were the sounds of hooves and voices. Ahead lay safety. He only glanced back once, just in time to see Anna driving her cart full speed at the charging soldiers.

They rode without stopping, all the way back to Gibraltar. Arriving breathless and exhausted, Richard slid off the horse and staggered toward the door. Aunt Cecily's manservant came running out and carried Ventura into the house. Richard stumbled behind.

"My dear boy," said his aunt from her seat in the small parlor. She jumped to her feet, hurrying to embrace him. "And this is your Ventura," she said, pushing a lock of hair out of the young woman's face.

Before he could answer, she had signalled to the servants. "Take them up to their rooms and draw their baths." The last words he heard from her were, "Rest as long as you like, my dears."

***

It was the smell of sausages that brought Richard down the stairs three days later for breakfast. Ventura was already there, her hair gleaming in the early morning sun. She looked like a shell of her old self, but a hint of liveliness lingered deep in her eyes. She was smiling, nibbling on toast in the breakfast room, and listening to Aunt Cecily tell her about Richard's father. "He was quite a ladies' man, my dear. I hope your Richard hasn't inherited those qualities."

Ventura looked up and saw Richard, her cheeks turning pink from embarrassment. "He's not my Richard, at least---"

Richard bent down and kissed her check. "Why, of course, I'm your Richard," he said, taking the seat beside her. "You don't think I would risk my life twice for someone unless she had captured my heart and soul, do you?"

"Let the poor girl finish her breakfast before you tease her so," said his aunt, pretending to be displeased.

He nodded, waiting patiently until Ventura finished her toast and tea. Finally, when he could contain himself no longer, he took her hand and said, "Well, are you ready?"

She smiled at him, the brave and beautiful woman he loved. "Am I ready for what?" she said, teasing him in return.

"Are you ready to come to the garden with me so I can ask you properly to be my wife?"

Ventura gasped, her eyes softening with love. Aunt Cecily embraced them both, then watched Richard and Ventura go out through the glass door to the gardens, the sun shimmering down on them from above.

***

On the day of their wedding, the sky was an intense clear blue and scents of roses and lilies filled the air. The priest waited, his fingers tracing over the rich brocade of the altar cloth. Richard stood in the mulberry shade, beneath a bower of tiny pink rosettes in the flower garden. His foot tapped nervously and his fingers played with the ruffles on his uncle's white silk shirt and the waistband of his black breeches. His eyes strained to see past the inner courtyard through the shaded roof of foliage. Ventura should have been there by then, unless she had changed her mind after all and decided not to marry him.

Then the door to the garden burst open and Sophia came out breathless and pink, her heart-shaped mouth working soundlessly. "Well, tell her to hurry. Richard's about to wear through the stone path," said Aunt Cecily, coming over to put her hand on her nephew's shoulder. "Now, now. Patience, patience. She is a beautiful woman, but all women take special care on their wedding day. The priest can be counted on to hold his tongue, now all we have to do is wait a few minutes and you two dears will be married."

Richard nodded, his eyes never leaving the door. A minute later, it opened again and out stepped Ventura. A shaft of sun gleamed off the wall behind her. She leaned into the light, eyes bright with love, face alive with a holy glow.

She wore a silk mantilla and the long flowing gown Cecily had been married in. It fitted her perfectly, Sophia had seen to that. Ventura and Richard stepped together and he took her hand. When the priest finished with their vows, Richard placed his golden ring on her finger and they were married. Doves wandered beneath the shrubbery, cooing and watching with their dark, curious eyes. Richard kissed Ventura softly on the lips, tasting the sweetness that was to follow.

An hour later, Richard sat at the linen-covered table next to his bride. The sunlight shown in her hair and her eyes saw only him. They dined on a meal of lamb, fish and sweet chunks of wedding cake, drinking sweet wine from studded goblets. Aunt Cecily sat next to the priest, eating and chattering away gaily.

Sometime later, Richard rose and took his bride by the hand. She gave him a passionate look, but before she could stand, another servant came by with yet another course. Then it was the violet hour when the earth was touched by the sun's last rays and still the servants came. Richard rose once more, but Aunt Cecily was on her feet again, lifting yet another toast to their union. The lamps were lit in the garden and Richard's mind was only on Ventura while he sat with his aunt, listening to her stories of his father.

When they finally escaped from the table, Cecily grabbed Ventura by the arm and steered her away to her own chambers, promising Richard with a hint of mischief in her eyes, that his wife would soon join him. Alone, Richard went to their bedchamber and waited by the silken bed, pulling back the draperies to peek at the moon.

When he thought he could wait no longer, the door to their bedchamber whispered open and Ventura entered. She was robed in a rich silk gown. Her long hair rippled around her shoulders as she walked. Her feet, encased in red-and-gold slippers, peeped out like nestlings under her softly rustling garment.

She came toward him slowly and he took her hands and pressed each palm to his lips. She stood immobile, waiting for him to take the lead. Neither spoke. It was as if the room was under a spell and they were statues, turned to stone by the enchantment of the moment.

Then she dropped her head, and when she did, her hair cascaded over her face like a shimmering river, covering her face and bosom. Slowly, very slowly, he reached out his hand and lifted her chin, catching a first glimpse of her angular cheek. Then her eyes, dark, endless pools of love, shaded by long dark lashes, looked up at him and his heart melted.

He kissed her petal soft lips and inhaled the perfume of her hair. Love ignited in his breast when she murmured his name softly. Another kiss, this one more intoxicating, and he pulled her to him.

Arms around her, they walked slowly to the bed. They sat side-by-side, looking into each other's eyes. A slow movement of his hand on her shoulder and her gown was pushed aside, freeing her full white breasts. Another slow movement of his hand and her legs, long and rounded, gleamed in the moonlight. She trembled and put her arms around his neck.

His hands explored her lovingly until they found the scars woven across her back like cruel serpentines. He pulled back from his bride, dumbfounded. He'd expected a perfect, unflawed body next to his. His surprise swiftly turned to anger at what they had done to her and tears welled up in his eyes.

He turned her gently and kissed each old hurt, whispering words of love for her. Tears of regret escaped from his eyes and ran down his cheeks. "I only wish I could have spared you this," he said.

They lay there for awhile, his body over hers like a protective covering. Then she lifted her lips and kissed him softly, rekindling his passion. Through gentle touches, he gradually showed her the joy and pleasure of the union of their bodies.

***

Richard and Ventura strolled through the gardens, the songs of countless birds mingling with the tinkling fountains. Flowering plants and shrubs were everywhere, releasing their scents into the air. It was their first full day as husband and wife and the afternoon slipped away into whispers and embraces, chews of sweet basil sprigs, bites of strawberries off the vine and slices of cool melon.

Behind the dark clumps of shrubs and trellised roses they found a winding path to a small patio. In the days that followed, the servants left trays of refreshments there for them, cool juices and tiny cakes and sweetmeats. The warm clear days drifted by, blending into serene indifference as Ventura and Richard planted small seeds, made wreaths for each other, coaxed small birds onto their fingers, and drew hearts and figures in the earth.

Sometimes they even forgot to go inside for meals, pretending the bell that called them had not rung. Not wanting to disturb the lovers, Cecily left them alone, peering out occasionally from behind the draperies and marvelling at their innocence and delight.

Then one day, Richard began to teach Ventura English. "You'll have to know it in the New world," he whispered, kissing her cheek softly and caressing a tendril of her hair absently. School was in session from then on, until she spied an unknown flower and scampered to pick a bloom, or saw a colorful butterfly and went chasing after it, or kissed him passionately and drew him to their bedchamber.

***

The letter laid on the desk of Hernando Sorell, the District Commissioner and parish priest of the tiny town that overlooked Gibraltar. He had read it several times. He wrinkled his nose, remembering the first time and how his hands had shaken when they broke the seal of the Inquisitor General.

Hernando had worked hard to be accepted for employment by the Inquisition. It had been necessary for him to provide a certificate of family purity, evidence that his own family had no heretical connections. He had even scraped together the extra money, realizing it was the applicant's responsibility to pay for all checking of records and questioning of witnesses to establish his purity. Even priests were not above this kind of investigation, and that was fine with Hernando, for it was well known that many priests had become fanatical and been labeled heretics.

Gaining the certificate had been expensive, forcing him to dip into his savings and even into the collection plates on two occasions. But he hadn't really minded the sacrifice. Already it was paying off for him. People were beginning to look upon him as a man of prestige. Many powerful families would eventually become indebted to him once he bargained with them to return a rebellious son or daughter caught with a forbidden book or accused of blasphemy or heresy.

Yes, soon he would be rich. Money and important possessions would be passed to him because of who he was. But the greatest privilege, the one he coveted the most, was that he was now immune from secular authority. Only the Holy Office had jurisdiction over his acts now, and the Inquisitor General was not likely to punish one of his own. Tight administrative organization and secrecy permeated every branch of the Inquisition's activity. That was how it had to be, for not even the King could demand information and expect to receive it unless the Inquisitor chose to supply it.

Yes, he would keep the secrets and do his job because he knew the rewards would be his. Already he had worked his way into the esteem of Dom Francisco and he must broaden it. He and his notary had formed a network of lay agents who supplied Hernando with information. Information led to more names and more witnesses, and eventually, to arrests.

When things were slow, Hernando carried out regular inspections. Functioning like a customs agent, he was always on the lookout for contraband. Hernando was especially interested in forbidden books. Only the other week he had confiscated the vernacular Spanish translation of the Bible.

At first, he had thought the letter from the Inquisitor one of congratulations for this seizure. That idea was quickly dashed when he saw the letter contained a list of escapees from the dungeons, and one in particular from an auto de fe. There was a note written at the bottom informing him that Richard Hasleton had helped her escape once before and may be involved in this escape.

Hernado settled back into his chair and tapped his chin thoughtfully. That would be a feather in his cap if he could catch the da Fonceca woman. Surely, she must be captured and made an example of. The Inquisitor General could not afford to be the laughing stock of Seville. And if he knew the peasants, the gossip had already spread the countryside. They were such stupid people, making light of their leaders and jokes about the economy. If they only knew how difficult and serious this ruling business was.

***

Cecily peeked out through the curtains as Hernando Sorell's mule cart came to an abrupt stop in front of the house. She motioned to Sophia and told her to show the priest into the small parlor off the breakfast room. By the time he arrived in front of her, she was sipping a cup of tea and pretending she had no idea why he was there. "Father, how good of you to come," she said, offering him some tea.

He eyed her up and down, probably wondering if she wanted to join his secret network. Yes, she'd heard about his work.

"I apologize for barging in this way," he said. Although he spoke acceptable English, his face reddened when he stumbled over an incorrect pronoun.

Cecily took another look at the local priest. What a silly creature he was. With that scimitar of a nose reaching into his cup like a ravenous bird and that beefy body. Surely he was slipping his hand into the local coffers to feed himself.

She forced a smile onto her face. "No need to apologize, Father. Is there something I can help you with?" Yes, she knew all his snoopy ways. He thought he had a secret network, but the peasant tongues clacked daily about who he was investigating and what he had already found out. That tickle on the back of her neck as she sat opposite this man was a sure sign something was amiss. Her neck only tickled when something bad was about to happen.

He looked at her with his beady eyes. "I---I wonder if you might have a relative, a Richard Hasleton?"

"Richard? Richard? No, I don't think there is anyone in our family by that name. Certainly not in Gibraltar." She handed him a tray of sweet cakes and watched him devour two before he spoke again.

"And what about in Seville? Is there a Richard Hasleton in your family who lives there?"

So, he was after her Richard. Well, he'd have to be a lot quicker than he had shown himself to be so far to trick her. "No, no Richard Hasleton in Seville either. Unless, of course, he is a very distant relative. No, it couldn't be. I would certainly have heard about him." Then just to be naughty, she threw in, "News travels fast from Seville, you know." He was a dolt. Her comment went right over his head.

He smiled at her and took another bite of cake before asking, "Do you travel to Seville often, señora?"

"I've never been there, Father. More tea?" She poured him another cup and waited. He chattered on, small talk about the village and Gibraltar. Then, his rotund body rose and she showed him to the door.

When she was sure he was well on his way, she went out to the gardens. "Children," she said, approaching Richard and Ventura who were sitting by the rose arbor. "Something extremely important has just taken place and we must discuss it immediately."

"Sit down, Aunt Cecily," said Richard, making room for her on the carved bench. "What is it?"

Cecily sat down and took her nephew's hand. "The priest from a neighboring village has just left. He was asking whether I was related to you and whether I went to Seville frequently. Things are getting very dangerous here. The priest is not too bright, but with all the men available to him, even he will figure out we are related. The Inquisitor General is putting out tentacles, trying to find you and Ventura. As much as I hate to say it, I think you two better think about leaving the country." She tightened her grip on Richard's arm. "Maybe even the continent."

"The continent?" Richard and Ventura said in unison.

"Word has it the Inquisitor General has a spy network that reaches from one end of Europe to the other. You might not be safe anywhere here."

Ventura's voice was filled with panic. "Then what are we to do?"

Richard grunted. "It's the New World for us, my darling."

Cecily nodded. "I think it will have to be the New World. I shall go and start making plans to book your passage. You two had better pack your things. I've already filled your closets with clothes that should fit you. You will have to travel separately to the ship. No telling how much the priest knows about your relationship. Ventura, you had better take the boxes with you, and wear a mantilla over your head in case you are stopped."

Ventura's eyes clouded with fear. "Why, I couldn't go alone, what about Richard?"

Cecily patted her hand protectively. "Richard will be fine. The priest probably doubles as a custom agent and he and his men will be on the lookout for a man and woman traveling together."

Ventura and Richard stood up nervously and clung together. "Another thing," said Aunt Cecily, "If I read the priest correctly, he won't take my word, and there are always servants and peasants eager to talk if they think they are helping the church. Poor devils. Why they can't see that the Church is corrupt is beyond me. I guess they fear that if they admit that, they will have nothing to cling to in this world. Why can't they see they have each other?" She crossed herself. "Oh dear, there I go babbling on." She stood up and motioned to them. "Come, you must start packing immediately! I'll send up some old trunks, ones that don't look like they would belong to a Hasleton."

***

The days dragged by and Aunt Cecily was unsuccessful in booking their passage. "It is very dangerous for you now, they are even looking on the docks. If Henry does not find a trustworthy captain, I will have to find someone to bribe."

Richard gave her a dark look. "Oh, Aunt Cecily, surely---"

"Bribing? But we can't pay," said Ventura.

"Consider it my wedding present to you," said Cecily, embracing them both.

Days later, Henry burst in from the hall and interrupted the English lesson Richard was giving Ventura. "I've gotten your passage. You leave in the morning, Señor Hasleton."

Richard pulled her into his arms. "Are you ready for this trip, my love?"

Ventura's eyes glimmered with a spark of challenge. "Have I ever missed an adventure with you?"

He laughed. "No, my dear wife, and I hope you never will." He pulled her even closer, until he felt her heart beating against his. Then he covered her face and neck with soft kisses before he carried her to the bedroom. Who knew when or if they would be together again?

***

It was before sunrise and the sky was a dull gray. Long black mantilla covering most of her face, Ventura kissed her husband good-bye at the door. She rushed back three times for more embraces before she finally tore herself away and wiped back the tears from her eyes. Henry helped her into the cart he had carefully packed with her baggage, then he climbed into the driver's seat.

Richard climbed up the side of the cart by Henry. Don't forget, Henry, take the most direct route to our point of departure. I'll draw any guards or soldiers away." He lowered his voice so Ventura could not hear. "Even if I do not survive, Ventura will make it to the New World."

Richard jumped down and ran to the other side of the cart. He grabbed Ventura's hand. "Be careful, Richard," she whispered. "Your route is long and dangerous. Maybe you shouldn't take the cliffs."

He pulled her close. "Everything is set. No time for new plans. We've gone over everything and it's the best we can do on short notice. You do your part and I'll see you in Cadiz at the ship." He didn't wait for her reply. He slapped the horse's rump and the cart jolted forward.

Half an hour later, Richard set off, wearing his hat low over his brow. He took leave of his Aunt regretfully. After he was mounted on his steed and ready to go, Cecily pressed his hand tightly and whispered, "If there is trouble, trust the peasants." Then she swatted his horse, forcing him on before he could ask her what she meant.

His Aunt's comment had alerted him and he said few words to the guide who rode beside him. The man led the horses past olive groves and through fragrant cork forests until they came to the dreamlike place that was Ronda. There, three bridges spanned an incredibly steep ravine. Richard looked down into the gorge. It was nearly a thousand foot drop in many places, down a silver-green gashed chasm. They started to cross one of the bridges, but Richard's horse shied. There was a roar of hooves and six soldiers galloped toward them, their steeds thudding over the bridge.

From behind a thicket of brambles popped the heads of three smiling peasant men. "Come with us, señor, they will be unable to traverse the gorge," said one with a sweat-sprinkled forehead and ragged hair.

Richard jumped down, signalling to Henry he was leaving. Suspicion sizzled in his mind, but if he didn't trust these men, he might soon be in the Seville dungeon.

The peasants led him down into the gorge to a nearly invisible cave. The men knew a secret way and they were soon inside. The dank, cool stone enclosed them like a tomb. From his vantage point, Richard had a good view of the soldiers. They were talking to his guide and pointing down into the gorge. Finally, the soldiers seized the guide and dragged him back across the bridge.

When the guards had gone, the peasants led Richard up the twisting, roughly-trodden path to the road. A cart stood waiting. Richard crawled in the back of it and they covered him with a rough blanket that smelled of dust and earth. He waited, heart thumping. He heard a boyish laugh and the creaks and crunches of men climbing aboard the cart. Then the donkeys moved on and they clanked and bumped over the rock-strewn road until his body ached.

Hours later he heard the din of a city--- shouts of tradesmen, criers making official announcements, asses baying and the hammering of coppersmiths. The cart clattered to a stop and his heart stopped with the idea they might have made it to Cadiz.

Harnesses snuffled and far away he heard a burst of drunken singing. More creaks and then footsteps. The blanket was pulled off his head and he sat up to the whistle of boat. The sail of a large ship loomed in the distance.

He was gently dragged out of the cart. "You are here, señor!" said a peasant with a boyish laugh.

Richard said a hasty good-bye and headed for the docks. He had not been given the name of the ship, but he would find Ventura if she was there. The sea air was a vast improvement over the blanketed cart, and he breathed deeply of it.

He had only been on the dock for a minute or two when he heard a familiar voice. "Señor, señor, do you not know me?" He turned, saw her smiling face, and embraced Ventura.

# BOOK II

## The Journey to the New World

## 1671 - 1672

# 10

Richard's arms wound tightly around Ventura. "Thank God, you're safe," he whispered, kissing her softly on the mouth. She lay her head on his shoulder and hugged him, snuggling into the wet wool of his cape. A minute later he asked, "Is the baggage on board?"

She murmured into his neck. "Yes, it's there. Let's go find it." Arm-in-arm they started up the gangplank.

Richard eyed the ship. "From the outside, the Merchant Cadiz looks adequate for the trip. She looks like about 250 tons of sea-going vessel."

Ventura nodded. She'd never been at sea and had no idea about anything to do with ships. "Why so many sails?" she asked.

He patted her hand and pointed to a sail with a cover and triangle sail. "That's the lateen mizzen, there's the fore course, and that one that looks like a feedbag for a horse is the spirit-sail."

All the new words swam around in her head "At least I know what the colors are," she said.

"Yes, we'll be flying the flag of Spain."

Her eyes shifted to the decks. "Why so many guns?"

"To keep pirates away, why did you think?"

"Pirates?"

"Don't you worry. We'll be well-protected and if the real ones aren't enough, we'll have the dummy guns on the lower deck. From a meter away, they look good as the real ones."

"Do you really think we'll run into pirates?"

"If they sense we have cloth and trade goods hidden in our hold."

A shiver of fear ran down her spine and she pulled him aboard just as the sun set and the cabin boy came around to light the candle lanterns on the poop deck. If their luck held, they'd see no pirates and the trip wouldn't be too bad. Except for the ship smelling of hemp and pitch and the overheated bodies of the crew, she might even enjoy it.

A very young sailor showed them to their sleeping quarters. He wore a blouse with a hood, stockings and a red wool cap over his burnished curls. His hands had been chafed raw by the sea and his eyes were big and dark, like a bear's. Before he left, he mumbled an invitation to eat at the captain's table that evening.

***

Ventura was rifling through the lavender-scented trunk, trying to find the red silk dress Aunt Cecily had given her. Each time the ship rolled, the heavy black trunk inched its way along the grimy floor toward their small cot. "Richard," she said impatiently, "will you please stop looking at that map and hold this trunk for me?"

The temporary canvas walls of their tiny cabin let in a heavy draft and Ventura clasped her hands across her chest and rubbed her arms while she waited for Richard.

He put down the parchment and his strong arms were soon around the chest. He looked at her and raised an eyebrow. "I don't think we're expected to dress for dinner."

Her jaw set in a stubborn line. "Maybe not, but this is my first opportunity to impress the captain and I'm not going to miss out."

He looked at her. The tendrils of her thick hair seemed to have doubled in the damp salt air. The lamplight shone down on her face, putting a glow into her huge brown eyes. A flame of passion coursed through him and he reached for her waist, thinking she was as lovely then as he had ever seen her.

She giggled. "Richard, there goes that blasted trunk again!" He silenced her with a long kiss and they fell onto the cot laughing.

An hour later they picked their way carefully along the deck and entered the dining room. Sitting at a crude wooden table, barely big enough for one, sat the captain. Ventura took one look at him and stepped back. Had not Richard's strong arm propelled her forward, she would have left the room. Although the captain's eyes were alert, they carried a wild-eyed gleam and his ruddy face was soiled and weather-beaten. His hair was prematurely white, probably from too many rough voyages and there was a strange way about him that frightened Ventura.

"Sit down, folks," he said, indicating their seats, "I'm Captain Diogo Dias." Ventura swallowed hard and squeezed into the spot next to Richard, directly across from the captain.

"Our fare is simple here. We have but one hot meal and it's served at eleven a.m. Tonight it's salted meat, cheese and biscuits. Tomorrow," he drew his coarse hand alongside his mouth, "if you're lucky, you'll get some bacon and salted meats. Friday is a fast day and you'll only get snap beans boiled in salted water. On important holidays, we're treated to codfish." He withdrew his hand and leaned toward them, smiling. "Most of the food is rotten anyway and its stinks like a savage's stew, but here, have a glass of wine."

They raised their glasses. "To a safe journey," he said, clinking his glass against theirs. The wine had a musty odor and tasted of vinegar. Ventura coughed and sputtered. "Captain, do you suppose I could have some water?" she managed to gasp.

"Water? Water?" He winked at Richard. "Tell your wife about the water supply here, will you, mate?"

Richard smiled good-naturedly. "Ventura, at sea, there is only an ounce or two of water for each of us. And that's only until the water goes bad."

Ventura felt her hopes sinking. "You mean the water is bound to go bad?"

The captain laughed. "I've been on many voyages and on all of them, the water went bad. You'll see. Remember when you came on board, forward of amidships?"

"Amidships?"

Richard smiled at the captain and said, "In the middle of the ship, my dear. The bilge-pumps are there. As the days pass, you'll smell a stench from them. If it gets bad enough, the crew will flush her out and wash the hold with vinegar."

The captain winked at Ventura, "Aye, but some old sailors swear that if the bilge water stinks, we will be happy, for it is a sure sign that the ship does not leak."

Somehow she made it through the meal, using several glasses of wine to make the food go down. They left the captain in the dining room and took a short stroll on the deck. The sea had changed from green to dark olive and the moon was a sliver amid fleecy clouds. Ventura held tightly to Richard's arm, afraid to look over the edge.

He showed her the galley and stores forward of the masts. "The hold is below. The wood and cargo are stored there." They walked to the fore bulkhead. Muskets and long-blade knives garnished the walls. Her arm tightened on his and she wondered what kind of battle the crew had prepared for.

The great cabin, on the main deck at the stern, had been divided by temporary partitions to form extra cabins. They hadn't been fortunate enough to secure one with windows, but at least theirs was dry.

They walked past their lodgings to the after-cabin. Inside, it smelled of ink and must and was full of shelves crammed with books, writing materials, telescopes and nautical instruments. From a beam high above swung a huge compass. Nearby were suspended charts of the sea. "These are used by the captain to---" She yawned and stretched. "You're tired. I can show you this later," he said, putting his arm around her and leading her back to their cabin.

Exhausted from the trip, Ventura climbed into their cot and tried to sleep, but the farther out into the ocean they got, the more she groaned. Richard's arms came around her. "My dear, are you all right?" she heard him ask.

She cupped her hands over her mouth and stumbled toward the rail. She lay on the deck, wishing to die, so seasick was she.

Richard picked her up in his arms and carried her back to their cabin. "This will never do." He went out and came back, dragging a large piece of roped canvas with him. After much hammering and cursing, he scooped her up from the bed where he'd deposited her, and placed her in a swinging cot.

Within minutes, her eyes fluttered and fell closed. She slept on and off that night, awaking to the creaking of the ship as it pitched and rolled through the surf. Her only thought that night was how long it would be before she could step on land.

***

Shaky and pale, Ventura walked on the deck the next morning. The worse of her seasickness was past. The ocean had calmed and the sun felt warm and friendly on her face. With the salty breeze rippling through her hair, she was ready for an adventure. She walked along, looking into the faces of her fellow passengers. They were old and young, dark and light-skinned, dirty and clean. Some belched openly, not even placing their hands to their mouths. There were no latrines, and the less modest ones relieved their bowels where they could. After a few moments among them, she ran for pleasanter quarters and found Richard in the great cabin. "I didn't realize things were so---so---" she said.

Richard smiled at her. "So what?"

"So primitive," she felt her cheeks grow hot with embarrassment. "No latrines for them."

"He laughed and hugged her. "It's better than the dungeon, isn't it? Besides, we're together."

She broke into a wide smile and hugged him back. Of course he was right. Richard was always right. They were together and that was all that mattered.

As the days passed, she got to know the crew. The pilot was a tall ruddy-cheeked man with a broad nose and gentle eyes. Ventura watched him for hours and finally asked Richard if she could see him at duty. As a favor to Richard, with whom he had once sailed, the pilot showed her his charts, compass, quadrant and sand-glasses. He held the thin round astrolabe at eye level, showing her how to observe the position of the celestial bodies.

Dialgo, the boatswain, was friendly, too. He went about his duties whistling and smiling. Frequently she waved to him as he inspected the rigging and gear or saw to it there was a fire in the fireplace at sunset. The secretary, a reed-thin, nervous man, kept to his office, preparing reports and keeping records and wills. The steward joked with her about the sad state of the wine and victuals on many occasions. He showed great patience when he taught the young apprentices how to box the compass and what prayers to say when turning the watch-glasses. One night when she couldn't sleep, she crept onto the deck and saw him poking the sailors on duty to keep them awake. The carpenters and caulkers kept the vessel water-tight and a cooper cared for the casks and barrels, making sure none of the precious drinking liquids or trading merchandise were lost due to damage.

The days at sea seemed to merge into each other, and she grew used to some of the ship's deprivations and crudities. Still, her fondest wish was that the ship would reach land. Then, when she realized she was with child, she wished it even more fervently. "How long is the trip to the New World?" she asked Richard one evening when they were in their cabin, getting ready for bed.

He put down the blanket he was holding and said, "Captain Dias says first we go to Jamaica. We'll be laying in that port a few days, trading goods, before we head up to Massachusetts."

"Massachusetts?" It was a new word to her ear and it delighted her to say it.

"Yes, that's where we'll finally settle. Are you in a hurry to get there?"

She put down her comb, hesitating. "Well---there is something---"

Seeing her state, he came over and took her trembling hand. "What is it?"

She looked into his eyes, trying to read what he might be thinking. "By the time we reach Massachusetts, there will be three of us."

His face registered puzzlement, then wonder. "Three of us? A baby?" He picked her up, carrying her around the room. She giggled and held on tightly, tucking her face into his neck. Winded, he stopped, but he kept holding her in his arms.

"I've watched a few birthings," she whispered in his ear, "but I don't know enough to deliver my own baby." Before he could answer she said, "But there is no surgeon on this ship, so we'll have to do it." She said it calmly, but inside she was a muddle of fears and doubts.

He set her down on the floor and looked frightened for the first time since she'd met him. "Me? Help deliver a baby?" His face went pale.

"Yes, you." She poked him on the chest, pushing him back a few steps.

He smiled then, and grabbed her, holding her close. "But men don't become involved in women's discomforts---"

She pulled away, pouting. "Well, you're going to have to. Besides, it's your baby. You helped make it and you can just as well help bring it into the world!"

Laughter bubbled out of him and he pulled her back into his arms. "I suppose I shall. After all, one of the reasons I married you was because you're an adventuresome spirit. So I suppose I shall have to join in, too."

She smiled, feeling happy for a minute until she remembered she had none of the herbs Clara and Anna had used. She smoothed down the collar of his shirt. "If only I had some herbs."

"Aren't there any on board?"

"I don't think so, but maybe I can remember some of the information that was in my notebook."

"Why don't you just start another one? You have many free hours aboard the Merchant Cadiz and it would be time well spent."

The next morning, when she awoke, Richard was gone, but lying beside their cot was a small black notebook. She picked it up and looked inside. Richard's hand had penned the words: Ventura's Notebook. She smiled and took it and her portable writing case on deck. She soon found a sunny spot near the galley. In her mind she went over the visits she had made with Anna and wrote down every bit of information she could remember.

***

Loud drunken voices and bawdy laughter awoke Ventura and Richard one night. She was already heavy with child and had to be lugged out of the swinging cot. Richard helped her, then stuck his head out of their cabin door. "There is a ruckus on deck. Shall we see what's happening?" She pulled her woolen mantilla over her nightgown and padded after him.

They ducked behind the foremast, watching and listening. The Master-at-Arms shouted and swore at a group of twenty men who were in a state of intoxication. The men swayed and talked with slurred speech, some nearly falling down with drink. A loud inquiry took place during which the Master-at-Arms ascertained that the sail-maker, aided by one of the foremast men, had broken open the door of the liquor supply room and had supplied themselves and their friends with rum. After a long question-and-answer session, the sail-maker and the foremast man were tied up to the main sail. Four others were put in irons, and the rest, suddenly sobered, were pardoned and ordered to return to their quarters.

Knowing a flogging was forthcoming, Ventura turned away. She tugged on Richard's sleeve. "Let's leave now, I don't want to witness any more violence." They crept back to their cabin. "Isn't there a better way to handle such behavior?" asked Ventura when they were safely in bed.

He kissed her forehead gently. "Probably, but we can't interfere. If I were captain, I'd find a better way. Since we're only passengers, we must be quiet or risk being thrown overboard. I want you alive and well with me in the New World."

Ventura finally fell asleep that night, after the wails and moans of the two men had ended. But for hours she lay awake, safe in Richard's arms, listening to the creaking of the ship.

It was about that time that Ventura began to notice a change in the meat. It had never been very tasty, being too salty for her. But now it was riddled with holes and one day she found a worm in it. From then on, she lived on cheese and chickpeas.

"But Ventura," Richard teased her. "It's only the cacara worm. It won't hurt you. Think of him as food."

She wrinkled her nose and gasped and that was enough to end his pleading. The next day the crew found stowaway rats pilfering food from the stores. The rodents were quickly killed and eaten by the famished crewmen. The odor of rat roasting on a spit over the portable galley did smell enticing, but the idea of joining in the feast mortified Ventura and she kept to her meatless diet.

The next day she went on deck and found Edward, the cabin boy, bound in irons. His swathe of yellow hair was matted on his forehead and his eyes were immense hollows in his face. "What happened to you?" asked Ventura.

"Oh, the bells have been ringing for me to arise at night and I couldn't take it no longer. I got some oakum and tied it about the clapper of the bell. That bell won't ring no more. Once I get out of these irons, I will lay quiet a-nights and sleep," he said, winking at her. She almost undid his irons and let him free, but she remembered Richard's words about being thrown in the sea, and let Edward be.

That night there was a great storm. The rolling and pitching became so violent that the crew poured oil on the sea to reduce the force of the waves, but still it beat savagely against the ship. The sea broke into the best cabins, smashing the windows into tiny shards, filling the rooms with water, and nearly drowning an infant that was forgotten when its nurse went out on the deck to escape. Somehow Richard and Ventura's cabin was saved, but through the night they heard the agonized screams of others. Once Ventura tried to rise and go out to help, but Richard held her back. She did the same for him a few hours later. "There is nothing we can do, just be glad we three are safe," she whispered to him.

The next day the captain and his crew inspected the ship and found hundreds of buckets of water had gone down between the decks and into the steerage. He set the crew to work, doing vital repairs in the hopes another storm would not come up before they had finished.

Richard came back from the deck later that day with a shy-faced, skinny young woman and her pale infant. "They're without a cabin until the work is finished and I've offered to share ours with her. Is that all right with you, Ventura?"

Ventura made a face, but quickly changed her mind when she saw the child. "I'm Felippa do Valle and this is my daughter, Anna," said the woman.

Ventura took the babe to the cot and laid her down, crooning its name over and over. The child's name brought back all her memories of her Anna and a few tears, too.

***

Ventura was in her usual writing place. The angled sun was beating down on the deck, bringing some warmth to her sea-chilled hands. The steward came to her side, his voice chattering with excitement. "Please come with me señora, the men are terribly sick." She closed up her notebook and followed, her heels clicking across the deck.

The men lay on their mats unable to get up, their skin livid with spots. Her mind ticked back to a conversation she had with Anna. According to her, there was only one disease that laid men so low and could be cured quickly. To make sure, she asked the men to open their mouths. When she looked inside, their gums were swollen and red and sore to the touch.

"Give these men some fresh vegetables or fruits and they will recover. It's the scurvy. I haven't seen it myself, but my teacher told me about it."

The steward shrugged. "I would give them vegetables and fruits, but we have nothing fresh on board. We reach Jamaica in a month or so, 'til then, they'll have to suffer."

Ventura stood thinking, but could not come up with an adequate solution. She walked away, shaking her head, full of frustration. That evening after their meal, they walked on the deck and Richard mentioned how moist the hold was. She stopped walking and said, "I want permission to go down there and look. With all that moisture, there may be some sprouts or buds we could use."

Richard came back the next day, an apologetic look on his face. "I'm sorry, Ventura, but the captain thinks your request is foolish. Besides, women are not allowed in the hold, you could get hurt."

She ran at him, arms pummeling his chest. "Now you listen to me, Richard Hasleton. You tell that stupid captain that if something isn't done soon, everyone on this ship will be dead from scurvy!"

Stunned, Richard retreated from the cabin. In minutes he was back. "Okay, the captain has agreed, but only if you go with the steward."

"Fine. Great. As long as he doesn't get in my way. When do we begin?"

The steward's on deck waiting for you now."

"Can I wear a pair of your breeches?"

"My what?"

"You heard me. I can't very well be crawling around on my knees in a skirt."

Richard was already digging through the chest for some old trousers. He threw her a pair and she pulled them on under her skirt. They were a little snug over her bloated abdomen, but she tied them on with a rope. "There," she said with self-satisfaction, "I'm ready!"

The steward pulled up the wooden door to the hold and led the way, carrying a lamp in his hands. He was a skinny man with stilt-like legs and a stiff walk. "Careful," he cautioned, "step on the small piece of wood when you climb down."

The hold smelled of damp wood and musty sailcloth. Pregnant and puffing, Ventura managed to maneuver the steps to the floor. She tripped over the cool metal of a spare cannon and knocked over a piece of firewood before she found what she was looking for. Down on her hands and knees, she felt along the wood bottom for sprouted plants. "Over here," she shouted to the steward, "bring the lamp over here He came at once and held the light where she pointed. Out of a barley seed, three little sprouts were growing. Pinching her fingers together, she snipped them off, being careful not to disturb the plant. "Don't destroy these little plants," she said to the steward, "more will grow here."

Arriving breathless back on deck, she accepted a kiss and a hug from a relieved Richard before she asked the steward, "Does anyone have seeds of any kind?"

He shook his head. "No señora, we're sailors, not farmers."

"That's true, but perhaps the men have a seed or nut in their pockets. Have everyone empty out their pockets and look in their knapsacks. We might be able to grow enough sprouts to cure the scurvy and keep the rest of us healthy."

He shook his head, but did as requested. Several hours later he came to her on the deck with the handful of seeds and nuts he had collected. She took them eagerly and went to her cabin. She found a warm, moist place in a dark corner and started her sprout farm in a tiny bowl. Moistening the seeds with the last of her water ration, she waited for them to grow.

Weeks passed and the sprouts flourished. Ventura fed the first batch to the sick men and when they multiplied, she and Richard ate them, savoring their nutty flavor. The following Tuesday, Ventura began to get vague pains. By that evening, they turned into nagging spasms and finally into bone-wrenching pain. "Richard," she called across their cabin, "It's time. Let's go up on the deck for a walk."

Richard gave her a confused look. "Walk? Shouldn't you lie down?"

"Don't argue with me now. Anna taught me that walking will help with the labor. Come on, now. All is well. Soon we will have a beautiful son or daughter."

Richard had his arm around her on the deck, stopping when a spasm came, and helping her walk when it passed. The crew watched, some coming to ask if she needed help. She smiled and shook her head.

When the pains were regular and strong, they went below and prepared for the birthing. Ventura took a few clean cloths and blankets out of her trunk and put them aside for later. Already they smelled of the sea and had hardened from the salty spray. They would just have to do.

She walked a few more steps in the cabin until her water broke. Richard stared in fear at the deluge of water running down between her legs, but Ventura nodded, reassured that the birth would come soon.

"Go and lower the bucket into the ocean and wash your hands," she told him. "You will catch our baby when it is born."

Richard hesitated, then started for the door, but came back to kiss her on the mouth before he was off on the run.

"Wait," she shouted, "here is some soap."

He took the bar from her hand and started off again, only to turn at the door when she said, "See if you can find a mat for me to lie down on."

He returned a few minutes later with a rolled up mat under his arm. He helped her lie down on it and then he sat beside her, holding her hand and stroking her hair back from her face.

She dug her fingers into Richard's arm and waited out the pain, her body heaving and twisting with each spasm until her body was bathed in perspiration. Inside her there was tremendous pressure, like a hundred heavy rocks weighing down upon her. She wanted to push so badly, but she knew that if she did, she would be ripped by the baby and then she might die. She muffled the screams that wanted to come out of her, digging even harder into Richard's arm. Then the world was slipping away and she had to hold on.

When the pain became almost unbearable and the panic gripped her inside, she blew out mouthfuls of air. When her belly swelled as the baby forced its way out of her, she blew. When she saw Richard's face contort in alarm, she blew. After the next spasm, she whispered with the last of her breath, "Go now and catch our baby."

With the next spasm, Richard's voice rang out with awe. "There is a head. It's coming---our baby's coming!" He laced his hands beneath her. "I can see shoulders. You should see this Ventura." She looked down at his joyful face and knew then that her work had been worth it. "She's out! She's out," he whooped, "our daughter has been born."

"Bring her here. Let me see her." He brought the baby to her and alarm gripped her heart like the jaws of some great monster when she saw how pale the baby's body was. "Clean out her mouth with a cloth! Hurry!"

Afraid to touch the tiny thing at first, Richard tentatively put one of his fingers in the cloth and pushed it into the tiny mouth. The baby lay still, inert.

"Rub the soles of her feet!" she shouted. Just as a feeling of terror suffused her body, the infant let out a strangled cry, then a more robust one. "Put her on my belly," she said excitedly. Ventura's eyes surveyed every inch of her daughter. She was perfect---no blemishes, no deformities. "Cover her with the small blanket and put her at my breast. It will help the afterbirth come out."

Richard did as Ventura asked, and then he sat by their side, watching his daughter suckle. The afterbirth came out easily and Ventura stuffed it in the blanket next to their daughter. "It won't hurt you, Richard," she said, pinching the cord between her fingers until the blood stopped coursing through it. "It will dry and fall off by itself."

He watched, entranced. Finally he said, "I think we should name her after my mother."

"What is your mother's name?"

"Verity.

"Truth. Verity means truth."

She looked into her daughter's face. "Verity? Do you like your name?" The infant gurgled and Ventura hugged her little girl to her breast.

The days seemed to disappear between dawn and sunset. Richard and Ventura were busy, watching their infant grow. Richard learned to care for his daughter and when Ventura saw the two of them huddled together, her heart felt a lightness she had never known.

Wanting to keep the babe with her while she worked, Ventura searched for a way. Sitting on the deck one day with Verity on her lap, her eyes fell on the sails and she began to hatch a plan.

First she had to get the attention of Louis, the sail-maker. She found him in the hold, with his supplies. "Some drunken sot has pissed all over this! Now what will I use?" His eyes glowered at Ventura and his finger quivered in the air, warning of danger.

But when he saw Verity in her arms, the wiry man's face puckered into what looked almost like a smile. "So this is the little one born on the ship. She's a right pretty little one." His hands, made for hard work, were long and narrow, and one of them reached out to chuck the baby's chubby chin.

"I can wash this cloth for you," she said, learning forward until she could see his bald head glistening in the dim light and smell its oiliness.

He looked at her thankfully. "You could?"

"Yes, I could and maybe you will do me a favor in return."

His eyes, which had no border of lashes or brows, were strangely sinister. "And what favor might that be?"

"Why, make me a pouch from your sailcloth so I can carry Verity on my back."

A strange sound, something between a guffaw and a snicker, came out of his mouth before he laid a hand on her arm. His fingers were claw-like, reminding her of the talons of a small bird. "Aye, I'll do it," he said. Then he leaned forward and winked at her.

Two days later he presented her with a small pouch made of sail cloth to which were sewn two straps long enough to fit over her shoulders. He held Verity while she put the contraption on, then put the baby in its holder, giving Ventura another of his puckered smiles. After that, whenever she saw him climbing the sails, he waved to her and pointed at Verity.

Richard awoke with a fever one gray day and Ventura had all she could do to care for Verity and him, too. He was soon delirious, ranting and raving about the dungeons and screaming about Dom Francisco. At one point, she had to hold him down so he wouldn't get up and try to walk. His fever passed in a few days and then Verity showed signs of the fever, but hers did not linger.

Late in the night, the steward came to get Ventura, claiming nearly everyone on the ship was delirious with fever. She rushed to help, Verity slung into the pack on her back.

Fever-racked bodies and wild eyes of passengers and crew were everywhere. She asked to see the captain. His assistant showed her to his cabin, apologizing for the baggage that nearly blocked their way. She burst into Captain Dias' cabin, pushing through the hovel to get there. She stood facing him, her child slung behind her, fists sitting boldly on her hips. "With so many people confined in a small place, it is no wonder the fever rushes like lightning through us," she shouted. "And your deck! It is a wonder air can even pass through there, let alone people!"

The Captain's eyebrows came together in an angry line. "And what is all this commotion about, Señora Hasleton? I know a trip is hard on a woman. They are, after all, not as strong as men."

She glared at him. "It is not me who is falling with the fever. It is your men, and your passengers and something must be done."

"What are you talking about? I know of no fever."

"Have you been out of your cabin today to see the men and women ravaged by the infectious fever? If you don't care about your paying passengers, you'd better care about your crew. With so many unable to work, I wonder how long this ship will be kept asail."

"My crew is sick? No one told me about this!" He stormed out of his cabin and came back with his secretary. "Is it true my crew is dropping like flies from this infectious fever?"

The secretary nodded, body quivering. "It is true that many are laid low, but---"

"Don't but me, mate. I am to be informed of the state of my crew. Now this good woman tells me the fever is sweeping over the decks like some ill-omen."

The secretary straightened his back. "I didn't want to bother you---"

"Bother me? What's wrong with you, mate? I have to be apprised of these things. They must be dealt with." The Captain started pacing up and down, his ruddy face nearly purple with exasperation.

Ventura stepped forward. "May I make a suggestion?"

"This is not woman's work, although I do appreciate that you came to me about it."

"But I am a healer and I know something about the fever. I don't have my herbs, but there are other things I can do to help."

He looked at her suspiciously. "A healer? Never did hold much with them."

The secretary's voice turned pleading. "But Captain, you have to do something."

Captain Diaz looked at the man. "What do you suggest?"

He shrugged and said, "Maybe she can help."

The Captain threw up his hands. "Very well, you may try your healing practices. But I warn you, if you do them more harm, you shall be lashed to the mast and made to pay."

She nodded. "I have taken an oath not to do harm and I will not." She turned to go. "There are a few things I will need."

The Captain looked at her. "Things? What things?"

"Some jugs of vinegar."

The Captain made a disgusted sound. "Vinegar? What in heaven's name are you going to do with vinegar?"

She smiled at him, knowing she had won. "It's part of my plan to stop the fever from spreading."

He shrugged. "Mysterious you want to be señora. Okay, I give you what you want. See the steward. I will tell him to help you." With that he waved her out.

The steward was nowhere to be found, so she left word with the boatswain and several others of the healthy crew and went to her cabin to feed Verity. Her daughter was a sweet child, given to long bouts of sleeping without waking and then coos, gurgles and smiles while awake. She seemed to love the salt air in her face and the sea wind blew her fine blond hair around until it stood out from her head like a fine-tufted halo. Her huge blue eyes gazed around her curiously and her cheeks were constantly pinked by the wind and spray. She was a lusty eater and hungrily attacked her mother's breasts when Ventura sat down to feed her.

Richard stood by, watching. "If I didn't know better," Ventura told him, "I'd say she loved the life of a sailor, just like her father."

"Of course. She was born at sea, maybe even conceived here. She is a true child of the ocean. I'll bet she even swims like a fish."

Ventura shook her head. "Oh no, you'll not be finding that out. I saw a young one nearly drown in just the overflow from the ocean. It's too dangerous."

"All right, we'll wait until we're on land. But then, I'll show you what I mean. I was always a water baby myself and I'm sure my Verity is, too."

When she finished feeding Verity, she told Richard about her visit to the Captain. Richard looked at her doubtfully. "And just what is your plan?"

"Come with me and help and you'll see. You seem to be fit enough."

Richard got up from his bed tentatively and then walked to the door. "Coming?" he said, walking out. Ventura slung Verity onto her back and hurried out.

# 11

Alvaro Ribeyra, the steward, was an easy-going man. But he should have taken notice when his nose began to twitch, a sure sign that something was brewing. He had spent many years at sea and he was used to strange requests from captains. Captain Dias was the fifth captain he had served under, and in his opinion, the best. He was a little wild-eyed and fiery, but a good captain had to be that way.

In battle against the Barbary corsairs, those crazy men, Captain Dias had been something to see. Everyone knew the corsairs regarded themselves as combatants in a war against the Christian world. They would have never have been so successful if the Church did not encourage them in their madness, hoping to injure trade for their enemies.

Thank God, the Barbary corsairs operated out of North African ports and not the Atlantic. Good thing too, because they used fast and formidable galleys and chebecs, ships that could give the Merchant Cadiz a run for her money.

There were pirates in Jamaica and the West Indies, but none around where they sailed. Just in case, Alvaro offered up a silent prayer, asking that their ship remain safe.

He sighed. Yes, Captain Dias was a good man. Alvaro had seen him do more than battle corsairs. There had been that mutiny last year when all provisions had gone bad and the crew had been nearly delirious. Forced to exist without food for days, it had taken almost a miracle for the Captain to restore order.

But Captain Dias was not only good in battle. That man had a heart. He had taken on the surviving crew and passengers of a shipwreck and fed them until he could drop them at a safe port.

Now his captain had summoned him and Alvaro looked forward to the command from him, whatever it might be. Señora Hasleton. Yes, he knew her, the one with the eyes of a deer and the body of an antelope. Just because she helped with the scurvy, didn't mean she could help with the fever. "You sure she doesn't have childbirth madness? Vinegar? Pah!" He twirled his finger in circles at the side of his head and rolled his eyes. "A little crazy in the head perhaps?"

The captain's eyes popped with anger. "That may be, but that is my order."

Alvaro took a step back and said hesitantly. "But she has no medicines or herbs to give them, so I thought---"

The Captain's voice came at him angry and decisive. "Well, you thought wrong. Unless you have a better plan, take six of the best men who can still stand and help her."

"Help her do what?"

"Whatever she asks you to do. The first thing is to fill some jugs with vinegar."

This was too much. Alvaro felt his stomach tightening. He was about to counter with a plan, but he scratched his head thoughtfully and none occurred to him. He wished a wonderful idea would hop into his head, but it didn't. So, against his better judgment, he was forced to accept his Captain's order. "Yes, Captain," he said as he left, grumbling to himself, not quite loud enough for Captain Dias to hear, but loud enough to release the frustration he felt.

Being ordered about by a woman, even a woman as beautiful as Señora Hasleton, was not manly. He had done it when the men had been stricken with scurvy, but then he had only to follow her to the hold and ask the passengers and crew for seeds. Now he had to drag jugs of vinegar around and do heavens knows what with them. But the Captain had given the order, and Alvaro Ribeyra was not one to go against orders. So, he made his way slowly to the deck and began choosing men to help. Of those who weren't already working to keep the ship asail, there were only ten or eleven healthy ones. He finally picked five and was about to march them to Señora Hasleton's cabin when she appeared, moving swiftly behind her husband, her tiny daughter giggling from the sack on her back.

He nodded. "We are ready to assist you, señora. Here is the vinegar. What, pray tell, do you plan to do with it?"

She smiled at him broadly. "Fumigate the vessel. We will scrub down every deck and cabin today and again in a few days. That will be done twice a week until we reach port." She started past him. "Well, let's get to it. Have some of your men take the jugs and cloths and start scrubbing. The rest of us can take the bedding and air it on the deck."

Alvaro folded his arms and expanded his chest. "Air bedding? But that is woman's work!"

She tossed her head. "That may be so on land, but there are not enough women here and those that are, lie sick with the fever. Of course, I will help, but you and your men must work also."

Alvaro was about to refuse, but then he remembered his Captain's words and he sighed, shrugged and motioned his men to pick up the jugs. Maybe his friends in the ports would never find out. But if they ever learned he had aired bedding, he would be a laughing stock. "When you've finished, mates, scour every room and deck," he said to his crew. "And remember, I'll be checking on you, so do as you've been told."

It was midday by the time they had finished the work, but he had to admit everything had lost its musty, sickly smell. The vinegar gave the ship a clean, invigorating smell. He gazed at Ventura with respect. Maybe she did know what she was talking about after all.

***

After Ventura's plan was set in motion, only two other passengers, and no crew members, came down with the fever. After that, she was consulted by everyone for their ailments.

Several weeks later, word spread through the ship that they were close to the West Indies and would soon arrive in port at Jamaica. Passengers gathered together, their excited chatter rising over the blasts and swells of the sea. Daily, their expectant eyes watched the horizon for a sign of land. Once Ventura saw a clump of weeds float by and a shout of joy went up. But then, more days passed and still no land. A week later, Richard spied a flock of birds, their black images startling against the bright blue of the sky, and Ventura's pulse quickened with the hope of walking on firm earth again.

Too excited to sleep that night, many of the passengers joined Ventura and Richard at the railing. The day dawned cloudless, with a sky of brilliant azure. Straining to see, Ventura spied a black clump of land against the horizon. The ship bobbed closer and trees and rocks poked their way out of the land mass.

A roar went up and boatswain called loudly, "Land ahoy."

Verity giggled and Ventura talked nonstop, telling her daughter about the land and trees. The little girl smiled and grabbed hold of her mother's hair, trying to look over the railing and see the birds on shore. Her tiny fists reached out to grab the trees. Ventura gazed down into the sea. The water was so calm she could see pink shells and moss-green seaweed lying on the bottom.

The anchors were thrown overboard. They splashed and churned into the brine. Along the shore, black-skinned people swayed between emerald trees and waved from behind shrubby banks.

The crew hoisted boats overboard, banging and scraping them against the side of the ship. Babbling passengers pushed and shoved to get on board, but Captain Dias stepped in front of them, stern-faced. He raised his hand for quiet. "Be careful out there, Spain no longer occupies Jamaica. The English have brought their African slaves here to do their work." He pointed to the shore. "You seem them. Their black cousins, the Maroons, were set free when the Spaniards fled to Cuba. They live in the mountains and fancy themselves free." Contempt crossed the Captain's face. "You will also see the Arawaks. There are still a few of those proud Indians here." His eyes narrowed and Ventura couldn't tell if he was pleased or displeased.

When he'd finished speaking, the Captain nodded once and stepped back. The passengers and crew rushed to the edge of the ship. In moments, they were slipping down the ladder, their hands holding tightly to the sticky guide ropes. Some shouted and whooped, others screamed at the speed of their downward trip. Their shaky legs stepped aboard wobbly wooden boats waiting alongside the Merchant Cadiz.

Ventura stood with Richard's arm around her, watching each boat load and head toward shore. They bobbed like a fleet of small playthings in the high waves. "I think we can safely go down now," he finally said. "Do you want me to take Verity?"

She tried to hand their daughter to him, but Verity clung to Ventura screaming and burrowing her curly head into her mother's breast. Ventura gave Richard a futile look. "No use. You go first and we'll follow."

When Richard was halfway down, Ventura put an unsteady foot over the edge and slowly lowered her body onto the first rung. The wind tore at the rope ladder, driving the breath out of her lungs and nearly slamming her into the side of the ship. "Grab Mommy's neck, Verity," she shouted. The little girl latched onto Ventura's neck, fingernails digging in. Ventura climbed down slowly, eyes closed so she wouldn't feel the pull of the sea below.

Strong arms grabbed her. "All right now, one more step," said Richard's voice. Her leg came down shakily, stepping onto the bouncing boat before she collapsed in his arms. "You can let go now, Verity," said Richard. But the child held tight to her mother, her tiny face a mixture of curiosity and fear.

Ventura took a deep breath and sat down. "It's all right, Verity. We're on an adventure." She kissed her small daughter's brow, then held her up so Verity could see the shore.

Beautifully decorated with carvings, a group of canoes hovered in the distance and then came straight toward them. Indians dressed in splendid feather headdresses and palm-leaf corslets filled each craft, their faces proud and solemn, their muscular arms holding wooden spears.

Ventura stared at them, wondering if this was a friendly mission or if they might attack. Heart beating frantically, she waited and watched.

A tall, brown-skinned Indian stood erect at the bow of the lead canoe. He wore a cloak of red feathers and a green-feathered coronet. A large stone and metal ornament hung from his neck. In one hand he proudly held a white banner that swirled above his head.

"They must be the Arawak," whispered Richard. She looked at her husband, wondering if he was as afraid as she was.

The Indians pulled their canoes alongside, handing all the passengers gifts of fruit and fish. Their brown faces did not smile, but they had a kind manner about them and a majesty that calmed Ventura.

The passengers' feverish whispers and gestures quieted. They took the gifts, holding them stiffly in their hands. "Shouldn't we eat something as a sign of friendship?" Ventura asked.

A thin man next to Ventura glared at her. "They're savages. I ain't eating nothing but what the ship's cook feeds me."

Ventura tried to sound pleasant. "You could use a little fruit and fresh fish." She looked at the rest of the passengers and crew. "What are you afraid of? They've come to us in friendship."

A man in soiled shirt mumbled, "The Captain said---."

Grumbling to herself, Ventura tore the skin off a banana, put the pulpy fruit in her mouth and chewed. Richard did the same. The rest of the passengers watched, wide-eyed, intent, as if they expected them to be dead any moment. Ventura smiled at them and peeled the skin off an orange and handed a section to Verity. The child took a bite, chewing with her mouth open and talking in singsong syllables through the mush of her food.

Whispers and words of encouragement started and then rose, running through the passengers until a few others took a bite of fruit, then smiled and chortled to the Indians. A flicker of bright energy in the Chief's eye made Ventura wonder if she'd done the wrong thing and angered him. Then the Chief nodded and raised his arm and the canoes turned around and headed for shore.

Richard smiled and squeezed her hand. Her eyes rose from beyond the creamy sand to the shadowy outline of mountains and lush vegetation. Then whiffs of flowers and spice scents drifted in from the coast. As their boats neared shore, black-faced slaves turned and ran into the bushes, not waiting for them to disembark. Ignoring the black men, the Indians jumped gracefully out of their canoes, extending hands and spears to help the first passengers ashore.

Their boat slid into the sand of the shore and Richard leapt out to help Ventura and Verity out. By the time they joined their fellow passengers, one of the crew from the Merchant Cadiz had already stepped forward. He looked like a starved dog, all stark and bony. He opened a small bag and took out hawk's bells, beads, red caps, cheap mirrors and scissors. He handed one or two to each of the Indians. They accepted their gifts as if they were gold.

Spying Verity's blond tresses, the Chief marched over, fascination reigning on his face. His brown fingers reached down carefully and touched a lock of her hair. Verity smiled up at him.

The Chief signalled and another Indian came over, bearing a special gift. A little rodent laid in his huge palm. "Hutia," he mumbled, "Hutia." Ventura didn't know whether that was the name of the animal or something else, but she smiled broadly and shook her head in agreement, repeating the word. Verity squealed with delight and put her tiny fingers on the little creature.

As swiftly as they had appeared, the Indians disappeared, leaving the passengers alone on the white sandy beach. Ventura's eyes followed the Indian's path in the sand to thick clumps of lush and verdant vegetation. Above that soared cloud-capped mountains, sectioned by deep wooded valleys. Higher up, a stream splashed down its silver spray in a cascading waterfall, turning into a rushing torrent before it found its way to the sea.

Ventura grabbed Richard's hand and pulled him along. "Let's have a look," she said, leading the way.

"Be sure to be back to this boat in two hours or you will be left ashore for the night," shouted the Captain's mate. "We cannot guarantee your safety if you do not return to the ship. The Indians may appear friendly, but they can change more quickly than you think."

Richard and Ventura set out, Verity on her mother's back, clinging tightly to the strap of her carrier. The vegetation was so thick in places Richard had to hack their way through, the blade of his knife glinting in the sun. Growing wild at every turn were seas of orchids of every color, brilliant scarlet and gold plantain, bright red scallions and luminous yellow poui. Ventura picked two of the most beautiful orchids, placed one behind her ear and the other behind Verity's.

They wandered among the many palms and thickly-growing trees. The air was fragrant with flowers, moist vegetation and damp earth. The well-shaded land rose to become a small mountain and they climbed for sometime until the heat of their exertion forced them to stop and rest.

Verity pointed to a small stream and Ventura set the little girl near it to squeal and pat its wetness, giggling and splashing with delight. Richard's eyes met Ventura's with a challenge. At the same moment they both jumped to their feet and dove into the cool water. They drank from it thirstily, washing their bodies and clothes in the overflow. They dunked each other like baby porpoises until they were exhausted.

Then Richard stood up and pulled Verity in. She pumped her chubby legs and arms, babbling and chirping. "See, I told you she'd love the water!" he shouted, grabbing his daughter in his arms. Ventura laughed and splashed water at him before he dunked her under the cool water. Gasping for breath, they climbed out and laid in the heavy underbrush.

Ventura heard it first, a slight rustling in the thick woods on the left. Words drying in her throat, she raised up on her elbow and pointed. Richard's eyes fastened on the spot. "What is it?" he whispered.

Ventura whispered back, "Probably some of our party, exploring." But it wasn't any of the passengers they had seen. Nearly hidden by the thick underbrush, Ventura counted thirty black bodies, running through the woods, making barely more sound than a slight breeze. They must have seen Ventura and Richard, but they made no sign and continued in their parallel course. "Maroons," whispered Richard and Ventura felt her heart click with fear.

"We'd better get back," he said, picking up Verity. They ran through the dense forest, hardly stopping for Ventura to scoop up handfuls of herbs and flowers.

Reaching shore, they found the others waiting for the boat to take them to the ship. Some scampered in the crystal clear blue ocean while others lay luxuriously on the white sand. Before leaving, Ventura tucked her samples in the small bag she carried. They would be useful in the future.

***

Ventura was up early the next morning, ready to accompany Alvaro to buy provisions. He had his list and she had hers. If she had anything to say about it, there would be fresh vegetables and fruits aboard when they set sail this time. But there shouldn't be any trouble. Captain Dias and Alvaro were behind her in this. Since the fever, they granted her every request and treated her with great respect.

Alvaro helped her into the boat. "Good morning, señora," he said. "The sun shines favorably on us this day." His weather-beaten face crinkled into a smile. "Let us see if we can find something more tasty for our table."

She smiled back at him, enjoying the feel of the sun lying warm and safe on her back. She breathed in deeply of the clear, salt air and took a seat next to two smudged-faced crewmen.

Clouds drifted across the mountains ahead, the sun stretching out over the hills. Richard stepped aboard and sat in front between two crew members. He held Verity on his lap, her tiny head bobbing against him until their boat pulled into a small bay.

The sun came through the trees in shafts of gold, melting onto the alabaster sands. The two crew members shouted to Alvaro and jumped out, pulling huge casks behind them. Once ashore, they rolled the barrels to a mountain stream and set to work, filling the wooden containers with fresh water.

Alvaro pointed to a nearby beach where puffs of feathery smoke rose. "The Arawak village. We will try them first. They are satisfied with trinkets while the British will try to take everything we've earned from selling what was in our hold."

Alvaro led the way, tottering on his skinny legs. They entered a small village and Ventura recognized some of the Indians she had seen in canoes the day before. They wore no cloaks and carried no banners and were naked except for palm-leaf corslets. The women wore only a little cotton swatch, no bigger than an orange peel. Some carried infants on their backs or suckled them at their brown breasts.

The village smelled of morning fires and roasting fish. The chief came forward, majestic in body and face. He welcomed them, offering gifts of oranges and cassava, his eyes latching on Verity's blond hair and refusing to let go. Ventura poked Alvaro. "Tell him we need more fruit and any vegetables he has. Ask him what this root-thing is and how to use it," she said, holding up the cassava. Alvaro frowned nervously and waved his hand to silence her. "Don't forget!" she hissed.

The steward spoke to him in another language. The words were garbled, mixed up in her ears. The Chief's low voice rustled like dry leaves across a stone walk. Alvaro's voice was animated, sometimes pleading, sometimes growling. At a signal from the Chief, four young Indian braves advanced and exchanged bags with the crewmen.

Ventura looked inside the bags. They were full of coconuts, bananas, exotic fruits and cassava. Smiling, she motioned to Alvaro that there was sufficient for their journey.

They were back on their ship by late morning and ready to sail, but puffy gray clouds and a wind from the northeast brought heavy rain. Ventura busied herself below, preparing seeds and making sure everyone had at least a small portion of fruit that day.

Some of the slaves and a few Arawak Indians gathered on the shore under tree cover to see them off. They chattered and waved at the ships. Captain Dias paced up and down on the quarter-deck in a fury of impatience, waiting for the weather to clear.

By late afternoon, the storm had passed and the wind came from the southeast. The voices of the crew rose in friendly banter as the men lifted anchor. At a gruff command from Captain Dias, the mainsail jerked aloft while the topsails fell from the lashings. A current of air filled the canvas with a rumble like thunder then the ship shuddered, and leapt ahead, heeling to the wind.

Ventura glanced back at Jamaica. Already the shape of trees and sand were beginning to merge, taking on an unreal and distant look of a painted picture. All on board seemed more content, more civil, as the ship slowly made its way north toward Massachusetts. The days dragged on like a string of donkeys, reluctant to move forward. They were sailing with a favorable wind when Ventura noticed an unusual smell. She and Richard were taking a short walk on the deck before breakfast that morning. Verity clung to her mother's neck, making babbling sounds only Ventura claimed to understand.

"Richard," said Ventura, feeling a slight flicker of fear, "do you smell smoke?"

He lifted his nose and sniffed. "Yes, and the galley fire has not yet been lit."

"It's not cold enough for the fireplace." She sniffed again. "Come on, she said, pulling Richard behind her. They ran to the greater hatchway. There, issuing from the panel was a puff of gray smoke. "Quick, go alert the Captain!" she shouted, hurrying in the other direction to find Alvaro and the keys to the hold.

She found the steward setting up for breakfast. He stared at her. "What is the matter, señora?"

"Come with me and bring your keys," she shouted. Before he could answer, she flew out of the cabin and set off for the hatchway. Alvaro was on her heels, his keys clunking together in his hand. "Do you have any extra sails? Maybe we could throw them over the hatchways and keep the air from getting in the hold," she shouted behind her.

His voice was breathless, resistive. "That would take an order from the Captain, and I don't think you should disturb him until---" He grabbed for her arm just as they arrived at the hatchway. Thick smoke poured through the opening. He turned on his heel and began running in the opposite direction. "I'll alert the Captain."

"Richard's already doing that. Can't we release some water between decks to stop the fire?"

Captain Dias' familiar face, jaw jutted out in annoyance, came swinging around the corner. "What the devil---" His eyes and nose took in the scene immediately. "Get the crew to restrain the passengers. Keep them in their cabins if possible. If they panic, we'll never be able to stop this thing."

Ventura shouted above the roar and crackle of the fire, "But maybe the passengers can help carry water. The crew can't do it alone."

Captain Dias shot her an angry look, but growled, "Fine, you get some of the calmer ones and have them grab buckets and form a line from the sea to the hatchway. I'm putting you in charge of this, so step lively."

He turned away and she ran to collect passengers. She hollered into the cabins, asking for their help. "Bring a bucket or a jar, anything that will hold water. Come immediately!"

Back on the deck, the Captain was shouting at his crew to get the yawl hoisted overboard. When it was safely away, Ventura lined thirty passengers up, handed them buckets and gave the signal to fill them with sea water and pass them back up the line to her.

Meanwhile, Richard stumbled down into the hold, but the heat forced him back up on deck, his shirt in flames. Giving a scream, Ventura threw a bucket of water on him and nearby passengers emptied theirs on his head.

Ventura dragged him to a safe place on the deck and made sure he was all right, before pulling Verity out of her carrying sack and putting her in his arms. When she returned to her post, all around her coughed and gasped, fighting their way through the smoke.

The flames from the hatchways shot up even higher. Captain Dias jumped in front of the crew. "All boats overboard!"

The fire spun up the main mast and a deep groan of fear escaped from the passengers. More joined the lines and more buckets were thrown on the fire until it was doused as quickly as it had started. A great cheer arose from the crowd before they slowly moved away from the smoke-filled deck.

The hatchways stood burned and smoke-damaged, but the hold below was untouched. The Captain shouted, "Get the carpenters and caulker to work. There is damage to the mast and main sail."

Then Richard was at her side and Verity was sobbing in her fist. Ventura swept the child into the bag on her back and looked at her husband. His face carried the marks of pain and fatigue and she was sure she looked worse. "Let's get to our cabin, your wounds need looking to." He placed an arm around her neck and hobbled along beside her. "A nice poultice of dried flowers and sea water is just the thing for those burns," she mumbled.

***

Captain Ann Bonny had been watching the Merchant Cadiz from the deck of her ship, The Pirate's Revenge, since its departure from Jamaica. She had been fully informed of the exquisite loot that filled its hold and even knew about the secret chest Captain Dias had hidden in his cabin. Very soon now, she would capture the ship, take their loot, and exchange it for provisions, arms and other necessities in the New World, just as she had with many other ships.

Ann pushed back a lock of her long red hair from her sea-seamed face and grunted. This one was not as easy as some. The Merchant Cadiz should have sunk when the fire broke out, but somehow they had managed to keep her afloat. Someone on that vessel had a brain or two. But still, even though they had repaired her, she was probably weakened and would yet be an easy target for her and her crew of pirates. Her lips moved into a smile of pleasure.

How she loved the challenge of the sea. Who would have thought that she, the daughter of an Irish lawyer who had settled in the New World, would have ended up captain of a bunch of pirates?

But then, marriage to Robert, a mealy-mouthed man her father had chosen for her, could never be enough. It was probably some stroke of fate that she had happened to be walking by that tavern at the precise moment when Calico Jack Rackham had been there, fighting with some other lusty pirate. Her smile broadened. Jack had nearly knocked her over in the scuffle and she slipped and fell in the dirt. She could still feel his kiss, warm and passionate on her lips, when he picked her up, held her to him, and forced his hard body against hers.

She was fascinated, thrilled by the whole incident. He was everything her husband wasn't. Robert was boring, shrill-voiced, stammering, and interested only in the sums he worked on daily. She, of course, had her father's violent Irish temper and was apt to let it loose on Robert, especially when he became quiet and subdued. He was so easily intimidated and she hated him for that.

Jack, on the other hand, wore bright patterned shirts, was a smooth talker, and not easily bullied. He was someone who promised adventure and romance. So she sailed away with him, not even leaving poor Robert a note of good-bye.

What fun they had had. Her smile deepened. It was Jack who had taught her to fight like a man. "You're a big woman. You can easily take a man your size and age. And you're quick, too. Move the way I move. That's right, you've got it." She had been a willing pupil, but who wouldn't be with a man like Jack?

Her smile faded. Then Jack had been stabbed in a fight and her heart had nearly jumped out of her throat. He could have died, but he didn't. And when she realized he would be sometime recuperating, she took command. Masquerading in his clothes, she became Jack, Captain of the ship.

He had only been a little angry that day when he finally had the strength to leave his cabin. His laugh boomed across the deck. "So, my pretty. I suppose I shall have to share command of this ship." After that, they were known as the Calico Twins.

Mary Read's high breathy voice disturbed Ann's reverie. "You haven't moved an inch since fire broke out on the merchant ship." Ann turned to face the woman who was as thin and short as Ann was tall and broad. Mary was an interesting pirate, too. Brought up as a boy, she fought as a soldier in England before she married. Widowed shortly afterward, Mary sailed to America with a West India man Jack and Ann captured. They had taken an immediate liking to one another and so Mary had joined the crew.

Ann put her arm around her friend. Mary had seen her through a bout of prison when an English Navy ship captured them. Those were grueling days, sentenced to death, not a prayer in the world until some of Jack's men broke in and rescued them. Even back at the ship, the King's men constantly harassed them until Jack finally agreed to move their seat of operations to the Atlantic Coast.

Ann smiled at her friend and gave her a squeeze "I'm keeping my eye on that ship, I am. Soon we'll board her and have enough loot to get ourselves whatever we need or fancy." She stared at Mary. "Then we'll put a little fat on those bones."

Mary nodded. "If we don't get food soon, they'll be a mutiny as sure as I stand here."

Mutiny. Ann shivered at the word. She didn't even want to think of what that would be like.

Jack's deep voice boomed behind them. "Mutiny, is it?" He filled the air with bellows of laughter. "You've never been through one have ya ladies?" He put his arms around their shoulders and hugged them. He smelled of rum and the sea. "Famine brings the most horrible excesses. I remember the time it happened to our ship when I was cabin boy on the John Drum. They was like beasts of prey, deaf to every representation, coolly meditatin' on the death of their fellow creatures," he whispered, black eyes snapping with some odd mixture of emotions Ann couldn't identify.

He looked into her eyes and said, "The wind had been favorable on the ship, only one night it suddenly shifted and violent storms, one after the other did much to damage the vessel. Despite our experience at sea, the masts went by the board and all the sails, excepting one, were torn to shreds. To add to our adversity, several leaks were discovered in the hold."

What happened?" Ann asked breathlessly.

"Well, the wind finally abated a bit, but we were driven way off course, and without masts, sails or rigging, she was unmanageable. We drifted to and fro, completely at the mercy of the waves." He took a swig from a rum bottle, wiped the excess from his thick black beard and handed the bottle to Ann. "That was the least of our troubles. When the steward went to examine the state of our provisions, there were none to be found."

Ann took a sip, feeling the liquid burn down her throat before she handed the flask to Mary. She turned to Jack. "What did you do?"

"We thought we were saved when the next day we spied two vessels. We knew if we could board them and take their ship and provisions, we would be safe. As luck would have it, the sea ran so high we were prevented from approaching the ships, and they soon were out of sight. I have never seen such disappointed seamen. They fell upon the wine and brandy, allotting the captain only two small jars of water. To add to the deplorableness of the situation, the crew appeased their painful cravings of hunger by incessant intoxication. I," he turned to Ann, "being only eleven or twelve years at the time, went and hid in the Captain's cabin, fearing for my life."

Ann nodded, hoping to console him. "You couldn't be faulted for that. Was that when mutiny was whispered?"

"Hush now woman, there's more to my story. Much more. On the fifth day, I observed a ship bearing toward us in full sail. No time was lost in us making signals of distress. A cry of joy rose from the decks when the crew saw our signals were answered. The sea was sufficiently calm to permit the two vessels to approach each other. Then something extraordinary happened, but then, given we was a pirate vessel, I suppose it wasn't that strange. The other ship crowded all sails and bore away."

"Is that when the mutiny occurred?"

"My dear girl, you are anxious to hear about such a dread occurrence as mutiny, aren't ya?" He grabbed her and kissed her full on the lips. "Be patient. There's more adventure to come." He grabbed the rum from Mary and took another deep slug. Ann smiled at him. Impatient as she was to hear the end of the story, she loved it when he told her stories of his adventures.

He wiped his lips and continued. "No language is adequate to describe the despair and consternation which then overwhelmed us all, my Annie. They were enraged, their eyes showing the terror and horror I've seen in trapped animals. They raced around the deck, looking for the only live things." He leaned toward her and said in a blood-curdling whisper, "The only creatures they found, other than men, were a couple of love birds and a cat. Those they devoured in an instant, without even taking the feathers off the birds or the fur off the cat."

"Ugh," said Mary, thinking about swallowing dry feathers and wet fur.

Jack winked. "But before they finished, they did do the captain the honor of saving him the head of the cat."

Mary shook her head. "What did he do with it?"

Jack took another swig from his bottle. "Well, later he declared it would have been a disgusting event at any other time, but just then, he believed it to be the most exquisite treat he had ever seen."

"Really, a cat?"

"That he did, my Annie. And from that day and for more than a month, it was impossible to tell in what manner we subsisted. The Captain, himself, was confined to his cabin, being in great pain from an attack of gout. I, as a young cabin boy, was with him nearly constantly. So, when the sailors came to him and declared that it was necessary to sacrifice one of their lot in order to save the rest, I heard them. And I must say, them was frightening words for such young ears. But it was even worse than that. They let him know that no matter what he said, they had decided, and they intended to cast lots for the victim that very night."

"What did the Captain say?"

"Well now Mary, the Captain was a humane man, and he started to shudder and rant about how we were to regard each other as brethren, and that if we did such a terrible deed, we would forever consign ourselves to universal execration."

Ann drew a tight breath. "Did they listen?"

"Of course not. He pleaded with them to relinquish the idea of committing such a heinous crime, but it was as if he was speaking to deaf men. They all replied in one voice that they planned to do it whether he approved of their deed or not, and they had only come to him out of respect for his station."

"What happened then?" The two women said in unison.

"Well, I left the Captain. He was nearly incoherent, raving about his men. I sneaked out on the deck and found the crew drawing lots as they had said they would. A young man, a negro, who belonged to the Captain was the victim. I don't really believe he was chosen by lot, they probably had him in mind all along, being as they hated the black people with a venom. Now, I myself have never felt that way, having had pirates with me who were as black as coal and who fought bravely by my side. But to them, black was inferior, and so they doomed him."

"Did they really eat him?"

"Of course. A big man, Brazen John, he was called, came forward and smashed the poor fellow to the ground with one blow of his fists. The black man was dead, having fallen against the cannon and split his head open. They dressed the body, lit the biggest fire in the galley I had ever seen and divided up the meal. They saved most of him for the rest of the month, being very economical about that, I must say. They even offered me some, but I trembled when I thought of what I would be eating, and declined. The Captain and I subsisted by mixing the rest of the water with a couple of bottles of spirits."

Ann pushed back a thick lock that had escaped from under Jack's black hat. "You must have been very hungry."

"We were, or maybe we were past hunger. For whatever reason, the flesh of a man was more than either of us could stand."

Mary nodded. "But the crew didn't feel that way."

Jack passed the bottle to Mary and said, "No, and once they had tasted human flesh and overcome their reluctance, when there was no more to eat, they went back to the Captain. But he stood fast. No more human meat was to be eaten on his ship."

Ann made a face. "Of course they didn't take his word."

"You can be sure of that. I think that was the first time I heard the whisper of mutiny, and I can tell you it was a terrible sound. They rioted and pillaged, taking what they wanted from the Captain's chest, finally throwing him overboard. Thank God, some other ships were traveling nearby and they came and fetched him out of the water and restored order. Many of the crew were killed. I think they went mad. In the end, they were fighting and killing each other."

Jack's words sent a shiver through Ann and she knew then that they must take over the Merchant Cadiz that very day. "There'll be no mutiny on this ship," she proclaimed.

Jack smiled. "Good, Captain Annie. My sentiments exact. Do ye have a plan?"

"Yes. Mary, will you pass the word and make the crew ready? Jack and I will make the final preparations."

They watched Mary's slender body retreating, then they huddled together against the mainsail, making plans. "We could dress ourselves as natives," said Ann. Remember when we outfitted ourselves as Moslems on that pilgrimage to Mecca? We lulled those British into believing we were a friendly vessel."

Jack stroked his chin. "Yes, that was an easy takeover But Moslems? In these waters? I think not. Let's go to our cabin and reconnoiter this." He took another swig of rum and began to sing a sea chant. They clunked down the steps, giggling and whispering, then sat for a while in their cabin.

Finally Ann said, "Judging from the cannon on that ship, we don't have enough firepower to win by coming aside her."

Her co-captain nodded. "You're right about that. But she is injured. I don't care how much repair they did, that main mast is weakened. They've even slowed their pace and we've cut back ours nearly hourly not to pass her."

A smile moved across Ann's lips. "Time to come astern her and take her over."

Jack nodded. "Yes, that will be our plan, Annie." He gave her a bracing bear hug and went out to supervise the preparation of weapons.

When the Pirate's Revenge and all aboard were ready, Ann and Jack gave the signal and they sailed up to the wounded ship, coming astern of her at an angle to her horizon where her cannon could do no harm. The Merchant Cadiz tried to come quickly into the wind to fire broadside at them, but in their condition, the ship lurched and moved too slowly.

"It's a bonny ship," cried Ann spying the great Castillian ensign flying from the castle above the balusters and the balconies and saints in painted wood swaying below high lanterns and a gilded crucifix.

"She's very confident, despite her wounds," shouted Jack. Just then, two rounds of cannon fire came through their stern ports even though the Pirate's Revenge had not yet hoisted a flag.

"Yes, but she'll miss." And Ann was right. The ship was swinging sideways and much too unsteady to be able to adjust their aim. Their cannon balls exploded with smoke and vanished in the waves before they reached the ship. "Unfurl the flag and advance!" she shouted.

"Unfurl the flag, maties!" shouted Jack. With that, the pirate banner rippled to full width, high above them. Ann looked down and saw her crew assembled with muskets and cutlasses, some carrying boarding axes and piles. All had hooks attached to their belts and several braces of pistols and knives. "Get on the foretop," Jack shouted to several of his sharpshooters. "Pick off the crew on the quarter-deck. You ten, up to the ship's head above the beak-head frame. Fire on every living thing you see. You men, behind them to pass loaded guns."

"They're getting ready to fire again," shouted Ann. The cannons sent two more balls blasting across the water. One hit the foresail, but before they could reload, the pirate ship drew close and fired on the cannon loaders.

The battle wore on, casualties falling on both sides. Neither Ann nor Jack were in a hurry to board. Their plan was to tire the enemy, not kill them all. They stayed in the wake of the other ship until evening of the next day, sometimes coming so close their bowsprit nearly shattered against the Merchant Cadiz.

Alert on the deck, Ann ordered the crew closest to the ship to fire into the windows of the Merchant Cadiz. They retorted with issues from their stern-frame cannon, but each time they did, the pirates killed so many that the crew of the Merchant Cadiz gave up for a while and retreated, running for the hold. At darkness, all crew and passengers left the deck and not a human thing was seen.

The next morn came in all violet and purple with just-felt breezes. Ann looked for the other ship, her mind turning with confusion. "Do you see her, Jack?"

He shook his head. "Not yet, but she can't have gone far. There. There she is. They've tried to change course on us to escape, but that old hulk can barely move anymore." For that whole day, the Merchant Cadiz sailed wobbly through the waves, the pirates following close behind. The crew and passengers hid themselves below, not daring to come on deck.

The pirates, anxious to fight, busied themselves cutting or firing at their prey's cables, ribbing, pulleys and ropes. The big guns opened fire and red hot shot peppered the air. Sparks ran up the rigging and puffs of smoke were everywhere. By late afternoon, the masting that had been put on the main sail fell with a great crash to the forecastle.

Jack signalled the pilot to come forward and then he fired two broadsides into their poop at short range. Jack laughed fiendishly when the carved saints that crowded their castle lost their heads and arms and their great flag was little more than a rag.

Just before noon, the Merchant Cadiz struck their tattered ensign. Ann and Jack put out a boat and headed toward the ship to receive the sword of the captain. Victory was theirs.

Halfway there, Ann turned to Jack and said, "You don't think they would deceive us, do you?"

"Nah, those Spaniards are infatuated with the idea of honor. They prefer to perish rather than break their word." To the crew he shouted, "Boarders away!"

Stationed along the bulkwarks of the pirate ship were twenty men equipped with grapnels and hooks. On the count of three, the grapnels went hurling across to the Merchant Cadiz and entangled in the rigging. "Haul, my maties," shouted Jack, and haul they did, drawing the two vessels together. Boarding planks were quickly shoved across and Jack and Ann sauntered over proudly, followed by a swarm of angry-faced pirates.

# 12

When the first cannon blast from the pirate ship shook the Merchant Cadiz, it sent clouds of scarlet smoke into the air. Ventura wanted to take Verity to the cabin and lock her there, but the child clung to her so tightly she could not dislodge her fingers. "Very well," she told the young child, "you shall stay with me, but if I am hurt, your fate is sealed." Then, before she could change her mind, Ventura hurried to the deck and took her place next to Richard, a pistol in one hand, a knife in the other.

Richard shouted to her above the din. "Are you all right?"

She nodded, "My knees are shaking, but otherwise I'm fine."

Richard laughed nervously. "My whole body is shaking. This is the worse I've seen. Stay close to me now and we'll stick this out."

When the cannon fire forced them below to their cabin, they lay awake all night, waiting for the inevitable. "Will they kill us?" Ventura whispered.

Richard tightened his arms around her. "Possibly. Pirates sometimes kill their prisoners and throw them overboard."

Ventura shuddered. Once again the heavy stone of death hung over their heads. But they were powerless to do anything except huddle together on the floor, like helpless animals, Verity locked between them in their trembling arms. The only sound in the cabin besides the distant rumble of cannon fire was the sound of Richard and Ventura softly praying.

Then, a knock on their door and they were summoned on board. "We are surrendering. We cannot win. The Captain wants you on deck," said Alvaro, his face full of shame.

They followed him quickly, taking a place near the railing. Across the plank, a ruggedly handsome man in a bright yellow shirt with a bold print smiled back at them. His black eyes snapped with energy and the scars on his face told the story of his battles. A thick red sash circled his waist and a bright purple scarf hung from around his neck. Round gold earrings swung from his earlobes and a red bandanna peeked out from under his wide-brimmed hat. The big woman at his side wore the same clothes, but her face was sterner and her dark eyes held a glint of hard humor in them. Her hair hung wild and thick below her shoulders as if she cared not what others thought of her.

The two pirates covered the distance between ships quickly. "We are Captains of the Pirate's Revenge," said the man in a booming voice and his chest puffed up with vanity. "I am Calico Jack Rackham and this be Ann Bonny." He bowed, sweeping his hat nearly to the deck.

Head hanging in shame, Captain Dias slowly surrendered his sword. Jack took it, smiled, held it in his hands for a moment, then promptly gave it back to him. "I give this sword back to you as a sign of our esteem for the fine defense you and your men put up."

Showing his large teeth in a genial grin, Captain Dias said, "I would appreciate it if you would not seek my flag as a trophy."

Jack looked at Ann and nodded. Ann spoke up, saying, "We prefer the riches that are below your decks. You can keep your flag."

Captain Dias bowed to her. "I am pleased to see you are not as cruel and debauched as I have heard."

Jack flashed a smile and said, "We wish you no further harm. You are free once we receive payment of a ransom. Now please, surrender your weapons." Ventura and Richard were the first from the Merchant Cadiz to hand their weapons over to the nearest pirate.

Captain Dias surveyed his ship and said, "Do I have permission to repair the damage?"

Jack waved a hand. "Yes, yes, go right ahead. Your men are free to proceed with their work. Meanwhile, you can take us below to see your hold and whatever other treasures you have." He winked and Captain Dias coughed loudly and long until his face turned nearly purple.

At that moment, one of the crew who had managed to keep a knife, jumped out of his hiding place and thrust the weapon into Jack. He missed his vital organs, but put a deep gash in his left arm. Before the crewman could retreat, one of the pirates grabbed him by a twist of bright cloth that clung around his waist. He killed the assailant with a swift hack of his sword, and threw him overboard.

Ann's face turned even harder. "For this indiscretion, all who do not cast their lot with us will be set adrift in small boats to make your way to land as best you can. Your ship will be set aflame and left to sink."

Seeing Jack had been made dizzy by his wound, Ann ran to side, quickly giving orders to the closest pirate to survey the passengers about how they stood. "And mind you," she cautioned, "no drinking! Now," she said turning to look across the deck, "is there a physician on board?"

Ventura, who had been raising wordless prayers to God, forced herself forward. "I am a healer. I can help. I've had experience with wounds."

Ann gave her a suspicious look, but signalled with her hand to let Ventura try. "I'll need my herbs, some water, and some clean cloths. Those are in my cabin. Perhaps he would be most comfortable there."

Ann raised her voice and her face pinked with anger. "Oh no, I'll not surrender Jack to you. Bring the things on deck. The rest of you pirates, set the cowards among them adrift. I will follow this woman to my cabin." With her pistol cocked in Ventura's ribs, they made their way.

Sensing something was wrong, Verity stayed wide-eyed and silent while Ventura moved along. Lips trembling with silent prayer, Ventura hoped to spare Verity injury.

Reaching their cabin, Ventura gathered what she needed and returned to the deck, still feeling the pistol cold and deadly in her side. She bent down by Jack. "I'll have to tear off his sleeve. I need to cleanse the wound and wrap this herb next to it." Her fingers moved expertly, cleaning and wrapping the wound. When she was finished, she stood and told Ann, "I will have to change this in a few hours. Meanwhile, I will make a broth for him to sip. It will give him strength."

Ann watched all of this, her eyes softening when she saw the tenderness with which Ventura worked. "Where have you learned all this?" she demanded.

"In Seville, where it is forbidden."

Ann let out a loud laugh. "Forbidden to heal? How can that be? Forbidden to kill or maim, but forbidden to heal? What madness has taken over there?"

"The Inquisition. They were to burn me at the stake for healing."

Ann nodded. "They were to kill me for being a pirate and taking what I earn by my wits. But as you see, they were too stupid to enslave me." She tapped Ventura on the shoulder. "You are a bright thing, you must join us."

"Join you?"

"Yes! At least until we reach the New World. There is much you can teach me."

Ventura searched her captor's eyes, wondering if she could be trusted. Something told her it would be safe and so she said, "I will be happy to teach you. But first, I will use my hands to help this man heal his wounds more quickly." Ventura rubbed her hands together quickly, closed her eyes and then held her palms above Jack's wound.

Ann Bonny leaned closer. "What is that, magic?"

When Ventura finished her work, she faced the larger woman. "Not magic. I can teach you how to use your hands to heal, too."

Ann Bonny smiled then, a warm and generous smile. "Yes, you shall teach me and anyone who wishes to learn about these powers you have. Now, let us find something to eat, for I am hungry."

Before leaving, Ann commanded Mary to see that Jack was settled comfortably in a cabin before joining the women in the galley. Mary nodded and did as she was bid. Ventura introduced Richard and Verity to Captain Bonny on their way across the deck.

Ann stopped and tweaked the child under the chin. "A beautiful child and very brave for one so young." Verity smiled shyly at Ann and then reached her chubby hand out to touch the pirate's scarf.

Ventura nodded. "She has been through much already in her short life."

Ann shook her head. "That's a pity, but it will make her strong." She grasped Verity's curled finger and shook it until the little girl giggled. "Come, let us find something to eat."

While they ate, the Hasletons sat with Ann and Jack in the galley watching the wild goings on around them. Ann shook her fist angrily at the sound above them. "I told the crew no drinking, but they never listen after a capture. I suppose it is their way of celebrating." Pirates paraded past the galley in all sorts of elaborate costumes. Ventura thought she even saw a man in one of her gowns, but discounted it as being due to her fatigue. Pirates danced everywhere, singing and shouting praise to each other. A few gambled or told stories in loud, liquor-filled voices.

After they had eaten, Ann led her dinner companions to the Captain's cabin. He had already been moved to smaller quarters. She turned and whispered to them, "I've heard about the chest your captain has been guarding."

Jack pushed forward. "Yes, I wouldn't miss this for anything." He made sure no other pirates were about, then he said, "I don't want my crew to see this yet. In their drunken state, there is likely to be a fight or two over it. Tomorrow, when they are sober, we will divide up the loot."

Ventura shook her head. "I've been in this cabin many times and I've never seen a chest."

Jack's eyes darted around the room until they came to rest on a box in the corner. He moved quickly, tearing off the soiled piece of cotton that had been covering it. "Aha! I'll wager twenty pieces of silver this is the chest!"

Empty, it must have weighed as much as a large man. Full, it probably weighted twice that. There were extra wide handles on each side for carrying. Jack fiddled with the lock until it sprang open. The inside of the lid was covered with a decorative iron shield and an intricate locking mechanism. The inside was full of silver and gold. Jack's hand reached in, dipping out handfuls of treasure.

"This will make up for the weeks of near famine," he said, laughing. "As soon as we get to the New World, we will buy new clothes and ample provisions for the crew." Returning every piece of gold and silver, he carefully closed the chest and returned the soiled cover. "Now, let us see what lies in store for us in the hold." He took several lanterns and led them from the cabin. In the hold, tucked behind a musty curtain, they found wine, olive oil, spices, raisins, many types of cloth and some jewelry. "Look here, Annie," he shouted, "these will make a fine start for our mansion in the New World."

"Mansion?" asked Ventura.

"Oh yes," said Jack with a wink. "We must have a home to go to, just as you will. We are not on the seas at all times. We like to come to land to feast and to purchase our goods. Sometimes we just need a place to rest."

Ann yawned and then said, "I think we all need some rest right now. Let us see if we can quiet down the crew and get some sleep."

The next morning, those who agreed to go with the pirates, returned to the Pirate's Revenge. Ventura made sure she and Richard and Verity were the first aboard the pirate's ship. From their vantage point, they watched many of their fellow passengers, and most of the crew, take a small parcel of food before climbing into a boat and heading toward shore. When everyone was safely away, one of the pirates set the Merchant Cadiz afire. Red tongues licked up from the deck and sparks ran up the rigging until the sails caught. A tremendous explosion followed and the ship shuddered mightily. Ventura's last vision of the ship was of its injured body, red with flame, slipping slowly into the sea.

The next weeks were busy for Ventura. She spent nearly every waking hour teaching Ann and Mary and a few others all she knew about healing. Verity was with her constantly, bright eyes watching everything. They talked about things other than healing. Sometimes they talked of Seville and what had happened there. One evening at dinner, Ventura asked Ann, "Why did you move to the Atlantic coast? The Indies must be more exotic, more exciting."

"They are and they aren't. There is a price on my head there and on poor Mary's too. But smuggling is even more profitable here than in the Indies."

"Why?"

Ann lifted a mug to her mouth and took a long sip before answering. "The British want to control the colonies and exclude foreigners, like the Dutch, from commerce with their possessions. So, the American colonials have to buy all their merchandise from England. Prices are high and quality is low. There are plenty of prosperous merchants and planters in the New World and they want luxury. They want spices and jewelry. Things I can furnish them."

Jack raised an eyebrow. "But it's a dangerous business."

Ann clapped him on the back. "Yes, but a real challenge. I can handle rough characters and I know the sea."

Jack interrupted. "And no one can fault her courage."

Ann smiled at him. "So there you are."

***

The pirates sailed directly up the coast, purposely staying out of any possible battles or inclement weather. The Captains dared not sail right into port, so Jack gave orders for the ship to be anchored near one of the small islands at the head of the bay near Salem. Those going ashore, including the Hasletons, prepared to take the small boat into town.

Ventura felt the bitterness at leaving her new friends behind. She drew a long sigh like a small child about to sob when she hugged Anna and Mary good-bye on the deck of the Pirate's Revenge. "I'll never forget you," whispered Ann.

"Nor I, you," said Ventura.

# BOOK III

## The New World

## 1673 - 1692

# 13

Misty flakes hung across the harbor like tiny ghosts. The sea spumed and sleeted in from the open ocean, piling water into foamy mountains at the edge of the headlands of the Cape. The wharf stood dark against the sky and tall ships rocked and creaked beside stilted buildings. A young boy stood waiting, shaking in the freezing air, thin coat icicled to his body.

Ventura crammed her fists deep in her pockets and turned up her collar against the April wind. It blew hard and wet, taking her breath away when she tried to speak, whipping snow into her hair and stinging through her clothes.

Richard stepped onto the water-soaked wharf and reached his arm back to pull Ventura up beside him. Cheeks pink and chapped, Verity cried into her mother's mantilla. Before Richard could pick up their two small bags, the young boy stepped forward and said, "Can I help you with that?" His voice was polite and delicate. He had a smudged face and tattered clothes and frost gleamed off his thin eyebrows, making his eyes appear the color of new straw.

Richard shook his head and said, "No, I can manage, but maybe you could watch these bags until we find a place to stay."

He nodded, his lanky figure dragging the trunk to the side. "Winter's back. Ain't we had enough of her?" He took a piece of paper out of his pocket and slapped it in Richard's hand. "Just ask at Nate Hubbard's there. Your trunk will be safe for a week."

Richard grabbed Ventura's arm and said, "Let's find someplace warm." Stumbling along beside him, Ventura's feet stung and her shoes rattled with the cold. She put her head down, pulling a small mantilla more tightly over Verity's head and wishing they were snug in a berth next to a warm hearth. They made their way toward town, dodging the snowy water that ran from gutter to gutter, sometimes stepping in ankle-deep slush. She huddled against Richard, walking gingerly on her toes, sliding occasionally along the cobblestones.

They moved slowly up the street, past a darkened warehouse with ice-covered windows and a short row of fishermen's shacks and ramshackle wharves with twisted pilings. The smells of cinnamon, coffee, fish and cloves mingled with the cold air. Slack-rigged one- and two-masted fishing boats clung beside the docks, bouncing in the sea, whining against its pull. Farther along, the noises of people eating and drinking in the little clutter of ordinaries blended with the odors of rum, stale beer and cooking food.

Richard guided Ventura toward one of the boozy eating establishments. "Shall we get something to eat and warm ourselves?" he said, guiding her closer. She nodded, smiling at the idea of something hot inside her and dry shoes on her feet.

The door opened, spilling light. The room smelled of freshly-filled oil lamps and cooking fish. Ventura bolted for the hearth and stood with her stiffened hands spread to the warmth of the blaze. She watched the great logs crumble while the flames leapt and hissed.

A man reached his gnarled hands toward the fire beside her. He was weather beaten as an old oak, with hair and beard of white, and skin brown as a dried apple. "Just come in, then," he said to Ventura. The firelight played across his face, polishing his cheeks and filling his dark eyes with a vibrant glow.

She nodded. "Is it always this cold here in the spring?"

"No." He paused and rubbed his hands over the heat. "It's a wintry night, then isn't it? Reminds me of when I was at sea and we had a winter storm that April." He looked at Richard. "You'll be looking for lodging, then?"

Richard nodded. "Yes. can you steer us toward a warm place that's not too expensive?"

The man looked back at the room. "Right here's about the best you'll find this time of night. That's Tom, the owner, over there behind the bar." The man at the fire looked in the direction of a tall man with an apron tied around his slim waist. "He'll put you up or I'll give him a what for." Then his mouth crinkled into a smile and he leaned closer and whispered, "He's my son, so let me know if he don't treat you right."

Richard left to arrange for lodging and to send for their chest, while Ventura sat down at a table in front of the fire with Verity. By the time Richard returned, a round-faced maid in a skirt and kerchief had set down steaming plates of fish stew and biscuits for them, and toast swimming in warm milk for Verity.

They ate to the accompaniment of the rattle of dishes and silverware from nearby tables. Verity took a few bites, then fell asleep in her mother's lap. Ventura sighed with pleasure, feeling warmth coming back into her feet. She savored each bite of her food, tasting the succulent fish, sweet carrots and potatoes. When the stew was gone, she dipped her biscuit into the thick thyme and sage broth, wiping her bowl dry.

Then with eyelids almost too heavy to keep open, she followed Richard up the high creaky stairs to bed. Neither the drunken noises below nor the moan of the wind intruded on Ventura's first night of blissful sleep on land.

***

With Verity slung into the bag on her mother's back, Ventura and Richard set out the next morning to find permanent lodgings. The cold made the porch boards snap and click beneath their feet as they made their way carefully along the slippery porch to the steps and street below.

The storm had blown itself out, leaving the morning sky blue and clear. The breeze warmed quickly, washing most of the slush and snow away and leaving the curbs and cobblestones clean and dry. Snow only remained in the hollows on the shady sides of houses or under tall evergreens, and even that had grayed and pitted.

They passed two men with bowed heads and glum faces who wore plain black garments and dark brimmed hats with buckles. From behind the gate of a barnyard, a sad-eyed horse and several mud-covered cattle watched them.

A slender girl in a white cap, and stiff-collared dress whisked her broom across the walk outside a clapboard house. Ventura walked toward her. "Hello," she called, "we are looking for permanent lodgings, do you know of any?"

The girl smiled faintly and beckoned them to come to the front door. She had violet eyes and a sprig of her ashen hair peeped out from under her bonnet. Her voice was barely audible above the flapping of the loose wooden shingles in the brisk wind. "You can speak to my mother," she said. "She will know."

The door creaked open and they stepped inside the house behind the girl. Across from them, a steep narrow stair ascended to a loft. On their level, several small rooms opened out from the side of a great chimney. A piece of pewter sat next to a Bible on a walnut chest. The girl led them past a room full of peas, barley, wheat, rye and oats in barrels.

Farther along, a woman in a long skirt and stiff bonnet bent over an open fireplace, and stirred a heavy iron pot. Above the crackling fire hung a long-barreled rifle and long-handled cooking utensils. The woman turned and smiled shyly. She was thin on top and plump as a beet below, with a square, strongly-proportioned face and a questioning expression. The girl spoke politely, "Mother, these people are looking for lodging."

The woman glanced at their clothes and started to frown. Then she saw Verity clutching a tiny cloth doll, and her eyes softened. "The widow Glover of Salem Village has died. Her house is empty." She pointed across the square. "I think Mrs. Griggs, her neighbor, can help you. I see her in her yard just now."

Ventura and Richard made their way across the square. Mrs. Griggs looked sharply at them from under shaggy brows. She was a tiny woman with faded blue eyes, an oval face, and a voice that rang brittle as glass. "Yes, the Glover house is for let. I have the key, let me just go in and fetch it." She returned and marched them over to the house next to hers.

It stood on a slight knoll next to the square. The house was made of sturdy clapboard walls and a high-pitched gabled roof with a massive chimney. In the corners, hanging under the roof, were carved drops, the only ornaments to be seen.

Inside, the house felt small and confining with a low ceiling and enormous summer beams that seemed to press down on them. Only the brick fireplace stretching across most of the inner wall of each downstairs room hinted it might provide some coziness on a cold winter's eve.

Even the hall with its spinning wheel and pine furniture wasn't very inviting, but at least maybe she could learn to spin. Richard took her hand and looked into her eyes. "Do you like the house?"

She nodded and smiled, thinking any place was better than a dungeon or a ship. He looked at Mrs. Griggs. "I guess we will take it."

"You'll like it here," she said, handing Richard the key. "Come over later and we shall talk about the rent." Richard gave Ventura a kiss and clunked down the steps behind their neighbor, on his way to fetch their trunk.

When they'd left, Ventura picked up Verity and spun her around. "Do you like your new home, sweet baby?" Verity gurgled and yanked a clump of her mother's hair.

***

That night after Verity had been properly tucked in, Ventura and Richard lay awake, giggling and talking about their new home. She already had plans for where the high-backed pine chairs should go and what to do with the pine chest and walnut table. Richard promised to cover the chairs that someone had painted a horrible dark green with a cheerier color and Ventura dreamed about spinning her own woolen mantillas. They could even have their own garden and animals. Her brain whirled with plans for their future together.

While she chattered on about fixing the house into a home for them, his hand traced the outline of her face, then began to explore her earlobes and the softness of her neck. Her fingers touched his arm softly, absently, while she thought about teaching Verity all there was to learn about living in a house.

His lips whispered words of love in her hair, on the back of her neck, down her shoulders and all thoughts of fixing their home dissolved into desire. Then she was in his arms, feeling the beat of his heart and the hardness of his muscles. Burying her face in his shoulder, she searched for the warmth there.

He kissed her, softly at first, then more urgently. An aching heaviness spread between her legs and her body yearned with eagerness. He stroked her back and her willing limbs, kissing her from her feet to her thighs until she pulled him next to her. They curled into each others arms, their bodies meeting like strong wine, all fire and spice.

***

A few days later Mrs. Griggs came to call, warm sweetcakes in her arms. "I hope I'm not intruding," she said, managing a small smile.

Ventura showed her to the kitchen and poured two cups of coffee. Halfway through her cake, Mrs. Griggs asked, "Are you of the Puritan faith?"

Ventura shook her head. "Puritan? I've never heard of it. I was raised Catholic, but I have long since come to question the ruthlessness of that religion."

"I'm sorry to hear that. You may find some comfort here. We Puritans believe in living a natural, simple life. We wear black clothes and do not delight in frivolity."

At that moment, Verity started to giggle loudly and bang two spoons together. "Verity, be quiet," whispered Ventura crossly.

Mrs. Griggs shook her head. "We are not that strict. Children must learn. It is only excess we deplore. Only brutishness and jumping around aimlessly is punished. And we never strike our children, except in case of obstinacy or stubbornness or some gross enormity. We are here to create an order on earth for the glory of God, don't you think?"

"I think---"

"Of course children are born in sin and must be educated to see the light of salvation. We adults work hard and use our time wisely, giving thanks many times each day to God for his blessings. We are firmly against anything that is unnatural or artificial." Her eyes fell on Ventura's frilly sleeves, darkened for a second with disapproval, and then darted back to look into her neighbor's eyes.

Ventura felt a flush rising on her cheeks. "I guess I should make my clothes more suitable. These were given to me in Spain."

Mrs. Griggs nodded with approval and said, "Prayer is very important, too. Beginning at sundown on Saturday, each family is expected to devote itself to prayer, contemplation and the reading of the Gospel. Naps, labor or even a stroll is forbidden on the Sabbath."

"Seems like a lot of rules, I---"

"That's only the start. If you're caught wandering by the harbor or standing in the street exchanging pleasantries, the tithesman will be upon you, urging you to meeting or to your home."

Ventura nodded and offered her neighbor the plate of cakes. "No, thank you. One is sufficient. Oh, and I forgot to tell you, if your husband wants to vote, you will have to join the Church."

"I don't understand, join the Church to vote?" Ventura picked up Verity and held her on her lap. The child smiled at Mrs. Griggs winningly and then hiccupped. A small dribble of her breakfast came out of her mouth and sat on her lower lip until Ventura wiped it away with a small cloth.

Mrs. Griggs smiled briefly and continued. "A freeman is one in good standing in the Church. To achieve that status, he has to have a letter from the minister declaring he is fulfilling his religious duties or he won't be able to vote at all."

Ventura nodded, trying to take in everything Mrs. Griggs had said. Finally she replied, "I think I could believe in all those things except perhaps that children are born in sin." She glanced down at Verity who was crawling out of her lap and onto the floor, dragging her doll behind her.

"Well then, there is no reason for you to fear. But I did want to tell you there has been an increase in punishment for heresy lately, so I came to warn you about it. If you do not embrace what I have told you, the clergy may punish you."

Ventura took a sip of coffee and thought about punishment. Visions of days in the dungeon and Clara burning at the stake flashed before her. She wondered if they had come to the wrong place.

Mrs. Griggs patted Ventura's hand sympathetically. "Don't worry, the punishment isn't severe. When you pass by the village common you will see how those who do not devote themselves to our teachings are punished. It is a simple punishment, nothing painful, but it is very effective."

Before Mrs. Griggs left, she touched Ventura's sleeve and said, "I don't want to frighten you dear, and I see no reason for you to be afraid since you seem a God-fearing girl, but you should be aware of what goes on here." Ventura thanked her neighbor and saw her out. Then she took Verity in her arms and went out to the garden to talk with Richard.

He stopped digging and gave her a concerned look. "What's the matter?" he said, sensing immediately she was upset. He left his shovel and came over and stood by her, the smell of moist earth heavy on him.

She looked at him hesitantly. "I've just had the strangest visit. Mrs. Griggs came to warn me about the goings-on in the common. She said people here are punished for their religious beliefs, too." Richard put his arms around her and Verity. For a moment, she leaned into him, feeling safe and secure. Then she looked up at him and said, "I suppose we should be happy that at least the Inquisition is not here. And she said the punishment wasn't painful. What do you suppose it could be?"

"I don't know," he whispered in her hair, "But it may be prudent to take her advice. We will have to be careful what we say about what we believe."

Ventura sighed and said, "Maybe it would be a good idea to join their church. She said there's a lecture there tomorrow."

He kissed Ventura's forehead and Verity's cheek. "Then we'll go to their church and find out." He looked into her eyes and said, "Now, don't go worrying. This is the New World, you know."

***

Ventura clicked her tongue and wiped the dampness from her forehead with a cloth. She had been ripping the lace off the darkest dress she owned. But no matter how hard she tried, it still didn't look plain enough.

Richard waited patiently for nearly half an hour, then he took her hand and said, "Time to go. The meeting will be over and you will still be fixing your dress."

Ventura pulled her arm away, feeling slightly cross that he didn't understand. "I don't want to appear too fancy," she said with a hint of frustration in her voice.

Richard's voice was coaxing. "Let's just go and show them we've made an effort. They'll understand that we've just come here and haven't had time to get suitable clothes."

She frowned. "I hope so, but what if---"

"Never mind what ifs, let's just go." He picked up Verity and started out the door. Mumbling to herself grimly, Ventura followed.

In minutes they were in the center of the square, watching a skinny man in wooden stocks. His face was an odd mixture of contempt and humiliation. His body was bent slightly forward so his hands and head would fit through the wooden openings. Next to him, a fat man sat on a short bench. His solemn eyes looked past them into the distance and his stubby feet stuck out from two holes in foot stocks.

Village people walked by on the rough cobblestones. They pointed their fingers and gaped at the two men. "I guess this is the punishment Mrs. Griggs was talking about," said Ventura. "Not half as bad as the strappado."

Verity pointed and giggled, then tried to wiggle out of her father's arms so she could investigate what was happening. Richard held her firmly and pulled Ventura toward the meeting house.

It was an impressive building with wood framing and stiff angle braces. Higher up rose the belfry, and above that, gleaming in the morning sun, was a thirty-foot spire topped with a cross.

Inside, there was an odor of old Bibles. Ventura gazed up the plaster walls to the exposed timber ceiling. Simple, but carefully carved pews faced a raised wooden pulpit. The pews were full of plain-dressed folk, their eyes riveted on the pulpit. Standing behind it, leaning over menacingly and pointing his finger at his audience, was the minister. His shoulder-length curls bounced angrily as he talked, and his piercing eyes stared accusingly. Except for the rise and fall of his gritty voice, the church was deathly still.

Ventura couldn't understand all of it, but he was saying something about Election passing through godly loins of parents. She didn't like the tone of the minister's voice, but maybe she could get used to it.

"Let's find a seat," whispered Richard, starting down the aisle. Venture tiptoed behind, Verity gurgling into her small fist. The minister looked up, eyes boring into their faces. Heat rose on Ventura's cheeks and her mouth went dry. The minister waited, scowl on his face, until they quickly took a seat.

Giving them a condescending blink, he began again, repeating many of the same rules Mrs. Griggs had spoken the day before. The parishioners listened respectfully, waiting until the minister left the pulpit before they moved down the aisle.

When Ventura stood up to leave, she heard a woman's voice behind her. "God speaks to me directly. I know he does, even though I do not follow the path this minister has so carefully laid down."

Ventura turned to see an intelligent-looking blonde woman, a few years older than she was, staring back at her. Her face was angular, with a long thin nose and wide eyes. Although she was a small woman, there was a steady, cool decisiveness about her. "Mary Hazzard," she said, extending a hand.

Ventura shook Mary's hand and introduced her husband and daughter. "New here, aren't you?" Mary said, leaning forward. Although she didn't look one bit like her, for an instant, Ventura was back in Clara's house, listening to Maria do Valle gossiping. "I can tell you're new from your clothes," she said, winking at Verity. The baby sucked her thumb and made happy noises. "Why not come back to my house. We can talk about the lecture. I have some delicious things to say."

Ventura looked at Richard questioningly. He nodded and they followed Mary home. Her house was like the others on the square, clapboard with a big fireplace. When Mary opened the door, the smell of strong coffee and the sound of female voices rushed out to meet them.

Six women sat around a long oak table, drinking coffee and chattering gaily. Ventura surged forward as if she was back in Clara's kitchen, feeling the warmth of so long ago.

Mary hushed the women and found a spot for Ventura and Richard. "Can it be true that we must be elected to the Church?" she said, her eyes flashing excitement. "Is it only through careful obedience and strict attention to religious duties that we can attain full membership?"

A plump woman with thick curls said, "But doesn't God choose who shall be in his Church through the minister?"

A woman with eyes of green and hair wavy with a coppery red said, "Yes, is it not necessary to follow as the minister has prescribed or suffer eternal punishment?"

Mary tapped her cup. "But isn't it possible that from my own meditations, I could communicate directly with God, like the sudden hearing of an inner voice, which could come to me, leading me in another path?"

There were a few gasps and then silence. The discussion finally picked up again and a few more women wandered in and took seats at the table. Mary came over and stood by Ventura. "Well, what do you think of our meeting?"

Ventura smiled. "I think you put some ideas in their heads and that's good."

"I thought you'd like it." She turned quickly and linked arms with Ventura. "Have you had some refreshment?" Ventura shook her head. "Your husband can get you something to eat while I take you to meet someone." Mary motioned Richard toward the coffee and sweetcakes, then she pulled Ventura to the side.

Standing by herself, leaning lightly on a cane, was an old woman with long white hair. She wore a pointed cap on her head and a tattered cape hung loosely around her narrow shoulders. Her eyes were big and dark with deep wrinkles at the corners. There was an open, trusting look on her face and something of Clara in her glance. "This is Sigrid," said Mary proudly.

The woman's fingers shone in the firelight, long and thin and graceful. Ventura took Sigrid's hand and shook it, feeling a surge of heat. The old woman smiled a toothless grin and said, "You liked what Mary said, didn't you?" Her eyes sparkled with mischief and energy.

Ventura nodded. "Yes, I liked what Mary said. I've seen too much bad done by people who claim to represent God. It is refreshing to hear that we may all be able to communicate with our Maker."

Sigrid smiled and patted Ventura's hand. "You have powerful hands, my dear. Have you ever used them?"

Ventura nodded. "I was a healer in Spain, but the Inquisition put a stop to that."

"And that's why you've come here, as we all have. But be careful, there are persecutors here, too."

"Yes, we saw the stocks."

"I believe there will be more evil things happening here than simple embarrassments, but no one believes an old woman like me." She shrugged sadly and ambled away, leaning heavily on her cane.

Ventura followed her. "Wait. I want to talk to you some more."

Sigrid stopped and turned to face the younger woman. "You want to return to your healing work again, don't you?" Ventura nodded. "Come to my house tomorrow and we will talk. I live past the square on Sutter Lane. Ask anyone, they will direct you." With that, she walked out of Mary Hazzard's house, leaving Ventura standing at the door.

***

Cotton Winthrop, minister for the Village of Salem, sat in his hall, fuming. He had heard the remark Mary Hazard had spoken in the meeting house that morning. He bit the skin on his fingers angrily. Blasphemy, that's what it was. Who did she think she was? If God's grace was free, why then almost anyone might reach Heaven. Besides, if people did not dress in black clothes and quote the Bible and respect the clergy, then how was he supposed to be able to tell when they were being good?

He clasped his hands in prayer, bowed his head, and asked for an answer. But no divine response was forthcoming. His anguished eyes looked up toward the low ceiling, searching the cracks and crevices, as if there might be a sign to be found there.

***

Richard came running down the street to the Glover house. He arrived in the hall, winded and red-faced to find Ventura spinning wool. He watched her fingers pulling the furry mass of dark fluff until thread whirled and clicked on the spindle. Gradually his breath slowed. Verity crawled toward him and he picked her up and held her, smelling her sweet smell.

Ventura looked up at him. He could see from her face that she knew something was wrong, so he said, "The news in the square is that Mary Hazzard has been ordered to leave Salem Village."

The spindle stopped clicking and her brow wrinkled. "Leave? Why she's one of the most interesting and intelligent people here. Why would anyone want her to leave?"

Richard shrugged and came over to put a hand on her shoulder. "Maybe that's the problem. She's stirring up people, making them question the Church."

Ventura clasped his hand. "Isn't there any place for people who have different ideas?" she whispered.

He bent down to embrace her. "I don't know, Ventura. I don't know."

***

Ventura stood at the window watching Richard farming in the field, his muscular body tensing as he worked. He stopped often to glance toward the sea. At first she thought he was only resting, but then the raw and painful moment arrived when she realized what he was doing. The air in the hall grew suddenly cold and she hugged herself, trying to keep the sinking feeling from deepening in the pit of her stomach.

When he came inside, she hesitated, fearful to say what she knew was true. She put down the apple she was peeling and looked at him. "You're not happy here, are you?"

His eyes met hers, searchingly. "I'm happy with you and Verity, but I miss the sea." He walked over and buried his face in her hair. His voice sounded soft and loving in her ear. "I hear there's a ship in Salem harbor for repairs and I thought I'd find out about what kind of jobs they may have." Then his voice turned to excitement and hope, "I don't think I'm a good enough farmer to make enough for us to live on, and if we want to buy the house---"

Ventura swallowed, helplessness lying out like white bones in the desert in front of her. "What am I going to do without you?" she said, tears brimming over in her eyes and running down her cheeks.

He gently wiped the tears away with his hand. She opened her arms, relinquishing just enough space for him. "Oh, Ventura---" he moaned, revealing the agony he felt about his decision.

She shook her head. "No, I'm not going to start an argument. If it's what you must do---" She looked away so he couldn't see the pain she felt. "Then it's what you must do." Her voice trembled and she fell against him and sniffed. Finally she said, "I won't claim I'll like it, but I'll manage." She sniffed her tears back, hoping she was acting brave.

He kissed her forehead tenderly. "You won't be alone. You'll have Verity and Sigrid and your healing---"

She wanted to scream and cry out and stamp her foot, but she saw the look in his eyes and knew it was no use. Softly she said, "I know I have them. But they're not enough, they're just not enough."

He went on in an impassioned voice. "Of course, they may not need me, and even if they do, I probably won't be gone more than a year or so."

She clung to him more tightly. A year or so. She didn't know if she could bear it.

***

Richard stood in Braddock's Boat Yard. The warm morning sun brought out the pleasant odor of fresh-sawn timber. It mingled with the scent of pitch a stocky man was applying to a newly-finished brig. The thundering of hammers filled the yard, punctuated by brief pauses when the chanting of rope-makers across the cove took over. "How long 'til she's seaworthy?" shouted Richard.

The man turned and Richard could see his sallow face and bulging eyes. "You can see the keel is done, but we've a lot to do yet." Richard looked at the mighty ship's skeleton reaching skyward amid the web of scaffolding. The shipwrights swarmed over it like so many ants. The man smiled at him, "Looking for work?"

Richard nodded. "Yes, I want to get back to the sea again."

"Ever been on a whaler?" Richard shook head. "No matter, looks like the sea is in you, and you could learn fast. The wages are high and you'd share in the profits of any whale that's speared." Richard nodded, feeling a shiver of excitement starting inside him at the idea of harpooning a whale.

A month later, Richard stood looking at the completed whaling brig, the Salem, his arm securely around Ventura. He was explaining the ship to Verity, pointing out the masts and standing gaff. Ventura made a half-hearted attempt to look, but her heart was aching with missing him already.

Verity giggled and pointed above her head. "Yes, my dear, those are the cranes we'll use to hoist in the whaleboats. And look up there, see the canvas thing? That's the crow's nest. The look-out will be up there watching for whales when we're out at sea."

He sighed and looked at Ventura. "Isn't she a beauty? And she's so strong."

Ventura felt a stab of jealousy. How could he talk so endearingly about a bucket of wood and a few sails?

Undaunted, Richard kept pointing out features of the ship to his daughter. "See the brig up there and all those barrels of oil." He squeezed Ventura. "What a beauty!"

She leaned against his body, taking in the smell of him, the feel of his arms around her and the sound of his voice. She couldn't believe they were really going to be apart again. Somehow, she had to survive without him.

***

George Veneble, first mate on the Salem, was a bully. He was a bear of a man, six feet tall and heavy and he smelled of medicines and tobacco. His hair and beard were black and curly and his eyes danced with fury. He carried a cat-o-nine tails with him as he walked around the brig, getting it into full working order.

Many of the men felt the scourge of that whip their first day out because they did not move fast enough to please George. Richard gritted his teeth and pulled at the long oar, feeling grateful that he was not one of the very young men aboard on their first tour on the sea. Their backs would be bloody until they learned how to move on the rocking deck.

When Richard's time at the oars was complete, George's growling voice was at his ear, saying something crude and threatening, ordering him to the boats. He and nine others stepped to the railing. They hoisted and grunted, forcing the small wooden boats over the side. They lifted and shoved until Richard's arms ached and his back rippled with pain. It was not until sometime later that the first mate let them go to their rest, satisfied they could work the boats.

Richard laid in his cot, mouth working in anger. He knew the crew had to be good at what they did. In pursuit of a whale, the men had to be handy with the paddles and stealthy in hearing the whale so as not to frighten it. Whales have poor eyesight, but their hearing is very keen. Even so, this first mate was going to be trouble.

The next day on his watch, the cry came loud and clear. "Men overboard!" Richard ran to the side just in time to see three of the younger men deserting ship. They were in one of the small boats, heading toward shore.

"She's a floating hell," one of the men shouted back to the ship, shaking his fist in anger.

Richard shouted at them. "Do you know where you're going?

"We'll drift into a friendly distant port," shouted one.

"Maybe we'll be beachcombers on some balmy island," shouted another.

Richard just shook his head. They were doomed. There were no friendly ports near, nor any balmy islands. Huge bulk shivering, the first mate let out a bellow of laughter at the stupidity of the men. Then he snapped his cat-o-nine tails over his head. "Back to work!" he shouted. Richard stepped back to his oar wondering if leaving his wife and daughter had been a good idea after all.

Weeks later, the cry came, hoarse and excited from the masthead. "There she blows. There she breeches!" Three times the length of the brig, the whale leapt far into the air and landed on his back with a blow so loud it shook the ship.

Before the whaling boat could even be lowered, the sperm whale dove deep, huge girth buckling and pouring water out wide around him. "He knows he's been spotted," shouted one of the men in a reedy voice.

Richard looked at Charters. He had a wiry body that believed its strength. Of all the men he'd met on this tour, Charters was the one he trusted. The mate had saved Richard a few times from the burn of the whip and was more knowledgeable than most aboard. "He'll stay under water one hour by the watch, said Charters. "That's when we'll get him."

The men danced around or jumped in the air, clapping and rubbing their hands together at the excitement that was to come. "Keep the ship close to the wind," shouted Captain Chadwick, a big man with slicked ebony hair and a quality of restless impatience about him. "And get the boats ready to lower as soon as he rises, for he's a big one and will put up a dandy fight."

Richard watched the sea until his eyes blurred. Then, with a tremendous shudder of the sea, the whale burst to the surface just feet from the brig. "Take in the light sails, haul up the courses, haul back the main yard and lower down the boats," shouted the Captain.

All hands streamed forward to lower the whaleboats into the foamy water. Thirty feet long and six feet wide at the center, the boats were light and made for speed in either direction.

Richard scrambled down the side of the brig toward his vessel, the ocean wild beneath. The whaleboat rose and lowered towards the bulkwards one minute and dropped down halfway to the keel the next in its fight against the waves. Richard clamored down the ladder expertly, but one of the younger boys paused, then slid down, finally falling into the whale boat, a gash of red deepening on his leg.

The boat ahead of Richard's moved out, buoyant and graceful, cutting through the water, dancing over the sea. Richard was in the first mate's boat and Venable was not about to let another boat beat him to his prize. He yelled and bullied, at times using his cat-o-nine tails on a crew member who didn't pull fast enough to suit him. Every man stretched every muscle to get to the whale. As their boats drew near, the whale dove down, tail splashing, water nearly capsizing them, before the huge mammal came up to the surface again in another spot.

Richard's whole body burned and he wondered how long he could keep up the pace. The crew grunted and rowed for three hours and still the whale dove and evaded them. "Pull away, boys!" shouted Venable, his whip whizzing over Richard's head and striking the man in front of him.

Backs to the whale, the men were totally dependent on the boat header to steer them. The skinny man cocked a defiant eyebrow at them, using a tiller and his deep voice to discipline them. The harpooner, a big man with a tangle of hair and sinister gate of teeth, pulled the forward oar until he was next to the whale. "Stand up and let him have it!" shouted the mate.

Against what he knew was good whaling form, Richard glanced behind him at the whale. The sight was enough to unnerve him. The creature was as big as any ship he had ever seen and its jaws were open, showing rows of horrifying teeth. The harpooner held steady to his weapon, then at the exact moment before the whale swallowed them, he drove the three foot long iron deeply into flesh. The whale took a violent plunge, reacting to the painful shock of attack, throwing his enormous tail high in the air and lashing the sea into a violent foam.

Richard's boat surged upward, then stopped, suspended in the air an instant, before it was pulled forward with such a ferocious jerk, he thought his head would come apart from his body. "Here we go on the sleigh-ride," shouted Charters, and they were towed, full speed, behind the whale.

"Peak your oars," shouted Venable and the crew rested their oars at an acute angle with the gunwale. Richard could see nothing but a blur while their boat thudded and trembled through the water.

Eventually the whale exhausted himself and the boats closed in for the kill. "When I tell you to, give 'er the dart solid!" shouted Venable, while the harpooner readied himself. "Now, boy, now!" shouted the mate, and the weapon spun into the whale to the hilt. Enraged, the whale reared up and headed for the boat. "Stern all, boys, for dear life, or he'll knock us into the briny deep and we'll be food for the sharks!"

The crew hurriedly reversed their oars and backed the boat away from the angry beast. "He's right on us!" Richard stared at the creature whose mouth was open ten canyons, ready to swallow them up.

By some miracle, the cavernous mouth missed them and the whale sped by. The boat overtook him and the lanceman hurled his razorsharp five-foot shank into the whale's pectoral fin. The prize was theirs. A thunderous din went up as the men saw their victory and shouted in relief.

Like a giant faucet opening its spout, the sea surrounding the beleaguered beast crimsoned with blood. It poured from all sides like rapids over a cliff, churning the white brine into a troubled, scarlet whirlpool. In desperate agitation, the whale swam furiously, wallowing in the seething red pond. He arched his body in rapidly narrowing circles until the flurry abated, then he rolled into view, spouting great gushes of body fluids into one terrifying fountain above them. "His heart's burst, we have him now!" shouted the mate.

A roar of pleasure and excitement went up. Richard felt better than he had since he left port. Maybe even better than his last night of splendorous passion with Ventura. With her, there had been that rush, that build-up of exquisite tension, then the release of unspeakable pleasure. With the whale, the release was more intense, having narrowly eluded death.

Sometime later, Richard laid in his cot wondering why such a marvelous beast had to be killed at all. Seeing the wondrous creature chopped and carved into pieces to be sold for oil in some port, he vowed this would be his first and last whaling voyage.

## 14

"Ventura, this is John Corwin," said Mrs. Griggs. Ventura turned and looked into the tall man's deep brown eyes. He was not a handsome man, but he was serious and polite, and he leaned down to look at her, gazing into her eyes for so long that she felt a rush of heat on her cheeks.

His voice was masculine, but soft. "What did you think of the meeting, Mrs. Hasleton?"

She smiled at him, feeling a tingly feeling rising in her body. "Well, I---" She felt confused. It was not like her to be at a loss for words.

He took her arm and guided her forward. "It was a complicated message, was it not?" He had a posture somewhere between a dignified churchman and a pirate, and people stepped aside, feeling his presence. "May I have the pleasure of walking you home?" he asked when they reached the door.

A surge of excitement and fear crept through her. It was wonderful to be with a strong man again, smelling his male odor, feeling his attentive voice in her ears. Wonderful and forbidden.

She lay in bed later that night, her mind a tangle of confusing feelings. She missed Richard so much her body yearned for his caress. Yet, this very day, she had stood next to John Corwin, stretching to feel the touch of his arm on hers and the sensation of his breath in her hair.

Unable to sleep, she crept out of bed. Feet ice cold on the hardwood floor, she moved quickly to the table in the hall. She pulled a mantilla over her trembling body and took out her writing case. She sat down and stared into the red embers hissing in the fireplace. She'd just write to Richard. That would relieve the terrible feelings of guilt plaguing her. She loved Richard and no one else. It was just being alone for so long that made her body ache for a man's touch. For John Corwin's touch.

She shook her head and then burst into tears. "No," she whispered. "I will not give in to it. It is but a passing flash of my weak body." She rubbed her burning eyes, then she slowly picked up her pen and began to write.

***

John Corwin's voice pleaded softly, filling the Hasleton kitchen. "But Ventura, let me help you. You're all alone here and a young girl like Verity needs a man's firm hand. I can see she has gotten the best of you already."

Ventura set her jaw. "Verity is a fine, bright child and she is just fine."

"But Ventura," he argued, "it is usual for a child of her age to be apprenticed. Of course, Verity is not a bad child, in fact she is a very dear girl, but it is time for her to begin to act like an adult."

Ventura looked at Verity. Her small daughter sat at the table, drawing a picture. Her tiny face twisted in concentration and her hands moved eagerly over the page. Verity was just a child. There was no need for her to go anywhere.

John Corwin smiled at Ventura, making it difficult for her to concentrate on his words. "But she could learn some very helpful skills as an apprentice." He turned and looked at the little girl. "Come now, Verity, wouldn't you like to learn to be a baker or a housewife or---"

Full of fear, Verity's eyes found Ventura's. "Mother, do I have to?"

"No dear, Mr. Corwin is just asking you a question."

Verity's eyes returned to her paper and John continued. "Ventura, can you really afford to feed two mouths? I know your husband is not here to provide for you. I would be happy to do so, but you have declined my offer many times."

Ventura looked into John's eyes. It was true she was having a difficult time feeding Verity with only her healing fees. Most people paid her with a few pennies or a piece of fabric or jewelry. Still, there were some things more important than money. She finally said, "No John, I know you're only trying to help, but I've made up my mind. Verity stays with me."

After Sunday meeting, Mrs. Griggs came up to Ventura and said, "If you want to be a respected member of the community, you should apprentice Verity to one of the better families. She will learn better manners when she is brought up in a home other than her own. Besides, you show that girl entirely too much affection, it hurts any discipline you hope to provide for her."

Ventura looked at Verity. "But affection is what she thrives on. Look at her. There is no better statement than that about the way she is being brought up."

Mrs. Griggs clicked her teeth. "But it's not right. Even the minister agrees in this."

Ventura felt a quaver of doubt, followed swiftly by anger. "You've spoken to him about this?"

Mrs. Griggs nodded. "Well, only in passing."

Ventura cleared her throat and said softly, but firmly. "Now, you listen to me. I've lost my husband to the sea and I won't lose my daughter, too. If I have to, I'll take on more work. I'll do whatever it takes to feed Verity. Now, if you two don't stop this, I shan't sit with you at meeting again." Mrs. Griggs nodded and stepped back.

John Corwin smiled at her. "Perhaps you're right, Ventura." He offered his arm.

She took it. And then she sailed out of the meeting house on angry feet.

***

John Corwin sat in meeting, staring at Ventura, taking in her lustrous black hair, luminescent skin and faultless profile. There was no woman in Salem Village who could evoke the feelings that Ventura did in him.

Her hands were so perfect in the way they moved across the hymnal, and her body so graceful as it arched and shifted when she stood to recite or sat down in her pew again. Why was God punishing him? He had to have this woman, yet he knew it was wrong. She was married.

He stared at the minister and thought about it. There must be some way he could have her. Perhaps her husband would die. But then again, he was young and healthy. Maybe he would be mortally injured on that whaling expedition.

But he couldn't count on it. If there were only some way he could guarantee such an occurrence without being directly responsible. He had to stay in the background. If he did anything that directly implicated him, it would be considered a sin. But maybe there was some way he could increase the chances of Ventura Hasleton becoming a widow.

He leaned back into the pew and sighed. She was such a beautiful woman, someone he deserved, so unlike the plain ignorant women in Salem Village. Since his wife had died in childbirth five years ago, he had been alone, consumed in grief.

It was only when he first saw Ventura Hasleton that the old sensations of want had crept into his loins. At first he had tried to pry that spoiled little girl away from her, but that hadn't worked out. He scowled at Verity. Ventura was high-spirited, that was true, and she had a mind of her own. Well, it didn't matter, there would be plenty of time when the girl was sleeping or in school for him to be with her mother.

He looked back at Ventura and felt his lust rise. He put his hands in his lap and tried to quiet his heart. It surprised him how intense his feelings were for this woman. They were stronger than anything he had felt for Ruth, and she had been his wife. When he wasn't with Ventura, she was all he thought about. It was a wonderful feeling, but so bewildering. His thoughts had even caused him to make a few bad business decisions and that couldn't be allowed to go on. It was time to end this and settle things so Ventura was his.

He glanced back at her and wondered if it showed, if she could tell how much he wanted her. He forced his eyes away, afraid she might see him looking at her and guess what was in his mind.

It wasn't until several days later that John hit on a plan to make Ventura his. He was walking home from his shop, thinking he was not without influence in Salem Village. After all, he was a wealthy merchant and well-known; that should count for something in this matter.

The smells of cooking food and stale ale reached his nose and he looked up. The dockmaster's dull gray eyes and ugly face grinned back at him from Fisher's Tavern. Of course, Sam Pritchard. He would be just the person to fix this thing.

John hurried inside and took a seat opposite Sam. The dockmaster's wild hair fell into his eyes, and his noise and motion filled the room with jokes, guffaws and rambunctious gestures.

John's quiet voice calmed him. "How do sailors receive their commissions on a ship?"

Sam took a bite of his lamb pie and chewed it coarsely, leaving a path of juice running down his chin. "Well now, that depends on the ship and the sailor." He picked up his ale and guzzled half his pint.

"What if you found out about an especially good sailor, would you recommend him to captains and first mates for their voyages?"

Sam glanced down at the gold pieces John Cowin had stacked on the table in front of him and swallowed hard. Then he wiped his mouth with the back of his hand. "That all depends on how the sailor is, see---"

John took a few more gold pieces out of his pocket, rattled them, and then added them to the pile of gold sitting in front of Sam. "How good would he have to be?" said John, winking at Sam and motioning to the tavern-master to bring over a bottle of rum and pour a drink. "Maybe you could let me know when he's a good enough sailor."

John kept adding gold to the pile until Sam put his hand up and shoved the glimmering pieces into his lap. John smiled and pushed the rum bottle toward Sam. "The man's name is Richard Hasleton. I want you to make sure he is placed at the top of your list of recommendations."

Sam smiled and picked his teeth with his finger. "Ah, Richard Hasleton. He's the best sailor on my list, yes siree."

***

The smells of fresh apple pie and bacon lingered in Ventura's kitchen. "What is it, Mommy?" asked Verity, pulling on her mother's sleeve.

Her mother's eyes scanned the letter, first for the words of love, then for a sign that Richard would be coming home at last. Halfway into the first paragraph she let out a whoop, picked up Verity and swung her around. "He's coming home. Your father's coming home!"

"When Mommy, when?" The little girl's eyes brightened and she rubbed her small foot against her mother's leg excitedly.

"He says here, the exact day and time are uncertain due to the weather, but it should be sometime soon."

Verity yanked hard on her mother's sleeve, pulling her arm down and making it impossible to read the rest of the letter. "Can we go to the harbor and wait, Mommy, can we?" she squealed.

"Umm hmm. Now just let me finish reading, will you?" She gave Verity a disapproving glare and Verity let go, but not without a little pout. "He says kiss my darling daughter for me," said Ventura, bending down to kiss Verity on the cheek and then hug her tightly. "Yes, we can go to the harbor. We'll go this very afternoon."

Wearing their best dresses, hair brushed and shining, Verity and Ventura went to the harbor. Above them, seagulls broadened out their wings and hung like kites in the damp salt air. Mother and daughter waited, pacing up and down the creaking dock until an ugly man with wild black hair stepped forward and waved his arms. "Waiting for a ship, Mrs.?"

Ventura nodded. "The Salem. My husband comes in on that ship any day now. I thought perhaps today." She looked up at the sound of the whistle of a ship.

The man consulted his dock-master's list. "Aye, the Salem. What be your husband's name?"

"Hasleton, Richard Hasleton. Do you know him?"

The man gave her a strange look, spit behind him and said, "No mam, I sure don't, but that ship hit some bad weather and won't be in today."

"Thank you," said Ventura dejectedly. She took Verity's hand and they headed back home, a feeling of sadness enveloping them both.

The next morning dawned bright and sweet with the smell of dew-laid dust, grass and herbs filling the air. A robin was busy plastering his house nearby and song sparrows sat on spotted eggs in the oak above. Ventura and Verity worked in the garden, their hands deep in the dark soil. A noise startled her and Ventura looked up. Pushing a clump of hair out of her eyes, she wiped her face on her apron and stared down the road.

She let the hoe drop to the ground and her heart surged in her chest. Then she was running, moving as fast as she could toward the tall figure. He was already coming at full speed, a big smile on his face. Then she heard him call her name and she ran into his arms, squeezing him tightly. The smell of sea covered his clothes and his whiskers tickled when she kissed his face.

A quick push from behind and they were nearly knocked off their balance. Ventura looked down to see Verity, butting her head into her father, grabbing his legs, squealing with delight, then begging to be picked up. The three of them stood together hugging for a long time until Ventura finally pulled back again to see his face. She traced the deep lines the sun had cut into his brow and drank in every detail about him. Finally she said, "You're so thin. Come inside and I'll feed you."

***

Long after Verity's soft breath of sleep had overtaken the room, Richard dazzled Ventura with tales of his travels to unknown lands. When the fire had burned down to ashes, he carried his little daughter to her room and lit the way to their bed.

Months of separation had not killed Ventura's passion. She sat beside him on the soft cotton quilt, drinking in the look of his brow, the shape of his nose, and the curve of his lips. Slowly, her eyes met his and she could neither speak, nor move. His arms reached out and pulled her close, his breath warm with words of love in her ear.

Her pulse quickened and warmth spread between her legs. She nestled close to him and he tucked her long hair away from the side of her face, promising never to leave her again. Her doubts evaporated and she celebrated the moment of their reunion. Hugging him to her, she delighted in his smell, praying that what he whispered to her was true.

Hooking his arm around her waist, he tightened his embrace and drew her closer. Lips parted, he bent to kiss her, sending her heart speeding. Sighing with urgency, she kissed him back, until her body tingled with desire. His hands touched her gently, coaxing her longing until her body shuddered with awe. Somewhere outside, the love call of a distant bird swirled in her head, mingling with the sweetness of the moment. Then a soft burst of love flowed through her and she clutched him tightly.

When she awoke in the morning, he was by her side, piling money on the quilt. A shaft of light from the window fell on his hair and she thought she had never loved him more. "There's enough here to pay for the house and still buy a few things for us," he said, kissing her ear lobe.

She leaned closer and hugged him, intoxicated by his smell of strong soap and cinnamon. When he said, "Let's go to the village and spend some of this," she ran to change her clothes and get Verity.

They wandered through the shops in Salem Village, buying up fresh fish, oranges and sausages. Richard picked out a bolt of the best linen so Ventura could make herself and Verity dresses for Sunday Meeting.

They spent many sunny days by the sea, picking berries and gathering shells. On the days Ventura helped at a birthing or brought herbs to someone in pain, Richard took Verity to the wharf or they worked in the garden, harvesting vegetables.

Ventura thought she couldn't be any happier until the day Richard turned to her with face flushed and eyes pleading. They were in the hall, drinking coffee and eating their morning cakes. Verity had already gone outside to play on the swing Richard had made for her. The shimmering maples caught rare shafts of light and sent them through the window.

Ventura's hand paused in mid-air when she heard Richard's words. "I've an offer on a merchant ship as first mate and I---" He lowered his voice and took her hand in his. He kissed her palm softly, then more passionately, awakening a deep yearning in her.

But she pushed passion aside and let anger grow. "You're going to accept the offer, aren't you?" she shouted. She pulled away and ran to their room, his words pulsating in her mind. Throwing herself on to the bed, she repeated over and over that he wasn't going to leave her again. But he was going to leave her again, she had seen it in his eyes.

Then he was beside her, pulling her into his arms. "My dear Ventura, it won't be so bad. I'll be away awhile and then I'll be back here again." He kissed the tears from her cheeks and tried to soothe her with soft squeezes and words of love.

But she pulled away, feeling the anger rising inside her like a giant animal she had suddenly unleashed. "It's not the money, is it? Is it?" she demanded.

"No," he whispered in her hair, "it's the sea. I have to be there, feeling the power of her, the---"

A terrible feeling of emptiness welled up inside her. "Don't you love me and Verity at all?"

"Of course, I love you both. Very much." He stared into her eyes and then his lips were burning into hers. Their bodies locked in mortal battle until passion overtook her and she reached for him hungrily.

Ventura laid in bed the night Richard left for sea, eyes tracing the empty place beside her in the bed. She shivered, not from cold, but from loneliness and anguish. And a terrible idea gripped her and would not let go: what was wrong with her that she could not hold him?

She tossed and rolled that night, trying to figure out the puzzle. Maybe it wasn't her at all. Maybe there was something in Richard, something in his background that made it impossible for him to stay with her, to commit to a family, to commit to her.

Time passed and Richard came back for a few months of bliss. But then, as always, the sea claimed him again and Ventura was alone and lonely. Her only pleasures were her healing visits and her time with Verity.

On one especially beautiful summer day, they planned a picnic and spent hours packing a wooden basket with cheeses and breads and fresh vegetables from their garden.

"Can we go to the ocean?" asked Verity, closing the basket and setting it on the table.

Ventura nodded. "It is a perfect day for it." She looked at her daughter. Verity was so much like her father, it delighted Ventura to listen to her talk and be with her.

Verity smiled. "Then come on, the ocean awaits!" She pulled her mother out of the house and down the walk. They stopped along the way to pick wild strawberries that gleamed and glistened from under their green leaves like priceless jewels. They ate most of what they had picked on their walk, savoring their sun-warmed sweetness.

They ate their lunch sitting on a sand dune. Afterwards, Ventura sat for hours, her hand shielding her eyes from the dazzling surf. She looked out and wondered where on that vast surface Richard was. The wail of the gulls reached her ears like flutes of sorrow and her body ached for his while her mind hungered for his companionship.

Verity was off to the rocks that lay near the shore, hunting gull eggs or digging for clams and crabs, her blond hair streaming behind her in the breeze, her slim body moving gracefully along the white sands. Then she darted back to her mother, cheeks pink from the salt air, bucket full of her catch. They sat together in the fading light, capturing the last rays of warmth from the sky.

They waited for low tide, rushing to collect the tawny rock weed that grew under high water. When the sun dipped below the horizon, they collected their things and hurried home to cook their clams and crabs in the great iron pot that hung in the fireplace. After their meal, Ventura cooked down the rock weed into an ash and saved the kelp to fertilize their garden.

***

Verity was with her mother on a healing visit when she discovered the gift in her hands. They shook with warmth, the full force of power tingling through her fingers. She ran to her mother.

Ventura put her hands next to her daughter's. "Yes," she said, "you have the healing power. I can feel it."

Verity danced around until Ventura grabbed her and hugged her. When their excitement died down, Ventura held her daughter's face in her hands and said, "Now listen. Your power is only to be used for good. And you must never hold your hands over anyone for too long. That will do harm."

Verity stared at her hands, a look of wonder in her eyes. "What else do I do?"

"You must practice on yourself first, or on me. Only when you know how to control the touch will you be ready to heal."

For days after that, Verity practiced. She was proud of the power in her hands. By then she was a young lady of sixteen, with her father's thick hair bursting out from under her white cap like spun honey and her mother's dark searching eyes. The other girls in Salem Village spurned her, partly because of her beauty and intelligence and partly because she had not been apprenticed out and they thought she was odd to stay home with her mother.

A few weeks later, Verity sat in the meeting house with her mother, trying to listen to Reverend Winthrop, but she kept losing track of what he was saying. It was so tiresome. He kept repeating the same things over and over. To make the time pass faster, she looked out of the side of her eyes, making sure her head remained facing straight ahead. That way, no one would know she was studying the people around her.

John Corwin always sat near them. He seemed pleasant enough on the surface, but what her mother saw in him, she did not see. There was something nasty about him, although he always tried to be nice to her when her mother was around. But he didn't fool her. He had some evil plan in his head, something that involved her mother. She couldn't prove it, but there was something about the way his eyes followed her mother that proved her reasoning.

Verity glanced at the next pew and Absalon Winthrop, the minister's son. Although she had looked at him many times before, that day he seemed to be the handsomest man she had ever seen. His face, which used to be so thin and marked, was now clear and engaging. And his eyes, when they fastened on her in passing, were gentle and deep, the color of the dark walnut chest in Mrs. Grigg's house. She smiled at him, feeling her heart thud heavily in her chest.

***

Absalon Winthrop gazed across the aisle at Verity Hasleton. He had admired her for two years, but he was not yet old enough to marry. He would complete his apprenticeship with the Parris family in two months and then he would be free to do as he chose.

This time, when he looked at Verity, he sensed something in her eyes he had not seen before. Usually she looked right through him or fluttered her eyes and looked away quickly. But at that moment, she gave him a look of interest, a look of longing. Then something passed between them that made him feel like he did when he stood on the beach and watched the wild ocean crashing against the shore. Only this time, there was no ocean, just two people giving each another a silent message that only the other could receive. He sighed deeply, glorying in the rush of excitement that filled his body and dreaming about what might come.

It wasn't until much later at the corn husk that Absalon was to become sure about Verity's feelings for him. Absalon badgered Farmer Jacob, finally learning that Verity Hasleton would be there. After that, he spent every waking hour, dreaming about what would happen between them at the corn husk.

So as not to miss a moment with her, Absalon was at the farm by a quarter to seven. He was the first one there and he wandered around the barn, the odor of hay and horses strong in his nose. He stood under the high wood beams, near a pile of corn, trying to guess where the best place to sit might be. He was too shy to sit next to her. Besides, what if he had misread her glance? Maybe she was just being friendly.

Before he could do any more wondering, the rest of the young people burst into the barn, filling it with giggles and whispers. They sat down on the floor, boys alternating with girls.

Everyone was seated, and still no Verity. Just when his heart started to sink, she came flying in the door, warming something inside him. Blonde hair shimmering in the lamplight and skirt rustling, she took a seat next to Farmer Jacob's son. Absalon looked at her, his heart racing, and his mind wondering if she would look up him and favor him with a smile. But she was too busy, adjusting her skirt and squeezing her slim body into the small space the burly Andrew Jacob allotted her.

Before she had time to settle herself, farmer Jacob lumbered in, his big frame twice the size of the corn pile he was pointing to. "There will be a prize for whoever husks the final ear, so move quickly. Remember, any young man who finds a red ear gets to kiss every girl in the circle. And you, young women, if you find a red ear, you can kiss the young man of your choice."

After much tittering and whispering, farmer Jacob continued. "I'll be passing some jugs of fresh cider around to quench your thirst. When I signal you, begin. And remember, keep husking."

The farmer raised his arm and signalled them to begin. Each one grabbed an ear from the pile in the center of the circle and began stripping the covering from it and breaking the cob free from the last bit of stem. Absalon ripped off the sticky silk and pulled the moist green covering off, releasing the smell of fresh corn. He threw the cob in the pile and scrambled to grab another. He moved quickly, working himself into a frenzy, grabbing for ears and stripping them as fast as he could, all the while praying he would get a red ear and be able to kiss her.

Although the barn was cool, as the evening wore on, his clothes became drenched in perspiration until water dripped off his brow. By then his stomach was full of cider and his arms ached from the work, and still no red ears had been found.

Just when he'd almost given up, a squeal arose from the other side of the barn and Verity held up a red ear triumphantly. Absalon's heart trembled with hope and fear. Maybe, just, maybe she'd choose him.

Before he could recover, Verity stood in front of him, face smiling and flushed, hands reaching down to him. Some of the others hooted and clapped, some whistled or shouted his name. Absalon stumbled to his feet, his legs gone to sand. Her clean, fresh scent surrounded him. She stood on her tiptoes and placed her sweet warm lips next to his. They were soft as a thousand rose petals, filling his heart with a deep, unending ache of love. The crowd exploded into cheers. Encouraged, Absalon slowly gathered her about the waist and kissed her again. This time, long and hard.

Then farmer Jacob stepped between them and he said, "Okay, son, back to the husking." Absalon and Verity held a long steady look. To him, she was more beautiful than a fawn at sunrise. "Come on, son," said the farmer, laughing and winking. "You can walk her home when we finish." Absalon tore himself away, a furious blush on his face. He slumped back to the floor and grabbed the husk someone thrust into his hands.

***

Banking in the sky were great clouds. The moon blinked through them, shining on the oak leaves. Stars entangled themselves in the tall treetops, gleaming off Verity's hair. Absalon held her hand tightly, heart chugging, words trapped in his throat. Ahead, the smoke of the Hasleton's evening fire rose heavenward and a lamp shone from the gate.

They stopped in front of the house, her face silver in the night. She peeped through her hair and he looked into the sweet darkness of her eyes. She gave him a secret smile and his eyes fixed on her, his lips repeating her name softly. Dropping her lashes she gave him another smile.

He put his arm around her and marveled at how well it fit. He touched her hair as he might a fragile flower and she looked up, her eyes reflecting him. Ideas savage and tender poured through him, Encircling her arms around his neck, she pressed against him until he felt her passionate heart beating to his desire.

He kissed her then, believing nothing in his life could be so filled with splendor. She kissed back, her body straining against his. "Oh Verity, I love you, I love you," he said, then kissed her again. This time more passionately, more fully. Then he whispered her name into the darkness of the night until he gathered his courage to say, "Marry me, be my wife."

She pulled back, a dazed look on her face. "Marry you?" she said, running up the walk and halfway up the steps. "Marry you?" she whispered, turning at the door. Then she turned and said, "Yes, I'll marry you!" Before he could catch her, she pulled the door open and rushed inside.

He stood numbly, blushing stupidly, letting her words sink in. Then he rushed toward home, happy heels clicking over the cobblestones.

***

Verity hurried inside, shouting excitedly. "Mother, oh Mother! Something absolutely wonderful has happened."

Ventura stopped her spinning and turned to face her daughter. "Not so loud now, you'll wake up poor Mrs. Griggs." She smiled up at her grinning daughter. "Can I assume it had to do with the corn husking?"

Verity ran into her mother's arms. "Oh, yes, and Absalon Winthrop. Mother, he's just the most---"

Ventura hugged Verity and laughed. "The most wonderful man you've ever met?" she finished.

Verity pulled back, surprised. "But---but, how did you know?"

She hugged her daughter again, not wanting to let go of her. "When a young lady of sixteen says something wonderful has happened, what else could it be?" She stared over Verity's shoulder, seeing a desert of loneliness looming up before her.

The young woman blurted, "And he asked me to marry him and---"

Ventura pulled herself away regretfully and sat her young daughter down. "Slow down, dear. Let's have some coffee and talk about it."

Verity nodded, then went to pour two cups of coffee and take down the sweetcakes from the drawer. When they were seated at the table she said, "I'm just too excited to eat, mother. This is just the best thing that's ever happened to me. I mean, he actually kissed me and everything!"

Ventura smiled a bittersweet smile. "I know, dear. I'm happy for you." Ventura listened to her daughter chatter on, but inside she felt a tug of sadness. Verity was growing up too fast. Soon she'd be alone without either husband or daughter.

***

Looking lame and bent, Sigrid came to visit late that night. The old woman gingerly placed her body in one of the high-backed chairs in the parlor and removed her tattered cape. In the firelight, her hair glowed, pure white and shaggy. Her heavy wooden cane fell with a click against the chair. "Would you like some tea or coffee, Sigrid?" Ventura asked.

The old woman's wrinkled face glistened in the light and her dark eyes stared fondly at her friend. "No coffee. I have just come to warn you."

Ventura felt a tremor of fear. "Warn me?"

Sigrid nodded. "Remember when I told you years ago that evil was coming to this place?"

Ventura swallowed, picturing her days in the dungeon. "Yes, I remember what you said, but since nothing has happened, except for poor Mary Hazard---"

Sigrid's eyes turned brighter and she leaned forward in her chair. "Something has happened now that foretells the future and urges me to warn you." She lifted her hand and placed a boney finger to her chin. "All healers must be very careful. There are two who can speak against us and cause great harm. We must be very careful who we tell about our powers. There are those who seek to destroy us."

Ventura looked at Sigrid, trying to tell if this was just an old woman's fears or if something really was going to happen. She considered her words carefully before asking, "Do you have any proof?"

Sigrid shook her head and sucked in her lower lip. "Proof is not easy to come by when foretelling the future. But I did have a dream. A black woman and two children were in it. The little girls had their fingers pointed at a healer and there was death in the dream. Someone will die and it will be soon."

Despite the blazing fire, a cold draft passed through the room. It was as if some ghostly figure had entered. Ventura shuddered and dug her fingers into the smooth wood of her armrest.

A patter of feet on the wooden floor startled her and she turned to see Verity in nightdress, sticky-eyed and yawning. "Verity, you're up late. Can't you sleep?"

Verity rubbed her eyes, sighed and sat down in a high-backed chair by the fire. She sleeked her body and when she spoke, it was like the soft purr of a cat. "Oh, it's you, Sigrid. Is something wrong?"

Ventura patted her daughter's hand. "Sigrid has come to warn me."

Verity yawned again. "Warn you? About what?"

"She thinks there is evil here and that someone will die soon because of it."

Verity's face turned from a sleepy yawn into an incredulous scowl. "Evil? Here? In this quiet little village?" She shook her head.

Ventura shrugged and Sigrid just smiled wisely. After the old woman left, Ventura made chamomille tea and they sat at the hall table sipping it and talking. "Don't you think Sigrid's a funny old woman?" asked Verity, giggling into her hand.

Ventura nodded. "She is strange, but many things she has foretold have come to pass. I think she knows the future and we should listen to her." She took a sip of tea, forcing herself to swallow at the thought of the warning.

A tender vulnerability shown out of Verity's fragile dark eyes. "Evil and death? Can it be possible?"

Ventura told her daughter about Seville and the Inquisition, sparing no detail of her torture and imprisonment. "So, you see, I've seen worse things and in a town I thought was safe."

Verity shuddered. "They actually were going to burn you at the stake for helping people?"

Ventura nodded. "Yes, anything is possible. The healers in Salem Village will probably have to meet in secret and be careful who they tell about their powers."

Verity stared at her mother, a look of fear and disbelief on her face. Ventura put her arm around her daughter, wondering if she would be able to protect them both from what was about to happen.

# 15

Lying on the maple chest in the hall of Reverend Cotton Winthrop, next to the Bible, was a copy of the Reverend Michael Wigglesworth's Day of Doom. Its worn pages described the blessed in heaven looking down with eternal joy on the torments of the damned.

Next to the maple chest, sitting in high-backed chairs were Elizabeth Winthrop, age nine, and her cousin, Abagail Goodfellow, age eleven. They resembled two small prim matrons in their long gowns, aprons and kerchiefs, seemingly absorbed in their knitting. Although they looked like quite ordinary children, presenting a picture of household duty and discipline, underneath, a storm was brewing.

With curly red hair pouring down angelically over her shoulders, Elizabeth was a sweet, biddable child who was ready to obey anyone who spoke with conviction. But buried deep in her blue eyes, like the devil's own treasure, was a glint that reflected the warfare in her soul. And Abagail, had anyone looked, had the makings of a true hellion. With her thick lashes and soft brows, and a forehead smooth and white as cream, she, too, looked angelic. But when she smiled, it was the grim smile of someone who had seen much evil or perpetuated it.

Enduring the rigors of a strict upbringing and being exposed to her father's hell-fire sermons, Elizabeth was convinced she was going straight to Hades. How else could it be when for all of her nine years she had been sinning with her hands and tongue and probably every other part of her? Damnation was a fact of life for her, and she quivered and sobbed in her pew when she listened to her father speak.

She had just recovered from smallpox and had survived unscathed, her fresh complexion and strong little body testifying to her physical health. Her spiritual well-being was another matter. She was, like most of the children in Salem Village, trying to cope with the inhuman strain placed upon her by being raised in an adult world that had little understanding of the needs and capacities of children.

Abagail was a different story. She was more robust, and though just as relentlessly catechized, she took damnation, death and other unpleasant incidents as something scheduled to happen to someone else, especially people she didn't like. She was a smug child, sure of herself, and apt to act more like a parent than a playmate to Elizabeth. Somewhere along the way she had taken on the attitude that she would inherit salvation in the same way she would the family pewter.

At that moment, Abagail was thinking about the sermon she had recently attended, and in her mind, she was back in the meeting house, sitting in the pew beneath her uncle's pulpit, watching him in his black robe, impressive and strong. Knitting one and purling two, she remembered his sterile discussion of damnation and licked her lips with relish, wishing she had yelled out and stamped her feet in accordance with what was being said. Someone needed to bring some fire to his sermons and replace the dull words he spoke. But it wasn't only the sermon she yearned to enliven, she ached to make an explosive noise in Salem Village, even if her youth and upbringing prohibited it. She knew she would have been severely punished if she'd tried. A young girl was not supposed to give way to her impulses, so for the time being, she had only her imagination in which to revel and scream.

Of course, she could read the Bible and listen to her uncle talk about the Devil. She thought of him as an arch-criminal in the everlasting detective story being conducted by the Church. So, she looked forward to the next meeting, hoping there would be a lusty description of him and his doings.

As young as she was, Abagail was attuned to local gossip. She knew there were quarrels that approached bloodless feuds buried deep in the village consciousness, and that her uncle's two predecessors had been hounded out of the parish by the harsh criticism of the congregation.

While Abagail and Elizabeth were knitting in the hall, Reverend Cotton Winthrop was in his study, stewing over the preparation of his Sunday sermon. His fingers pulled the white curls of his wig into messy lumps while his piercing eyes flickered over the pages, pausing now and then to allow his thin lips to smile or his skinny hand to make a correction.

The room gave off a musty sourness, suggestive of hours spent cloistered away in clerical musings. It was a small and cold place, made large by the sparse furnishings. Believing suffering to be good for the character, he refused to let the slaves start a fire when he was working.

He wished more of his congregation were suffering. He was angry with them, and maybe even a little angry with God for what had happened. Since they had moved to Salem Village, it had been one calamity after another. First, the smallpox, then the ongoing Indian raids, which had taken some of his parishioners. Word was that John Stuart had been attacked on the road in front of his house by one of the savages. Then, of course, there was the growing uncertainly swirling in Cotton Winthrop's head and discussed in whispers and sometimes out loud by his parishioners, that New England had lost forever the near-independence it had enjoyed under the charter.

For all these reasons, the Reverend dropped his weary head into his hands and prayed. "Why have you forsaken us, Dear Lord. Why have you turned your countenance from us? Are we unworthy to be chosen as you have once chosen us?" Cotton Winthrop searched his heart for the cause of God's withdrawal. Was doomsday really imminent as he so often cautioned his parishioners? All signs pointed to the coming of the Kingdom of God at the close of the century.

"Repent," he regularly counseled his congregation, "for the Kingdom of God is at Hand."

But before that happened, before God took him to be with him or sentenced him to eternal damnation, Cotton Winthrop planned to get even. His parishioners did not show him the proper respect, and for that, they must pay.

It wasn't Christian the way they had pried and picked at his past when they had hired him. Yes, he had begun theological study at Harvard with all good intentions of taking a parish, but the idea of going into trade with the Barbados had pulled him way for a few years. Of course, it hadn't worked out all that well financially, so at the age of thirty-five, after much nagging from his wife, he had been bullied into accepting the call to Salem Village. It was a matter of profound humiliation that the only employment he could find without the benefit of a Harvard degree was this obscure little hamlet.

He closed the Bible, pushed back his chair and gazed out the window at the two men held captive in the stocks below. A small smile escaped his lips. He had already gotten somewhat even by keeping the congregation dangling for nearly a year, hinting he knew about their quarrels and history of not paying their ministers appropriately. After much wrangling and bargaining, he had demanded clear and permanent title to the parsonage and grounds. Somehow the dumb farmers had outsmarted him, misleading him so he finally agreed to a small salary, use of the parsonage only during occupancy, and denial of even such common courtesies as a wood spell.

He slammed his fist on the table, not even noticing the red welt that grew on his hand. Well, he would settle things very soon. Really, making him find even his own firewood. Blood pounded in his ears and anger filled his heart.

He had already punished them to some degree by refusing to ordain the deacons, and requiring they submit anew and undergo a long probation under his supervision. Some parishioners had been punished, too. His eagle eyes had searched out all iniquities in his church members and had made as many as possible do public penance in the stocks for the most trivial and excusable of offenses. Even at that moment, one of them sat on the bench below, his ugly face scowling at the jeering crowd.

While the Reverend gloated in the remote regions of his study, Bituba, one of his two household slaves, completed the household chores. Her huge brown hands pounded the freshly-washed linen, inhaling the clean soapy smell. Then she fetched water from the well, emptied the slops and scrubbed the floor she had recently sanded. She nodded in approval at the soft surface beneath her hands.

As she worked, she hummed a melodious island tune. Her wide face pinched with effort and her heavy bosom heaved as she moved in her characteristic waddle. Whenever she could, she stopped to smile or chat with Jim Indian, the other household slave.

Jim attended to the livestock and wood lot, gave a hand in Deacon Whitworth's ordinary and worked with him in the field. All the while, Jim's muscular body strained under his thick cotton shirt.

How she adored that handsome man. Reverend Cotton had brought the two of them from Barbados when he returned to the New World. She didn't know how she would have survived without Jim Indian watching over her during the day, sometimes helping her with the more difficult chores when the Reverend wasn't looking, and turning her body into a bewilderment of passion at night.

He would sneak into her bedroom on tiptoes, his thick finger pressed tightly against his lips, indicating the secrecy of the thing. Then he would drop his trousers and jump quickly into her bed, ready for the hours of pleasure he would provide her.

How that man could use his hands. He extracted every drop of her passion and pent-up tension. She loved Jim Indian as she had no other, and he was the only other living person she trusted. Whites were okay, but there was no telling when they would turn on you and leave you alone in your suffering.

Frosty New England was not to Bituba's liking. She was accustomed to a sunnier and more languid clime. To ease her load, she idled with Elizabeth and Abagail, who were under her direction during the many hours Mrs. Winthrop was out on errands of mercy. Bituba never asked the girls to help with the heavier household chores. Instead, she reserved the simpler tasks and errands for them. As a consequence, the little girls lived more like pampered princesses than Puritan children.

On that particular day, when Bituba finished her chores, she sought out Abagail and Elizabeth and tucked them away by her side in her snuggery by the fire. Elizabeth cuddled next to her, craving the touch and affection she never got from her mother. Bituba stroked her hair, pulling her to her ample breast in hugs. Her cushiony arm wrapped around Abagail cozily and the girls sat, listening to Bituba's slurred Southern speech. Old tales and nonsense rhymes wove out of her mouth like spun cloth.

At that moment she was telling a story about witchcraft. Bituba looked at the two girls and said, "There was a half-human thing in the corner. She had placed a spell on her cat sure as we sit here."

They shuddered, wondering if such things actually could happen. "How did she place a spell on the cat?" asked Abagail bravely.

Bituba tightened her arms around the girls. "Why, she made a little doll out of some cloth and a few sticks and she stuck a pin in the middle of it. And the very next day, that cat was bleeding and half-dead." The fireplace popped a cinder out at that moment and all three of them nearly jumped out of their seats. "Hush now, babies, it's only a fire plug. Don't you worry. Bituba will fetch it." She got up from the wooden bench and swept the cinder back into the fireplace. When she returned to her place, the girls were still trembling in fear. She cuddled them against her, humming softly.

After the girls recovered from their fear, Bituba continued. "'Course there was a few times I used wax to put my spell on someone who had done me wrong."

"How do you use wax?" asked Abagail.

"Why honey, you get a piece of wax that looks like what you trying to cast your spell over. Then you just close your eyes real tight like this." She squeezed her eyes tightly shut, wrinkling brown folds into her face. "Then you say your spell and light the wax and watch it burn." She paused for a minute, either for effect or to catch her breath, then she continued, her voice dropping down to a velvet smoothness. "Sure as we sitting here, that person will waste away to nothing until they fall down and die."

Silence ruled the room, the girls sitting entranced, fearful. Elizabeth was nearly hypnotized by the warmth radiating from Bituba and by the scary tales of voodoo and spells. She knew it was wrong, but inside her a battle was raging. Part of her said it was not the upright Puritan thing to do, and that she must be tampering with what her father would surely forbid. The other part of her was spellbound, and unable to resist. Eventually, the mystery of it all drew her under Bituba's spell like a fly into a spider's web. Those hours spent with Bituba were the only exciting times she knew, hours that made that part of her life a thrilling dream.

Abagail was more sophisticated about such matters. She knew for sure that what was being discussed was not God's work. She even felt a pang of guilt now and then, but that only added to the zest of the adventure. So, she listened, intent on learning to work some of the magic that Bituba knew.

"What else, Bituba, what else do you know?" whispered Abagail.

Bituba shook her head and said, "No, now that's enough for tonight. You little ones must be up to bed."

"One more thing, Bituba," begged Abagail.

Elizabeth's voice echoed insistently. "Yes, yes, tell us."

Bituba finally gave in. "All right, but then you little darlings must go off to bed." The girls nodded and smiled. "One thing I can do is go into a trance."

"What's that?" asked Elizabeth.

"Yes, show us!" shouted Abagail.

"First you close your eyes, like this." The brown-skinned woman closed her eyes and leaned back. Her breathing became slow and labored. As the girls watched, Bituba began to twist and contort and out of her mouth came strange raspy, animal-like sounds.

Elizabeth screamed, but Abagail shook her head in disapproval. "Don't be so afraid. Be quiet now."

Then as suddenly as the noises and movement had started, they stopped, and Bituba opened her eyes. "What happened? Was he here?" she demanded of the girls.

Abagail said, "Was who here? You made a lot of funny noises and shook your body all over. But I didn't see anybody."

Bituba smiled. "Oh mercy---I was back in Barbados and my daddy, yes, my very own daddy who has been dead these many years, came to visit me. He spoke to me just as clearly as I'm speaking to you now." The girls looked at each other and giggled, covering their mouths with their hands so Bituba wouldn't hear them. She scowled at them and pulled her body up straight. "All right. I can tell when somebody don't believe what I say. Off to bed now, my tricks are over!" She swatted each one lightly on the bottom and they disappeared up the ladder to their beds.

After that evening, Elizabeth was never quite the same. By the end of the month, she looked sickly and drawn. Bituba nursed her constantly, rubbing her down with wet cloths, oiling her skin and bringing her bowls of nourishing broth she brewed over the fireplace. In a few days Elizabeth recovered from her fever, but then other symptoms took over.

Instead of doing the small chores or errands assigned her, she began to forget things she was told to do, and her eyes took on a stare as if she were some place else. Sometimes she sat with her knitting for hours, hands poised, but motionless, eyes staring at the chest across the room or at the Bible resting on it.

Once when the Reverend found her sitting in the hall, staring straight ahead, he scolded her. Instead of eliciting the apology he expected, her limbs went rigid, her tongue fell out of her mouth and hung to the side, she barked like a dog, and her body arched backward.

To make matters worse, Abagail joined in, babbling and making rasping sounds, her body dropping down to the floor where she ran around on all fours. She barked and brayed until she fell on her back, writhing and screaming as if she were being tortured by the Devil himself.

Reverend Winthrop stood by, his mouth open, unsure of how to proceed. When both girls quieted down, he stumbled over to the chest, took the Bible in his hands, knelt beside them and began to pray. "Our Father, who art in heaven---"

Elizabeth screamed wildly, her voice a piercing screech. It set off Abagail who covered her ears, rose to her feet, stamped loudly, and drowned out his prayer.

Panicking at their reaction, Reverend Winthrop handed the Bible to Elizabeth. She hurtled it away, sending it bouncing across the floor. Face twitching with fear, the Reverend ran from the hall and out of the house.

When all was quiet inside, the two little girls got up, smiled at each other, and went back to their knitting. The episode was never discussed between them, but on some childlike level, they knew what they had done and were pleased with its outcome.

As the days passed, whenever Bituba or their father requested their help with a chore, the girls fell into a seizure or barked like a dog. Bituba never seemed fooled by these episodes. She merely walked away, leaving the girls where they fell. But Revered Winthrop took the occurrences seriously. Early one evening, totally bewildered by what was happening, he decided to take a firm hand on the situation.

***

The fire had burned down to red coals and the scraggly gray cat in the corner mewed, wanting to go out. Dr. Benjamin Hanover sat in his study, his rangy body hunched over his massive desk. His wide-mouthed face of agreeable ugliness twisted in a nervous tic and his thick hands pulled roughly at the iron gray of his full-buttomed wig. Looking at the large stack of unpaid bills in front of him, his tic twitched all the more. He had no idea how he was going to pay them.

He peered out through the dingy windows into the night. Salem Village was a small town, and although people were sick, wise women seemed to be stealing his practice out from under him. He had protested to Reverend Winthrop one day after meeting, but the man had only shook his head as if commiserating, while his eyes and mind were on other things.

A loud knocking on his door interrupted the physician's reverie. One glance at Reverend Winthrop's anguished face and he knew something terrible had happened.

"You must come and see my daughter, she---

"What's wrong with Elizabeth?"

"She's throwing fits and barking like a dog. And her cousin is similarly afflicted."

The physician nodded. "Sounds very strange." He threw on his velvet cloak to protect him from the chill wind blowing, then grabbed his cane, checking inside the head to make sure it was sufficiently filled with pills. Before leaving his study, he surveyed his book shelf, settled on a few volumes and quickly threw them, along with *Memorable Providences Relating to Witchcraft and Possession*, into a bag he had slung over his shoulder.

The two little girls were waiting for them in Abagail's bedroom, calm and pink-cheeked. They sat like two cherubs on the lamb-embroidered quilt, surrounded by a halo of bed curtain, holding each other's hands primly.

When Dr. Hanover stepped into the room, Abagail's body twisted in half, becoming so rigid he could not get her to sit up. She choked so badly that he thought she might stop breathing. She also shrieked and shouted, "The pain, the pain," and pointed to her abdomen.

Usually competent and self-confident in simpler emergencies such as broken bones, scaldings or smallpox, Dr. Hanover scratched his head and wrinkled his nose, sure this case was quite outside his experience. He prodded Abagail and peered into her eyes, hoping to find some evidence that would help him decipher the mystery. He turned from her twitching body to thumb through books.

"Epilepsy," he mumbled, tracing the words as he read. "No, not epilepsy." After looking up several other entries, he opened his cane and withdrew several pills. With trembling fingers, he crushed two in a glass and added water. With difficulty, Abagail finally swallowed a small amount, but not without gulping and swishing her body about.

The physician watched his patient anxiously, waiting for a response. Nothing. He tried another mixture, forcing it into her mouth between her squeals and posturings. Still no change.

Dr. Hanover scratched his chin and slowly withdrew from the bedroom, his eyes nearly receded into his skull. Reverend Winthrop and his wife awaited him in the parlor: he, sitting in a high-back chair, pulling at one of his fingers, she, pacing in front of the fire. "Well, what is it?" Reverend Winthrop demanded, his face having aged considerably since the physician came into his home.

The physician shrugged. "I'm not sure. I've ruled out epilepsy and everything else I can think of. There is only one diagnosis left."

Mrs. Winthrop nearly shouted at the man. "What is it?"

"Yes, what is it?" asked the minister.

Dr. Hanover sniffed and then said, "The evil hand is upon them." He scraped his feet on the floor nervously, not sure how his diagnosis would sit.

"What?" shouted Mrs. Winthrop. "Are you out of your---"

Reverend Winthrop drew himself up to his full height. "Do you mean the Devil?"

The physician winced. "Let me explain. I have in my possession a book by Mather detailing the strange case of the Goodwin children in Boston. It happened nearly four years ago. John Goodwin had four daughters and they were well-behaved and God-fearing until the day the family laundress stole some linen from Mrs. Goodwin's chest. When the eldest daughter questioned the laundress, her mother, Mrs. Bond, came to her employee's defense and bestowed some very bad language upon the Goodwin child."

Mrs. Winthrop started to wring her hands and pace even more quickly. "Yes, well, what does that have to do with our little girls?"

The physician made every attempt to remain calm. "Let me finish my story. Immediately after that, Dolly Goodwin began to have strange convulsive seizures. Before long, all three of John Goodwin's daughters were writhing on the floor and barking like dogs."

Mrs. Winthrop looked at her husband. "Why Cotton, that's very much like our Elizabeth."

He nodded. "So it is."

The physician, gaining confidence minute by minute, said, "Wait, there's more. Three physicians examined the little girls and they concluded it was nothing but a hellish witchcraft. You must realize that not all illness is physical. Some," he looked at them gravely, letting the rest of his sentence fall of his tongue, "is spiritual."

Mrs. Winthrop turned to her husband, her face flashing him a warning look. The Reverend's face was perfectly controlled, if slightly ashen, until the pulse at the side of his temple began to throb visibly. "Are you saying the girls are bewitched?"

The physician nodded. "That's exactly what I'm saying. Now, you can call in more physicians, but I'm afraid their answer will be the same." Dr. Hanover placed his books back in his bag and prepared to go.

His heart was considerably lighter as he returned home, knowing that his reputation as a physician had been enhanced. Just to make sure of it, he made plans to pass the word around that the girls were bewitched. With a little luck, more girls in Salem Village would become bewitched, as it seemed to be contagious matter similar to smallpox. He smiled and stepped up his pace. What a stroke of luck that Cotton Winthrop had come to his house that evening. As a result, his practice would be substantially enhanced and that large stack of unpaid bills on his desk would soon be paid.

***

Reverend Winthrop sat in his study, pen poised above his sermon, hands shaking at the thought of Abagail's and Elizabeth's predicament. He eventually bowed his head in prayer, hoping to receive spiritual advisement. But no loud and terrifying voice of God came to him with an answer. He was going to have to solve this problem himself.

By Sunday meeting, after two nights without sleep, haggard and near exhaustion, he stepped before his congregation and before he knew what he was doing, he began to describe what had happened to his two little girls. The faces of his parishioners froze in fear. Spurred on by their reaction, he shouted and waved his fist. "They are bewitched and need your prayers."

Leaving the meeting with his wife, he mumbled to her dazedly. "What am I to do? I will be a laughing stock!" As soon as the words were out of his mouth, he regretted them, for admitting his true feelings was something he rarely did.

"My dear," said his wife, putting a consoling hand on his arm, "why not consult with some of your colleagues. Perhaps they have the answer."

He looked at his wife as she were a stranger. In all the years they had been married, she had not come up with a single helpful idea. Now, here she was, making a perfectly sound suggestion. Not bothering to stop to thank her, he hurried her home, went to his study and locked the door.

His trembling hands took out a list of nearby ministers, tracking down the names until he found Reverend Boyes from Salem Town. Joseph Boyes was his first choice. Of course, he would have to address the invitation to Samuel Bigginson, since he was senior pastor, but everyone knew Bigginson was too old for travel and turned most of his tasks over to his assistant, Joseph.

He leaned back in his chair and took a deep breath. Now, Joseph Boyes was a man after his own heart, preaching the evils of the world and never missing a change to bring in the disastrous effects of listening to the Devil.

He leaned forward and looked at the list again. He'd have to ask Nicholas Hale, although to his mind, the man was too soft. Ah, well, if he was to survive this calamity unscathed, he most follow church protocol.

Pulling out paper and quill, he wrote them similar letters, addressed each and gave them to Indian Jim to deliver. The brown-skinned man took the mail, shook his head deferentially and hastened to do his master's bidding.

***

Reverend Joseph Boyes was on his way to his superior's office. He was a slightly-built man with red-rimmed eyes and eager face. He had the look of a brown fox: sly, quick and impossible to outdo.

His feet clicked along the cool corridor. What silly errand was old man Bigginson about to send him on now? Since he had come to First Church as second pastor, he had been sent on many a merry goose-chase. He supposed it was all part of winding his way to the top, but he wished the overly benevolent first pastor would seek his Maker and be done with it.

Pausing outside Reverend Bigginson's office, Joseph took a deep breath and pulled open the heavy door. It was what people called a cozy room with book-lined walls, bowls of fruit and nuts lying about haphazardly and the flicker of flames from an immense fireplace. They were all the things Joseph despised. A minister should expose himself to deprivation and certainly shouldn't be a glutton.

Samuel Bigginson beckoned his young associate in the room with his corpulent arm. "Joseph, come in. Have a seat. Would you like some tea and cakes?"

Reverend Boyes looked at his plump employer overflowing the large high-backed chair he was sitting in, and forced a slight smile onto his lips over a layer of disgust. "No thank you, Reverend. How can I assist you?"

Samuel Bigginson handed his younger associate the invitation. "Reverend Winthrop from Salem Village has sent for aid."

Joseph harumphed softly. Salem Village, that tiny hamlet, what would Reverend Bigginson from the more prestigious Salem Town want to do with him? After gazing at Reverend Bigginson's face for an answer and receiving one, Joseph reluctantly read over the letter quickly, his heart quickening when he read the word, bewitched.

This could be his chance to prove himself. If the girls repented of their sin and named the witch, he would be gentle and forgiving. But heaven help them if they did not. Then he would damn them to the eternal fires. Either way, everyone would know he was the one who had decided their fate and his career would be made.

Joseph nodded benevolently. "I will be most happy to go in your stead." He said it much more quickly than he usually agreed to errands, so he watched his employer's face carefully to see if there was any sign he had been too hasty in his acceptance.

Moving up in the Church required carefully calculated moves and it wouldn't do at all to show his hand too quickly. He held his breath and searched his employer's face, but all he saw on Samuel Bigginson's face was relief. "For that, you will surely find your place in heaven. Thank you, dear boy, thank you."

Joseph Boyes hurried out and wasted no time setting out for Salem Village from his solitary dwelling. Not that he minded living alone, it was just a fact that he did. He had never been drawn to women and they certainly hadn't made any fuss over him.

He put some extra clothes in his saddle bag and was up in the stirrup and away within the hour. Straining from effort, temper barely under rule, he coerced his nag along through the nearly impassable ways that were filled with flood and slush from the February thaw. The lights of Salem Village lay ahead and he began to wonder what he had gotten himself into. He was in no mood to see anyone, let alone two bewitched girls.

***

Reverend Nicholas Hale's wife intercepted the invitation from Salem Village when a small black boy peeped into the room and she motioned to him. She was a carefully dressed woman with hair so shiny it shone on her skull like a painted doll's and fingers so slim they nearly disappeared from view when they picked up the sealed paper from the silver tray and carefully peeled it open.

Mr. and Mrs. Hale sat in the parlor, the darkest room in the house. It was a cold room of uneven floor and uncomfortable furniture. Reverend Hale, slumped into one of the heavy armless chairs, was so engrossed in his Bible reading that he did not even notice his wife put down her embroidery and whisk the letter into her lap.

It was a dreary room, although the curtains were flung wide to let in the sun, and a dreary relationship, arranged primarily for convenience. Mrs. Hale talked furiously at her husband much of the time, trying to push him under with words, while he retreated farther and farther into his Bible. Despite her bubbly speech, there was something ugly and hard in her gaze.

"It's from Reverend Winthrop, dear," she said, not bothering to apologize for opening his mail. "Why do you suppose he would be writing to you? Maybe it's about the annual churchmen's meeting or the latest biblical interpretations. I've heard from my friend, Betty Anders, they are not at all what we thought they would be."

Nicholas Hale sighed and waited. He was used to sighing and waiting around his wife. He was an ugly man with bulging eyes, snub nose, pitted face and a head too big for his body. He supposed he listened to her harangues because he thought himself fortunate to have married such a pretty and well-bred woman, one whose family connections had helped him advance in clerical circles.

Although from time to time, and this was one of those times, he wasn't exactly sure whether it was all worth it. "Give me the letter, my dear, and I shall see." She stood up stiffly, back ramrod straight and advanced on him, passing the dignified, but sparse furniture and the potted ferns dying a slow death from over-watering.

Nicholas Hale read the message, his brow furrowing more deeply the farther down the page his eyes went. He felt a strong sense of guilt when he saw the word, bewitched. Twice in the last ten years he had been called upon to deal with such charges against women and both times he had been able to clear the accused.

Now he wondered if he had misplaced his power. This witchcraft thing was becoming too widespread. It was almost a plague now, and while he sat reading the letter, he began to wonder if he hadn't been a little hasty in those earlier occasions and wronged the innocent. What if Dorcas Bishop and Bridget Hoar were witches? What if they were the cause of this new mischief? He didn't want to jump to any conclusions in the matter, for he was not an impulsive man, but he began to steel himself against the awful moment when he might have to accept the humiliation of a public reversal of his former position, should God reveal he had taken the wrong path.

Clearing his throat, he stood and left hastily, hardly giving his wife any explanation. The less she knew, the better. That way, there would be fewer tongues waggling in Salem Town that evening.

Hale was a much better rider than Boyes, and more muscular, but the roads were a bother for him, too. He arrived hungry and tired, several hours after Winthrop and Boyes had supped. Nicholas received neither food nor rest, and being the easy-going and self-denying man he was, he demanded none. Upon his arrival, Reverend Winthrop proclaimed, "We shall have a day of public fast to prepare us for what lies ahead. And now, let us meet privately with my daughter and niece and apply the therapy of prayer."

The men tiptoed into the little girl's room. The cherubs perched on their quilted bed, all rosy smiles. The three reverends sat down on straight-backed chairs and began to pray. Winthrop's face showed a mixture of anxiety and anticipation. Even in prayer, Boyes' face gave off a reflection of superiority and disdain, while Nicholas Hale looked as if he were going through an internal battle.

The three of them prayed for several hours, but the results were discouraging. Elizabeth sat dully insensible to their words, while Abagail shrieked as if being slapped by a heavy hand whenever a sacred word was uttered. Completed embarrassed by the goings-on, Reverend Hale kept one eye open, staring at the girls, bracing himself for the next scream, while the other two muttered on, seemingly oblivious.

After their prayer session, the three reverends retired to the Winthrop study and faced one another in silence. Finally, Joseph Boyes spoke. "We must have a trial. Have the little ones name their tormentors. It is well known that witches do not work alone, they work through go-betweens. We must ferret out these witches and bring them to justice."

Reverend Winthrop quickly took up the cause with zest. He was in a delicate position because the outbreak had occurred in his own house, in his own daughter and niece. It was of the utmost urgency for him to clear himself and his household. Besides, the idea of direct confrontation with the forces of evil appealed to him.

Reverend Hale picked at his face, weighing what the two other men suggested.

"Well, Reverend Hale," began Reverend Boyes, his voice full of condescension, "what is your decision?"

Nicholas looked away, trying to sneak a quick prayer for help off to the Almighty. "This calls for more than an easy answer--" he finally said, when the Lord refused to answer.

Reverend Winthrop spoke up, his voice implying that any rational man would have decided by now. "We've prayed with the girls and spoken our minds with each other. What else is there to do?"

Reverend Hale cleared his throat and examined the shadows on the ceiling. "It is a decision I make with great reluctance. I have been through two trials and know what misery they entail."

Reverend Winthrop nodded. "Of course, it shall be difficult for all of us, but is there a better way?"

The collar of Reverend Hale's cravat suddenly became painfully tight and he thrust his fingers beneath it, trying to loosen its hold on his throat. "I can't say I've come up with a better idea."

Reverend Boyes spoke smugly, folding his hands into his lap. "There you have it, then."

"It's settled then?" asked Reverend Winthrop, standing.

Reverend Hale nodded reluctantly. "Well, I guess---"

Cotton Winthrop smiled. "Fine. Then I will set the trial date."

***

Abagail giggled devilishly when the three ministers left her room. Elizabeth's face showed the pressures she was under. She stood up and wandered to the window. The clouds were widely spread in starlight, and she looked up, hoping for some advice from her Maker. It was a night of bitter frost and cold cisterns of night air bit at her through the window. Shivering, and with no greater wisdom than when she'd arrived, she found her way back to the fireplace.

Rubbing her arms for warmth, she turned to face her cousin. "We must tell the truth, Abagail. We have to tell them we have been playing some tricks Bituba taught us. We must stop now or God will surely punish us."

Abagail cocked a defiant eyebrow. "But what is the truth? And if we tell it, will anyone believe us? Do they want to believe us? There will be more excitement in this village because of us than there ever has been or ever will be again. It will make us famous and people will remember our names forever." Abagail's face took on a glaze of dreaminess and she swayed and hummed to some rhythm only she could hear.

Elizabeth looked at her cousin in horror. "I know the truth and I don't want to be damned to the everlasting fire. I'm going to tell them."

Abagail's usually pretty face twisted into an evil combination of angles when she said, "If you say anything other than what I tell you, I'll say the whole thing was your idea and you made me go along."

Elizabeth burst into tears. "But, but, you can't---" She began to sob hysterically.

Abagail threw her arms around her cousin. "There, there, little one," she said, using the soothing voice she had heard Bituba use. "I will take care of you. No one will hurt you, just do as I say and everything will be fine."

Elizabeth dried her tears and clung to her cousin. Then, she promised never to speak of the truth again.

The next day, the three reverends sent for the girls. They entered the Winthrop study for pre-trial questioning. "Who has afflicted you so, Elizabeth?" demanded Reverend Boyes.

Body quivering and eyes full of tears, the little girl answered, "I do not know, sir."

Reverend Winthrop gave a stern look to his niece and said, "And you, Abagail, surely you have some idea who has done this terrible mischief."

Abagail raised her eyes to his and said, "No one afflicted me. It just happened."

The three reverends continued their questioning for hours, but to no avail. The girls simply could not or would not name their persecutor. Totally baffled, the three men finally left.

When Abagail was sure they were out of hearing range, she pulled Elizabeth to the corner. "We must choose some people to name, otherwise they might begin to suspect it is our own tricks we are up to. Start thinking of people you want to get back at."

Elizabeth cowered in the corner, her body hunched over in fear. "Oh no, I couldn't get anyone into trouble. They might be horribly punished."

Abagail shook her. "You'll do what I say or we'll be horribly punished. Now, let's make a list and decide who to accuse."

***

Verity sat in front of the hot biscuits and coffee, waiting for her mother's voice of praise for her accomplishment. She waited until the coffee had gone cold and the biscuits sat like rocks on the plate. Wondering what was wrong, she tiptoed up to her mother's room.

Ventura laid in the bed, groaning softly, her body twisting in the bed. Verity grasped her hand. It was so cold, so limp. "I have a terrible pain in my stomach and it won't go away. It feels like the Devil himself has reached in there and is pushing down on my insides."

"What can I do, Mother," said Verity, frightened something terrible had happened.

Ventura moaned again, this time more loudly. Her eyebrows pulled together in agony and her voice was a mere whisper. "Fetch me some chamomille tea, that may help."

Verity ran downstains and made the tea, hurrying back up again with a large cup of steaming liquid. "What else can I do?" she asked after setting the tea aside her mother.

Ventura shook her head. "Just stay with me."

Verity sat on the side of the bed, listening to the pounding of her heart and her mother's labored breathing. There had to be a way to help, but she just couldn't think what it was. Finally she said, "Maybe I should call Dr. Hanover or Mr. Corwin."

Ventura shook her head. "No, just help me downstairs. I will be all right in a minute or so."

"I think you should---"

"Never mind that and help me."

Somehow they managed to maneuver the stairs, although Verity thought they both might fall at any moment. "Help me over by the window. I want to be by the light." A shaft of sun hovered against the wall, falling on her mother's dull hair. Ventura limped over to a straight-backed chair, leaning heavily on Verity's shoulder. "I wish Sigrid were here, she has powerful hands for healing." Ventura slumped into the chair, perspiration standing out on her brow.

"What about me Mother, you told me I have strong powers too."

Ventura managed a weak smile. "But, of course. Yes, you can help."

Verity did as her Mother had taught her, closing her eyes, breathing deeply and picturing a protective shield around her. When she was ready, she moved her hands slowly over her mother's abdomen until she found a burning hot spot. She worked for several minutes, fluttering her fingers out to the side until Ventura slowly opened her eyes and her face released its tension.

"The pain is gone," her mother said softly, then closed her eyes and fell asleep. Verity covered her with a heavy blanket and tiptoed to the kitchen.

Then she heard a knock on the back door. When she opened the door, she found Absalon standing there smiling at her. "Come in," she said, feeling her face go hot with embarrassment at what she was thinking.

In an instant, his arms were around her and the freshness of his face came toward her until she tasted the sweetness of his lips. "Verity, dear Verity," he murmured into her hair. "How I've missed you. When will you marry me so we won't have to be apart?"

***

Abagail and Elizabeth became instant celebrities once the household learned what had happened. Even Elizabeth's mother seemed to pay more attention to the girls. At first they gloried in it, then Abagail began to grow tired of her aunt's doting. Watching the light stream in the window that day, she hit on a new plan. She turned to her aunt and asked, "Can we go outside and play?"

Somewhat in awe of the girls, Mrs. Winthrop was now unable to deny them anything. Since her husband was busy with the other reverends, she quickly granted their request.

Soon they were playing hide-and-seek and Elizabeth was it. Abagail, even more brazen than before, ran up on the Hasleton's porch and hid behind a pile of wood. When Elizabeth didn't find her after a few minutes, Abagail grew tired of the game and wandered toward the nearest window.

Fascinated, she watched Verity moving her hands above her mother's body. Abagail realized what was happening immediately and she signalled to Elizabeth, who had just come around the side of the house. "Come over here and look at this," she whispered to her cousin.

"What is she doing?" whispered Elizabeth, joining her cousin on the porch.

"Trying to help her. See how pale Mrs. Hasleton is. She must be in very bad pain."

"Shouldn't they call Dr. Hanover?"

"Maybe they already have. Look, she's better, the pain is gone out of her face."

Elizabeth pushed her face against the window, trying to see. "Do you suppose it's magic?"

Before Abagail could answer, they heard footsteps on the path and hurried to hide behind the woodpile. Absalon Winthrop covered the stairs to the back door in seconds. They watched him go in the house and followed his vice to the nearest window. "Look, he's kissing her," said Elizabeth, giggling and looking away.

"He can't be. Not my cousin!" Although Abagail knew she was too young yet, all her life she had planned that some day she would marry her cousin, Absalon. He hadn't taken much interest in her of late, but when she was smaller, he used to carry her on his shoulders and dry her tears when she hurt herself. He was the handsomest, bravest man she knew, and she meant to have him for herself. Somehow she had to prevent Absalon from marrying Verity.

Abagail jumped off the porch, pulling Elizabeth behind her. "Where are we going?"

"Home. Just you hurry or I'll tell." Their feet crunched along the road and Elizabeth quivered with fear, not knowing what kind of mischief Abagail was up to now.

When they arrived at the parsonage, the three reverends were still in the study, but Bituba was waiting for them in the kitchen. Her face was angry when she said, "You girls were supposed to help me with the cornbread. Where have you been?"

Puzzled by the scolding when she'd been used to only adoration, Abagail turned on Bituba. "Who are you to question me? You're just a slave anyway."

"Why you!" cried Bituba, coming after Abagail with a broom. The girls ran screaming out of the kitchen.

Reverend Wintrhop came out of his study when he heard the ruckus. "What is this? What's going on? Come in here, girls," he said, sending Bituba cowering into the kitchen with his stern glance. "Now sit down girls, and tell us what has happened."

Abagail started to speak, but Elizabeth clamped her small hand over her cousin's mouth. "It's nothing, Father," she said sweetly, "we were late, that's all." Before she removed her hand, she gave her cousin a piercing look, one Abagail had never seen on her face, a look that silenced even her.

Reverend Winthrop said to the girls, "Please go and have your supper. Tomorrow is the trial and we have a great deal of work to do before then."

***

After the girls left, the ministers returned to their work. They had been consulting the Bible, or more aptly, ransacking it, trying to find something that would set them clear about the nature of witchcraft and how to recognize it. To their consternation, nowhere did the Bible define witchcraft. It named the offense, along with sodomy, lying and idolatry, but no descriptions were given. The only references to witches and witchcraft they could find was, "Thou shalt not permit a witch to live."

Reverend Boyes nodded. "There is no doubt about God's will on this subject.

Reverend Hale shook his head. "Yes, but we need a more practical guide. Something to help us cope with this emergency."

Reverend Winthrop turned to his bookcase and pulled down a number of legal volumes. Not trusting lawyers, they would conduct their own trial. He handed *Guide to Jurymen and Collection of Sundry Tryals in England and Ireland* to Reverend Boyes to read. To Reverend Hale, he entrusted *Common Law and Certainty of the World of Spirits*. For himself, he retained, *Kingdom of Darkness and Memorable Providences*.

"Gentlemen," he said, "seek out the chapters that apply and we shall meet later this evening to agree on the principles of evidence." With that, he opened his book and began to read.

Several hours later he began their discussion. "I believe one principle to be accepted as proof of guilt is the finding of any teat or devil's mark on the bodies of the accused."

"But how will we discover them?" asked Reverend Hale.

Reverend Noyes answered. "It's a simple matter. I read here that the suspect is stripped by women and examined minutely. Pins are run through any abnormality found."

"Isn't that a bit brutal?" asked Reverend Hale. "I'd like to suggest we refrain from the water test, it's superstitious and unchristian."

"What, pray tell, is the water test?" said Reverend Boyes, wiping his nose with his handkerchief.

"It was used in Beverly in a case I was associated with," said Reverend Hale, opening a book to a page he had found. "Mather has written a scathing opinion of it. Did you see it?"

Reverend Winthrop turned a few pages in the book in front of him. "Ah, yes. As I understand it, in the water test, the accused is tied and thrown into a stream. If she floats she is considered guilty, since pure water rejects someone who is impure. If she sinks, she is innocent, but many have been lost in the current of the river even when shown innocent by this method." He closed the book and looked at his companions. "I agree we should not use it. Have either of you found any other principles?"

Reverend Hale tapped his finger on a book. "I believe we should accept as ground for suspicion of guilt any mischief following anger between neighbors."

Reverend Boyes frowned. "That was used in Beverly, and to a bad outcome. The entire village compiled histories of atrocious spites. This principle makes a memory for petty quarrels a virtue." His voice rose in the closest thing to anger either of the men had heard. "I say no to it."

Reverend Winthrop pushed away the books in front of him on the table. "But we must have some principles---"

Reverend Hale set his jaw. "We'll have our hands full for months if we take every squabble that has been followed by a breaking of a cartwheel, the loss of a scythe, the sickening of a hog, or the drowning of an ox."

Reverend Boyes raised his voice. "I say keep it. And I have another principle that must be placed on the list. The most important one to date, I might add. It is the principle of spectral evidence. As we all know, the devil cannot assume the shape of an innocent person. Therefore, dreams and reports of visitations from a suspect shall stand as factual proof."

Reverend Hale shook his head in disgust. "Yes, yes, we used that in Beverly too, and it only proved to me that hallucinations and mere fancies can be accepted as proof. I've heard accusers say, 'Your shape came to my room last night,' and they were believed. Now what defense can the accused have for that? There is no conceivable alibi for the whereabouts of someone's shape. It's only an airy substance."

In the end, Reverend Hale was voted down on all counts. All the principles discussed were listed as proof of witchcraft.

# 16

Abagail had taken to watching the goings and comings from the house, afraid of what might happen should anyone figure out what she and Elizabeth were up to. That was why she was the first one to notice Mrs. Sidle coming up the walk.

Mrs. Sidle, a fat woman with snake-pale eyes and barrel hips, knew every bit of gossip there was to know in Salem Village. She knew when Sarah Creepot was pregnant and when Elsie Glover's mother fell down and broke her ankle. When anyone in the Village wanted to know what was what, they consulted Mrs. Sidle.

In the summer, she sat on her porch, listening for gossip, offering weary travellers a glass or two of cider or iced tea so they'd sit on her porch and tell all. In the winter, she was at the meeting house, her heavy body leaning forward to catch any whiff of scandal that might pass close enough to her ears. It was to Mrs. Sidle that Reverend Winthrop had turned when he wanted publicity about the upcoming trial and to whom Dr. Hanover deferred when he wanted the village to know he had diagnosed Abagail and Elizabeth bewitched.

From her hiding place, Abagail watched Mrs. Sidle enter the kitchen, throw her soiled cloak on a chair, open the old book and shove it in front of Bituba's staring eyes. That was when the little girl realized the old woman was up to no good.

Bituba's brown face took on a look of sheer terror and her body began to shake when she looked at the pages. "This is voodoo, sure and simple. Uh, uh, I can't do it, no ma'am, I sure can't."

Mrs. Sidle gave her a stern eye. "You silly woman. Of course you can. Reverend Winthrop wants the girls to name their persecutor, doesn't he?" Bituba nodded. "Then bake it and do whatever else the recipe says."

"No ma'am, no ma'am!" shouted Bituba.

As if taking her cue, Abagail came running into the kitchen, yelling, "What is it Bituba?"

The brown woman's eyes flashed. "No, no, Miss Abagail. I won't do what she says." Large body shaking with fear, she hurried out of the kitchen.

Abagail shrugged and looked at Mrs. Sidle. "What is wrong with Bituba? Let me see that book." It was an old English volume containing recipes for special conditions. On page forty-three appeared directions for making the bewitched speak out against their persecutors. "Hmm," she mumbled, reading aloud to herself in a singsong voice, "Bake a cake of rye meal and mix with the urine of the bewitched. When saturated, feed it to a dog."

Mrs. Sidle snapped up the book and said, "You do want to name the person who is tormenting you, don't you dear?"

Abagail cringed. Inside her, for the first time since she and Elizabeth had begun the charade, fear started to grow. This was magic, no question about it. What would happen to them if they failed to heed it? Running like her life depended on it, Abagail scooted out of the kitchen and went to find Elizabeth. They had to settle on their list of people to accuse and they had to settle soon.

She knew her cousin was partial to the new colt that had been born and was likely to be visiting it. That was why Abagail ran in the direction of the barn. "Elizabeth! Elizabeth!" she shouted, pushing the door open and inhaling the sweet smell of hay and moist animals.

She found her cousin by a stanchion, face nuzzling into the colt's neck. Somewhere nearby a horse's whinny echoed and hooves clacked uneasily. Elizabeth turned and looked into Abagail's face. "What is the matter with you?"

"Mrs. Sidle has been here and she tried to get Bituba to work magic on us to tell who has bewitched us."

"Bituba?" Elizabeth shook her head. "She wouldn't do something to hurt us."

Abagail harumphed. "Not yet, but she probably will. We better name her first."

Elizabeth let go of the colt and pulled on her cousin's skirt, tears already wetting her cheeks. "Not Bituba. I love her."

Abagail tightened her jaw. "It's her or us. If she tattles, we will be in real danger. Now, come on, we have to tell your father." She grabbed Elizabeth's hand and dragged her behind, pulling her toward the house.

They found Reverend Winthrop in his study with the other two ministers. Abagail spoke first, her eyes never leaving Elizabeth's. "Uncle, Uncle! We are ready to name our persecutors!"

The minister smiled and motioned them inside. "Come in, girls. What delightful news. Tell us who has done this terrible thing to you."

Before Elizabeth could say a word, Abagail blurted out, "It was Bituba and Verity Hasleton!"

Reverend Winthrop looked stunned. "What? My own slave has done this?" He staggered backwards and fell into his chair. "I don't believe it," he kept murmuring.

Reverend Boyes stood up. "Get hold of yourself, man. We must question this Bituba. Where is she?"

Reverend Winthrop looked up, dazed and mumbled, "Down in the kitchen, I suppose."

"Then, to the kitchen!" shouted Reverend Boyes as if he were leading a battle charge, with Abagail at his elbow, dragging a sobbing Elizabeth behind her. Nicholas linked arms with Reverend Winthrop and helped the blubbering man down the steps to the kitchen.

Bituba was bending over a pot of soup, just replacing her stirring spoon, when the group descended upon her. "Why have you bewitched these girls?" shouted Reverend Boyes. "You will be sentenced to eternal damnation and will burn forever!"

Her eyes went black and dull as coal and she ran from the kitchen, out into the field, toward the woods. "She has wax images and dolls she works spells on in her room," shouted Abagail, storming to the place where Bituba slept. Just as she had reported, a waxen image of a woman sat on the fireplace mantle and a tiny cloth doll lay on the floor under her bed.

"Aha!" cried Reverend Boyes, eyes flashing with hellfire and damnation while his hands quickly gathered up the evidence. "Now, what of this Verity Hasleton? Where is she?"

Abagail smiled sweetly. "She lives nearby. I'll show you. We saw her using her hands to do a magic spell over her mother."

A smile of self-satisfaction creeping across his thin lips, Reverend Boyes led the group outside. "Bewitching her own mother. She is an evil one. Well, let us get the warrants for the arrest of these women so the trial can begin."

***

Ventura saw them coming down the road. Out in front, silver-knobbed canes at the ready and swords at their waists, marched the local constabulary. Next came Mrs. Sidle, the town busybody, her long skirts bustling over her ample hips. Then followed Dr. Hanover, with his long wig bouncing off his shoulders and his face somewhat embarrassed. Abagail pranced beside her Uncle Cotton Winthrop, her pinched face flushed with anger and revenge while the fires of eternal damnation blazed in his eyes. There were others, but Ventura could not identify them because a fear had gripped her and a strange coldness crept up her legs when she saw the ill humor on their faces.

She had heard rumors that the Winthrop girls had been bewitched and something told her to protect her daughter. "Run Verity, leave the house through the fields."

Her daughter's eyes looked up questioningly from her knitting. "But why, Mother?"

Ventura raised her voice. "No time to discuss this. Just leave!"

Then the loud and constant knocking told her it was to late to run and she opened the door and stepped out on the porch. A tall man with a cane and wide-brimmed hat addressed her. "We've come to arrest Verity Hasleton in the matter of bewitching Abigail Goodfellow and Elizabeth Winthrop," he said. "Step forward please, or we will be obliged to come inside." His cane tapped impatiently on the porch.

Ventura blocked the way. "No, this is ridiculous. Verity is not a witch. She is but a girl."

He looked at her sternly. "Send her to us or you will be arrested, too."

Verity rushed out onto the porch. "It's all right, Mother. There is no proof against me. I am innocent." Ventura grabbed her daughter's arm, but Verity pulled past her and walked down the steps confidently, head held high.

Ventura watched her go, remembering the day so many years ago in Seville when she believed authority would do the right thing. Now, she knew differently. She had to do everything in her power to save her daughter. The first thing to do was to get in touch with Richard. If she could find him and bring him back home, all of them could leave this evil place.

Throat tight with fear and anger, she went in the house and dashed off a letter. It told of Verity's imprisonment for witchcraft and begged him to come home as soon as possible. Pulling her heavy mantilla around her, she hurried to the wharf. The biting sea wind dried her face and swirled through her hair, but her eyes continued to search for any ship which might be able to contact Richard.

She knew his ship was due to stop in Virginia in the next few days. What she didn't know was how to send a letter that could reach him by then. She went from vessel to vessel until she found a ship with the same company name as the one Richard had sailed out on. At last her eyes found the insignia: Great Eastern Company.

Ignoring the seagulls who protested her arrival with their mournful cries, she ran up the gangplank, feet thudding plaintively on the wood. She stopped every sailor she saw, asking where the captain might be. Most ignored her, some just shrugged and pushed her away.

"The captain hasn't come aboard yet, miss," said a deep voice. She whirled around to see a burly man with a beard thick as bear's fur, "Can I help?"

His eyes flashed with vigor and just a hint of compassion. "Thank you," she said. But I must see the captain, I have this letter and it's a matter of life and death." She waved the paper in front of him.

"Maybe I can help. I'm Henry Jordan, the first mate." He smiled at her in a friendly way.

She nodded and decided to trust him. "This letter has to reach my husband, Richard Hasleton, as soon as possible in Jamestown. I understand your ship will be sailing there first."

"That's true, mam. I'll be happy to take the letter and see that he gets it. What ship might he be on?"

"The Glouchester."

"Aye, the Glouchester," he said dreamily. "I've sailed her myself. She's a fine vessel." His eyes drifted back to hers and held there. "Now just what exactly is this life and death matter of which you spoke?"

"Our daughter is going to be killed if he doesn't intercede. She's been imprisoned wrongfully and hanging is in their minds. He has to come back home right away."

The mate shook his head in a concerned way. "That is wrong. I have a wife and two daughters myself, and I worry about them all the time. I know if they were in danger, I'd appreciate anything someone else could do to give aid."

"That's very kind of you, but even if he gets the letter, I'm not sure there's any way he could get back here in time."

"Don't you worry now, ma'am, if there's a way to get your husband back here, I'll find it, yes, ma'am, I sure will."

***

Bituba stumbled through the fields like a wild boar, running away from the white people. She had to find Jim Indian. It was turning dark and she was alone. She shivered and stared into the dark. She'd been afraid of it since she was a little girl. That was why she kept her fireplace stoked and her lamp lit at night.

She shivered again, hearing the distant howl of some mournful creature and knowing she wouldn't be able to stay outside the whole night, not without some food and warmth to comfort her. Trembling with fear, she headed back toward the Winthrop house. Maybe they'd forgotten about her by now, or at least given up for the night.

Moonlight spilled through the trees, casting eerie shadows on the house. Her heart thumped, then stopped. She slowed down, squinting to see in the dim light. Out of the shadows stepped two constables. "This is her, ain't it?" one of them said.

Before the other one could answer, he grabbed her arms and tied her hands behind her. Then both men threw her in the back of their cart. She lay, bruised and frightened, smelling the odors of dung and rotten vegetables.

In minutes, the cart lurched ahead, scraping the skin off her arms. All the while, her mouth was moving in silent curses. "You just wait, you big fellas. Bituba gonna cast a spell on you just as soon as she close to some wax or cloth."

When she got tired of that, she thought about Jim Indian. If he were there, he'd know what to do. Without him she was powerless against the strong constables. She lay down and started to cry, wishing with all her heart that she had stayed in Barbardos.

It seemed like days later when the cart stopped and the two constables slid her off the cart. No one said a word to her, but she was thrown into a cell and given a crust of bread and some water.

When she awoke the next morning, she thought she had been dreaming. But the filthy cell, crawling with insects and rodent life, was not a dream. When she screamed for help, the jailer told her to quiet down. He pushed a tray under the door and she ate hungrily, shooing a rat away with her hand.

Minutes later the constables came to get her. They put her back in the cart and started driving. An hour later a wheel hit a large rock and nearly threw her out onto the road, but she held herself in by grabbing the wooden side.

An idea started to form in the back of her mind. At the next corner she flung herself off and fell to the ground with a thud. Brushing her skirt off, she limped toward the woods. She had only taken a few steps when the cart screeched to a halt and she heard the sound of two pairs of footsteps on the dusty road.

She tried to get away, but they overtook her. "Think you can get away, huh? We'll show you." One of them punched her in the stomach and then they threw her back behind the driver. This time they chained her in. Hands bleeding and stomach burning, she was driven to Ingersoll's Tavern in Salem Village.

***

Abagail sat in the hall knitting. Since Verity and Bituba had been arrested, she had been the picture of discipline and propriety. Inside her, she was composing an argument for her uncle. She had to do something to keep Absalon out of this matter. He was away for only a few days and when he returned, he would be at Verity's side, trying to help her. He might even be considered guilty by association if the town's people saw him with a witch.

She went upstairs and knocked on her Uncle Cotton's door. When she saw his concerned face, she knew she had a chance to achieve her purpose. "Dear uncle, may I please speak with you for a moment," she said in the sweetest, softest voice she could muster.

He asked her in and when they were seated, she said, "I saw something the other day, something I think you should know about---"

Her uncle followed each of her words intently, moving his chin closer and closer to her. "Yes, yes, speak up girl. What did you see? Another witch perhaps?"

"No dear uncle. It was Absalon and---"

"Absalon and who dear?" He signalled with his hand for her to hurry up.

Finally she said, "Absalon and Verity Hasleton."

"Yes, and---"

"They were doing something that might be a sin."

"What was it?"

"They were---they were---"

"Come girl, what was it they were doing?"

"Kissing. They were kissing!"

Her uncle's eyes widened and then receded. "Kissing? You're sure? You sure they weren't doing something else and you thought they were kissing?"

Abagail shook her head. "No sir, I'm sure. Absalon kissed her on the mouth and told her he couldn't wait until they were married."

Reverend Winthrop's face changed instantly from pale to crimson. "Why that is most extraordinary." He fell back against his chair. "Kissing? Getting married? But why hasn't he told me about this?"

"Maybe because he's afraid to."

"Afraid to tell his own father? I doubt that very much, my dear."

"Maybe he's afraid because he knew you wouldn't want him to marry a witch."

"A witch? What are you talking about?" He grabbed her arm and squeezed it until it burned beneath his touch. She squirmed and tried to get away, but his hand held her in place.

Finally she screamed, "Verity Hasleton is the woman you arrested today!"

Her uncle released her and nodded. "So it is. This is terrible. What disgrace that would bring to this family if she is a witch. Something must be done."

Abagail nodded. "That's why I came to tell you."

He stared at the ceiling. "And you were right to do that, but what am I going to do now?"

"Keep him out of the village until after the trial. By then we'll know if she's a witch or not and if she is, you won't be disgraced."

Reverend Winthrop gazed at his niece with a look of delight. "Out of the mouths of babes. That is a very good idea, Abagail. An excellent idea." He started rummaging in his desk for pen. He didn't look up when he said, "Thank you my dear, you've been very helpful. Now, run along and play."

***

John Corwin sat in his study completing a letter. The pungent amalgam of paper and ink filled the room. He stretched his long legs and thought of Ventura. A knock on his study door disturbed his reverie and a scrawny black servant boy stood waiting, huge black eyes riveted on his master. "Yes, what is it," John said.

"Miss Hasleton is in the parlor. She says it's 'mergency, can you come quick."

John pushed past the black boy, heart leaping into his throat. The fact that she'd come to his home could only mean she had come to be with him at last. Perhaps her husband had been shipwrecked or drowned. Maybe he'd even been taken with scurvy. He really didn't care the cause. All that concerned him was that she had come to him.

He rushed down the hall. He had wanted her for an eternity, pined for her until it seemed only the sight of her or a word from her soft lips could set him into the exquisite pain of longing.

She walked to the fire. He missed nothing, taking in the sway of her gait, the fall of her silky hair across her neck, the way her simple gown gathered winsomly around her lush breasts and tiny waist. He took her hand and wanted to kiss her, but she gave no encouragement. Gazing into her eyes, the perfume scent of her warm flesh swam through his head.

It was all he could do to restrain himself from taking her in his arms and kissing her. The idea of the touch of her lips on his, dazzled in his mind. She looked so young and beautiful that the years of waiting seemed to melt away. It was as if he was seeing her for the first time, his love was so new and shining.

She hesitated, then said, "John, I've come---"

"I know, I know and I'm so glad---"

"But I must explain---"

"Don't say anything, just let me---" He moved even closer, desire burning inside him.

"But I need---"

"I know, and I need you, too." He dropped to his knees beside her, his lips finding her palm in a hungry kiss.

"But you don't understand---" She pulled her hand away.

But he did understand. It would take time for her to get over the loss of her husband, but he would be at her side, waiting patiently, just as he had waited all these years. His thigh edged closer to hers.

"Dear John, you don't understand," she said softly. "I've come here for your help."

"Help? What kind of help?"

"They've taken Verity."

"Taken Verity?" Wonder of wonders. That damnable girl was even going to be out of their way. This was the happiest day of his life. He looked into her eyes and said, "You'll miss her, but we'll be together---"

"You don't understand at all. The constables came and arrested her, not more than a few minutes ago."

"Arrested her? What for?"

"Witchcraft." A single pearl-shaped tear made its way down Ventura's cheek.

Even better. That meant she would be hung. This was no short visit to a relative, she was going to be dead, out of Ventura's life forever. But he must not show his glee. A simple, noncommittal, "Oh," found its way out of his mouth.

"But we have to do something, stop this, she's not a witch." Ventura's hand grabbed his shoulder.

The heat from her touch increased his desire. "Then you have nothing to fear, dear Ventura. She will be acquitted."

Anger flowed across his beloved's face and she pulled her hand away. "You expect me to just sit and wait for her to be tried? I know about these things, nearly the same thing happened to me in Spain. There is no justice when the masses seek an outlet for their despair. There must be a victim and Verity is it. We have to rescue her before she is tried. It is the only way."

"Rescue her? But my position in this village---"

"Your position," she nearly pushed him to the floor, her finger shaking in defiance only inches from his eyes, "your position. You don't really care about her, do you?" Her pale cheeks turned an accusing pink.

He stood up, wondering how he was going to salvage this. "I care about you, Ventura," he said carefully. "You're the only thing I care about. She is doomed. Let us just leave Salem Village, the two of us, go somewhere else and start anew."

Her eyes darkened. "Leave? Now? That can never be. I love Richard and I am his wife. I have no intentions of being with you. Ever!" She turned and fled, heels clicking away from him.

"Wait! I love you Ventura!" He rushed after her, hands clutching for her cloak.

The door slammed shut behind her. She was gone, her anger and total separation flung behind her in a draft of iciness.

He was alone now, her words whispering in his ears. She didn't love him at all. He slumped into a chair. After all he'd done for her. All the years he'd waited, even put up with that spoiled daughter of hers. This was the thanks he got. Very well, not only wouldn't he help, he'd see that Verity got what was coming to her.

That very day he'd apply to be a magistrate on the court. He knew as much English law as anyone else in the village. Although he'd never shown it to her, he could be very cruel when the occasion called for it.

***

On the morning of March 1, 1692, the road to Salem Village was filled with farmers, housewives, children, oxen, carts, dogs, and nearly every living thing from the surrounding towns of Beverly, Ipswich, Topsfield, and Salem Town. It was a sunny morning, but the boughs of the trees were loaded with ice. A great snowy mist of clouds had blown over earlier and its remains dazzled on tree stumps and road hollows.

The local constabulary and some of the guards set up watch on the road to Salem Village. They stood around, joking, pulling on their leather shoulder straps, clicking their leather boots together to ward off the cold and pulling their hats down in front for warmth.

Some of the town's people were there also, some banging on drums or waving pennants. All eyes strained toward Salem Town, hoping to catch a glimpse of the magistrates who would join John Corwin and the three reverends in trying the two women.

It was a small boy sitting on his father's shoulders who caught the first sight of them. "It's them. They're coming!" he shouted and the crowd came alive in one large, yelping cheer. The horsedrawn cart came down the road slowly, the magistrates' brocaded coats visible from a great distance. It was nearly noon, and many of the crowd had been there for hours, but their energy had not flagged.

Pennants waved more ferociously and a flutter of clouded drums encouraged the townpeople to fall into line behind the cart. They marched into Salem Village, the procession coming to a halt in front of Samuel Ingersoll's tavern.

Being a deacon of the Church, Sam had petitioned, and received agreement to hold the trial in his establishment. Throngs of people waited outside, hoping to get a chance to see the proceedings. Farmers stood around uncomfortably, the smell of dung and hay lingering on them. A few rigidly corseted housewives cuddled their babies in their arms while men dressed in felt hats and blue coats chatted with one another in small groups, gaping and exchanging stories of witches and trials. Excitement and near panic swirled through the crowd as their wildest fantasies neared release.

John Corwin stepped forward to greet his fellow magistrates and the crowd swelled with pleasure. "Come in gentlemen. We shall hold the trial here."

Ezekial Hawthorne, one of the magistrates, surveyed the tavern with contempt. "There's not enough room for all these people. Don't you have a bigger room?"

John stared at the magistrate. The man's right eye turned toward his nose and he had an unpleasant laugh, but he was in charge. It had been John's assignment to choose the trial building, but he had underestimated the crowds. His mind spun with reverberations from Hawthorne's question. There had to be a bigger place somewhere,but his mind was completely blank.

"What about the meeting house?" chimed in Henry Osbourne, the other magistrate. He was brown-haired and flabby with a small brown spot near the end of his nose.

Reverend Winthrop nodded. "John, perhaps you'll go ahead and prepare it for our court."

"I'm on my way," said John, hurrying across the square. Several strong farmers followed him, anxious to do more than stand around.

John put them to work immediately, moving back the pulpit and setting up a large table and chairs for the magistrates and their secretaries. Amid scraping and grunting, the room was soon transformed into a bar of justice.

Stepping back outside, John invited the magistrates and reverends to their places. Faces somber and self-satisfied, they marched in and took their seats. Heads down and skirts held demurely in their hands, Abagail and Elizabeth were brought in and seated in the foremost pew, facing the bar.

When all was ready, Reverend Winthrop nodded and two constables opened the door. The throng came in, loud and brash, some laughing and pointing, others gossiping and giggling.

Someone called for silence and eventually everyone quieted down. Then, only the wind was heard, rattling at the leaded casements and wailing under the eaves as the crowd waited for the first accused. Eyes glued to the floor, Bituba came in between two constables, her ample frame shaking. They kept a tight grip on her arms and whispers ran through the crowd. "Did ya hear how agile she is? Said she jumped out of the constable's cart," said an old man.

"She's agile enough to ride a witch's broom," whispered a voice that seemed to choke back a laugh.

Jim Indian sat in the back, huddled down between two other slaves, his dark eyes following Bituba's body. Joseph Boyes watched too, face eager to show how quick his mind worked. The look in his eyes said he knew she was guilty and he was ready to bully her into a confession if need be. His voice rang out biting and loud. "Bituba, what evil spirit have you familiarity with?"

She thought for a minute, looking up to the heavens several times and once at Jim Indian before she said, "None. I don't know no spirits."

Joseph's eyes narrowed. "Have you made a contract with the Devil then?"

"No sir, I don't even know him." Bituba's eyes fell on Mrs. Sidle and she staggered backwards, hands clasping her chest. The crowd gasped and two constables came forward to steady her.

Reverend Boyes continued. "Then why did you hurt these children?" Jim Indian stood up, his body shaking in anger. Before he could speak, two men beside him pulled him back down and whispered in his ear. After that, he not attempt to rise, but fury blazed in his eyes.

Glaring at the crowd, Reverend Boyes repeated his question. "Why did you hurt these children?" He pointed to Abagail and Elizabeth. The girls sat quietly, heads bowed.

Bituba looked at the girls. "I don't hurt them. Only if they is bad."

Reverend Boyes looked down his nose at her. "You have heard of familiars, have you not?"

"Oh no, sir," she said, standing up straighter so the constables let go of her arms and stepped back.

Reverend Boyes smiled caustically at the audience. "Familiars are objects or animals witches employ to do their wicked work. Have you used," he shuffled his papers about and began to read, "a family pet, rats, toads, yellow birds or spiders?"

Abagail began to moan and wail. Then she stood up, flapped her arms like the wings of a great bird and ran around in front of Bituba. Her feet moved with such incredible swiftness they hardly touched the ground. Bituba stared at Abagail, her body quivering in fear.

The audience came alive, gasping and crying out. Eventually Abagail came to rest and Reverend Boyes turned to her and said, "Is this one of the persons who has tormented you?"

Abagail pointed her finger at the slave. "Yes, Reverend. I have seen her melt down waxen images of us and fly on a broom." The crowd gasped. "She is a witch. A witch!" Then the little girl clutched her side and screamed, "The pain. She is giving me such pain!"

Reverend Boyes turned back to the accused. "Bituba, do you not see what you have done? Why do you thus torment these poor children of God?"

Bituba shook her head violently so the folds of fat under her chin fluttered like an imprisoned bird. "No sir. No sir!"

Reverend Boyes' questions kept hammering at her, asking her to confess until finally, perhaps out of desperation, or maybe when her brain hit on a way to save herself she said, "I will admit the Devil came to me and bid me serve him."

Reverend Boyes smacked his hand on the table. "So, you admit making a contract with the Devil." He turned to the audience with a complacent smile.

Bituba nodded. "Yes, but he promised me many fine things---laces and jewelry and a fine carriage. And he made me sign in his book that I made a contract with him."

The reverend winked at the audience. "You signed in his book. Um hmm. And just what kind of book was this?"

"A big black book and there were other marks in there, too. I saw them, yes sir, um hmm, yes I did. Nine from this village alone."

"There were marks of other witches right here in Salem Village?" His face looked as if he couldn't fathom the idea.

The audience was abuzz with whispers. Jim Indian started to clap and smile. He knew his beloved Bituba had outsmarted them all. The thought that the Devil's attack was even more widespread than anyone thought was overwhelming to everyone but Jim.

Reverend Boyes gave the audience an angry look and silence was restored. But each one looked at a neighbor, wondering if the other was a witch. The reverend's voice turned nasty. "And just whose marks were they?"

Bituba shrugged. "I can't say sir, they was only red marks, just like mine."

"I see," said Reverend Boyes, looking as if he wasn't sure what to ask next. Then he spun around and faced her. "What was your contract with the Devil?"

She sniffed and said softly, "He wanted me to harm the little girls. He told me to. Sometimes he came to me in my sleep."

"Just what did he look like?"

"He was all dressed in black and wore a tall hat, just like that man there!" She pointed to a fellow in the audience and the crowd exploded.

When order was finally restored, Reverend Boyes said, "Is that the man?"

Bituba shook her head. "Oh no sir, the Devil don't look like that."

"Do you see anyone in this room who looks like the Devil?"

She looked over the entire audience, seeing some who slunk down in their seats or covered their faces with their hands. Finally she said, "No, sir. There's nobody I done seen who looked like him."

The crowd gave a visible sigh of relief and Reverend Boyes was silent, consulting his notes. Finally he said, "What else did the Devil tell you?"

"Oh, he came to me many times. One time he whispered in my ear, 'Kill the children.' Sometimes his spirit appeared in the form of a hog or a big black dog that could change just like that," she snapped her fingers and the crowd smiled appreciatively. "The Devil has many powers, you know." She winked at Reverend Boyes.

He flushed and cleared his throat before asking, "Did the Devil say anything else to you?"

Bituba stared up at the ceiling as if recollecting. Finally she said, "Not as the Devil, but he did appear to me as a thing with the head of a woman, two legs and wings. Another time he was hairy all over and about three feet high. But he walked just like you or me."

Reverend Boyes eyed her wearily. "Did these, ah, creatures say anything to you?"

She shook her head. "Not them, but there were two rats, a red one and a black one. They asked me to serve them."

"Have any of these things you talk about affected Abagail or Elizabeth in any way?"

"Oh, sure. These things have hurt the little girls, but I never would. I love those precious children. He made me do it."

Reverend Boyes consulted his notes again. "Is there anyone in the village of Salem who is a witch?"

Abagail and Elizabeth remained strangely quiet as they had since Bituba began her confession. The audience had quieted also, listening to her story in fascinated horror. Then Bituba put herself in a trance and she spoke in a raspy, frightening voice. "Rebecca Corey and Sarah Goody are witches."

The audience burst into terrified screams and Bituba fell on the floor, her body convulsing. Only Jim Indian had a worried look on his face, for he knew Rebecca Corey and Sarah Goody were two women who had spoken harshly to his Bituba. His body started to shake with the fear she might name him next for the times he had hollered at her.

When silence was restored, Bituba moaned from her place on the floor, "She's pinching me now, it's Rebecca Corey and Sarah Goody, she's biting me."

When Bituba recovered, Reverend Boyes held up his hand for quiet. "Is there anyone else in this village who is a witch?"

Bituba licked her lips and looked the audience over. Her finger slowly came to rest on a woman in the audience. "Mrs. Sidle, she's a witch." The accused fell in a heap on the floor. Bituba nodded. "Yes sir, Mrs. Sidle. She came to me with a witch's brew and asked me to make it for her, that's what she did. She's a witch, no question 'bout that."

The next day, Mrs. Sidle was examined. She named Dorcas Wently and several others with whom she had quarreled. Not wanting to soil her new gown, she did not wrestle herself to the floor in convulsions, but she did cackle like a hen and moo like a cow.

The trials proceeded. More and more people in Salem Village and surrounding towns were named until the jails in all available burgs were full of people accused of being witches. No one felt safe travelling on the roads at night, for they feared they might meet a witch or be accused of being one. It was even rumored about that the wife of the Reverend Nicholas Hale was a witch and that the governor's wife had sympathized with a prisoner accused of witchcraft.

Nicholas Hale had lost weight and he was jittery as a pregnant horse. He feared that what had happened in Boston and Beverly would soon happen in Salem Village---innocent people would die on the gallows. The Reverends Winthrop and Boyes seemed to be warming up to a fever pitch, their eyes gleaming like rabid dogs and their faces dripping with the sweat of self-righteousness. The magistrates were more subdued in their questioning, but they still held firm against Hale's pleadings to stop.

Meanwhile, Verity languished in Salem Town jail. Ventura went to visit as often as she could, bringing nourishing soups and stews with her. But she wasn't able to see her daughter and she never knew if the food even reached her.

***

Governor William Easty sat in his chambers examining his stockings. It was clear they didn't match. His wife, Mary, or that dreadful servant girl had been at it again, making him look like a fool. How could someone of his stature be expected to meet and greet dignitaries and make important state decisions with two stockings that didn't match? Perhaps if he remained behind his maple desk, no one would notice. But, then, he did have that dinner with the governor of New York that evening. Still, if he planned things right, he might find time to sneak home and change. That would give him a chance to chastise Mary at the same time.

It was a commanding office and Bill Easty looked a little silly in it, sitting in front of the massive green velvet draperies and the giant window seat overlooking the formal gardens. He was dwarfed by the large corner fireplaces and the dark wood paneling with its marble surrounds. Even the bronze bust of his predecessor, standing on a high rosewood table and the Chinese jars of gold, were more imposing than he.

Pushing away his anger, he smoothed back the sides of his thin mustache and fiddled with his beard. His short-sighted eyes read through the pile of letters lying on his desk.

He was fond of smelling a letter before he read it, seeing if he could tell anything about it from sniffing it. Of course, the ones written in a woman's hand were easy, they usually smelled of lavender or roses and plead for leniency in the cause of their husband or family. He shuffled through the pile until he chose one.

He sniffed it. "This one is of a diabolical nature," he muttered, pulling more furiously on his dark beard. "Smells of religion, too." The governor was not given to deep and involved thinking about religious matters and had not been enthusiastic about the witch trials in Salem. It wasn't until he began to read the letter written in a perfectly round and childish style that he sat up straight, his face hot with rage. "Accusing my wife of being a witch? This must be a mistake or a child's prank!"

He stood up and hastened to find his assistant, Oliver Stone, who at that moment was reading a love letter from the wife of his best friend. Oliver's freckled face had already twisted into lines of passion when Governor William Easty walked into his office. Caught in a compromising position, Oliver leaped to his feet, shoved the letter in his desk and closed the drawer with a resounding bang.

"Oliver, come into my office immediately," the governor said, neither noticing nor caring about Oliver's affairs.

When they were both sitting in the governor's office, William Easty began to speak in a low-pitched drone. "Oliver, what do you know about these witch trials that have been going on in Salem?"

Oliver brushed a knot of red hair back from his face. Oliver was the governor's assistant because he remembered almost everything he heard, saw, or read, and William Easty was notorious for his forgetfulness. Sometimes he even contradicted himself twice in the same speech because he couldn't remember what he'd said earlier. But Oliver could always remember, unless he was embarrassed.

In that case, everything he ever knew, heard or remembered flew right out of his head. He sat staring at the governor.

Not noticing Oliver's hesitation, William Easty continued. "It has come to my attention that this matter may be getting out of hand. I want you to go to Salem Village and sit in on the trials. Apparently there have been some accusations against," he coughed loudly into his hand, "my wife. Something about being a sympathizer with witches, if you can believe such nonsense."

He smiled benignly at Oliver. And Oliver, knowing his place, smiled back. "Report to me immediately concerning the state of affairs there. Then wait for further instructions. He nodded at Oliver, a sure sign their discussion was at an end. Oliver stood to leave, tugging at the back of his breeches, which always seemed to lodge themselves in the most uncomfortable positions.

"Oh, and one thing more, Oliver," said the governor, "take ten or twelve soldiers with you in case there is any trouble. Tell them to keep well-hidden outside Salem Village, but within easy reach to you, in case there should be any resistance to my orders once I decide what to do."

# 17

Ventura hurried to Sutter Lane to see Sigrid, the only person she knew she could trust. Sigrid was not the kind to watch other people suffering, so surely she would be at home, not at the trial.

The smell of burning wood and the stream of gray smoke ascending from Sigrid's chimney confirmed it. Perhaps seeing Ventura come down the lane, or maybe even sensing her arrival, Sigrid waited on her porch, smiling. Her outline stood out, black against the front of the fine old oak door. It was one of the finest homes in the parish, yet Sigrid lived a simple existence, ministering to the poor and dressing like a pauper.

"Come, let's have some tea," said Sigrid, putting her hand on Ventura's shoulder and ushering her into the house. "I've been expecting you." Ventura searched her friend's face for a sign of how she knew, but the only things there, shining out from the cracks and crevices of her face, were compassion and love.

They went into the kitchen and settled into chairs by the fireplace. Sigrid nodded to her visitor. "I heard Verity has been arrested."

"Yes, and I don't know what to do. It's like Spain all over again."

Sigrid put her hand over Ventura's. "I knew something like this was coming."

Ventura nodded. "Yes, you did tell me, but I didn't believe you." Sigrid's hand was warm and comforting. Tears welled up in Ventura's eyes and she set her cup down. "I wish I had believed you." She clenched her fists. "Maybe we could have left this terrible place before Verity was taken."

Sigrid nodded. "It is horrible that someone so pure should be accused."

"Can't they see she only wants to help? Why must anyone who is different suffer?"

Sigrid shook her head sadly. "I don't have the answer. It may go on for centuries, bursting forth when people are oppressed and angry and latch onto revenge as the answer to their problems. Or, it may be stopped here, in Salem Village."

Sigrid rose slowly, rubbed her crooked spine, picked up a log and put it on the fire. It sputtered, then blazed into sudden brightness, throwing shadows across the old woman's face. When she returned to her chair, she said, "There is something you need from me. What is it?"

"I do need your help. She will surely be found guilty, and once done, she will be hanged."

"What is it you want me to do?"

A wave of calmness settled over Ventura when she thought about her daughter and the minister's son "Verity and Absalon Winthrop are in love and hoped to become engaged. I'm sure after this, even if she is found innocent, Reverend Winthrop will not bless the marriage."

Sigrid shook her head sadly. "Men of the cloth are not always forgiving."

"Absalon is away on an errand and Verity's trial begins tomorrow or the next day. If I could find him and bring him here, maybe he could stop this terrible thing. Reverend Winthrop must know where he is, but I can't---"

Sigrid nodded. "I can bring him here." She rose, moving her stiffened body slowly. "Come here early tomorrow and I will have your answer."

Ventura hurried home, wondering what Sigrid planned to do. She kindled the lamps in her bedroom and crawled into bed with the moonlight bright on her. Dreams of Seville haunted her. Someone was binding her arms and the sound of bones cracking was heavy in her ears. She woke with a shudder, drenched in sweat, wondering if Verity would soon be swinging from a rope.

While it was still dark, she dressed and hurried to Sigrid's. The wings of dawn flew over the horizon, opening up great shafts of light just as Sigrid welcomed Ventura inside. "He's coming here before the trial," Sigrid said gaily, dipping her biscuit in coffee.

Ventura swallowed. Now that the plan was upon her, a dry fear crept up her throat. "How did you manage it?"

Sigrid winked. "Donations are always first in the heart of the reverend."

Before she could ask Sigrid what she meant, someone knocked on the door. Ventura's heart froze. Sigrid signalled her to hide in the hall while she went to the door.

Ventura jumped up and ran across the floor. Breath whistling in her ears, she peeked from her vantage point next to the wall. She leaned forward carefully, watching the parlor through a crack in the door.

Squinting, she could just barely make out Sigrid's bent frame and Reverend Winthrop's tall body. He sat down by the fire while Sigrid tended the falling fire, bringing renewed light into the room.

They sipped their tea slowly while Ventura's impatience built. Just when she thought she would burst, Reverend Winthrop spoke. "My dear Widow Cloyce, I was delighted to hear you have another donation for the congregation. What is it this time?" His eyes greedily surveyed the parchment she handed him. "The deed to your house? This is a fine gift indeed."

Ventura took a step forward, but Sigrid's hand reached out and snatched the parchment out of the reverend's hand. Holding it tightly, Sigrid's berry-stained fingers stood out in relief from the dull white paper. Her voice was firm, determined. "The only requirement I make is that when I die, a plaque commemorating my husband be placed on whatever edifice you construct. You will see I've written that below and it has been notarized, so I'm sure you will follow my directions."

"Most explicitly, Mrs. Cloyce, most explicitly." He stood up and reached for the parchment. "Now, I'm afraid I must be going. The trial is continuing in the meeting house and I must be there."

Sigrid held tight to the paper. "Before you go reverend, perhaps you might tell me something."

He sat down quickly, never taking his eyes off the deed. "If I know what you want, I'll be happy to tell you."

She leaned toward him. "It is about your son, Absalon. I've known him since he was a small boy. My husband used to take him fishing. How is the boy?" The parchment dangled within inches of the reverend's hand. "By now he must be a young man."

His eyes stared at the paper. "He's fine. Off to do an errand for me in Beverly."

She nodded. "Beverly. An errand?"

"Family business with his uncle. Now I'm sure you can understand that I have to leave." He stood up again and reached for the deed, but Sigrid's hand didn't budge.

She inclined her head. "And what is his uncle's name?"

Reverend Winthrop gasped for breath, holding his annoyance at bay. "Why Matthew Winthrop, of course!" With that, he rose, jerked the paper out of Sigrid's hand and bolted out the door.

A minute later, Sigrid motioned to Ventura to come out. Ventura smiled for the first time in days. "Sigrid, you are a tease."

"I had to find out about Absalon and if I'd given him that deed a moment sooner you can be sure he would have been out the door before I could ask. Now, on your way. Take a horse from the stable if you like."

Ventura embraced her friend, feeling herself enveloped in the smell of spices and old things. When at last she let go she asked, "How can I ever thank you?"

Sigrid smiled. "By keeping safe, so you and Verity can continue your healing ways." She waved the younger woman on. "Now hurry!"

Ventura started to go, then turned at the door. "One more thing. Would you go to the trial tomorrow? Verity needs someone there who cares about her. She acted very brave when she was arrested, but I know she's terrified.

Sigrid patted her arm. "If it will help you, I will go. Now hurry on."

Ventura was up on the black stallion and on her way in minutes, a small cake and some cheese tucked in the saddle bag. Urging the horse to a canter, she rode for a while with gnats humming around her head. Then the sky darkened and filled with angry black clouds. The wind switched, filling the air with the smell of rain. She pulled her mantilla more tightly over her head and prayed it would pass over.

Ahead, lightning tore across the sky in a ferocious yellow bolt. Seconds later, a terrific crash of thunder shook the earth. Whinnying in fear, her horse bolted, throwing Ventura to the ground. She lay there, semi-conscious, on a carpet of decaying leaves, feeling the patter of drops against her face and listening to the moan of the wind in the trees above her.

Sometime later, she tried to move, but pain shot up her leg. Straining and grunting, she forced herself to her feet. Wobbling and shaking, she made it a few steps, then her ankle buckled and she fell to the ground, unconscious.

***

When Ventura opened her eyes, the sky was clear and her ankle throbbed painfully. Her horse stood a few yards away. She moved her legs, trying to crawl to him, but each movement brought brilliant shafts of pain up her leg.

The horse gave her a worried look and swished his tail. Then his eyes caught the moonlight before he whinnied and trotted away. A nightingale's song, piercingly sweet and low filled the silence. Shadowy lines of trees made their eerie presence known on each side of her, and she shivered with fear, wondering what to do.

She pulled her cloak around her and went to sleep. She awoke to the sound of leaves stirring nearby. The sun had already moved part way across the sky. A few houses clung to a nearby hill and in the distance black crows talked loudly.

A man came out of a small cottage next to a wall. He gave a shrill whistle and a dog dove out from behind him. In seconds, the black creature was on her, sniffing and growling, pushing his snout into her roughly and showing his teeth. She tried to push him away, but the dog was strong and determined. The man came closer and her heart raced like a runaway horse.

The man stood over her, his face a horror of scars. The mouth was pulled to one side in a grotesque sneer and the eyes were reduced to crooked slits on his mottled face. She bit her lips so tightly to muffle her scream that the tang of coppery blood filled her mouth.

She was helpless against him. If he wished to be cruel, she had no defense except her fingers. He smelled of tobacco and biscuits and when he stooped beside her, she closed her eyes, praying to the Blessed Virgin for aid. His hands roamed over her body while she moaned with fear. Without so much as a grunt, he pulled her to her feet, flung her over his shoulder and carried her to his cottage. From her upside down vantage point, she caught sight of the piled fire wood and the door latch. Then, the porch lurched beneath her and for the second time in twenty-four hours, she lost consciousness.

When she awoke, she was in the cottage, lying on a tiny bed by the window. Arrows of sun came at her through the paned glass. From the other room, she heard muted wheezing and she wondered if the man was sleeping. The odor of fresh coffee made her stomach jerk with hunger.

She pushed off the thick coverlet, her hands exploring for injuries. Only her ankle throbbed. It had swollen to twice its normal size and was wrapped in a soft cloth. With great effort, she swung her legs over the edge of the bed and tried to stand, but bolts of pain forced her down again.

She heard shuffling footsteps and turned to see the man who had carried her to the cottage. His white shirt and dark breeches were old, but clean. Her throat went bone dry when she looked at his face.

He stared at her leg. "I'm Andrew Martin. I wrapped your ankle. Are you hungry?"

She looked into the slits that were his eyes. This time she saw compassion and concern. She told him her name and said, "Yes, I am hungry."

He nodded. "I'll bring you some food." He turned and started to leave the room.

She shook her head and said, "No, I want to get out of bed and see if I can walk. There is someone I must meet, someone---"

His strong arms went around her. "We will eat first, then we will talk of meeting." She leaned against his body, placing her injured foot on the floor cautiously. Her body shook with pain, but she managed to hobble across the dirt floor. He helped her into a chair, placing a soft pillow behind her shoulders. The red logs in the fireplace snapped and glittered, beating back the cold and throwing a half-circle of warmth out into the room. The black dog eyed her with interest, snout on paws, fur shining in the light.

Andrew handed her a piece of cake and a cup of steaming coffee, then sat down by the dog, petting it slowly while he watched her eat. "More?" he asked when she finished.

"No. I am indebted to you for your kindness, but now I must leave. My daughter is in great danger."

He nodded. "Then it is a matter of great importance."

"Yes. But first, I must find my horse. He threw me yesterday and I haven't seen him since."

He nodded again. "Blackie. Yes, he is in the stable."

She looked at the man feeling confused. "Blackie? Is that his name?"

"It is my name for him. I give all the animals names so I can talk to them. Sometimes they are of more comfort than people." He pointed to his face.

She nodded. "People can be cruel. I know I thought you were going to hurt me because of the way you look." A grimace, which she supposed was his way of smiling, started across his lips. "Will you take me to my horse?" she asked.

"Of course, but it is much farther than from here to the bed. Do you think you can make it?"

She looked down at her leg. "Maybe not." She tried to stand, but the pain was too much to bear. She started to whimper. "I have to meet Absalon and get his help."

"I have a cart. I could drive you."

"No, you---" She looked at his face and saw he was sincere. "You'd do that? For a stranger?" It was the first time since she'd left Sigrid's that she felt a glimmer of hope.

"Yes, I'll drive you. Wouldn't you do that for me?"

The heat of embarrassment rose on her cheeks. "I'm afraid I didn't have very Christian thoughts about you when we first met."

He cocked his head. "And now?"

"I trust you and would be eternally grateful if you would drive me to Beverly."

Sadness crept into his voice. "Beverly. Yes, I know the village. I used to live there a long time ago." The room filled up with painful silence and Ventura wasn't sure what to say next. Finally Andrew said, "I will hitch up the cart and come back for you." He looked at the dog. "Come, Champion." The animal leaped up and followed his master out the door.

Ventura had barely finished her coffee when he was back in the kitchen, scooping her out of the chair. He helped her to the cart, picking her up easily to set her on the small bench in front next to him.

Hitched to the cart were two horses, her black stallion and a dapple gray that had to be his. Andrew tucked a small bag of food behind them and whistled for Champion. The dog bounded into the back and sat waiting, ears cocked ahead. Andrew signalled the horses to move and the cart creaked off.

She looked at the man, wondering how his face had been so brutally disfigured. As if he guessed her thoughts, he kept his eyes on the road and said, "It was a fire."

She swallowed, then said, "What was?"

"Everyone wants to know about my face. I figured you do, too."

"Sorry, if you'd rather not talk about it, that's all right."

"It's all right. Our home in Beverly caught fire. Someone was careless with the fireplace, I suppose. I was on my way home with Champion when I saw the burst of flames and smelled the smoke of burning books and clothes. I ran inside and---" his voice cracked. "I tried to save them but---"

"And your face got burned."

"Yes."

"How horrible."

"After I buried them, I went to live in the woods. The children teased me and played tricks, thinking I was some kind of monster. Their parents weren't much better, shunning me in the meeting."

Ventura felt tears welling up inside her. Despite the many injustices she had suffered, she counted herself fortunate compared to Andrew. At least she had Richard and Verity. Andrew lived alone, with no one to love him but Champion.

They rode the rest of the way in silence, their cart splashing through the muddy thoroughfare and bumping and swaying over the ruts cut out of snow by yesterday's rain. At times, between the forests and thick underbrush, she could see the ocean and the tiny streams that ran down to it. They passed small villages with handfuls of houses surrounding a town square. In several places, they had to go around the road because the mud and water were too deep to ride through. Andrew drove the cart alongside the deep hollows of murky wetness, turning it expertly through the shrubs and bushes until they could regain the road.

Sun-down shadows lengthened and they moved through fragrant cedars and ghostly pines until the day dissolved into twilight. By the dim light, she saw a small wooden sign tacked on a stake announcing the town of Beverly. The evening turned purple in the evergreen forest and they wound gently down hill from the main road, between rocks studded with bushes and heavy undergrowth.

They found the Winthrop home. Like so many of the houses in Salem Village, it was a two-story gray clapboard with wooden shingles and an immense chimney spouting gray smoke.

A young girl in Puritan black answered the door. She was slim and dark-haired with a tender mouth and blue eyes. Ventura told her who she was. Behind her, Absalon's soft masculine voice said, "Come in." Seeing the pain on Ventura's face, he moved quickly to place a chair beneath her. He had good bones, a steady gaze and dark eyes that didn't look away from trouble.

It was a sparse Puritan home, but the fire seemed friendlier than most. It crackled and hissed invitingly, giving off the pleasant aroma of burning wood. Champion headed for it immediately. He dropped down and put his face in his paws.

Absalon offered them coffee and cheese and they accepted gratefully. Only once did the young man glance suspiciously at them. "This is Andrew," she told Absalon. He helped me when I was thrown from my horse. He can be trusted."

Absalon smiled at the other man. "Thank you for helping Mrs. Hasleton, sir. I am sorry my uncle and aunt are not here to greet you, but they have been called out on parish business."

Ventura nodded, happy to see the young man's manners. After hours in the cart, she ate and drank with vigor, taking just enough to revive her. "Absalon," she said, putting down her cup, "I've ridden here to get you."

His face clouded, his eyes turning dark. His small cousin was trying to tickle him at that moment and he shooed her away before saying, "Something's happened to Verity."

Ventura nodded and told him about her daughter's imprisonment. "I am certain she will be hanged if you do not come and save her."

His handsome face took on a look of bewilderment. "Hanged?" He jumped to his feet and began to pace in front of fire. "But why would anyone want to hang my sweet Verity?"

"Your father has started a witch hunt and I'm afraid there is no telling where it will lead. Elizabeth and Abigail may have started this whole thing as a prank, but it has gotten out of hand. Many people have been accused and are in prison."

He stopped pacing. "But Verity's not a witch, we plan---"

"I know of your plan to be married. Of course she's not a witch, but she does have remarkable powers. If anyone who wishes her ill has seen her working with hands, they can do her much harm. I have seen it happen in Spain---burned at the stake, garrotted---"

He started pacing again. "But this is America. We are free here." He stopped and banged his hand on the back of a chair.

Ventura leaned forward, her words spilling out. "I know this is hard for you to believe, but it's happening in Boston and other places, too. You have to believe me that Verity faces certain death unless you come with me now."

Absalon gulped and his face turned a pasty white. "If what you say is true, how can I stop it?"

"Rescue her. Take her away from Salem Village. She will never be safe here now that this terrible thing has happened."

Absalon's face dissolved into thought, seeming to age him to full adult status during that moment. Finally he said, "Yes. I will do it. We will leave right away." He went to the desk and wrote a short note, folded it and set it on the table. Before they left he called to his cousin and told her where he was going. He kissed the little girl good-bye, stuffed some food in a bag, pulled on his winter cloak and ushered Ventura and Andrew out the door. "I'll get my horse and meet you in front," he called behind him as he headed for the barn.

Before she could reach her horse, Andrew was already unhitching the black stallion from the cart. "You will want to ride sidesaddle, Ventura, to make better time." He turned and looked into her eyes. "Can you manage with your ankle?"

Pushing the pain from her mind, she nodded. Before he helped her into the saddle, she grabbed him into a hug. "You are a good man Andrew," she whispered. "If there is anything I can do for you---ever---I will do it." Just as he was about to help her up on her horse, she reached up and kissed him on the cheek.

Just then, Absalon came trotting around the house on a white horse. "Good-bye Andrew. Safe journey," she shouted as they rode away.

***

The journey back was treacherous. They goaded their horses into a fast gallop, ducked under thick overhangs of branches, pushed back tickling shrubs and dove around muddy puddles. When there was time, Absalon's mind was absorbed in what lie ahead.

His father was pompous and often acted in his own best interests, rather than those of his congregation, but hanging innocent people seemed out of character for him. Absalon puzzled over how he had sat so many years in a pew beneath his father's stern gaze, listening to sermons and never had heard the judgment in his voice. His father was not the man he had respected and loved. What he was doing now meant that underneath his religious clothes lurked a man who thought God wanted him to punish people rather than love and support them.

He would rescue Verity and take her away from the horrible place Salem Village had become. But first, he must settle things with his father. They had argued before. Absalon secretly believed it was his refusal to submit to his father that led to his being apprenticed out. Father was patient in many things, but one thing he would not abide was anyone who disagreed with his opinions. Now they would clash as they had never clashed before and he must prepare himself for the inevitable.

***

Richard's ship pulled into Jamestown harbor. They had been to the West Indies and back. Now they were preparing to exchange some of the silks, jewelry and spices they had bought for guns and ammunition They would fetch a pretty penny in Jamaica.

He was looking forward to being in port. Surely a letter from Ventura awaited him. Sometimes there was one from Verity too, written in her careful round hand. Every word made him cry, and after he read them, he tucked them in his shirt until he returned to his ship. Sometimes he kissed them first, or sniffed them to extract any hint of perfume that might have been on Ventura's hand when she wrote it. After that, they were locked in his black chest, next to his other valuables.

When he was full of longing for them, he took out each letter and reread it, pretending he was sailing home that evening. More and more lately he had come to question the life he had chosen. He loved his wife and daughter dearly. It made no sense to him any longer to be away from them.

That was why when the first mate from The Boston Frigate tapped him on the shoulder that evening in White's Tavern, Richard wanted to turn away and forget everything that reeked of the sea. But the man would not be overlooked. He grabbed hold of Richard's hand and shook it firmly. "I'm Henry Jordan, from your sister ship."

If it hadn't been for the man's friendly eyes and persistent ways, Richard would have left and found another place to weep into his ale. But Henry Jordan shoved a soiled piece of parchment into Richard's hand and said, "This is from your wife, mate. You'd better read it."

Richard stared at the man, not believing his words. "My wife? You know her?"

"Aye, matie. I met her at the wharf in Salem. She's a beautiful woman and bright as a button." Henry took a swig from his mug and set it down decisively.

Richard looked at the parchment and then back at the man by his side. How could this man know Ventura unless she and he---But no, Ventura would never interest herself in another man. She loved him. Pushing back his ale, Richard's eyes devoured the message.

Henry put his hand on Richard's shoulder. "Bad news, aye?"

Richard bolted from his stool. "Yes, I've got to---"

"Hold on there. I can help," shouted Henry from behind him, quickly catching up and grabbing his collar.

Richard pulled away. "You? How are you involved in this wretched thing that plagues Salem?" He stared into the man's face, then pushed him aside. "Leave me alone. Richard took a swing at the man, but Henry blocked his punch and pushed him back.

He shouted in Richard's face. "Listen to me! I can help!"

Finally understanding the other man's words, Richard stopped struggling. "What can you do? My daughter's in prison, about to be hanged!"

"You have to get back to Salem, right?"

"Right."

"And you're committed to be first mate until the end of the term, right?"

"Right."

"What if we exchange posts?"

"You'd take my ship?"

"Yes. I'm taking the short tour this trip. From the looks of you, a little time on land is exactly what you need."

Sailors were not always a trustworthy bunch and so Richard said, "What's in it for you?"

"Listen mate, I've got a family too. Besides, your wife deserves your help." Henry reached out his hand and Richard shook it. Then they stood and smiled long and hard.

Feeling better, Richard clapped Henry on the back. "Let me buy you a drink."

Henry smiled and shook his head. "Not until we clear this with our captains. Come on, let's go see about it."

After some discussion, both captains agreed. The next morning, Richard was on The Boston Frigate sailing up the coast to Salem. He only hoped he would get there in time to save his dear Verity.

## 18

Verity paced back and forth in her cell as well as the small space would allow. Her mind buzzed with questions: Where was Absalon, and why hadn't he come to see her? And her mother, had she given up on her, too? Tears tracked down the dust and grime on her cheeks and a moan of hopelessness escaped her lips. She stopped pacing and leaned against the coldness of the wall, feeling the ache of loneliness building inside her.

Wasn't a month in prison enough to try anyone's soul? She tried to pray, but her cracked lips refused. So, she looked through the dim light at her companions.

The cell was barely big enough for one, but all five of them had eventually ended up in the tiny space. When they laid down, there was no space left for walking. And when Bituba slept at night, as she rarely did, she walked in her sleep, stepping on top of anyone who lay beneath her feet. As a result, Verity slept lightly, always vigilant for Bituba's foot. But while Verity could never sleep once the sun's rays penetrated the dank cell, Bituba slept well during the day. Even now, she was curled up like a small baby in the corner. Rebecca Corey and Sarah Goody snored against the far wall, and Mrs. Sidle stood in a corner, peeking at her from behind her knots of thick twisted hair.

At least they had been fed regularly, but it was never a sufficient amount. Verity looked down at her gown. It hung on her like the dress of a much larger woman. Mother had sent a package or two of food and for that Verity was thankful. Receiving them, she had ripped open the paper, jamming pudding and bread into her mouth until she choked. Seeing the pain of hunger in her cell mates' eyes, she had recoiled in shame and handed them chunks of bread and cheese and fresh apples until there was precious little left for herself.

She had never been allowed to see a lawyer, but had learned a lot about the Puritan way of doing things. They were ruled by the Word of God, not the English legal system, and their form of law was outdated. From what she could make out from talking to Mrs. Sidle, the law they used antedated the Magna Carta by at least two millennia.

Seeing a lawyer was the least of her problems. Never seeing Absalon or her parents loomed large in her mind. Suppose she never again saw the sun or a blade of grass. Another moan, this time one of desperation, and she crumbled into the corner, escaping into reverie, reliving Absalon's kisses again, hearing his perfect voice in her ears.

***

Verity Hasleton's trial began on a warm, sunny spring day. The robins were chirping cheerfully in front of the meeting house and the tulips were just beginning to poke their red and yellow heads out of the ground.

When the guards came to get her, she was eager, looking forward to seeing sunshine and being with someone other than her foul-smelling cellmates. She walked willingly beside the soldiers, looking forward to her first whiff of fresh air.

At first the daylight was more than she could bare, and her eyes burned, clamping shut in protest. Stumbling along with the guards' rough arms on her elbows, her eyes slowly began to adjust.

She heard their jeers before she could make out their faces. Men and women and children of all ages gathered outside the jail, depositing themselves along the road to the meeting house. Some played drums and sang hymns while others waved and taunted her. Her eyes darted through the crowd, searching in vain for the face of her mother and Absalon. Head and spirits dropping, she wondered if they had abandoned her to the court.

The constables hurried her into the meeting house where hundreds waited to see the spectacle. Some shoved and shouted, others stood by quietly, eyes riveted on Verity. In the first pew sat a demure Abagail, her eyes blazing with what looked like revenge. Next to her, Elizabeth hung her head, looking embarrassed and a shade guilty. The onlookers in the back gossiped noisily or sucked on oranges or sausages, while they waited for the officials to convene the hearing.

Unbeknownst to any who waited breathlessly for the proceedings to begin, the officials were locked in mortal combat. The cause of the delay was the mighty schism that was developing among the judges on questions of procedure, particularly the interpretation of spectral evidence.

"Gentlemen," Nicholas Hale's voice rang out, pleading and strong. "Had spectral evidence been barred from admission, Bridget Brown would have been convicted for little more than standing nearby when James Cary's oxcart fell into a hole, wearing scarlet, and getting herself talked about." He paused and dug a finger into his pitted face. "Granted, these are offenses, perhaps---,"he glanced at each member. Ezekial Hawthorne and Henry Osbourne were nodding and smiling. John Corwin looked as if he was thinking the matter over. Joseph Boyes and Samuel Bigginson sat stone-faced and cross-armed.

"No perhaps at all," sputtered Joseph Boyes, "those are offenses."

"I'll grant you that," continued Nicholas, "but hardly worthy of hanging."

"What you say has merit," said Ezekial, "what do you propose?"

"We could get the governor's opinion on the matter."

Henry Osbourne winked at his colleagues and said, "But that would delay us for sometime. And if I know the governor, perhaps forever."

Ezekial shook his head. "What other recourse do we have?"

Henry spoke up boldly. "What about consulting the other reverends present today. They are scholarly and ethical men."

All heads shook in agreement and a messenger was swiftly dispatched to bring back Reverent Winthrop and three other guardians of the flock from neighboring villages. Reverend Richards was the most outspoken on the issue. He was a short round man with a severe look and bow-shaped nose. "We must face this issue with critical and exquisite caution," he said gravely, "lest by too much credulity of things received only upon the Devil's authority, the door be opened for a long train of miserable consequences."

"Yes," agreed the rotund Reverend Johnson, "we must manage the proceedings with an exceeding tenderness towards those that may be complained of, especially persons formerly of unblemished reputation."

Over the continual opposition of the Reverends Winthrop and Boyes, it was agreed that spectral evidence was to be handled with care, and conviction should be on evidence certainly more considerable than that the accused was represented by a specter unto the afflicted. That agreed, the magistrates retired to the courtroom.

***

John Corwin strode to the front of the meeting house and took his seat with the other magistrates. Although not a muscle in his face moved to indicate what he was thinking, he was barely able to contain himself. Now it was his turn. He had sought and received approval from the magistrates and reverends to be the main questioner of Verity. The moment of his triumph was at hand.

His eyes searched the crowd, looking for a sign of Ventura. How delicious it would be to watch her face while he questioned her daughter. He would bring her to her knees, show everyone that her daughter was guilty and should be sentenced to hang. He squinted, staring at the crowd, thinking he saw her in the back. No, that woman had none of the beauty of Ventura.

No matter, she would be there soon enough. She would not miss seeing her daughter sentenced to death. His lips pulled into a vengeful smile. After the way she had led him on and then cast him aside, she deserved to feel pain. He only hoped it was one-tenth of the pain she had caused him.

He had been cloistered in that meeting house daily for more than a month and he had come to know every creak of every pew, every board that rattled under foot, every conceivable type of smell that emanated from the unwashed bodies of folk who came to jeer and laugh, getting their enjoyment out of watching their fellow human beings suffer. It wasn't for nothing that he had endured all this. The moment of sweet revenge was near.

Two grim-face guards yanked Verity's thin body before the bench. She looked up at John, sunken-eyed, dazed, pale-faced. The honey-haired beauty had changed much in a month. Too bad, but that was what she and her mother deserved. Relishing the moment, he pointed an accusing finger. "Verity Hasleton," his voice rang out, "are you a witch?"

She struggled to speak several times before any words came out. "I can say before my eternal Father than I am innocent, and God will clear my innocence," she bowed her head meekly and the crowd sighed.

John Corwin nodded. "If you be guilty, I pray God discover you." Without taking his eyes off Verity he said, "Abagail Winthrop, is this the woman you saw performing witchcraft?"

Abagail stood, angelic face, evil smile, body rigid, finger shaking at the accused. "Yes, I saw her using her hands in witchcraft to heal or harm her own mother!" The crowd buzzed. "She put her hands over her mother's belly like this," Abagail thrust her hands in front of her, innocent eyes growing wider, "and lightning burst out of her fingers and cackles burned out of her mouth."

Verity's breath came short and fast. "I have never afflicted anyone in my life. I heal people, not hurt them with lightning."

"Is it true you held your fingers over your mother as Abigail has said?"

Verity sighed. "Yes, sir." Her mouth began to tremble and her eyes to plead. "But you don't understand. I was helping her, not harming her."

John Corwin grunted softly. "Are you an innocent person relating to this witchcraft?"

His answer came not from Verity, but from Abagail. She fell onto the floor, legs and arms banging with such rapidity that the floorboards shook beneath her. Elizabeth fell to the floor next, barking and running across the floor on all fours, her thick red hair standing out behind her. Then sour-faced Sarah Pettengill and pink-cheeked Darcy Winewood started to wail and scream until all the girls in the meeting house were screeching loudly. Beads of perspiration popped out on John Corwin's forehead. This was more than he had bargained for. Things were getting out of hand.

The crowd was in a panic. They screamed and jumped about, many pointing the finger of accusation at Verity. They had been in the meeting house for many days, but never had anyone seen such a reaction to an accused witch. An infection of demonism was running across the whole assembly. Children barked and fathers clucked. Plump mothers in chaste white collars shrank from the touch of their linen-capped daughters, fearful of who was the witch and who the bewitched.

Above the clamor in the meeting house, John Corwin's voice rose mightily. "Verity Hasleton. Did you consort with the Devil?" He wiped streaks of perspiration from his brow and struggled to keep his voice calm.

Verity opened her mouth, but no words came out, only the silent incantation, "Oh Lord, help me." She spread her hands out helplessly, eyes appealing to the Almighty. Abagail, who had been watching Verity intently, jumped to her feet and spread her hands out helplessly, mimicking Verity. Elizabeth watched for a minute, then she jumped up and spread her hands out. In seconds, every girl in the meeting house was on her feet, holding the exact posture of Verity. Their rigid bodies and glazed eyes stood out in stark relief to the pointing fingers and shaking fists of their parents.

When the onlookers saw what was happening, the din in the meeting house rose to a roar. The accusations made by Abagail and Elizabeth may have been false, but deeds were known to be truthful. If the bodies of so many were being controlled, the court could not discount the evil power Verity Hasleton held over every girl in the room.

Caught up in the panic, John Corwin jumped to his feet. With fists shaking and a face hot with emotion, he shouted, "Confess your sin, girl. You are a witch. Say it!"

Verity rolled her eyes toward heaven and said softly, "I do not know what a witch is." Following Abagail's lead, one-by-one, all the girls in the room rolled their eyes to heaven. The crowd burst into screams and Maggie Dodson and Angelica House fainted, their scrawny bodies crumpling to the floor.

John Corwin ran to the table and thrust a jar above his head. "Is this not what you use to cast spells over others, you witch!" he cried.

Verity stared at the herb jar from her healing box. She swallowed. "Where did you get that?"

John Corwin's eyes blazed with fury. "Never you mind where I got it, miss, just answer the question." Verity stared at the jar, confusion and anger crisscrossing her face. Without waiting for her answer, he shouted, "Are these not the potions you use to cast spells on others?"

She took a step forward, arms extended, eyes pleading. "No, they're healing herbs. They help people. They have nothing to do with casting spells. I am a Christian." A sob cracked her voice. "I read the Bible and go to meeting."

Abagail jumped in the air and shrieked, "Gospel witch! Gospel witch!" The other girls took up the chant, clapping their hands and stomping their feet until the floor boards rocked with their evil cries and outrageous feet. Verity bit her lip, face torn with helplessness.

Abigail shouted, "She's biting me. Oh, the pain!" Elizabeth and the other girls bit their lips and shouted of the pain.

Verity took another step toward John Corwin. "Don't you see what they're doing? They're playing a silly game of follow me." Her voice rasped in utter woe.

"I can see a black man whispering in her ear. It's the Devil!" screamed Abigail, before she fell to the floor, then rolled across it, her heels banging and her arms flailing.

Sigrid stood up and raised her voice to a shout. "Yes, it is the prank of the young. Many of these confessions and accusations are lies. They have been made by foolish young girls and ridiculous women after they have been arrested and tied neck and heels together until the blood gushed out of their noses."

A few women in the crowd applauded, but were quickly silenced by the angry looks of their neighbors. Sigrid tried again. "They have already been condemned before they have been tried. Is this justice, good people? We must join together and demand the trials be moved to Boston or the judges be changed. There can be no more shedding of innocent blood."

Sigrid turned her withered face to the crowd. "Joseph, Ann, Samuel. Can you truthfully say this young woman is a witch? Hasn't she helped you when you were sick?" They nodded, but turned their timid faces away, refusing to look Sigrid in the eye.

On a signal from John Corwin, two guards stepped forward and seized Sigrid. They dragged her to the bench. "Who is this woman?" John asked of his fellow magistrates.

Reverend Winthrop gave Sigrid an embarrassed smile. "She is one of my parishioners. One who has just given me the deed to her land when she dies." John Corwin pounded on the table. "Well, I believe she has been bewitched today and the Devil himself must have done it!"

"She's a witch!" shouted Abagail and the cry was quickly taken up by the other girls. A few of the older ones fell to the floor or gobbled like turkeys.

Nicholas Hale rose from his seat. "Isn't this going too far? This happened in Beverly---"

John Corwin's voice rose above Nicholas Hale's. "Are you a witch, Verity Hasleton?" The crowd went wild with shouts.

When the hall had quieted, John Corwin looked back at Verity. "Do you not see what a solemn condition these children are in?" He pointed to Abigail and Elizabeth. "When your hands are loose, you afflict them. And you stand dry-eyed while many in the crowd are weeping. How do you explain that?" Verity looked at him blankly. "Do you not know it is a fact that witches lack the ability to cry?"

Verity's chin trembled and her words shook out of her. "You do not know my heart. It is very sad this day." Her eyes raised heavenward.

Reverend Winthrop stood up then, shaking his arms and grimacing with hellfire in his eyes. "Satan is representing his internal forces. The devil is armed and among us. I am commanded to call an alarm unto you. Arm and see that you are in readiness as faithful soldiers under the Captain of our salvation. Arm that ye may resist the fiery darts of the wicked."

"Send the witches to the whipping post!" shouted a bearded man in the front row.

"Hang the witches!" shouted a portly matron in the rear. Soon most of the crowd were on their feet, roused to fight a mortal war with the Devil himself.

John Corwin's voice rose above all others. "I believe we have heard all the evidence against Verity Hasleton. We will now retire and come to a conclusion about her guilt." With that, the magistrates stood up and got ready to leave.

Nicholas Hale scratched his face and mumbled to himself, "No good will come of this. It is Beverly all over again." He raised his hands in prayer, his head shaking sadly.

"Come, Reverend Hale," said John Corwin. "It is time to retire." He left the bench and Nicholas followed, a look of befuddlement on his face. Verity burst into tears and two guards grabbed her and dragged her out.

As soon as the accused and the court disappeared, shouts and fists were gone and onlookers busied themselves pulling picnic baskets out from under their pews. They chewed on coarse bread and crunched on red apples, gossiping about what the verdict would be. The odor of spicy sausage, bread, and strong cheese permeated the meeting house.

***

Oliver Stone sat in the back row, red hair standing out in knots about his head, freckled nose twitching in disbelief. The proceedings had been shocking. The young woman, Verity, hadn't done much, but it was clear that the little girls had it in for her. It was true she had tried to heal someone with her hands, and that was forbidden. But was it a hanging matter?

While they waited for the verdict, Oliver turned to the men and women around him, trying to find out the latest gossip. One old crone offered him a slice of sausage on a chunk of bread and told him she had heard Reverend Hale's wife was a witch and the governor's wife was a witch sympathizer. "And that young woman. She's a witch, too, mark my words."

Before he could ask the old crone how she knew all this, two guards clunked back in. The jury followed and two more guards came behind, dragging Verity in. John Corwin rose ceremoniously and his voice rang out. "Verity Hasleton," his eyes searched the hall frantically for Ventura.

Reverend Winthrop pulled on John's sleeve. Still his eyes searched. Reverend Boyes cleared his throat. John Corwin blinked, then sighed. He shook his head quickly and the fire returned to his voice. "Verity Hasleton, we find you guilty of being a witch."

Verity's face twisted with pain and her scream echoed and ricocheted around the hall. Then her feet slid from under her and she fell in a heap on the floor. The guards pulled her up and held her. The crowd sighed, then went silent.

John Corwin's voice rose in the quiet of the hall. "Will you repent your sins?"

Chest heaving and tears streaming, she shouted, "I have not sinned. I am not a witch."

"Will you repent?" Verity shook her head. John Corwin's fist came down decisively on the table. "You are sentenced to hang tomorrow unless you repent in jail before that time."

The hall filled with cheers, shrieks and stomps. Some shrunk back, stunned. A few meek cries of protest rose, but they were silenced by the roused anger of the mob.

Oliver was the first one out of the meeting house. Pushing and shoving his small body forward, he made his way to the door. He had work to do and he better get at it. He jumped on his spotted horse and urged it quickly to a canter. The square and stables on the way out of town were a blur in his eyes and still he kneed his horse, forcing it forward.

The ferns and oaks thickened and moved closer to the road. Two of the soldiers came into view. They were leaning against a tree, warming themselves by a small fire. He could of done with more men, but two would do.

"You there. Take this message and deliver it to the governor. Neither of you is to stop until word is in his hands and his hands only." He thrust the letter into one guard's hand.

The men looked at each other, puzzled, then back at Oliver. "Well, if one of you doesn't make it, the other one will for sure." Nodding, the two men ran to mount their horses. In seconds, they were out of camp.

Oliver stood watching them, praying he had done the right thing. When they were out of sight, he got back on his horse and headed back to Salem Village. He rode down a gully, then past a high hill. The dark outline of several men stood out against the harsh sky. They were working there, their muscular bodies heaving and pushing, their strong arms constructing a wooden platform.

Oliver reined in his horse and pulled to a stop. "Hey, there," he shouted to the men, but they ignored him. Oliver dismounted and walked up to one with powerful shoulders that stretched the seams of his shirt. "What are you doing?"

The man turned around and glared at Oliver. "This here's Gallows Hill and we're readying it for the hanging tomorrow." He said it matter-of-factly, spitting into a small bush behind him. "See that there ladder? The accused will use it to walk to their death." Oliver followed the man's finger to the high platform.

Hanging from the top was the noose that would be used the next morning to hang Verity Hasleton.

***

Verity leaned against the damp gritty wall of the cell, her shoulders shaking with sobs. Low voices sounded behind the door and boards creaked outside. The latch opened and rough arms pulled her down a dank passageway to a small windowless room lit only by a dim lantern.

Reverend Winthrop's angry face looked into hers. "Confess you're a witch or face eternal damnation."

"But I'm not a witch. How many times do I have to say it?"

The guard thrust a lantern into her face and the reverend's words and questions jumbled in her mind until she fell silent, unable to answer anymore. "Ach! She will never repent!" said Cotton Winthrop, looking at the two constables.

A burly officer stepped forward and grabbed Verity. "A good dangle will bring repentance to her lips, you can be sure of that," he said, bending down and shoving each of her feet into a roped circle. Before she could speak, she was dangling by her ankles, upside down, the room spinning dizzily beneath her. She neither wept nor prayed, only a thin shrill shriek came out of her mouth before she shouted, "Let me down!"

But the harder she screamed and kicked, the higher they raised her until her head buzzed and her legs felt as if they would come out of their sockets.

"Repent Verity Hasleton!" shouted Reverend Winthrop.

"Lookie there," shouted a constable, "she's bleeding from the nose. Maybe she's had enough, Reverend."

"But she hasn't repented---"

The constable shook his head. "You don't want her to die before the hanging, do ye?"

The reverend's voice was sulky, disappointed. "No, take her down. Put her back in her cell."

Verity's body collapsed into the sandy earth with a thud. She wondered if something had broken. Her legs were wooden and her head thumped. Before she could figure it out, mean hands pulled her to her feet and dragged her to her cell. They dumped her inside like a lump of coal.

She laid there wondering how much more would have to be endured before the suffering ended. Then the tears came and she cried like a sorrowful flute.

***

A dove cooed outside her window and Absalon's smiling face appeared. Verity ran to greet him, but someone grabbed her and held her down, pushing the breath out of her, squeezing her lungs still.

Her eyes fluttered open and she sat up with a jolt. The stench of her jail cell filled her nose and with it came the realization she wasn't home after all. She would probably never see her mother again, let alone Absalon. She tried to pray, but her lips dissolved into sobs.

The sounds of clacking boots and loud voices came down the corridor. Her cell door opened with a creak and she was grabbed and propelled into the passageway. "Come now, miss," said a gravely voice, "it's a nice day for a hanging." He laughed out loud and another guard chuckled.

They forced her outside. She shielded her eyes, feeling giddy from the light, even though it was an overcast day. The clouds were heavy with rain and a thunderstorm was brewing in the east.

Hundreds of men and women lined the way. They jeered and pointed at her. With her hands tied behind her, the guards could only jostle her along by her elbows, making their way through the crowd. Ahead, Reverend Winthrop and the other magistrates stood at the base of the gallows. The wind came up, whipping their clothes to the side and blasting dirt particles into their somber faces.

Verity lifted her eyes above them. Standing on top of the structure, next to the noose, was a tall man. His arms were crossed over his shirt. His sleeves were rolled up as if he had been working hard and he wore a wide-brimmed hat. He was unshaven and raw in appearance and his eyes carried the look of destruction. Between his teeth, she saw the stem of a pipe.

The wind gusted, blowing her gown up and taking her breath away. Forcing and pushing, the constables made their way to the platform, dragging Verity along with them. At the ladder, they shoved her feet up a rung at a time.

A flash of lightning rippled across the sky, followed seconds later by boom of thunder. "I won't do it. I'm not guilty!" she screamed, refusing to go up the ladder. But strong arms lifted her until she stood on the platform for all to see.

"Verity Hasleton," said a gruff voice. She looked in his direction. The pipe-smoking man held the noose in his hands, adjusting the rope. Cinders blew into her eyes and the sweet smell of his tobacco was dizzying.

Another flash of lightning struck. Seconds later, another crash of thunder. Dry mouth, shivering body, eyelids trembling, Verity clutched her head, terrified of what was about to happen.

The coarse rope settled around her neck and she knew nothing could stop her death now. She closed her eyes and let death approach her, then she opened them, steadying her gaze on the horizon.

Two figures appeared on the hill. They were galloping toward the gallows with determined faces, their horses lathered from a ride of many miles. With a whoop of recognition, she called the names of her mother and Absalon, just before the noose tightened around her neck.

In the blur before her, the clattering of hooves and the whinny of a horse, drew her eyes to Absalon. He rode right at his father, ignoring Reverend Winthrop's look of shock, and grabbed the Bible out from under his father's arm. Absalon held the book high in the air, his voice ringing out in anger. "Where in here does it say you can sit in judgment of others? Judgment is God's job, not ours. Verity is no more a witch than you are. If you do this thing, God will surely punish you and I shall never again call you Father."

An even more frightening bolt of lightning ripped off the meeting house steeple. It was followed by a crash of thunder so terrible, the onlookers trembled, covering their ears from the sound while their lips mumbled fearful prayers.

Before Reverend Winthrop could speak, four more horses rode up to the platform. A small red-haired man dismounted. Ventura's eyes caught her daughter's and they exchanged a secret message of love.

"By authority of the Governor of Massachusetts," shouted Oliver Stone, "I command these hangings to cease. Further, I order you to release all those in prison sentenced to hang." The hangman yanked the rope off Verity's neck and slunk off down the ladder. A feeble cheer went up from the crowd of fearful men and women gathered there. Without another word, they dispersed and hurried back to their homes, heads down, bodies quivering.

Verity's eyes fastened on Absalon. He reached up, claiming her from the gallows stand and pulling her onto his saddle. She perched behind him, holding tight to his waist, while she buried her face against the strength of his shoulder. She babbled and wept, calling his name again and again.

"Hush now. I'll explain everything as soon as I have delivered you safely." For an answer, Verity snuggled against his body like a small puppy against its mother's warm belly.

Another horse appeared on the horizon. Galloping at full speed, blond hair and black cloak billowing behind, the rider came closer, eyes glowing with a deep fire. "It's Richard, it's your father!" shouted Ventura. She jumped down from her stallion just in time for him to leap off his horse and gather her into his arms. They locked in each other's embrace, mouth seeking mouth, unmindful of the raindrops, the reverends, of everything but themselves.

Absalon urged his horse toward them. "Mr. Hasleton, sir." His voice was so earnest, so dear, that Verity choked back her tears, she felt such a sense of relief and love for him.

But Richard's mouth was locked onto Ventura's and his eyes were closed in gentle bliss. It was Ventura who disengaged herself, tapping her husband's shoulder until, with great reluctance, he released her.

"I am Absalon Winthrop and I plan to marry your daughter, sir." The air tingled with expectation while Verity waited for her father's response.

Richard looked at Ventura. She smiled and nodded, tears tracking down her beautiful face. She reached up and hugged her face against her daughter's thigh. Verity leaned down and kissed her mother's hair. "I thought I'd never see you again. I thought I'd never---"

Ventura patted her daughter's leg. "Hush now. Everything's all right. Absalon is here and your father is here and everything is going to be just fine." She looked up at her daughter, eyes shining with love and hope.

Richard nodded, face full of a warm smile. "Not just fine! Wonderful! Come home with us and tell us all about it."

***

The wounds of Salem Village healed slowly after that. Ventura sailed off with Richard when he became captain of his own ship. They often visited his Aunt Cecily in Gibraltar, and Verity and Absalon who settled in Virginia, not far from the mansion of Captains Ann Bonny and Jack Calico.

Abagail and Elizabeth became strangely silent after that day and gradually faded from public notice. The members of the church decided Reverend Winthrop had been at fault in encouraging Abigail and Elizabeth to name the persons afflicting them. He and his wife were driven from Salem Village and never heard from again, although there was a rumor they returned to Barbados, along with Bituba and Indian Jim.

As the witchcraft fever died down, the men and women of Massachusetts recognized that the trials had been brought on by suspicion, fear and over-excitement. The Massachusetts General Court set aside January 14, 1697 as a day of fasting and forgiveness for what the people had done.

Several of the magistrates, including Nicholas Hale publicly acknowledged their error in convicting people unfairly and asked for forgiveness. Of all the persons involved, only John Corwin never expressed remorse about what he had done, but one day he was found, a bullet from his own pistol in his brain and a suicide note by his side.

The meeting house steeple was never repaired. It stood until the building was condemned a century later, a testament to God's judgment.

Power tends to corrupt and absolute power corrupts absolutely. Great men are almost always bad men, even when they exercise influence and not authority.

Lord Acton

EXURGE DOMINE ET JUDICA CAUSAM TUAM. PSALM. 73.